Disclaimer:

Although *Sweetwater* is set in a real time and place, it describes a West that the author wishes had existed and not the historical reality of many situations.

Sweetwater

Mickey Minner

Yellow Rose Books

Nederland, Texas

Copyright © 2006 by Mickey Minner

ISBN 978-1-932300-63-5

First Printing 2006

9 8 7 6 5 4 3 2 1

Cover design by Katherine Smith

Cover Photo by Micky Minner

Published by:

Regal Crest Enterprises, LLC
4700 Highway 365, Suite A, PMB 210
Port Arthur, Texas 77642

Find us on the World Wide Web at
http://www.regalcrest.biz

Printed in the United States of America

Acknowledgements:

This book would never have come about if it wasn't for all of the wonderful people who read my early efforts and encouraged me to continue writing. It is truly an amazing feeling when someone you have never met takes the time to send you a message of praise and support. Without those words of encouragement I would not have had the confidence to take my writing to the next level. The fact that *Sweetwater* is being published is a tribute to their support.

This book is dedicated to my grandfather, Charley F. Stetler, who inspired my love for the old west which has never faded but only continues to grow. To my grandmother, Edith M. Stetler, who always said I should be a writer. And to my parents, Bob and Madelyn Minner, who, even when they didn't understand, continued to love and support me.

Chapter One

THE MOON SLIPPED behind the drifting clouds as Jennifer crawled over the windowsill and gingerly stepped out onto a narrow section of roof. Though she was glad for the extra cover to help conceal her movements, the deepening darkness did make her immediate journey that much more difficult. Tentatively, she stepped to the roof's edge and, without giving herself any time to reconsider what she was about to do, she made the short jump onto a sturdy branch of the massive oak tree that had stood outside her bedroom window for as long as she could remember. Carefully using the tree's many branches as hand and footholds, she climbed down the rough trunk to the grassy yard below. Pausing only long enough to untie the small canvas travel bag strapped to her back, she quickly crossed the yard and passed through the waist-high cast iron gate before disappearing into the night's long shadows.

As she briskly walked toward the business district, she gave little thought to the fact that she was leaving behind the quiet neighborhood where she had been born and raised. Instead, her attention was focused entirely on the distant whistle of the midnight train chugging into the town's station. She quickened her steps because the last thing she wanted was to miss being a passenger on that very same train when it left the depot a short thirty minutes after arriving.

Even at this late hour, the business district was alive with activity. Freight wagons stood in the street at the side of the station, prepared to load any cargo the train delivered. Representatives from the town's hotels and boarding houses rushed onto the wood-planked platform that circled the brick depot building, all of them eager to greet late-arriving guests. Music from pianos, most of them badly in need of tuning, floated on the night air from the numerous drinking and gambling houses that shared the district with more respectable businesses.

This was not a good place for a single woman to be,

especially at night, and Jennifer kept her eyes focused straight ahead as she rapidly made her way to the relative safety of the station's platform. She reached the station just moments after the train rolled to a stop and the loud hiss of released steam momentarily drowned out the other noises of the busy depot. She started up the depot's steps, looking back along the route she had just traveled to see if anyone had taken any undue notice of her. Relieved to see that no one was paying her any attention, Jennifer turned to find a place to wait while the disembarking passengers gathered their luggage and moved off the platform and into the night. Trying to be as inconspicuous as possible, she pressed into the shadows cast against the depot's brick wall, forcing her body to remain still, afraid that any movement would give her away and spoil her plans. Jennifer was determined not to relax until she could feel the large steel wheels of the train moving beneath her.

The night's shadows and the floppy lace hat she wore did a good job of hiding her features, her long hair braided and tucked up and into her hat. Her dark blue satin dress easily blended into the shadows where she stood, and she hugged her travel bag close to her chest to conceal her frame that much more. If anyone had taken the time to pay the young woman any attention, they would have noticed that her eyes continually scanned the activity on the platform, looking for any recognition in the faces passing by her. But the people moving about that night were much too concerned with their own affairs to notice her as they scurried past.

"All aboard!" The conductor's cry interrupted Jennifer's surveillance.

"Finally," she whispered to herself as she pushed away from the depot's wall and nervously took another glance around the corner of the building. Again, she was relieved to see that she had drawn no attention, and she hurried across the platform to the conductor. By the time the man had finished calling out the names of the train's next few stops, she was standing next to him, waiting for her ticket to be punched.

"Going all the way to Denver?" The conductor eyed Jennifer suspiciously as he took her ticket. "Alone?"

"Yes." Jennifer tried to remain calm under the man's questioning gaze. "I'm going to visit my aunt. My brother was to escort me but he took sick yesterday, and Father is away on a business trip. The tickets were already purchased..."

"You can turn them in on others. Best you wait until your brother or father can accompany you."

"Yes, you are right. But my aunt is so very much looking

forward to my visit. And I'm sure I'll have no trouble. I'll just stay to myself until we reach Denver."

The conductor didn't look as though he agreed with the girl's positive attitude, but she had a ticket and there was little he could do to prevent her from boarding. The sound of the train's whistle seemed to make up his mind. "You'll be wanting the sleeper car, then. Just continue right through this car and into the next. Take any bunk you like. I'd suggest one of the upper ones in the back."

"Thank you." She retrieved her punched ticket and tucked it securely back into her bag.

"Mind that you do keep to yourself." He would be paying close attention to make sure she did just that.

Jennifer mounted the high steps and, without a look back at the only home she had ever known, entered the passenger car and made her way to the sleeper. When, a few moments later, the engineer blew the steam whistle warning of the train's imminent departure, she was tucked behind the securely closed curtains of the top bunk at the front end of the sleeper car, waiting anxiously for the train to begin moving. Caught off-guard by the sudden motion, she was thrown against the car's side as the locomotive lurched to life, jerking the passenger and cargo cars behind. But she quickly resettled herself on the lumpy mattress as the train started to gain speed.

With each passing click-clack of the coach's wheels on the rails beneath the rumbling train, Jennifer left behind the comfortable life of her childhood. She was both excited and nervous about the new, unknown future waiting for her at the end of her trip. Stretching her body out, she rested her head on her canvas bag, allowing her thoughts to gradually replay the events that had led to this moment.

Five Days Earlier

"NO!" HIS DEEP voice boomed. "I will not have a daughter of mine working. Absolutely not." He paced about the room.

"But, Father..." Jennifer tried again to make her father understand her feelings even though she doubted she ever could. She'd had this *discussion* many times with her father and his response was always the same. "Respectable women do not work. Your mother never worked. She married, as was her duty, and you will do the same."

Jennifer's father was a large man, well over six feet tall and solidly built. Seeing him storm about the elegant furnishings in their home's small sitting room would have been amusing under different circumstances. She was anything but amused.

Martin Kensington was a successful businessman, having inherited a prosperous shipping company from his father who had, in turn, inherited it from his father. Her three brothers worked in the company, and she had thought that she could, too. Not on the ships or down at the docks where cargoes were loaded and unloaded, but in the shipping office where her skills with numbers and writing could be of use. She had listened as her father constantly complained of inadequate help in that area and she wanted to make a contribution to the family business. Not to mention the money she could earn would help fund her dreams of traveling; she longed to explore the country's western territories.

The last thing she wanted was to be the wife of one of the countless suitors her father continually arranged to call on her.

Watching her father cross and re-cross the room, Jennifer took a deep breath and tried again. "Just a few hours a week, Father. Just enough to make me feel useful and allow me some spending money."

"No!" Martin's shout rattled the room's windows. "You do not need money. A silly thing like you would not know how to handle money. Look at your mother—" He came to a stop directly in front of Jennifer and pointed at the small woman sitting without expression in the corner of the room. "She has never had two coins to rub together and she has never needed them. I see to all of her needs, just as your husband will see to yours."

Jennifer said nothing as her mind raced, searching for just the right reason that would convince her father. But her shoulders slumped; she finally understood that she would never make her father understand. She sighed deeply, and her head dropped to her chest in defeat.

Her father moved quickly to reinforce her apparent capitulation. "I never want this subject brought up again. Do you understand?" He leaned down until he was mere inches from his dejected daughter's face, waiting for her reply.

"Yes," she whispered.

"Good." Martin straightened back up, towering over Jennifer. "I have a shipment to see to." He nodded to his wife. And after one final look at Jennifer as if to say, *This matter is settled,* he turned and left the house.

Jennifer sat in the now-deafening silence and for several minutes studied her mother.

In contrast to her husband, Mary Stancey Kensington was a

woman of slight stature and delicate features. Born into the well-respected Stancey shipbuilding family, Mary was only seventeen when Jennifer's grandfather had arranged for her marriage. Jennifer knew that her mother had not loved her father at the time of their marriage but, over the years, had since come to "adore him," as she often said. Jennifer was never quite sure what her mother meant when she spoke of her husband in that way.

Mary Kensington spent most of her days seeing to the running of the Kensington home and supervising the small staff of domestic help. She attended few social functions unless her presence was required for her husband's benefit, instead spending her free time participating in sewing and reading circles, which were, in actuality, nothing more than gossip sessions.

Jennifer studied the woman who had raised her and her brothers with as much love as any mother had ever given her children. And yet, in her own sixteen years of life, Jennifer could not recall her mother ever voicing an opinion that had not been first uttered by her father. In fact, it was hard to remember a time when her mother had voiced any opinion at all. Mary Stancey Kensington lived her life in her husband's shadow and was seemingly content to do so.

No, Jennifer vowed, *I will not end up like her.*

She rose from the chair and crossed the room to where her mother still quietly sat. Leaning down, she kissed her mother gently on the forehead.

"I'm going to the library. Don't worry, I'll be back in time for dinner." Her father required the entire family's attendance at evening meals unless demands of their shipping business interfered. She covered the few steps to the front door, and then stopped. Turning back, she told her mother, "I'll make my dreams come true no matter what Father says."

And with that, she left, never seeing the single tear slowly making its way down her mother's cheek.

"I pray that you do, daughter." The soft voice was barely audible in the silence of the room. "I pray that you do."

JENNIFER PUSHED OPEN the heavy oak door that greeted visitors to the Kensington Library. Her father's gift to the town was a massive sandstone building with oak-framed windows, oak bookshelves and oak reading tables. "Genteel understatement," she had sarcastically observed at its elaborate opening ceremony. Its design was for one purpose only: to impress the town with her father's generosity.

Of course, she knew the real reason behind the gift. Her father had wanted to increase his dock space and, in order to sway the town council to his way of thinking, had donated the library and was providing a yearly stipend to employ a librarian and purchase books. In return, he had, not surprisingly, received permission to expand his docks.

Jennifer really didn't care why her father had donated the library, she was just glad that he had, as she spent as much time as she could at the building. In fact, the library was the best thing her father had ever done for her. She had developed a rich friendship with the young man hired as the librarian and she had read almost every book its shelves held. Her dreams had taken root in the library, and its many books repeatedly nourished them. She had kept her dreams to herself, though, because she knew her father would seal the massive oak doors shut if he knew the role the library played in them.

She trudged across the oak floor and slumped down into one of the large overstuffed chairs provided for reading.

"What did he do now?" Matthew, the young man who served as librarian, looked up from his work cataloging the latest delivery of books. Though he was a few years older than Jennifer, he had found her friendship a welcome bonus to his official duties.

"He turned me down again," she grumbled, sinking further down into the chair.

"You know that he'll never change his mind, don't you?"

"Yes."

Matthew rarely had to guess the cause of his friend's dark moods, as it was not uncommon for her to come to the library after arguing with her father. Having had this conversation with Jennifer several times before, he knew she would need some quiet time, so he went back to his work, leaving his friend to her own thoughts.

Almost an hour passed before Jennifer straightened up, pulling her legs up under her to get more comfortable in the large overstuffed chair.

"So, Matt." Her mood had improved, and she playfully asked the librarian, "You planning on letting me see today's delivery?"

"Maybe." He smiled, knowing she was fully aware of what the latest delivery contained since she had helped him make out the order weeks earlier. It was a favorite game of theirs to argue over the book orders. Jennifer was fascinated with the western frontier and would lobby for more books covering the West, while he would insist the library provide a wider range of subjects for the town's other readers. Then, after the order was finalized, he would always add one or two additional books as surprises for his young friend.

"Got something here that might just bring a smile back to your face." He reached down into a box at his feet and pulled out a rolled-up newspaper.

"What is it?" She rose out of the chair and made her way to the librarian's desk.

"All the way from Denver." He handed Jennifer the paper.

"This is great. But how did you manage it?" She knew that it was hard enough getting copies of newspapers from cities on the East Coast, let alone one from the western territories.

"A chap I know at the publishing house mentioned they sometimes send books out West. I asked him for a favor and that's what he sent, only a month old. Not bad, huh?"

"Not bad. I'd say it was fantastic. I can't wait to read the whole thing."

"Go on." He motioned her to one of the large oak reading tables, pleased he had been able to surprise her with the newspaper. "Spread it out and enjoy. I've got to finish cataloging the rest of these books."

A comfortable silence fell over the library as Jennifer read the Denver paper and Matthew finished the job of cataloging the recent arrivals.

She finished the news part of the paper and began reading through the advertisements at the end. "Oh, my," she gasped as she read a small ad at the bottom of the back page.

"Are you okay?"

"Yes, I'm fine." She reread the ad. "Matt, do you think I'd make a good schoolteacher?"

"You'd make a great teacher. Why do you ask?"

"There's an ad here. It says they need single women to teach school in towns out West."

"Jennifer," he pushed up from his desk, "you're not thinking..."

"Matt," she was getting more excited the more she read and re-read the ad, "it's perfect. I would be able to live in the West like I've always wanted and make enough money to be on my own. You said yourself that I would make a good teacher." Her confidence grew as she rolled the idea around in her mind.

"Great." He leaned over her shoulder to read the ad that had captured her attention. "I said that you would make a great teacher. But there is no way your father will allow you to travel west to be a schoolteacher."

"I don't plan to tell him."

"Jennifer, you can't...."

She thought for a moment before deciding. A sense of purpose grew inside her, and she twisted her head in order to face her friend. "I'll be seventeen in two months. Father is already complaining that I am taking too long to choose a suitor that will benefit the business and has decided that I shall be married by my eighteenth birthday whether I agree or not." She looked into his eyes. "Please promise me you won't say anything."

"I don't know." He started to pace, reminding Jennifer of her father's movements only a couple of hours earlier.

"Promise me."

"But he is..." Matthew returned to stand beside her. "I mean, technically, he is my employer, and — "

She grabbed her friend's arm, preventing him from ending his thought. "Please, this is a chance I have to take. I may never get another."

Matt sat on the arm of the chair Jennifer occupied, studying the girl looking so hopefully at him.

Jennifer was willowy and taller than most women the librarian knew, but not quite as tall as his own five feet eleven inches. Her ginger hair set off her sapphire blue eyes and he believed her to be one of the prettiest young women in the town. Indeed, she could have her pick of the town's many eligible bachelors but, for reasons he had never understood, she continually turned down all requests to be courted.

He had come to regard her as the sister he never had; he had watched her grow from a naïve child into a young woman with a fierce independent spirit who was not afraid to have hopes and dreams. He was convinced that her inner strength could wear down the strongest of men. Yet, did she have the fortitude required to survive the kind of challenging life she was now talking about? Not to mention doing it in a part of the country so different from the only way of life she had ever known.

As he continued to study her, Matt realized that Jennifer was right. Her dreams were too precious to destroy by forcing her into a future that would only bring her unhappiness. Being forced into a marriage by a father who was only seeing it from the standpoint of a good business deal was definitely not the right life for the young woman watching him so intently.

"All right. But how do you plan to get to Denver? You have no money," he reminded his friend.

"You're due to get your monthly stipend soon."

"Oh, no." He shook his head halfheartedly. "Your father

would hog-tie me and throw me on the next ship to the Orient if he found out that I not only kept your plans a secret from him but also gave you the money."

"He'll never know. I'll save the money I make and, as soon as I can, I'll send you enough to make up what you give me. Please, Matt." Her dreams were within her grasp and she was not going to let them slip through her fingers.

"Gosh, I know this is wrong." Matthew ran his hands through his hair fretfully. He looked into Jennifer's eyes and knew that he would not, could not, refuse her. "Your father is due to come by the day after tomorrow with my stipend. That should be enough for you to buy a ticket to Denver and have some left to see you through until you get to whatever town your teaching position is in."

"Thank you!" She threw her arms around his neck, kissing him on the cheek. "You're the best friend anyone could ever have."

"Just promise me one thing..." Concerned what it would look like if someone happened to enter the library just then, he quickly unwrapped her arms from his neck.

"Anything." She blushed shyly, realizing what she had just done.

"Promise me you'll make your dreams come true."

"I promise."

Taking a quick look at the library's door, he wrapped his arms around her and briefly hugged her close. "If anyone can, Jennifer, I know it will be you. You better be getting home. It's almost dinnertime, and you don't want to be late."

"Yes, you're right." Jennifer nodded, her eyes brimming with tears. She did not want to leave the refuge of the library, but she also did not want to give her father any new excuse to rage at her. She turned to leave, then stopped. Uncertainly, she looked at her friend. "Matt, one more thing."

"You want me to buy the ticket." The librarian grinned, knowing that she could not go to the train station and purchase a ticket to Denver without raising suspicions.

"If you don't mind."

"Just remember me when you're out West enjoying yourself." Matthew laughed.

"Don't worry. If this works, I'll never forget you."

"DID YOU GET it?" Jennifer slid to a stop at the librarian's desk, breathless after running all the way from her house.

"Just got back." Matthew handed her an envelope holding a

single ticket for the next scheduled train and a few dollars of spending money.

"Did anyone question you?" She clutched the envelope to her chest.

"No. I can honestly say that I've never seen any of the folks at that end of town within these walls. And since I don't get to that end of town very often, it's not too likely that anyone knew who I was. They probably assumed I was just another businessman traveling west."

"Good." She stared at the ticket in her hands.

"Are you sure about this?" Matthew asked. "I mean, it's not too late to change your mind."

"No." Jennifer rested her hip against his desk. "This may be my only chance. I have to go."

With a sigh, Matthew dropped into his chair. He knew she spoke the truth. In a way, he was jealous of her. Not because she was doing something to make her dreams come true, but because she had dreams. He was content with his life and really had no desire to change it. He would miss Jennifer after she left, but he had other friends and would happily take whatever life provided. But Jennifer was different; she would never just settle for what life handed her. No, she wanted to go out and reach for her dreams, forcing life to bend to her wishes. And he had no doubt she would do just that.

"Okay, I purchased a round-trip ticket. That way you can cash in the return trip when you get to Denver and you won't need to carry so much money on the train. Next train leaves in two days, just after midnight. Are you sure you'll be able to get out of the house to make it?"

"I'll make sure."

JESSE REACHED DOWN, grabbing the corners of the fifty-pound sack of flour and effortlessly lifting it from the scarred wooden floor of the general store to settle it across her broad shoulders. She carried the heavy sack outside, placing it in the back of the buckboard waiting in the hot, dusty street. Returning to the store, she asked, "Is that all of it?"

"Yep," the storekeeper replied. "Everything on your list, Jesse."

"What's the damage?"

"Give me a minute to finish this."

Ed Granger was a big bear of a man, but was one of the gentlest souls Jesse had ever met. A beard covered handsome features that would easily break into a broad smile and hearty laugh when given the slightest reason. His head was topped with graying hair that matched his eyes, sparkling with his ever-present good humor. And a leatherwork apron stretched over a growing paunch; "Too many good meals at the Silver Slipper," Ed chided himself every morning as he wrapped the apron around his growing middle. Always willing to help out anyone down on their luck, he was well liked and respected as an honest businessman in an occupation not always known for honest dealings.

"Take your time." Jesse rested her tall, sinewy body against the worn wooden counter in front of Ed. She crossed one booted ankle over the other and waited patiently for Ed to finish adding up her charges.

The storekeeper finally scratched a number on the page of his ledger. "Should I add this to your account?"

She glanced at the figure, then reached into the pocket of the faded flannel shirt she wore, pulling out the coins she had placed there earlier that morning and tossed them on the counter. "Here, you can put the change on my account."

"Thanks." He made a notation in the store's ledger before closing the large book and putting it back in its place beneath the counter. "Want me to walk over and help you unload?" He knew what the answer would be, but it didn't hurt to offer.

"No, thanks. I can manage."

Jesse walked out of the store, stepping back out onto the covered boardwalk that lined the front of the building. Heat waves were rising from the dirt-packed surface of the street and it wasn't yet mid-day. She knew the town was in for another scorcher; the sky was completely cloudless and there was no indication that rain would be forthcoming anytime soon. Not wanting to leave the relative coolness of the shaded boardwalk just yet, she leaned against the nearest support post and observed the town she now called home.

Sweetwater was located at the northern end of a river valley, and nestled up against the forest that separated the valley from the looming Rocky Mountains. The town had taken its name from the sweet-tasting waters of several creeks that flowed out of the nearby mountains to form the river running down the center of the valley. The constant supply of fresh water made the valley an ideal place for ranching, and kept the town alive during long summer months of drought. The town itself wasn't much by anyone's standards. It had been built around a stage station with its main reason for existing to serve as a supply point for the ranches and mining camps in the surrounding valley and mountains. A dozen buildings of various sizes and shapes lined the stage road that doubled as the town's only street. The original adobe stage station still served that purpose and was located directly across the street from the general store.

Jesse had lived in Sweetwater just shy of a year. She had arrived with nothing but the clothes on her back and the horse she rode. In her shirt pocket, she had carried the deed to a saloon and gambling house she had won in a Denver poker game. Never having heard of Sweetwater before the night of the game, Jesse had come to the small town intent on making a fast sale on the Silver Slipper and leaving town with some gold in her empty pockets. But as the fates would have it, Jesse had fallen in love with the town and the surrounding valley. So instead of selling the establishment of questionable repute, she had decided to stay and make it into a respectable business.

After assuming ownership of the Silver Slipper, Jesse had immediately thrown out the dishonest card dealers and gamblers. She had shut down the second-floor rooms used by the "working women" and had turned them into boarding rooms. The main floor had been split into three sections; her office took up one end of the building while the middle section had become a quiet place for diners to enjoy a well-cooked meal. The other end remained a saloon and allowed the use of the gaming tables for anyone interested. The women who had once plied their trade in the upstairs rooms had become the Slipper's card dealers, maids, and cooks. It hadn't taken much persuasion on Jesse's part to win the women over to the new way of doing business. Those who weren't happy with the changes had been given ten dollars and a one-way stage ticket out of Sweetwater. Those who decided to stay soon found they liked serving meals, cleaning rooms, or dealing cards much more then they had their previous horizontal profession, especially since Jesse made sure they were taken care of.

Cattle and horse buyers coming to Sweetwater to do business with the valley's ranchers quickly discovered they could obtain a clean room and good meal at the Slipper and made it their primary place of business when in town. Folks riding the stage to and from points further west enjoyed the atmosphere they found at the Silver Slipper much better than staying at the old adobe station and willingly spent the extra money to rent a room for the night. And once word got out that the tables at the Silver Slipper provided fair games of chance, there was no shortage of customers in the saloon.

Jesse had quickly found herself with a thriving business. Best of all, the Silver Slipper's profits had provided Jesse with enough money to purchase a small ranch just outside of town where she was beginning to slowly build a cattle herd.

It had always been her dream to own her own ranch. Growing up, she had thought she would take over the running of her family's ranch from her father. After all, she had no brothers, and it seemed like the natural thing would be for her father to let her assume operation of the ranch. But that was not to be.

After months of drifting around the western territories, Jesse had found herself in Denver and, being low on cash, decided to sit in on one of the poker games taking place in the saloon where she sat nursing a glass of whiskey. Lady Luck was with Jesse that night, and by late in the evening she had won most of the money on the table. Jesse wanted to take her winnings and leave the game, but one player, having consumed more than his share of whiskey during the evening, insisted on one more hand.

"Only fair to give me a chance to win back my money," the inebriated gambler told the rest of the players, his words slurred from the liquor.

"Ah, call it a night, Johnson. You ain't got nothin' left to bet with."

Reaching into his coat pocket, Johnson pulled out a crumpled piece of paper and placed it on the table, smoothing the sheet with his rough hands. "I can bet with this."

"What is it?"

"Deed to the Silver Slipper. Best whorehouse in Sweetwater."

Hearing the loud boast, the other men at the table and those at nearby tables burst into laughter.

"You mean, the only whorehouse in Sweetwater. Broken-down wreck. Even your whores ain't much, from what I've heard."

"It's worth enough," Johnson shouted, his face beet red in anger at the jeers directed his way. "Come on, what have ya got to lose?"

"I'll play." Jesse had remained silent up to this point, being content to leave the game with her winnings. But she didn't take kindly to the talk about the women. It disgusted her, the way men were always mighty glad to have the ladies share their beds but were loathe to have the same women share their table.

"I'm in." It took half of the money from the neat stack on the table in front of her, but she figured she could chance it; even if she lost, she would still have a great deal more than when she had entered the saloon.

"Now we're talking." Johnson placed the deed in the center

of the table next to Jesse's bet. "Anyone else want in?" He looked expectedly at the other two men sitting at their table.

"Nope, I'm out."

"Me too. If I don't get home soon, my woman will meet me at the door with her frying pan again." A second man rose to a chorus of sniggers and catcalls from the saloon's patrons now crowding around the table. It wasn't often that this kind of money was bet on one hand and everyone wanted a good view, knowing that the game would be talked about for months to come.

"Okay." Johnson glared across the table at her. "We'll cut the cards to see who deals."

"I have a better idea. Barkeep, a fresh deck of cards." If she was going to play for these stakes, she wanted to do so with a deck that hadn't been marked. Then, looking around the crowd of faces circling the table, she pointed to a boy who didn't look old enough to be out this late at night, let alone in this type of establishment.

"You deal," Jesse instructed the boy.

The boy found himself being slapped on the back and pushed toward the empty chair at the table. Several in the crowd laughed and scoffed at his instant celebrity. He sat down heavily on the chair, gulping audibly as the barkeep handed him the fresh deck.

"Why him?" Johnson demanded. If he couldn't deal, he wanted to pick his own dealer, one that could slip him a card or two from the bottom of the deck.

"Looks honest." She glared at Johnson, daring him to voice an objection to the neutral dealer.

Johnson studied the woman who sat across the table from him. Though her body showed all the curves he would expect to see on a woman, it also showed evidence of strength built over time from long days of hard work. He saw a woman who could possibly be more than a match for his own fighting skills and decided that this night was not the time to put his theory to the test.

"Fine." Turning to the nervous dealer, he barked, "Deal, damn you."

The boy broke the seal on the pack of cards, then shuffled the cards. After a couple of shaky shuffles, cards were dealt out to the two players.

Jesse picked up her cards and gave them a long look as she cradled them in her hands so no one else could see what she held. Leaving the cards in the order they had been dealt, she placed her hand face-down on the table. Her gaze turned to her opponent.

Johnson was staring at his cards. Beads of sweat had formed on his upper lip and he wiped at them with the back of his hand.

He looked at Jesse, trying to find any hint in her expression as to what cards she held in her hand. Seeing nothing, he grunted and studied his hand again. He removed two cards from his hand and discarded them. "Two."

The boy dealt two cards to Johnson before turning to Jesse.

"One," she quietly informed the dealer, and placed a card in the center of the table.

A wave of mumblings swept through the people crowded around the table as Jesse added the new card to her hand. She nodded to Johnson to play his cards.

"Three sevens. Looks like Lady Luck decided to change sides," he gloated, reaching for the pot in the middle of the table. He wasn't going to lose the Silver Slipper after all.

"Let the lady show her cards," someone in the crowd called out, forcing Johnson to withdraw his hands.

"Go on," Johnson snarled. "Show 'em you ain't got enough to beat me."

Jesse gave him a half smile, half smirk, as she started to turn her hand over, one card at a time. A hush fell over the room as a king of hearts followed a king of spades. Next, a two of diamonds was turned over and then a two of clubs.

"Told ya," Johnson crowed. "She ain't got nothin' but two pair."

Before he could get the words out of his mouth, Jesse turned over her last card to reveal the two of hearts.

A loud shout broke the silence and members of the watching crowd whooped and hollered at Jesse's victory. She gathered the money and deed from the table, carefully folding the paper before placing it into her shirt pocket. Jesse pushed a few coins across the table to Johnson.

"No one should leave the table broke," she offered.

Johnson picked up the offering and flung it back at her. "Don't want your money, bitch." He stood so fast that the people standing in back of him did not have a chance to move, and several were knocked back into others crowding behind. The table was jostled and would have tipped over had the young dealer not grabbed on with both hands to steady it.

Handing two bits to the boy who had dealt the cards, Jesse watched Johnson force his way through the onlookers and out of the building. Then she rose from her seat and smiled at the many patrons shouting offers to buy her drinks.

"Sorry, boys. It's been a long night and I think a nice, warm bed is a better idea."

Some of the men immediately changed their offers from whiskey to sharing her bed. She politely declined and, working

*her way through the celebrating crowd, made for the same door
that Johnson had exited moments before.*

*Once outside, Jesse stood for several minutes enjoying the
cool night air after the stuffy heat of the saloon. Her horse,
Dusty, stood patiently at the hitch in front of the saloon. She
stepped off the boardwalk and walked to the waiting horse,
patting the mare gently on the neck.*

*"Looks like we own a house of ill repute in Sweetwater.
Didn't think I'd ever be returning to Montana." Untying the
reins from the hitching post, she pulled herself up into the
saddle. "By the look of Johnson, seems best to hightail it out of
Denver. So I guess we'll be heading north tonight."*

*Dusty turned to the street, breaking into a trot without
Jesse's urging.*

*"You know something I don't?" She laughed, tightening her
grip on the reins.*

*Standing in the alley by the saloon and hidden in the night's
shadows, Johnson watched as Jesse mounted her horse. He
reached for the pistol in his holster, but before he could get a shot
off a group of men, still talking about the card game, exited the
saloon, blocking his view. When the men finally walked past,
Jesse was no longer in sight. "This isn't over, bitch." He
slammed his gun back into its holster.*

"'Bout time for the stage to arrive." Ed's words broke into
Jesse's thoughts as he stepped out onto the boardwalk and stood
beside her.

"Yep." Looking across the street, Jesse noticed that a few of
the local ranch hands were beginning to gather at the stage
station.

"New schoolteacher is supposed to be on the stage."

"Yep." *That explains the crowd waiting for the stage today.*

For the past several weeks, since Mayor Perkins announced
that a schoolteacher would be arriving from Denver to take on
the duties at their schoolhouse, there seemed to have been little
else to talk about.   The town had built the school during the
previous summer, but it had remained unused because the valley
lacked a qualified teacher. Each day, the demands had grown
from parents with children who needed educating. Finally, the
mayor had been left with no choice but to contract for the first
available teacher.

Jesse's sharp ears picked up the sounds of beating hoofs,
slapping leather, and the cries of the stage driver yelling
commands to his team of straining horses—noises that
announced the stage's impending arrival. Moments later, the

coach came into view at the point where the road broke from the forest. The stage thundered into Sweetwater and skidded to a stop in front of the station; a choking cloud of dust filled the air and covered everything and everyone it came into contact with.

She looked across the street as the passengers stepped out from the stage. A young woman was helped from the coach and the gathering of single men surged toward her. *That must be the new schoolteacher.* She reached up and removed her Stetson, releasing a shower of shoulder-length reddish-brown hair. Using the sleeve of her shirt, Jesse wiped the sweat from her brow, then waved the hat in front of her face to clear the dust kicked up by the stage.

At the same moment, the young woman stepped away from the stage. Getting her first look at the town of Sweetwater, she turned to observe the side of the street where Jesse stood. The motion of Jesse's hat attracted her gaze and her eyes fell upon the most beautiful woman she had ever seen.

A pair of sapphire eyes locked onto a pair of soft brown eyes and the world seemed to stand still for both women.

"Hey, are you all right?"

Jesse drew in a startled breath, sagging suddenly against the boardwalk's post. The sound of Ed's voice forced her to break her gaze. She jammed the Stetson back on her head and stepped down into the street. "Yeah, I'm fine," she mumbled as she walked around her buckboard. Climbing up onto the seat, she immediately urged the draft horse forward.

Ed shrugged his shoulders at Jesse's rapid departure and then stepped off the boardwalk, crossing the street to join the crowd by the stage.

"What the heck?" Jesse muttered to herself as she left the new schoolteacher and her crowd of instant admirers behind. Attempting to concentrate on the dusty road in front of her, she instead found herself trying to figure out what had just happened and why her hands were shaking so hard she could barely keep hold of the horse's reins.

Jennifer stood in the dusty street surrounded by several young men all speaking at the same time, but she heard nothing except the beating of her own heart. She watched as the buckboard carried the beautiful woman away from her and wondered why she had an almost uncontrollable urge to run after it.

"LET ME THROUGH!" A man elbowed his way through the young men surrounding the new arrival. He finally came to a stop directly in front Jennifer and grabbed her slender hands in his beefy ones, shaking them heartily.

"Miss Kensington, it is so nice to finally make your acquaintance," the man said enthusiastically. His arrival took Jennifer's attention away from the retreating buckboard.

Jennifer turned to face a middle-aged, balding man not as tall as she, but much wider. A bushy mustache hung down hiding his mouth, its thick hairs billowing out from his face with every word he spoke.

"Please allow me to introduce myself," the man continued, pumping Jennifer's hands up and down. "My name is Perkins, Miles Perkins. I am Sweetwater's mayor and it is I who arranged for your position." The mayor, as always, was ready to take credit for any project he had any part of, no matter how small his contribution might be.

Jennifer smiled sweetly at the man as she extricated her hands from his, her arms feeling like the bones had come loose after the vigorous shaking. "I'm pleased to meet you, Mr. Perkins."

"You can call me Mayor. Everyone does." The mustache billowed as several not too well hidden groans could be heard from the crowd pressed around them. "Do you have any luggage?"

"Just this." She indicated the small, canvas travel bag she had removed from under the seat inside the stage. Many of the young men surrounding them offered to carry the bag for her, but she insisted on taking it herself. It wasn't very large and she could easily carry it. Besides, the last thing she wanted was for a brawl to break out among the young men juggling for her attention.

"Go on, now," Mayor Perkins instructed the uninvited men. "I'm sure your employers expect you to be earning your pay and not lollygagging about. Now scoot, the lot of you."

Mayor Perkins took Jennifer's arm and started to walk down the street in the same direction that the buckboard had taken. As they walked, he explained the purpose of each of the scattered buildings they passed.

"That is, as you know, the stage station," the mayor pointed to the small adobe building that looked to be ready to fall in on itself, "and telegraph office. The telegraph hasn't reached Sweetwater yet, but you can have a message sent by stage to the nearest telegraph office. You will probably want to send your folks a message letting them know that you have arrived safely in Sweetwater."

She nodded in agreement to the mayor even though she had

no intention of sending a telegraph to her family, as that would provide her whereabouts to them.

"That there, as you can see, is the general store." He pointed across the street where a man was standing in the shade of the covered boardwalk. "That's Ed Granger, he runs the store for his no-good brother-in-law."

Jennifer smiled at the storekeeper.

"Now that's the jail and town hall." Mayor Perkins indicated the building adjoining the store. "And next to the town hall is the town's newspaper, The Gazette. Over here." He was now pointing to the near side of the street again. "That's the Oxbow Saloon, and not a decent place for a young lady like yourself. Behind the Oxbow are the stables, livery, and blacksmith. Most of the town folk live up at this end of town. You'll have a chance to meet everyone at the social in your honor tomorrow evening."

Jennifer believed his description of "this end of town" rather an overstatement for a community not much bigger than a couple of city blocks back home. But she kept her thoughts to herself. "And where is the schoolhouse?"

"Right over there."

A building sat atop a small knoll on the other side of a creek that ran out of the forest behind the stables and flowed past the Oxbow before turning to parallel the road out of town. A footbridge allowed access across the creek and a gravel path led to the schoolhouse.

"We'll be having the social there, so you can get acquainted with it then. It's all ready for you to start your lessons. Books and supplies are already purchased and waiting for you."

She had wanted to see the schoolhouse first, but decided that tomorrow would be soon enough. The sun was reaching its peak in the cloudless sky and she was more than ready to get out of its blazing heat. Without comment, she continued to follow the mayor down the dusty street. Other than what were obviously private homes, there was only one other building in the direction they were walking. A two-story structure that looked to be newly painted with new curtains hanging in its many windows. A large, painted silver slipper graced the side of the building facing the stage road.

"This is the Silver Slipper. The town has arranged for you to have a room here. It's the closest thing Sweetwater has to a rooming house. Don't worry, we'll put you up with a family just as soon as the proper arrangements can be made."

"I'm sure it will be fine." Secretly, she was happy not to be boarding with a family. She didn't want the responsibility of helping care for someone else's children and home. She had run away to make her own life, and she wasn't too eager to have her dreams shattered before she had a chance to fully experience them.

She looked away from the mayor to see her new home. In the shade in front of the building stood the buckboard. Jennifer gasped as her heart nearly jumped from her chest.

Mistaking her reaction for uneasiness, the mayor hastened to add, "No reason to fear, Miss Kensington. The Slipper is a very respectable place now that Jesse is running it. Clean rooms and the best food in town. Jesse will take good care of you. You have my personal guarantee on that."

She followed the mayor up the steps to the Silver Slipper's wide porch. It wrapped entirely around the building, providing places to enjoy the coolness of its shade regardless of the time of day or the season. Solid support posts held up the porch's roof and between the posts, rails were nailed in a crossing pattern. The rails were topped with a wide, flat board providing a sturdy place to sit if one so desired. The shade of the porch felt wonderful after the heat of the street and Jennifer had to stop herself from flopping down in one of the many comfortable-looking chairs scattered about the porch.

"Afternoon, Miles," a stout woman opened the building's front door, "and this must be our new schoolteacher." The woman smiled broadly as she held out a hand to Jennifer.

"Yes, this is Miss Kensington. I believe you are to have a room ready for her."

Jennifer noticed that the mayor addressed the woman rather arrogantly, but she seemed not to take any offense to his rude manner.

"Of course." The woman gently squeezed the hand Jennifer offered before releasing it. "Welcome ta the Silver Slipper, Miss Kensington. Come on in. I've jus' finished makin' some lemonade, and it'll taste mighty good after bein' out in that heat." The woman opened the door wide to allow Jennifer and the mayor to enter.

Jennifer was disappointed that this was not the woman she had seen earlier. This woman appeared to be of the same age as her mother, but had obviously seen a great deal more of life. She stood of average height and though she looked to be somewhat frail, Jennifer was sure that the woman leading her into the building could easily outwork most men. She seemed genuinely friendly towards Jennifer, unlike Mayor Perkins who accompanied the two women inside, and Jennifer instantly liked the older woman.

"Thank you, Miss Jesse."

"Oh, lordy," the woman chuckled. "I ain't Jesse."

"I'm sorry. I thought Mayor Perkins said..."

"I said that Jesse owns the Slipper. This is Bette Mae. She helps run the place for Jesse."

"Oh," Jennifer blushed. "I apologize."

"There's no need," the woman stopped her. "Now, sit and have some of this here lemonade. Jesse is workin' in her office, but you'll have plenty of time ta meet her later."

Jennifer dropped down into the closest chair, placing her bag on the floor. "I'd love a glass."

"Good." Bette Mae poured a large glass and handed it to Jennifer. "How 'bout you, Miles?"

"No, thank you. I must be getting back to my other duties. A moment of your time, please, Bette Mae." The mayor motioned that he wished to speak to the woman privately.

"I'll be right back. You jus' help yourself to refills." Bette Mae pushed the pitcher closer to the new arrival before following the mayor back out onto the porch.

Jennifer studied the room in which she sat. Several tables similar to the one she occupied were spaced about the room. Each table was covered with a linen tablecloth, and a small arrangement of fresh flowers was placed in the center of each. Silverware was set out ready to be used by any diner that might request a meal. This was obviously the dining room of the establishment, but it was also much more.

She was astonished to see, built into one wall, bookcases overflowing with books. In front of these, a varied arrangement of overstuffed chairs and settees made an inviting place to spend a few moments, or hours, enjoying the written word. Curiosity got the better of her and she rose from the table, crossing the room to see what kind of books would be found on the shelves. She was amazed at the wide range of titles and authors.

"Ya like ta read?" Bette Mae asked on returning from her talk with the mayor. "Lordy, tha's a mighty silly question ta be askin' a schoolteacher, now ain't it?"

Startled from her search, Jennifer smiled at the woman. "What is that saying? No question is a silly question as long as you are really interested in the answer." She returned to the table and her glass of lemonade. "This is wonderful, thank you. And to answer your question, I love to read. I must admit that I'm pleased to see such an extensive library. Are the books available to anyone?"

"Yep. And ya can thank Jesse for them. Travelin' salesman came through some time back, talked her in ta buying a couple. He's been sendin' 'em regular since and she jus' keeps payin' for 'em. Says the town needs a library."

"That's very generous of her. We have a large library back home. I've spent many an hour there reading. Some of the best afternoons of my life."

"Oh." Bette Mae seemed surprised that a girl as pretty as the schoolteacher would spend her afternoons within the stuffy walls of a library. "And where would your home be, Miss Kensington?"

"Please, call me Jennifer." Not wanting to discuss the place she had so recently left, she quickly changed the subject to the mayor's private discussion with Bette Mae." Is everything all right with the arrangements?" Jennifer hoped that what she had heard about folks in the West not asking questions about one's past was true and the woman would not pursue any more about the life she had so recently left behind.

"Everything is fine. He was jus' makin' sure Jesse understood the importance of lookin' after ya whilst you're stayin' at the Slipper. As if she would do any less," Bette Mae snorted. "Mayor Perkins can surely be a pompous ass given half a chance. Oh, 'scuse my language, child."

"I don't mind." Jennifer chuckled. She had heard much worse than that when her father was on one of his numerous rampages. "I imagine he takes some getting used to. He about shook my arms right out of their sockets before I could get my hands out of his." She rubbed her arms, remembering the mayor's energetic greeting.

"That he mos' definitely does. I 'spect ya'd like ta see your room and freshen up. Maybe even take a nap. I swear ridin' that stage can shake the fillin's loose in ya teeth. Not ta mention the dust them horses kick up."

"It certainly wasn't quite what I had imagined."

"Let's git ya settled then." Bette Mae picked up Jennifer's bag, refusing to listen to her protests. She led Jennifer to a staircase in the middle of the bookcase-lined wall.

As she climbed the stairs, Jennifer noticed, for the first time, an alcove tucked behind the staircase with a closed door marked *Private*. She wondered if it led to the office of the mysterious Jesse.

Reaching the top of the staircase, Jennifer followed Bette Mae down a long hallway. They walked past the doors facing both sides of the hall; Jennifer assumed they led to the boarding rooms Mayor Perkins had mentioned. Bette Mae led her to a room at the far end of the corridor, where she unlocked a door, then handed her the key before pushing the door open.

The room was smaller than her bedroom back home, but it was furnished with everything Jennifer would need in her new life. In one corner a four-poster bed sat, its thick mattress covered by a warm-looking quilt. Pushed against the wall next to the head of the bed stood a small chest of drawers. In the opposite corner of the room, there was a well-traveled trunk that could double as a sitting bench where she could store her personal belongings. A small desk sat against the other wall; neatly stacked writing paper and sharpened pencils lay on its surface ready for use. For light, there was an oil lamp atop the desk and another on the dresser.

The room was located in the corner of the building and had windows on both outside walls. Jennifer especially liked this and quickly crossed the room to enjoy the views. When she looked out the window facing the front of the building, she saw the auburn-haired woman retrieving items from the back of the buckboard below.

"Who is that beautiful woman?" The words were out of her mouth before she even knew she had been thinking them.

"That'll be Jesse." Bette Mae continued to empty her travel bag, placing the few items it held neatly into the top drawer of the chest next to the bed.

Jennifer watched until Jesse disappeared under the porch's roof on her way back into the Slipper before turning away from the window. "I'm sorry, I did not intend for you to do all of the work."

"Hush, child, ya didn' have enough in that bag ta be needin' two people ta unpack. Looks like ya need a few things 'fore ya can start teachin' school." It was obvious that the only dress Jennifer had was the one she was wearing.

"I was hoping to buy a couple of dresses once I arrived."

"Heavens, that won't do for the town's new schoolteacher. Now take it off so's I can have it washed while ya take a nap. No argument, hand it over." The look Bette Mae was giving Jennifer made it obvious she wasn't moving until she had the dress.

Jennifer pulled the dirty garment over her head and handed it to the older woman.

"Now git yourself into that bed. A nice long nap will do ya good."

Jennifer removed her dust-coated shoes and stockings before crawling between the cool sheets on the bed. She hadn't realized how tired she was after being tossed about on the long stage ride from Denver, and she snuggled down into the softness of the feather mattress and pillows.

Before Bette Mae reached the bottom of the stairs, Jennifer was fast asleep, dreaming of a woman with the most beautiful brown eyes.

BEHIND THE DOOR marked *Private*, Jesse sat at her desk.
The sound of the schoolteacher's laughter floated into her office
from the dining area and she knew she should go out and greet
the young woman she was providing lodging for. But before she
could get up the nerve to do that, the sound of footsteps on the
stairway told her Bette Mae was taking the new arrival upstairs
to her room. Unable to concentrate on the ledgers spread out
before her, Jesse went to retrieve the supplies remaining in the
buckboard. She had just settled back in behind her desk when
she heard a knock at the office door.

"Come in, Bette Mae." She knew the older woman would be
coming to fill her in on the Slipper's newest guest.

"Brought ya some lemonade. Figured ya might could use a
cold drink." Bette Mae entered the room with a tray holding a
half-full pitcher and two empty glasses. She set the tray down on
a table and filled both glasses, handing one to her employer and
friend.

"Thanks." Jesse smiled her appreciation.

"You should do more of that."

"More of what?"

"Smile. Makes ya look years younger." Bette Mae grinned at
Jesse's obvious discomfort.

Jesse changed the subject. "Is she settled?"

"Yes, she's taking a nap."

"Room okay with her?" She had been unsure as to what
requirements the schoolteacher would need in a room and had
decided to give her the best room in the Slipper. After all, the
schoolteacher would be spending a lot of time in the room, and
Jesse figured she might as well be as comfortable as possible.

"Her name is Jennifer. Jennifer Kensington. And she'll be
needin' some clothes 'fore she starts with her teachin' duties."

"What?" Jesse was confused as to why that should be of
interest to her.

"This is the only dress she has." Bette Mae held up the dress
she had carried into the room with the tray.

Jesse had assumed it to be a rag the woman would use to
clean up after they finished with their drinks. "That's it?"

"Yup. It probably was brand new when she left home. But
now it ain't decent ta wear."

"There's no seamstress in town." Jesse drained the last of
the lemonade in her glass. She was surprised at the condition of
the schoolteacher's only dress, but still wasn't sure what she was
supposed to do about it.

"Ruthie can sew." Bette Mae refilled both glasses. "I'm
guessin' we can find a dress or two at the general store and

Ruthie can alter them ta fit the lass. That'll do until Ed can order some material from Bozeman."

Jesse cringed at the mention of the town where her parents now lived. "Okay, get what you think she needs and tell Ed to put it on the Slipper's tab."

"Best find Ruthie and git over ta Ed's then."

Leaning back in her chair, Jesse watched the woman leave her office and wondered why she had just agreed to finance a new wardrobe for the schoolteacher. She had no obligation to the recent arrival except to provide her room and board, but somehow she felt a need to take care of the young woman.

Why?

As she pondered her dilemma, the image of the most beautiful blue eyes invaded her thoughts.

JENNIFER SAT ON the Slipper's porch, enjoying the slight afternoon breeze. For the umpteenth time, her hands brushed smooth the new dress she wore. A smile crossed her face as she remembered how she had been presented with it after waking from her nap.

A knock on the door to Jennifer's room announced Bette Mae and the young girl, Ruthie. No matter how strongly she protested that she could not accept, much less pay for the sorely needed clothing, Jennifer had been unable to prevent being presented with the recently altered garment.

The simple gingham dress was the only one the storekeeper had in stock. It did not come close to the quality of the dresses she had left hanging in her closet back home, but to her it was the most beautiful dress she had ever worn. She had thanked Ruthie for altering the dress so it would fit and promised Bette Mae she would pay for its cost. She had been surprised to be told that the Slipper's owner had been the one to purchase the dress. Anxious to thank the elusive woman, she waited impatiently for supper and her chance at finally meeting the beautiful Jesse.

AT SUPPER, JENNIFER found herself eating alone. Bette Mae and Ruthie were seeing to the paying customers, and Jesse had yet to appear from her office. Jennifer finished the excellent meal and decided that she might as well return to her room, since it was obvious that her benefactor had no intention of joining her. With a heavy sigh she rose from her chair and, deciding to take a book back to her room, crossed the room to the bookcases. As she passed in front of the alcove leading to Jesse's private office, the door opened and the mysterious woman stepped out.

"Oh, Miss Jesse." Jennifer was startled at the sudden appearance.

"Evening." Jesse nervously nodded to the young woman.

"I'm sorry I missed you at supper," Jennifer said shyly. She was close enough to reach out and touch Jesse, and it took all the self-control she possessed not to do just that.

"Sorry, I lost track of time."

"Oh, I understand. I'm sure running a business like the Silver Slipper must take up most of your time. Perhaps you can make it some other night."

"Perhaps." Jesse wondered what the schoolteacher would say if she knew that she had purposely remained in her office through supper. Unable to bring herself to face the young woman who seemed to have such a strong effect on her, she had stayed hidden in her office until she was sure that Jennifer would have finished her meal and returned to her room upstairs.

Jennifer sensed Jesse's unease. "It's been a long day and I'll bid you a good night, Miss Jesse." Then remembering the new dress she wore, she rushed to add, "Thank you for the dress. You really didn't have to go to such trouble. I'll talk to Mayor Perkins tomorrow about an advance on my salary so that I can pay you back."

"No need."

"Oh, no. I insist you let me pay you back, Miss Jesse." Jennifer reached out and lightly placed a hand on Jesse's arm.

Both women were startled at the sensations radiating from the touch.

"I'm sorry, Miss Jennifer, but I really should be getting back to the ranch." Jesse jerked her arm from Jennifer's grasp. She immediately eased past the schoolteacher, her long legs carrying her quickly to the Slipper's front door. As she reached the door, Jesse turned and looked back at Jennifer. The schoolteacher stood where Jesse had left her, her light brown hair backlit by the oil lamps that provided the room's illumination. Jesse rubbed her hand over her still-tingling arm, then she turned and was out the door.

Jennifer slowly followed Jesse outside, standing on the porch until long after Jesse and the buckboard had been swallowed by the night's darkness.

Chapter
Two

JENNIFER EXCUSED THE children at the end of her first day of class, grinning when the previously quiet schoolhouse filled with the sound of laughing and talking children running from the schoolhouse. Was it really only two days since she had stepped from the stage that had carried her into Sweetwater? It seemed like she had been in this small western town all of her life.

At her welcoming social the night before, she had discovered her schoolteacher responsibilities would require her to instruct twelve children, ranging in age from six to sixteen, with learning skills and knowledge coming in every combination imaginable. After spending her first day with the children, she knew it would take her a few days to uncover each student's strong points and weaknesses and develop study plans that would benefit all the students. She was quickly learning that teaching school with such a diversified class was to be much more of a challenge then she had anticipated. But the students seemed determined to work hard at their lessons, and Jennifer was just as determined to succeed as their teacher.

She had been surprised to learn classes could only be held from mid-morning to early afternoon, as the children were needed to help out with chores at home. This would leave her with most of the afternoon free, and she planned to make use of the free time by getting a second job to earn enough money to pay Jesse back for her new dresses.

She closed the schoolhouse door and hastily made her way back to the Slipper, anxious to ask Bette Mae about the employment opportunities in town.

"There must be something that I can do. Are you sure that Miss Jesse couldn't use some help in the office? Or I could help you in the kitchen. I'm a pretty good cook, even if I say so myself."

"Oh, no. Jesse would have my hide if'n I put ya ta work

around here. Not fittin' work for a schoolteacher."

"I must find something." Frustrated, Jennifer collapsed back in the chair she occupied. "I must pay Miss Jesse back for the dresses." *Not to mention, the extra income would help pay Matt back for my train ticket.*

"If you'll excuse me, ladies," a man sitting at a nearby table said to the two women, "I might just have a solution."

Jennifer sat up straight and looked at the man. He was of middle age, with graying salt-and-pepper hair and deep brown eyes. It appeared that he had forgotten to shave that morning, and light stubble covered his cheeks and chin. His shirtsleeves were rolled up to just below his elbows, and both the shirt and his hands were blotted with ink stains.

"You're Mr. Newby." Jennifer remembered having met the man at the social. "You own the Gazette."

The newspaper editor wiped his hands on the napkin, then stood and crossed to stand next to the table Jennifer and Bette Mae occupied. "Thaddeus Newby." He extended an ink-stained hand. "Yes, I own the Gazette and serve as its editor, reporter, typesetter, and anything else that might be necessary, including sweeping out the office."

"Please join us, Mr. Newby. You mentioned you might have a solution?"

"Thaddeus, please," the newspaperman took a seat in the chair between the women. "Yes, I could use someone at the Gazette to help me."

Jennifer was intrigued. "But I have no newspaper training, Mr. Newby."

"You're a schoolteacher and, therefore, I assume that you can read and write. That's all the training you need."

Grateful for the offer, she spent little time wondering what she had done to be so lucky and stuck her hand out to the editor. "You have a deal. When do I start?"

"Just as soon as you learn to call me Thaddeus," the newspaperman laughed as he shook her hand.

"Looks like Sweetwater has itself a new reporter," Bette Mae added. "I'd say that calls for a drink." She filled three glasses with lemonade and they toasted Jennifer's new position.

"WHAT DO YOU think, Dusty?" Jesse patted the mare's neck. "Looks like three riders." Her eyes followed the hoof prints until they disappeared into the creek several yards from where her horse stood drinking.

She had been out checking on her small herd when she first

spotted the tracks. Since she worked her ranch alone, it was unusual to find evidence of other riders on her land. It was likely that it was just some cowboys cutting across her property to one of the neighboring ranches. But it was also possible that it was drifters up to no good. Either way, it wouldn't hurt to check them out. Something about the tracks and the unknown riders that left them was making her uneasy.

Dusty raised her head, water dripping from her muzzle, and twisted her head to look at her mistress. The mare cocked her head as if to ask what her mistress was waiting for.

"Yeah," Jesse mumbled, swinging herself back up into the saddle. "Let's see if we can figure out who made them."

She urged her golden mare forward at a slow walk. Hanging her head down low next to Dusty's shoulder, she tried to locate the mysterious hoof prints further upstream. After riding up the small creek bed for almost a mile, Jesse spotted tracks leaving the creek and climbing up a stone-littered bank. She followed them away from the creek and back toward the ponderosa pine forest that bordered this section of her ranch, wondering what riders would be doing this far into her land.

Strange. There are no other ranches this side of the valley.

She continued to follow the trail left by the unknown riders until she lost them where they crossed a rocky stretch of ground between the forest and the valley. The riders could have traveled in several different directions from that point, and with nightfall not too far away, she decided to return to her ranch house rather than try to track them in the dark.

"I'll have to ask around town. Maybe someone saw three riders heading this way," she muttered, turning Dusty back in the direction of town.

After spending most of the day walking, Dusty was ready to stretch her legs, and Jesse encouraged her to do so. If anyone had come across them that evening, they would have seen the mare running like the wind, her golden tail and Jesse's hair flying behind as they raced the growing darkness home.

"RUSTLERS." CONRAD BILLINGSLEY slammed his fist down on the bar, rattling several glasses and knocking a few onto their sides. The sound of glass shattering could be heard as a couple rolled off the bar and fell to the saloon's wood floor.

"Can't be," Sheriff Monroe answered. "The valley is too small for rustlers to go unnoticed."

"I'm telling you, I lost a dozen head this past week and some of the other ranchers said they're missing cattle, too. So,"

Billingsley jabbed a finger into the sheriff's chest, "you better get off your lazy butt and go find out what's happening."

Conrad Billingsley stood half a foot shorter than the sheriff, but was not afraid to stand his ground. He had seen more action than he cared to remember during the conflict between the North and South, and had headed west as soon as his discharge papers were signed. He felt being the first to stake a claim in the valley after the stage line was pushed through gave him more influence in Sweetwater's affairs than the others that had arrived later. And he was not shy about trying to force his will whenever he believed it necessary.

"Now, hold on," the sheriff protested.

Appointed by the mayor, William "Billie" Monroe had served as Sweetwater's sheriff for the past three years. He had dealt with countless bar fights, numerous ranch hands needing a place to sleep off a night's drunk, and the occasional busted gambler looking for trouble, but not much in the way of serious crimes. Sweetwater was just too small to attract much attention from the seedier side of life, especially since Jesse had cleaned up the Silver Slipper. The Oxbow was now the only place in town to draw card sharks, and that usually didn't provide enough action to make it worth their time. But no matter what the threat, he performed his duty, and he wasn't about to let Conrad Billingsley talk to him like he was the town's lackey. And he didn't care if Billingsley owned the biggest ranch in the valley and was old enough to be his father.

"I'll do my job. But rustlers in this valley don't make sense. Hell, you know there's only a couple of ways to move cattle in or out of this valley, aside from the stage road. How could they get the cattle out without being caught?"

"That's your problem." Billingsley again slammed his fist down on the bar, disturbing more glasses.

"Before you bust up all of my glassware —" Jesse entered the saloon of the Silver Slipper, having been attracted by the loud voices she heard all the way across the dining area and into her office. "Maybe I can shed some light on this. What say we sit down and give the bar a rest?" She sat at a table, motioning for the men to join her.

"What have you got, Jesse?" Billingsley lowered his stocky body into a chair.

"Found tracks of three riders on my land yesterday." She signaled Sally, a tall redhead who tended bar in the Slipper, to bring a bottle and glasses to the table. "Picked them up at the far end of the meadows and trailed them southeast until I lost 'em in the granite fields. It was gettin' too dark to try to find where they came out."

Sally approached and placed three glasses and a bottle of whiskey on the table before returning to the bar and cleaning up the broken glass.

"That's pretty deep into your spread, Jesse." Billingsley pulled the cork from the bottle and poured the brown liquid into the glasses.

"Any idea who it was?" Sheriff Monroe lifted a glass to his lips, emptying its contents in one swallow.

"Nope." Jesse left her glass on the table; having never really acquired a taste for the strong liquor, she preferred a glass of milk to whiskey any day.

Sally read her boss's thoughts and disappeared into the kitchen, coming out moments later with a tall glass of cold milk that she placed in front of Jesse.

"Thanks." Jesse smiled at the redhead, who nodded before she retreated back behind the bar. "No one's been near my place for some time. Can't say why anyone would be passing that way." She took a long gulp of milk, wiping her mouth with the back of her sleeve.

"Don't know how you drink that stuff, Jesse." Billie grimaced as Jesse emptied the glass with a second long swallow.

"It's good for ya, Billie. You ought to give it a try sometime." She grinned as the sheriff shuddered at her suggestion. Since arriving in Sweetwater, she and the lawman had become good friends, and they both enjoyed teasing each other.

"So what do we do?" Billingsley grumbled, attempting to draw the conversation back on track, not amused with the playful bantering when he had cattle missing.

"I'll go out and see if I can pick up those tracks," the sheriff offered.

"You'll be wasting your time." Billingsley poured himself another shot of whiskey. "You can't track worth beans."

"I'm not going to sit here and listen to you insult me!"

"Sit down, Billie. You getting your tail feathers in a twist won't solve this problem."

"Both of you back down," Jesse quietly said. She glared at the sheriff until he resumed his seat. "Conrad is right, Billie. It would be a waste of time to try to find them now."

"Now, just a minute," the sheriff started to rise again. "I can track just as good as most can."

Jesse held up a hand to calm the sheriff. "That's not what I'm saying. I know you can track, but those tracks were already old and the wind we had last night probably wiped away what was left of them. If those riders were just passing through, they're long gone. If they were up to no good, they could be holed up in any number of places. You know the south end of the valley hasn't been explored much. Hell, if one had a mind to, they could hide out in the badlands for months before anyone took notice."

"Yeah, you're right."

The southern end of the Sweetwater valley was a maze of box canyons and twisted ravines with little vegetation and almost no water. Ranchers took care to keep their cattle well away from the serpentine chasms and arroyos. And with no cattle roaming the area, there was little reason for anyone to travel in the region known locally as the badlands.

"So what do we do?"

"How many ranches have reported cattle missing?" Jesse asked.

"Well let's see, there's mine," Conrad started to tick off his fingers, "Kelly, McPhillips, and Butler, that I know of."

"Guess talking to them would be a good starting point," Billie concluded, and the others nodded. "I'll head out now. It'll probably take a day or two to cover all the ranches."

"In the meantime, I'll have my riders keep a lookout for any strangers in the valley."

"Might be a good idea to have Ed keep an eye out as well."

"Good idea, Jesse. I'll have a talk with him before I leave."

"Guess that about does it." Conrad put the cork back into the whiskey bottle. "How much do I owe for the broken glass, Jesse?"

"How many, Sally?"

"Only two broke, Boss."

"Looks like you got lucky this time." Jesse slapped Billingsley on the shoulder. "Not enough to worry about. Just take it easy on the Slipper next time."

"You've got yourself a deal." Billingsley laughed. "Watch yourself out at your place, Jesse. You've got no one watching your back."

"I'll be careful." She carried the bottle and dirty glasses over to the bar as the sheriff and rancher left. After talking to Sally a few moments, she turned to return to her office. It was only then that she noticed another person was in the saloon. Sitting quietly at a table near the door leading to the dining room was the schoolteacher.

Jennifer had heard the loud voices when she came into the Slipper after completing her teaching duties for the day. Although she couldn't make out all that was being said, she had heard the word "rustlers" and, understanding what that meant in cattle country, she had grabbed a pencil and pad from the bag she used to carry lessons to and from the schoolhouse. Dropping her bag on the floor next to the door that separated the dining area from the saloon, she carefully pushed the door open. Slipping inside, she had taken a seat at the nearest table to listen to the conversation between Jesse and the two men, scribbling notes as they talked.

Finding herself under Jesse's glaring scrutiny, Jennifer was now unsure of the justification for her eavesdropping. When she had first entered the room, she told herself that, as a reporter for the Gazette, it was her duty to find out if there was a story that needed reporting. Watching the rancher slowly approach, she now wasn't quite so sure.

"Miss Jennifer." Jesse cocked her head to one side, scratching the back of her neck as she acknowledged the schoolteacher. "Something I can do for you?"

"I-I... Well, I..." Jennifer stuttered. Normally, the schoolteacher had little difficulty coming up with something to say, but with those gorgeous eyes staring at her she found herself tongue-tied.

"Yes, Miss Jennifer." Jesse stood patiently, waiting for a coherent response, quietly amused by the schoolteacher's unease.

"I'm working afternoons at the Gazette, and I heard the talk of rustlers, so I thought..."

"That there might be a story here."

"Yes. I know I shouldn't have been eavesdropping, but..."

"It's a public place," Jesse shrugged, smiling. "Guess if we had wanted a private conversation, we could have gone into my office. I don't think you would have followed us in there. Would you?"

Jennifer was sure that she had angered the other woman until she looked up and saw the barest of grins on Jesse's face and the twinkling in her eyes.

"No." She smiled up at the rancher. "I would not have followed you into your private office."

"Good. I would have hated to have to boot your pretty little butt out of there." Jesse immediately blushed, realizing what she had said.

Jennifer's eyes grew wide at Jesse's words. *Why had Jesse referred to that part of her anatomy, and why in that manner?* Whatever the reason, Jennifer decided, she liked that the rancher had. "May I ask you a question?"

"Go ahead," Jesse muttered, looking down at her boots in

hopes she wouldn't say anything else to embarrass herself in front of the schoolteacher. *Why do I react to her this way,* Jesse was thinking and missed hearing Jennifer's question.

"Miss Jesse, are you okay?" Jennifer asked when Jesse didn't answer.

"I'm sorry," Jesse mumbled. "What did you ask?" *Get some control, girl,* Jesse chastised herself as she concentrated on listening to Jennifer.

"I asked if you think there is a rustler problem in the valley."

"Can't say," Jesse truthfully answered. "Some of the ranchers say that they're missing cattle. The sheriff is looking into it. Guess maybe you should ask him."

"Have you lost any cattle, Miss Jesse?"

"No."

"Thank you." Jennifer made a few notes on her pad. "Guess I should let you get back to your business, and I should get over to the Gazette before Thaddeus thinks I'm not working today."

"School-teaching doesn't keep you busy enough, Miss Jennifer?"

"With classes ending so early, my afternoons were left open. Thaddeus needed help at the Gazette and was kind enough to offer me a position." She didn't want to tell Jesse the real reason she had needed a second job.

"I see."

"I'd best be going."

Jesse watched her leave, thinking that Thaddeus was one lucky man to be able to spend every afternoon with the pretty schoolteacher.

"ARE YOU SURE about this?" the tall, lanky boy, barely old enough to shave, leaned closer to the fire. He could hear the cattle settling for the night around the camp he and his companions had set up earlier. The sun had given way to a full moon and, as was common in the Rockies, the heated air of the day had turned cold with the night. He rapidly rubbed his hands up and down his arms in a futile attempt to warm them, but gave it up after a few moments when it didn't seem to help.

Pulling his coat tighter around his body, Johnson glared at the boy. He had planned his revenge for months, and now that it was within his grasp, this kid was getting cold feet. He reached into the pile of gathered firewood, pulling free a couple of the larger pieces and throwing them onto the already blazing fire. "You havin' second thoughts, Jimmy?"

"No. Just askin' if you're sure. Seems like we're puttin' ourselves in a tight spot if'n we have to get out of this valley in a hurry." Rustling cattle didn't bother Jimmy, but the threat of a rope necktie did. And being camped in the open with a couple dozen stolen cattle seemed like a good way to get caught and end up the guest of honor at a lynching.

"I know what I'm doin'," Johnson assured the boy. "So quit worryin'. Besides, by the time anyone figures out what's goin' on, we'll be in the Slipper celebratin'. Now get some sleep. Your watch starts in a couple of hours, and I don't want you fallin' asleep again."

"All right." Jimmy lay down on his bedroll, placed as close to the fire as he could get it without the cloth igniting from the heat. For several minutes, he quietly watched Johnson move about the campsite.

A month earlier, Johnson had approached Jimmy and his older brother, Clinton, offering them a generous payoff if they would help with his plan to get the Silver Slipper back. Jimmy hadn't liked Johnson from the start, and wasn't at all sure that Johnson could deliver on his promises. But Clinton had gotten into some trouble in Denver and it was quickly decided that helping Johnson was better than spending time in the jailhouse. Jimmy wasn't sure they had made the right decision, but, figuring he couldn't do anything about it until later when he could talk to his brother, the boy pulled his bedroll tight around his body and promptly went to sleep.

Johnson tossed another piece of firewood onto the fire. "How can it be so damn hot during the day and so damn cold at night?" he grumbled to no one in particular. As he stared into the flames, he again recalled the poker game that had cost him the Slipper. Each time he replayed the events, he became more convinced that somehow the tall woman had cheated. *Ain't no way that bitch won fair.*

Standing to stretch out his cramped legs, he walked to where their horses were picketed. After making sure the rope was secure, he grabbed his own bedroll on his way to a large boulder that provided a good view of the grazing cattle. He pulled the blanket tight around his shoulders, preparing to spend the next few hours perched on the cold stone. Thoughts of revenge would keep him occupied for the hours of his watch and, hopefully, help him forget the cold.

AFTER HER CONVERSATIONS with Billingsley and Sheriff Monroe, Jesse returned to her ranch to keep an eye on her small herd while the sheriff checked with the other ranchers in the valley. She spent the remainder of the day working on the leaky roof of the ranch house, quitting only when it became too dark to see the new sections of roof she was hammering into place.

Sitting in front of the fireplace that warmed her home during the cooler evening hours, Jesse aimlessly stared at the flames.

As her father's only child, she had been taught to ride before she could walk. Jesse loved the ranch where she had been born, and loved working it with her father. Over the years, she had come to think of her father's small patch of land as her own, and dreamed of the day when her father would pass the ranch over to her. That dream had been shattered when she found out her father had sold the ranch and made plans for a future that didn't include her as she was *of legal age and showing no inclination to marry.* As she wandered from one frontier town to the next, she had thought little of her own future. But that had changed the night she won a card game and the Silver Slipper.

Taking a day off from her work refurbishing the Slipper to ride Dusty and explore the valley that was becoming her home, she had discovered an abandoned ranch, deserted after its original owner disappeared from the valley one night and was never heard from again. The bank in Bozeman was only too glad to sign the paperwork when she asked about purchasing the property, and her childhood dreams had come back to life.

Allowing Bette Mae to manage the operations of the Slipper left Jesse with the time to concentrate on rebuilding the ranch. She worked to restore the neglected ranch, putting a new roof on the barn to keep hay dry for winter, replacing the broken corral fence, and topping the old well with a functioning pump. There was still a lot of work to be done, but it was livable and, most important, it was hers. A dozen cattle purchased from other valley ranches spent the summer days grazing on the rich grasslands she owned. To increase the herd, she hoped to purchase a breeding bull before much longer.

Even as she thought about the ranch, she couldn't shake the uneasy feeling that had nagged her ever since she came across the mysterious tracks. If there were rustlers in the valley, why were they on her property? *Why my land?* She kept turning the question over and over in her mind, but no answers were forthcoming.

Somethin' just ain't right. She watched the fire, her eyes growing heavy.

THE MORNING SUNLIGHT slipped through the east-facing windows to find Jesse asleep in the chair where exhaustion had claimed her the night before. The fingers of light spread across the ranch house floor, slowly crawling up her body as they lengthened across the room. She woke with a groan when the bright sunbeams reached her face.

Stretching her long limbs, she tried to loosen the numerous kinks that had developed during the night. She twisted her neck from side to side to ease stiff muscles. Slowly, she pushed herself up and out of the chair, pausing to stretch her long frame some more. After satisfying her aching muscles, she picked up the fire poker, stoking the embers before adding a couple of split logs, then standing back to watch as the fire burst back into life. Grabbing her coat off the back of the door, she pulled it on as she left the house to fill a large cooking pot with water at the water pump in the yard. She carried the pot back inside the ranch house, placing it on a spike over the fire to heat while she completed the rest of her morning chores.

Jesse loved this time of day. The sun was just beginning its long journey across the big Montana sky. The forest animals were beginning to wake, and the songs and calls of several different birds filled the morning air. Jesse could hear the chatter of squirrels in the trees around the ranch buildings. And far in the distance, a coyote greeted the morning with a long, mournful howl. A smile crossed her face.

Pushing open the heavy door to her barn, she made her way to Dusty's stall and was greeted with a warm muzzle being pressed against her chest.

"Morning, girl." She handed Dusty the apple she had snatched from a barrel just outside the barn's door. Dusty munched happily on the treat, and Jesse led the mare out of the barn and into the adjoining corral.

Free of the confinement of the barn, the mare raised her head to test the scents on the breeze. The normally calm horse sidestepped nervously.

"You can feel it, too." Jesse scratched Dusty's head to comfort the horse, her eyes scanning the far end of the valley. "Someone is out there. Maybe we should take another ride out that way and see if there's any fresh tracks." She smiled when another idea came to her mind. "Or maybe we should ride into town and see if there's any news."

Dusty nudged the daydreaming Jesse on the arm.

"Okay, let me get you fed, the rest of the chores done, and me cleaned up. Then we'll head to town."

With that decision made, Jesse headed back into the barn to

finish her chores and to wonder why the thought of seeing Jennifer was so appealing this morning.

THE SUN HAD been up long enough to begin chasing away the night's chill. Jennifer sat on the wide porch of the Silver Slipper sipping coffee from a large mug. It was going to be another hot, dry day, and she was intent on enjoying the morning coolness while she could. From the Slipper's porch she could look down the entire length of Sweetwater's dusty main street, where not much activity broke the morning's stillness. Ed was getting the general store ready for business by sweeping the boardwalk, and she could see smoke start to pour out of the livery's smokestack indicating the forge had been fired up. A horse was hitched in front of the jailhouse, the rider having already disappeared inside. Lights were on in several of the houses at this end of town, but she had yet to see any of their occupants.

She loved this time of day. It was peaceful and quiet, except for the chirping of morning birds in the surrounding trees. She could think of no better way to spend the morning than welcoming the waking day. Well, maybe one thing would make it better. Perhaps if Jesse were sharing it with her.

Whoa, where did that come from?

Jennifer was so startled by the sudden appearance of Jesse into her musings that she spilled the contents of her cup. As she rose from the chair to go back to the kitchen and get more coffee, she wondered why the beautiful rancher seemed to be sneaking into her thoughts more and more.

"I'M TELLING YOU, Sheriff, the tracks led to Jesse's land." Pete, a wrangler for Conrad Billingsley's Rocking B spread, paced opposite the sheriff's desk.

"Why would Jesse be stealing cattle?" Billie was more than a little perturbed at his morning beginning with the cowboy banging on the jailhouse door. He sat at his desk, trying to rub the sleep from his eyes.

"All I know is that Mr. Billingsley told me to ride in and get you. He said I should drag you out there tied over the back of your horse if I have to."

"You can go back and tell that..." Billie decided that taking his anger with the rancher out on the cowboy was probably not the best way to handle his frustration. "Look, Pete," the sheriff leaned back in his chair and ran his fingers through his uncombed hair. "Go back and tell Billingsley that I'll be out after I get breakfast. Maybe by then Jesse will be over at the Slipper and I can ask her about those tracks.

The cowboy wasn't about to return to the Rocking B without the sheriff. Not with the mood his boss was in after losing more cattle overnight to the rustlers working in the valley. "Nope, I ain't leaving here without you. The boss would shoot me on the spot."

"Have it your way. I'm going to wash up and go over to the Slipper. You can wait for me here or join me. Your choice." He poured water into a bowl. Several minutes later, the sheriff left the jail and headed down the dusty street for the Silver Slipper.

The cowboy angrily trailed behind, his stomping boots kicking up puffs of dust.

JESSE THREW DUSTY'S reins over the hitching rail at the side of the Silver Slipper's porch. She climbed the steps and crossed the wide porch to the Slipper's front door, hesitating for a moment to consider the cause of a wet spot in front of one of the chairs. She reached for the door's knob, and just as her hand touched the metal, it was pulled away from her grasp.

"Oh," Jennifer gasped when she saw Jesse standing before her.

"Good morning, Miss Jennifer," Jesse greeted the schoolteacher while thinking that seeing the young woman was a wonderful way to start the morning.

"Good morning, Miss Jesse. I was just coming out to clean up the coffee I spilled." She pointed to the drying stain.

"Don't bother. The sun will dry it before long." Jesse paused. "Have you had breakfast yet? Perhaps you would like to join me if you haven't," she heard herself say, surprised she had spoken out loud.

Before Jennifer could answer, the women were interrupted by the approaching sheriff.

"Jesse, glad to see you," Sheriff Monroe called out from the bottom of the steps. "We need to talk. Join me for breakfast."

"I, uh, I was just asking..."

"It's okay." Jennifer reached out, gently squeezing Jesse's forearm. "You have business with the sheriff. We can talk later." She nodded to the sheriff and cowboy before turning and retreating to her room.

Jesse was surprised at Jennifer's touch, and even more surprised at how her skin tingled where Jennifer's hand had rested. She wanted to protest Jennifer's departure, but her mouth refused to form words. She could only watch mutely as she disappeared up the stairs.

Greatly disappointed that Jennifer would not be her breakfast partner, Jesse joined the sheriff.

Jennifer hurried up the stairs and down the hallway. As soon as she entered her small room, she collapsed against the closed door. Her heart was beating so fast that she was sure it would burst from her chest. When she had touched Jesse's arm, a jolt of electricity had surged through her body. She had never felt anything like it before, and she was sure by the look on Jesse's face that the rancher had felt it too. She'd had to get away from Jesse before she embarrassed herself even more. Yet, as she leaned against the rough wood of the room's door, she had to admit that, as unexpected as her reaction had been, it had most assuredly been a wonderful feeling. And one she would like to experience again. Soon.

By the time she had regained her composure and returned downstairs, Jesse and the sheriff were finishing their morning meal. She took a seat at a table across the room where she could watch Jesse without being too obvious. Bette Mae came out of the kitchen with a pot of coffee. After refreshing the cups at Jesse's table, she crossed the room to where Jennifer sat.

"Thought ya changed your mind on havin' breakfast." Bette Mae filled a cup with coffee.

"No. Just wanted to freshen up a bit. But I'm ready for it now."

"Good. I'll be right back."

Jennifer returned her attention to the conversation between Jesse and the sheriff.

"Can't be," Jesse was saying. "I don't have any cattle on that part of the ranch. It's too far from the house to keep track of them."

"That's what I've been trying to tell this cowpoke." Billie cut a piece of ham into bite-size pieces.

"The tracks are there. I saw them myself. Must have been forty head moved up there."

"They aren't mine." Jesse finished her last bite of egg before washing it down with coffee.

"Never said they were," Pete mumbled. He was more than annoyed that he was still sitting in Sweetwater when he should be riding back to the Rocking B with the sheriff.

"Guess it won't hurt to go out and take a look. You can come with us, Jesse. If you want."

Jesse emptied her cup before responding to the sheriff's offer. "No, Billie. I think I'll give the meadows another look. See if those riders have been back through." In the back of her mind, she debated whether to tell the sheriff about the feelings she'd had earlier that morning, but decided against it. It probably wasn't anything anyway.

Bette Mae returned with Jennifer's breakfast just as the sheriff and cowboy stood to leave. As she thanked Bette Mae for serving her, Jennifer heard the sheriff's parting words.

"Be careful out at your place, Jesse, until we can find out what's going on. Come on, Pete. We've kept your boss waiting long enough."

Jesse watched the sheriff walk out the front door with the cowboy trailing behind, mumbling under his breath about how he could explain the delay to his boss. As she stood and turned away from the table to go to her office, her eyes fell on the schoolteacher. She smiled, remembering her earlier reaction to the young woman's touch.

Jennifer saw Jesse look her way and watched as a smile covered the taller woman's face. Brown eyes met blue and the world narrowed to just the two women caught in one another's gaze. Bette Mae stood watching, and grinned when she realized that the women were unaware of anything except each other. Someone bursting through the front door broke the enchantment and both women self-consciously looked away.

"My usual, Bette Mae," Mayor Perkins demanded as he sat at one of the empty tables.

Jesse quickly made her way to her office door, disappearing inside.

Jennifer waited several minutes before the butterflies in her stomach settled down enough for her to eat the breakfast cooling on the plate in front of her.

"HURRY UP AND finish the rest of 'em," Johnson growled at the brothers. He kept a constant vigil on the scrub-covered walls that formed the sides of the small box canyon. Sagebrush was the only vegetation in the canyon and it provided little cover. Even though they had yet to be disturbed, he was nervous, and wanted to get away as quickly as possible.

Jimmy and Clinton were heating a running iron in the fire.

The hook-tipped piece of iron was the tool of rustlers, used to change brands on stolen cattle. If done properly, the change would not be noticed until after the animals were butchered and the inside of the hide could be seen. But the brothers had never used a running iron before and their attempts at changing brands were anything but unnoticeable. It was a shoddy job, but that was part of Johnson's plan; he didn't want any doubts that brands had been altered.

A few feet from the fire, recently re-branded cattle were bunched behind a makeshift rope barrier. There was barely enough room for the cattle, and they were constantly jostling for position. The canyon had no water and the thirsty animals loudly bawled their unhappiness at the conditions. Another half dozen were waiting their turn with the branding iron.

"Come on." Johnson yanked on a rope pulling a cow closer to the fire. "Let's get this done and get out of here before anyone shows up."

Jimmy walked to the cow and roped its feet. As the cow struggled to free itself, it lost its balance and tumbled to the ground. Clinton removed the red-hot iron from the fire and pressed it against the cow's hide, burning a new brand over the top of the animal's original marking. As soon as he finished, the cow was released and another was pulled near the fire and the process repeated. In short order, the remaining cows joined the rest of the rustled and re-branded herd behind the barrier.

"Make sure them ropes hold 'em," Johnson ordered the brothers, who were busy throwing dirt on the fire to put it out. "No, leave the iron in the fire," he shouted when Clinton started to remove it.

Jimmy rechecked the ropes that made up the barrier; it wouldn't hold the thirsty and hungry cattle long, but that was also part of Johnson's plan. The sooner a few of them escaped, the sooner the rustled herd would be discovered. After securing the rope fence, the men mounted their horses.

"Fire's still smokin'."

"That's okay," Johnson informed him. "Makes it easier to find. And we want to make this as easy as we can." Johnson kicked his horse into a trot, riding out of the narrow box canyon and back into the open valley. He knew that the other two would follow.

"He's crazier than a rabid dog, Clint."

"Yeah. Let's just hope we can get out of this without a rope around our necks." Shaking his head, he urged his horse to follow Johnson. He wondered if a couple of months in the Denver jail might not have been such a bad idea after all.

"Yeah." Jimmy hesitated just long enough to consider his chances of reaching the dense forest a couple of miles away before Johnson put a rifle shot into his back. The odds weren't all that good, he decided, and held tight to the hope that his brother was right, and they could escape the hangman's noose.

JESSE WALKED OUT of the Silver Slipper not long after the sheriff and cowboy left. As she mounted Dusty, Jennifer came out of the Slipper and crossed the wide porch.

"Where are you going?"

Jesse took a deep breath and studied the woman leaning against the porch railing, her delicate hands spread before her on the flat board. She wondered what it would be like to have those same hands exploring her body. A light blush started to crawl up Jesse's neck as she recognized where her thoughts were leading.

Jennifer saw the blush and wondered what Jesse could be thinking to cause it, but didn't ask.

Each woman studied the other, both of them experiencing strange new emotions for the first time. They wanted to express their feelings, but neither had the nerve to do so.

"Thought I'd take a look around."

"Why?"

Jesse was puzzled by the concern in Jennifer's eyes. "Just a feeling. I think there may be someone down in the badlands."

"Shouldn't you have told the sheriff?"

"I will if I find anything."

"Be careful."

Jesse smiled. "I'm not going out looking for trouble."

"I know. But if someone is out there, you'll be all alone."

"Don't worry. Dusty is the fastest horse in the valley. She'll get me out of any trouble I might find myself in."

"Still," Jennifer smiled shyly, "be careful."

"I will." Jesse rode away from the Slipper thinking how nice it felt to have someone worry about her.

Jennifer watched until she disappeared from sight. "Be safe," she sighed before returning back inside the Silver Slipper.

"WHAT DID I tell you, Billie?" Billingsley pointed to the hoof prints of several cattle moving up a trail that eventually led to the badlands at the south end of the valley. "There's another group of tracks about a half mile that way." He pointed to the west. "It leads in the same direction. I don't run cattle up at that end of the valley. No one does. Ain't enough grass in those canyons to keep 'em fed."

"I know, been up there a time or two myself. It's rough country for cattle." The sheriff spoke from where he was kneeling next to the tracks. "Looks to be no more than a day or two old." He stood and shook out the cramped muscles in his legs. "You send any riders up that way?" The sheriff remounted his horse.

"A couple. Came back just before you got here. Said they saw smoke coming from the canyons down toward the end of Jesse's land." Billingsley mounted his own horse and signaled his men to do the same.

"Jesse ain't no rustler."

"Never said she was. But the tracks lead that way and the smoke was coming from her land. She's been building her herd up a lot the last few months. Kinda makes you wonder where she's getting the money. Slipper can't be doing that well, what with all those women she's keeping employed." Billingsley pulled his rifle from the saddle scabbard and checked to make sure it was loaded and ready for use. His cowboys followed his example.

"Let's hope we don't need to use those." Billie watched the men prepare their weapons. He knew Jesse would never steal, but he was smart enough to know that one man, even if he was the law, couldn't do much against a dozen armed and angry cowboys.

"Law says we can hang rustlers," Billingsley stated as he shoved the rifle back into its scabbard.

"Let's get this straight right now." Billie raised his voice so all of the men would have no trouble hearing him. "If there are rustlers out there, we are bringing them back alive. The circuit judge will decide their fate, not you." He stared directly at Billingsley as he spoke the final word.

Billingsley returned the sheriff's stare for several moments, his ranch hands waiting quietly. Not too many people spoke to Conrad Billingsley in that manner and got away with it. He glared at the sheriff and considered his options. Sure, they fought and exchanged words on many an occasion, but the truth was that Billie Monroe was a good sheriff, and the rancher had to admit that he liked the man. Finally, he decided that having the sheriff on his side would be a lot easier than having to fight rustlers and the sheriff.

Billingsley gave in. "We'll do it your way, Billie."

JESSE STOOD IN the stirrups to get a better look at the thin wisp of smoke rising out of the maze of canyons and arroyos that made up the badlands. With her view mostly blocked by the gentler rolling hills of the valley floor she and Dusty were riding through, she missed seeing the three riders leaving the chasms and racing to the safety of the forest to the east.

"Looks like we were right, Dusty. Someone is up in those canyons." She pulled her canteen free of the saddle horn and tipped it up to her dry lips. "Best find a place to fill this up before we head into those canyons." She wrapped the canteen's rawhide strap back in place. "Bet you could use a drink, too. Let's go see what we can find."

At Jesse's urging, the mare started walking.

"Good girl." She patted her mount on the neck when the mare carried her over a rise to see an irregular line of small bushes marking the banks of a lazily flowing, shallow creek. Stopping beside it, she slipped from the saddle before dropping the reins, allowing Dusty to enjoy a long drink of cool water. Kneeling down to refill her canteen, she scooped a handful of the liquid up to her own mouth. The rancher froze as a disturbing sound reached her ears. Abruptly standing, she looked around trying to identify the direction of the cries.

"Damn." She grabbed the mare's reins. "It's bouncing off the walls of those canyons. They could be up any one of 'em." Remounting, she nudged Dusty toward the badlands.

It wasn't long before the grassy, rolling hills gave way to the mostly barren, rocky ground leading into the dry, scrub-covered gulches and box canyons that marked the southern boundary of the Sweetwater valley. As they neared the badlands, the bawling of cattle grew louder and more incessant.

"They sure don't sound too happy." She led the mare toward the nearest ravine. "Let's find 'em."

The dry, stony ground yielded few tracks to follow, and the rancher searched several branch canyons only to find them empty, forcing her to backtrack. After numerous dead ends, she cautiously rode up the rocky floor of another canyon, its rock walls less than twenty feet apart. The heat in the canyon was almost unbearable and Jesse frowned as she considered the animals confined somewhere within these same walls.

"Those cattle have to be here somewhere, girl." She was apprehensive and reached down to pull a pistol from her saddlebags. Not knowing who or what she might encounter when she finally located the cattle was nerve-wracking, and the rancher hoped her search would end soon. Picking up her rider's unease, Dusty whinnied softly as she cautiously worked her way further back into the canyon.

Gratefully, Jesse sensed an end to their quest. A bend near the back of the canyon prevented her from seeing the cattle, but as Dusty moved closer, their cries grew louder. And there was no mistaking the increasing stench of cattle sweat and dung.

Dusty stepped around the protruding wall.

Bunched against the box end of the canyon were the miserable, hot, thirsty and hungry animals, held in place by ropes tied from one canyon wall to the other. Seeing that the area was unoccupied except for the cattle, Jesse replaced her pistol before slipping off the mare's back. She quickly covered the distance to the rope fence and climbed up onto a boulder that secured one end of the ropes. Pulling a knife from her boot, she cut through the restraints, and the freed cattle lost no time in escaping their stifling prison.

Once the cattle had fled the makeshift corral, Jesse surveyed the rustlers' work-site before dropping lightly off the boulder. She walked over to examine the remains of a fire that had been built at the base of the opposite wall. A running iron lay atop the ashes. Jesse lifted it up, turning it over in her strong hands.

"Looks like Conrad was right." She examined the rustlers' tool. "Guess we better let Billie get a look at this." She carried the running iron over to Dusty, jamming it into her saddlebag. "Ground is too hard in here to leave many tracks, and the cattle probably took care of any that were around." She pulled herself back into the saddle. "Let's see if we can pick up something out in the open."

As she rode out of the badlands, she scanned the ground for any sign of horses or men. Knowing rustlers would most likely not ride back into the valley and chance meeting up with the ranchers they had stolen from, she headed for the forest in the opposite direction. She was halfway to the trees when she saw recently made hoof prints and turned Dusty to follow them. As Dusty reached the forest's edge and continued further into the trees, Jesse, concentrating on the tracks she was following, missed seeing Billie and the cowboys appear as they rode to the top of a small rise.

"Look." One of Billingsley's men pointed out the single rider in the distance.

"Hey!" Marcus Butler, another rancher missing cattle, cried out excitedly. "Ain't that Jesse?" He and several other ranchers had joined the sheriff's group as they rode through the valley.

"Looks like her horse," Billingsley commented. "Only one golden palomino in the valley that I know if."

"Wonder what she's doing out here?" Butler questioned.

Before the sheriff could voice a reply, another shout went up.

"Look!" One of the riders had spied the cattle grazing on the valley grasses between the forest Jesse had now disappeared into and the badlands opposite.

Billingsley urged his mount forward. "Let's go see what they're doing here."

Sheriff Monroe followed the rancher and other riders, more

than a little concerned at what might happen if the cattle turned out to be their missing stock. The group, now joined by the other ranchers and their ranch hands, numbered over thirty armed men, and he wasn't sure he could control them if they decided to take the law into their own hands. He hoped Jesse was aware of the danger she might be in and was riding somewhere she would be safe if the worst happened.

"THIS ONE'S BEEN changed, too."

"Looks like they've all been changed. Not a very good job. Must have been someone new to the game," Lucas Kelly, who owned one of the smaller ranches in the valley, commented.

"Like Jesse."

"Hold on." Billie knew where this conversation was headed, and he didn't like it. "We don't know that Jesse had anything to do with this. After all, this is her land. She could have been out checking on her own cattle."

Two of Billingsley's cowboys rode up at a gallop, abruptly pulling up their mounts as they reached their boss.

"It was done up there," one of them pointed back to the badlands. "Found the remains of a fire and ropes where she held them in the canyon.

"Wait a minute—"

The other cowboy cut the sheriff off. "Only one set of tracks in the canyon. They lead in the direction we saw Jesse ridin'."

"Well, Sheriff," Billingsley snarled as he addressed the lawman. "How much more evidence do you need? We found the cattle on Jesse's land. They were re-branded in a canyon on her land, with only her tracks in the canyon. And she was riding away when we spotted the cattle."

"Seems pretty clear cut to me," Kelly agreed.

"I say we go after her."

Things were getting out of hand. Billie knew he had to do something, and fast, before a lynch mob rode after Jesse. "All right, you found your cattle. I suggest you take them back to your spreads."

"What about Jesse?"

"I'll go after Jesse." Before the ranchers could protest, Billie added, "I'll bring her in. The circuit judge is due next week. She can tell her side of this to him."

The ranchers and their men looked at the sheriff skeptically, unsure if they could trust Billie to arrest his friend.

The sheriff, reading their skepticism, hurried to remove any doubts from their minds. "I said I'd bring her in, and I will. Now take your cattle and go home."

Billie mounted his horse and rode off in the direction Jesse had last been seen before anyone had a chance to object further.

Chapter
Three

JESSE FOLLOWED THE rustlers' tracks for a couple of miles before coming to the spot where the three riders had split up, each taking a different route deeper into the thick pine forest. Nightfall was rapidly approaching and she debated the wisdom of continuing to follow the rustlers after dark. Perhaps she should return to Sweetwater. Remembering her conversation with Jennifer that morning and the look of concern on the schoolteacher's face, her decision was made. She gave Dusty her head and the two made short time in covering the distance to town.

Back in Sweetwater, Jesse headed straight to the Silver Slipper, arriving just as Sheriff Monroe was stepping out of the building.

"Evening, Jesse." Billie stood at the top of the steps leading up to the Slipper's wide porch. "I've been looking for you." His voice was more tense than normal. He had lost Jesse's trail soon after entering the forest, and returned to Sweetwater expecting Jesse would check in at the Slipper sooner or later. He was glad to see that he had made the right decision.

"Evening, Billie." Jesse swung down from the saddle. "I just rode into town. I've got something for you." She reached for her saddlebag to remove the running iron she had found at the rustlers' makeshift branding camp.

"Hold it, Jesse." He knew the rancher carried pistols in her saddlebags, and wasn't about to take any chances. "Leave your guns be."

"Wasn't reaching for them." She turned back to face the sheriff, carefully resting her empty hands on her saddle where the lawman could see them. "What's the problem?"

The sheriff placed a hand on his pistol, ready to pull it free of its holster should he need to, as he cautiously made his way down the steps to where Jesse stood warily watching him.

Jennifer came out of the Slipper. Seeing the sheriff's grip on his pistol, she hurried to the edge of the porch.

Jesse felt her body go cold with terror when she saw the schoolteacher rushing toward the sheriff.

"Stay on the porch, Jennifer." She had seen more than one person shot accidentally when someone with a gun over-reacted to an unexpected movement. There was no way she would let Jennifer fall victim to a similar calamity.

The sheriff kept his eye on Jesse while he spoke to Jennifer. "Suggest you go back inside, Miss Jennifer. This is official business."

"Are you arresting Jesse?" Jennifer's voice quaked as she waited for a response. Every instinct was telling her to run to the rancher's side, but the look of fear on Jesse's face kept her feet rooted in place.

"That's a good question, Billie. I'd kinda like to hear the answer myself."

"I need to ask you some questions and I don't want any trouble while I do that."

"Never needed a gun before to ask me questions, Sheriff." Jesse didn't like being at the wrong end of a gun, especially one in the hands of someone she considered a friend. "You mind telling me what's different now?"

"We found the stolen cattle today. They'd been held in a box canyon on your land."

A cautious smile crossed Jesse's face at the sheriff's words. "I know. I came across them and cut 'em loose, figuring they'd find their way home. Followed the rustlers' tracks until I lost them when they split up in the trees. Came back to town to tell you about it."

"Only found one set of tracks, Jesse. They were yours."

"Wait a minute!" Jennifer exploded off the porch. Planting herself right in front of the sheriff, she poked a finger into his chest. "You're not accusing Jesse of stealing cattle, are you?" Her blazing eyes bore into the sheriff.

Surprised by the speed of Jennifer's movement and by having the woman jabbing him in the chest, Billie was momentarily confused as to how to react.

"Hold on there." Jesse gently wrapped Jennifer in her arms.

At the unexpected touch, Jennifer forgot all about the sheriff and could only focus on the warmth generating from where she was being held. She allowed the rancher to pull her away from the sheriff.

"Billie hasn't accused me of anything. Have you?"

Seeing Jesse holding Jennifer, the unsure lawman thought he had to do something; he pulled his pistol from its holster. "Back away from her, Jesse."

She looked at the man pointing a six-shooter at her head, and her eyes went cold. She prudently moved Jennifer off to the side and backed further into the street, putting even more room between herself and the schoolteacher.

"Go back inside, Jennifer."

"No." Jennifer held her ground.

By now, the commotion in the street had attracted the attention of the Sweetwater citizenry. Many people had stopped their evening's routines and were watching from various locations along the town's street. Bette Mae stood on the Slipper's porch with the rest of the girls. Most of the folks in the Slipper's dining room had willingly interrupted their evening meal to see what was happening. Leaving their drinking and gambling tables in the Slipper's saloon, cowboys poured out onto the porch and into the street. While Bette Mae, the girls, and diners stood mostly in silence watching the drama unfold before them, the cowboys, encouraged by their consumption of liquor, were calling out for the sheriff to shoot Jesse.

Cautiously watching the rowdier cowboys in the growing crowd, Jesse listened as similar comments were shouted from the direction of the Oxbow and recognized the situation could quickly get out of the sheriff's control. "Why don't we go to your office, Billie? You can lock me up if you see fit." She could tell that it wouldn't take much for the intoxicated cowboys to stir up a big pot of trouble.

"All right," the sheriff growled. "You can all go back to your business. This matter doesn't concern any of you."

Seeing no one move at the sheriff's words, Bette Mae took matters into her own hands, shooing people back inside the building. The diners went without complaint, but the cowboys were a different matter. They insisted on accompanying the sheriff to make sure Jesse was "good and locked up," as one of them shouted. It wasn't until Bette Mae offered the first round on the house that most of the cowboys decided a free drink was better than a thirsty walk to the town's jail.

Once the porch was cleared of onlookers, Bette Mae turned her attention to the people still facing off in the street. A look of distress clouded her face as she started to walk toward Jesse, hoping to have a few words with the rancher before the sheriff escorted her to his office.

"It's okay, Bette Mae." Jesse held up a hand to stop the older woman from approaching. "Take Jennifer inside. I'll go talk with Billie and get this all straightened out."

"All right." Bette Mae reached for Jennifer, only to have her hand slapped away.

"I'm going with you."

"Stay here." Jesse's eyes locked onto Jennifer's, pleading with her to obey.

"No." Jennifer was adamant. "As a reporter for the Gazette, I have a right to be there." She stomped to face the sheriff.

"I'm sorry, Miss Jennifer. I can't let you come."

Meeting the sheriff's gaze, Jennifer said in a shaky voice, "You'll have to shoot me to stop me."

Before the sheriff or Jesse could respond to Jennifer's challenge, dozens of horses thundered into Sweetwater and surrounded them. At the front of the group rode Conrad Billingsley, followed close behind by the other ranchers and their cowhands.

Billingsley jumped down from his horse before the animal had come to a full stop. "Why haven't you arrested her yet, Sheriff?"

Billie pushed Jennifer aside so he could face the angry riders. "I told you I'd handle this, and I will."

"What's to handle?" Butler questioned as he swung from his saddle to stand beside Billingsley. "We saw her leaving, her tracks were the only ones in the canyon, and her brand was on the cattle. Arrest the bitch and get it over with." Butler spat dust from his mouth. He, unlike most others in the valley, had never liked Jesse. He didn't think much of women being business owners, except maybe of a boarding house or other domestic enterprise. But no way was it proper for a woman to run a ranch. *"Went against nature,"* he had been fond of saying when Jesse purchased the run-down property.

"I was just takin' her to the jail when you rode up." Billie tried to pacify the new group of potential troublemakers.

The uproar caused by the riders brought most of the occupants of the Slipper and Oxbow back outside where they eagerly added their opinions to the confusion.

Wanting to avoid a full-scale riot, Billie grabbed Dusty's reins and started to lead the horse and Jesse down the street. "Come on, Jesse." He pushed past the ranchers and cowboys. "We'll finish this in my office."

Jennifer marched after the sheriff and the woman she had an unexplainable need to defend. The ranchers and cowboys fell in behind Jennifer.

Sheriff Monroe stopped and faced the crowd. "Stop! No one but Jesse is coming with me. The rest of you, go home!"

Stopped by the sheriff's tone, the crowd broke up, most going back into the Slipper and some heading back toward the

Oxbow. The rest gathered their mounts to do as the sheriff had ordered and go home.

"What the hell is this?" Butler's voice shattered the rapidly growing silence as the crowd was dispersing. As Jesse, Jennifer, the sheriff and others turned, they saw him pulling the running iron from Jesse's saddlebag. Dusty sidestepped uneasily as the crowd of men packed in for a closer look at Butler's discovery.

"Trying to hide the evidence, Jesse?" Butler held the iron high above his head for all to see.

"Damn." Jesse knew that in freeing the cattle and carrying the running iron back to town, she had quite possibly provided all the evidence necessary to hang her for a crime she hadn't committed. She slowly shook her head, angry at herself for not even bothering to check what altered brand the cattle carried before setting them free.

Cries proclaiming Jesse's guilt grew among the men. Here and there, a suggestion to find a rope could be heard coming from the angry mob.

Jennifer instinctively reached out for Jesse, the enraged voices frightening her to the core of her being. She couldn't allow anything to happen to Jesse, but the throng was growing more uncontrollable by the minute and she knew she had no chance of stopping them if they decided to grab Jesse and drag her to the nearest tree. She had to do something.

Without realizing it, her hands were no longer reaching for Jesse, but had instead reached for the gun now back in the sheriff's holster. Jennifer pulled the pistol free. Holding it in shaking hands, she pointed it into the dark sky above.

Bang!

Everyone froze.

Dusty reared at the sound of a second shot, and Jesse grabbed her reins to keep her from injuring anyone.

Jennifer had never held a gun before, let alone fired one. The noise was louder than she had expected. Her voice quivering with emotion, she turned on the crowd. "Billie told you to go home." Her voice trembled and the men strained to listen to the schoolteacher holding a gun that looked extremely large in her hands. "I suggest you do as he says. Jesse is not a rustler, and I'm sure once she has a chance to tell her side, you'll see your mistake. Now go home and let the sheriff do his job."

The men stood, unsure what to do. Standing in front of them was a woman who had stolen their cattle and re-branded them with her own brand. They had the evidence to prove that. Or so they thought. But between them and that woman was another woman. A sapphire-eyed bundle of raw courage who, it seemed, was not afraid to take them all on.

As the men stood mulling over their options, Bette Mae shoved her way through the crowd and wrapped Jennifer in her arms. Removing the gun from the schoolteacher's shaky grasp, she handed it to Billie, then took Dusty's reins from Jesse.

"Go," Bette Mae commanded.

Wasting no time, Billie and Jesse ran for the jail. Once they were safely inside, Billie bolted the door. Dropping into the chair behind his desk, he placed his face in his hands. Nervous energy shook his body as he tried to catch his breath and slow his racing heart.

Jesse collapsed into the other chair in the room. Her heart was fluttering for a completely different reason, her thoughts full of the ginger-haired woman who had defended her against the mob of cowboys. A smile slowly crossed her face. "Damn," she sighed.

BETTE MAE WRAPPED a comforting arm around Jennifer's trembling shoulders and led her back to the Silver Slipper. Reaching the stairs, she threw Dusty's reins over the nearest hitching rail, not taking any time to secure the leather straps as she knew Dusty would wait until her mistress came to retrieve her. Once inside the building, Bette Mae directed the schoolteacher into Jesse's private office.

"Come on in here, child." Bette Mae opened the office door and gently guided Jennifer through it.

Ruthie followed Bette Mae and Jennifer into the Slipper to offer her assistance, but Bette Mae stopped her at the office door.

"See ta our supper guests, Ruthie," Bette Mae instructed the girl. "Miss Jennifer needs some time ta herself right now." Bette Mae softened her voice. "Keep an ear out, and tell the other girls ta do the same."

Ruthie nodded, then scampered to the kitchen to pass the request on to the rest of the Slipper's staff.

"Do you think they'll try to hurt Jesse?" Jennifer had overheard Bette Mae's instructions, and her body stiffened in fear.

"Probably not." Bette Mae crossed the office to a liquor cabinet standing against the far wall. Opening the cabinet's door, she removed a bottle left by the previous owner of the Slipper. Grabbing two glasses, she carried the items back to the couch Jesse kept in her office for late nights. Sitting, she set the glasses on the small table in front of it and poured a small amount from the bottle into each glass.

"Sit down, child," Bette Mae encouraged Jennifer. "Come on and sit 'fore ya fall down."

Jennifer wanted so much to run from the room and out of the Slipper to the jailhouse. She wanted to see Jesse. Wanted to touch her. Wanted to assure herself that Jesse was all right. But, instead, she collapsed onto the couch.

The thoughts scrambling around in her brain were making no sense as they raced about, bumping and crashing into each other. Why did she have such a need to see Jesse? What would she say to the rancher if she did go to the jailhouse? Could a woman even feel about another woman the way that she was feeling about Jesse? None of it made sense, and Jennifer groaned as she propped her elbows on her knees and dropped her head into her hands.

"There, there." Bette Mae reached over, patting Jennifer on the leg. "Don' ya go frettin' 'bout Jesse. She can take care of herself." Bette Mae picked up one of the glasses and held it out to her. "Here, drink this."

Raising her head to see what was being offered, Jennifer looked suspiciously at the mud-colored liquid. "What is it?" She hesitated before taking the glass from Bette Mae's hand.

"Jus' a little somethin' ta settle your nerves. You're still shakin' from firin' that gun."

"First time I've done that." Jennifer looked down, examining the glass and its contents. "First time I've even held a gun." She watched as Bette Mae emptied her glass in one large gulp, shaking her head and releasing a long hiss as the liquor slid down her throat. Jennifer handed the glass back to Bette Mae. "Uh, thanks, but I've never tasted spirits before, and from what you just did to get this stuff down, I don't believe I want to start now."

Chuckling, Bette Mae took the glass and replaced it on the table. "I told Jesse ya was a smart one."

Jennifer smiled at Bette Mae's comment. Then, thinking of Jesse's current dilemma, the smile faded. "What are we going to do about Jesse?" Her head dropped back against the couch. "I know she didn't steal those cattle. Why were the ranchers so angry? Jesse has never done anything to them, has she?" She knew so little about the woman who was stealing her heart.

"Jesse has never taken anythin' that didn't belong ta her. But it only takes one or two hot-heads ta stir a crowd up, and that Mr. Butler never has liked her." Bette Mae shook her head at the memory of some of the things she and the other girls had heard the man say about their friend. "Doesn't think a woman should own a business, 'specially not a cattle ranch."

"But that doesn't make sense." Jennifer sat up to face Bette Mae. "Jesse is the kindest woman I know. And look at what she's done for the women who work here, giving them a decent life."

"Don' have ta convince me 'bout Jesse's goodness. But some men jus' don' see any good in women except ta have their babies and cook their meals."

Jennifer fell back against the couch, memories of her father flooding into her mind. "Yeah, I know what you mean. But what about Jesse?"

"She has an explanation. Them men jus' haven' given her a chance ta say her piece."

Several long minutes went by, the silence broken only by the ticking of a clock that occupied a prominent spot on the fireplace mantel.

Jennifer studied the room. She had never been inside Jesse's office, and she found that the room had a warm, welcoming feel about it. Most of the furnishings were made from the local ponderosa pine and were covered with soft leather of a matching reddish brown. The large desk sat almost in the exact center of the room, attesting to the fact that this room was used for work, not entertaining. Shelves filled with ledgers hung on the wall behind the desk. At each end of the desk sat a lamp to provide light when Jesse worked late into the night. The couch that the women occupied sat against the wall in front of the desk and to the side of the room's door. A small chair sat on the other side of the door and provided a comfortable seat to anyone that might have business with the Slipper's owner. The more she looked about the room, the more she thought of the woman whose office it was.

A deep sigh from Jennifer finally cracked the prolonged silence.

Bette Mae looked at the young woman and saw the dreamy smile on the schoolteacher's face. "You like Jesse, don't you?"

Confused by the question, Jennifer's smile quickly disappeared as she turned to Bette Mae. "Of course I like her. She's done so much for me."

Bette Mae reached over and took Jennifer's hands into her own. "No. I mean you really like her. You have feelings for her."

As the meaning behind Bette Mae's question started to dawn on her, a blush inched its way up Jennifer's neck. "I, uh, I-I don't know what I'm feeling. When I'm near her, I just want to touch her. And when I touch her, my skin tingles at the contact and there's a kind of warmth I've never felt before that spreads through my body. I need to be near her, but when I am, I don't know what to say or how to act."

Jennifer was shocked to hear herself repeat what some of her girlfriends back home had described when they spoke about the boys they were courting. She turned, looking into Bette Mae's eyes. "Is it possible?"

"...ta love another woman," Bette Mae finished for her.

Jennifer nodded reticently.

"Yes, child," Bette Mae smiled. "It most definitely is."

Before Jennifer could ask any of the questions that swirled around in her brain after Bette Mae's statement, the door to the office opened and Ruthie slipped in before quickly closing the door behind her.

"What is it, Ruthie?" Bette Mae turned to the girl.

"Sally sent me to tell you that there's trouble brewing."

"What kind of trouble?" Jennifer quickly rose from the couch.

"A cowboy is talking up to the others that they shouldn't wait until the circuit judge comes next week. Says they should take Jesse out tonight and hang her."

"Dammit ta all blazes," Bette Mae cursed, then remembered the schoolteacher's presence. "I'm sorry."

Jennifer waved off the apology and addressed Ruthie. "What cowboy?" She couldn't believe any of the locals would be calling for Jesse's lynching.

"Sally says she's never seen him before."

"What do we do?"

"Someone needs ta go alert Billie that there may be trouble so's he doesn' git surprised."

"I'll go," Jennifer offered before she even had a chance to think it.

"All right. I'll go see if I can calm things down in the bar." She placed a motherly hand on Jennifer's arm. "Be careful."

Jennifer had the oddest sense that Bette Mae was talking about more than her going to the sheriff's office. Assuring Bette Mae that she would indeed take care, she was out the door before Bette Mae and Ruthie could say any more.

She hurried across the porch and down the steps, taking notice of Dusty still patiently waiting at the hitching rail. She veered the few steps to Dusty's side, retrieving her reins. "Come on, girl. Let's go get Jesse."

A whinny and soft nudge in the shoulder encouraged the schoolteacher on.

AFTER TELLING HER side of the day's happenings to Billie, who was now even more convinced of her innocence, Jesse knew that she would still have to be held in the jail's only cell until the circuit judge arrived. It would be up to the judge to hear both sides and to make the final ruling.

"Hate to do this, but I'm going to have to lock you up."

"I know." She rose from the chair she had been occupying and crossed the small room to the door leading to the even smaller jail cell behind. "Guess this means you won't be getting any sleep the next few nights." She laughed, knowing he lived in his office and slept on the cot in the cell.

"Yeah. Look, I'm sorry about what went on out there. I should have never drawn my gun on you, Jesse. You're too good a friend for that."

"Thanks, Billie. I won't say it didn't bother me, but I guess neither one of us has had to deal with something like this before. No harm done. Just do me a favor. Next time, let's talk it over first."

"You got it." The lawman smiled, glad that his actions hadn't destroyed their friendship.

Reaching down to her boot, she pulled a knife from its scabbard and handed it to him. "You might want this."

"Thanks." He took the knife and nodded for her to enter the cell. Once she was inside, he closed the door and locked it. "Sorry about this."

"Just doing your job." Jesse could see how much locking her up was hurting her friend. "That's what the town pays you for, isn't it?"

"Yeah, but times like this, it don't pay me nearly enough."

"Once the judge gets here, this will all be over and I'll buy you a drink."

"I think I'll be the one buying." He moved to his desk and placed Jesse's knife in the drawer for safekeeping. He was about to ask Jesse what she wanted for her evening meal since the town had an arrangement with the Slipper to provide meals for all prisoners and she was an official prisoner of the town of Sweetwater. Before he could ask, though, someone knocked on the jail's door.

"Miss Jennifer." He was surprised to see the schoolteacher when he eased the heavy wood door open to see who was knocking. "What are you doing here?" He opened the door wide, quickly pulling the schoolteacher inside before re-securing the door.

"Bette Mae sent me." Jennifer's eyes sought out Jesse, and once they had located the tall woman, they never left her. Jennifer crossed to room to stand next to the cell.

The sheriff knew he shouldn't let anyone that close to a

prisoner, but he shrugged it off, wondering what harm it could possibly cause.

"Why did Bette Mae send you?"

"There's a stranger in the Slipper's bar trying to stir up a lynch mob." Her shaky voice and concerned eyes conveyed the fear she felt for the woman who occupied the cell.

"Damn. I'm going to have to go over there. I'll need to find someone to stay here while I'm gone."

"I'll stay."

"Thanks for the offer, Miss Jennifer. But I don't think it would be safe to expect you to face down those men if they decide to come this way."

"I did it once before. And I can do it again, if—"

"No." Jesse's quiet voice stopped Jennifer's protest. "Billie's right. It's not safe. Go back to the Slipper and let Billie handle this."

"I'm not leaving," Jennifer declared, looking into Jesse's eyes. "I won't leave you."

Not having any other options, and seeing the resolve on the schoolteacher's face, the sheriff went to the cabinet that held his shotguns, pulling one out. Checking to make sure the weapon was loaded, he placed a few extra shells in his pocket. "I won't be long. Lock the door behind me and don't unlock it for anyone but me."

As soon as the sheriff left the building, Jennifer locked the door, and for an extra measure of security, she started to shove his desk against the door.

"What are you doing?" Jesse listened to the woman grunt and groan as the heavy desk moved begrudgingly across the wood-planked floor.

Jennifer didn't stop to answer. Once the desk was where she wanted it, she rummaged through the desk drawers. "Ah-ha," she declared, pulling a ring of keys from its hiding place.

"Do you plan on telling me what's going on?"

Jennifer crossed to the cell and unlocked the door. "I'm breaking you out."

"Oh, no you're not." Jesse stepped back from the door, vigorously shaking her head from side to side. "Are you crazy? Do you know what they'll do to you?"

"Don't care. Now come on, we don't have much time." Jennifer swung the metal door open.

"No, Jennifer." Jesse held her hands up, with the palms facing Jennifer. "I'm in enough trouble as it is." She backed as far back into the cell as she could.

"Jesse, did you steal those cattle?"

"No," Jesse snapped, hurt that the schoolteacher would think her capable of such an act.

"I know you didn't." Jennifer softened her tone. "But there are several drunk men over at the Slipper that don't care if you did or didn't. All they care about is lynching someone, and guess whose neck they plan to put their noose around. Please, Jesse. Come with me."

Without thinking, Jesse reached up and rubbed her neck, where she could almost feel the rope's coarse fibers tightening around it. She made one final attempt at stopping the unstoppable. "We can't go back to the Slipper. And we can't just walk out of town. They'll catch us in no time."

Jennifer grinned, knowing she held all the aces, and was ready to lay the last one on the table. "Dusty is waiting for us out back."

Jesse knew the right thing to do was to stay put. But if she did, there was a good chance she would hang for something she didn't do. If she ran, she knew she shouldn't involve the schoolteacher, but then Jennifer was already involved.

"Well, then. What are we waiting for?" She joined Jennifer outside of the cell, and the two moved quickly to the back door of the jail.

"Wait." Jesse stopped and crossed the room to the sheriff's desk.

Jennifer watched as she opened the top drawer and removed a knife, then bent to place it in her boot. "Yours?"

"Mine." Jesse rejoined Jennifer and carefully opened the rear door. Seeing only Dusty standing patiently in the moonlight behind Sweetwater's tiny business district, Jesse opened the door wide enough for Jennifer to pass though. Dusty raised her head in a silent greeting to her mistress and stood quietly as Jesse mounted her. Without a word, she stretched a hand down to Jennifer, who took it and was swung effortlessly up into the saddle behind the rancher.

"Hang on."

Jennifer gladly wrapped her arms around Jesse's waist.

AFTER A NERVE-WRACKING ride from Sweetwater, they reached the hillock that overlooked Jesse's ranch. Expecting to be detected at any moment, neither woman had spoken a word on the ride from town. Jennifer had never loosened her tight hold on Jesse's waist, not even after she had become accustomed to Dusty's gait and could have held on with a looser grip. She found that she liked the feel of her arms wrapped around Jesse.

It felt, well, it just felt right, she decided. Besides, Jesse didn't seem to mind.

Jesse had ridden from Sweetwater with both ears attuned to any sound that would indicate the jailbreak had been discovered and they were being chased. She was relieved when only regular night sounds of an occasional owl hooting or coyote howling in the distance interrupted the quiet. Nothing else had disturbed her concentration.

Well, almost nothing.

As much as she tried to disregard the feeling of the arms wrapped tightly around her waist and of the breathing at her back, she could not. She found herself liking the feel of Jennifer riding behind her. Somewhere between Sweetwater and their present location, she had placed one of her own arms atop Jennifer's, and had decided it felt more than right.

Cresting the top of the rise, Jesse turned so she would have an unobstructed view of their route from Sweetwater. Even though the night was dark, there was enough of a moon to allow her sharp eyes to scan the trail for any sign of a dust cloud that would reveal a posse in pursuit.

While the rancher surveyed what was behind them, Jennifer took the time to check out what lay ahead.

Nestled in a small basin at the bottom of the hillock sat Jesse's ranch. A one-story cabin, the ranch house, stood in the middle of the basin and faced west with a clear view of the mountains in the distance. It looked to be not much bigger than the dining area of the Silver Slipper, with a similar wrap-around porch. Flanked by chimneys at its north and south ends, the house sat in front of a long, neglected garden. About one hundred feet beyond the garden stood a barn more than three times the size of the house. The moonlight reflected off the new portions of roof and the newly rebuilt corral fence encircling three sides of the large building. There were a couple of other buildings, too, but not being familiar with ranches, Jennifer could only guess as to their purpose.

Jesse turned Dusty back toward the ranch and encouraged the horse to continue down the road. Just where the road flattened out at the bottom of the hillock, two large logs stood on either side of the path. Arching from the top of one log to the other was a bowed tree trunk with the side facing incoming visitors cut flat. Carved into the flat surface was the name Jesse had given the ranch, J's Dream. Dusty carried her two passengers under the arch and to the ranch house.

Slipping out of the saddle as soon as Dusty stopped, Jesse turned to help Jennifer down. "We don't have much time." She stepped up onto the porch, opening the cabin's door and urging Jennifer inside. "They have no doubt discovered us missing by now." She crossed the open room to the sleeping area, where a trunk rested at the foot of the bed, pulling items out of it and discarding most of what she took out until she held an old pair of denim pants and a worn flannel shirt. "Put these on." Digging further into the trunk, she pulled out a pair of boots. "These, too." She placed the boots on the floor, then slammed the trunk closed.

"These don't look like they belong to you." Jennifer held the clothes up in front of her.

"They don't. Found the chest after I bought the place. Figured it was left by the previous owner." Seeing that Jennifer had not moved, she snapped, "Hurry up. Get those on if you're coming with me."

Not wanting to give the rancher any excuse to leave her behind, Jennifer jumped into action. She removed the dress she wore. "What's wrong with my own clothes?"

Jesse had crossed the room to the kitchen area and was filling an old flour sack with supplies. "You won't be very comfortable in that dress and those shoes where we're going," she answered without pausing in her task.

"Where are we going?" Jennifer pulled on the denim pants. They were too long for her legs and she bent to roll the cuffs up.

Jesse's breath caught in her chest as she turned to answer, her eyes falling on the half-dressed body of the schoolteacher. She tried to look away, but her eyes would not follow her commands and stayed focused on Jennifer as she rolled the pant legs up to free her feet. "You're so beautiful," she murmured, thinking she had spoken to herself.

"Did you say something?" Jennifer turned her head to look in Jesse's direction. Her eyes locked onto Jesse's.

For several long moments, both women absorbed the varying and changing emotions flashing in the eyes of the other. They might have remained locked in that moment forever if Dusty hadn't whinnied outside.

Jesse finally pulled her eyes from Jennifer. "Um, I, um..." She couldn't make her mouth form the words she wanted. She finally gave up and went back to filling the sack.

Jennifer smiled to herself as she returned to her task of dressing.

After dropping the full sack at the cabin's door, Jesse walked to a chest standing against the rear wall of the cabin. Opening its doors, she reached inside and filled her hands with ammunition for her rifle and pistols. "You about ready?" she walked back to the cabin's door and pulled it open.

"Yes." Jennifer stuffed the bottom of the too-big shirt into the top of the too-big pants. Surprisingly, the boots seemed to be the right size for her. She felt like a little girl wearing her big brother's clothes. At least, she thought that was what she felt like, since she had never in her life worn pants before. One more firm tuck to secure the shirt and she crossed to the door. Since Jesse was busy placing the bullets into Dusty's saddlebags, Jennifer bent and picked up the sack Jesse had filled.

"I'll get that," a tender voice whispered into Jennifer's ear, sending a warm shudder through her body. Jesse carefully took the sack from Jennifer's hands. After tying the sack to Dusty's saddle, she swung herself up into it. "Make sure the door is secure," the rancher instructed the teacher, who stood waiting on the porch.

After doing so, Jennifer quickly re-crossed the porch and took Jesse's offered hand to be again lifted into the saddle. Not needing to be told, she wrapped her arms around Jesse and hung on as Dusty took off at a fast trot.

As they rode away from the ranch, Jesse laid an arm atop Jennifer's and was rewarded with a soft sigh. To the east, the morning sun was beginning to disperse the night's lingering shadows.

IN THE TOWN of Sweetwater, Billie left the jail after Jennifer brought word of a growing lynch mob in the Slipper's saloon. He could see several men loitering about the porch and in the street in front of the Slipper. He didn't have to get too close to them to know that they had consumed more than enough liquor to make them dangerous. As he walked toward the Slipper, he was joined by Thaddeus Newby, who was returning from his monthly visit to the surrounding mining camps in search of news for the pages of his newspaper.

Thaddeus left his horse tied up outside the newspaper office and met the sheriff in the middle of the street. "What's going on, Billie? Heard lots of talk about a hanging when I rode past the Slipper."

"Billingsley and Butler are accusin' Jesse of being a cattle rustler," he explained without breaking stride.

"That's a pile of horse poop and you know it. Where is she?"

"In jail."

"You left her alone?" Thaddeus was incredulous at the seeming lack of protection the sheriff was providing to his prisoner.

"Didn't have much choice. Couldn't stay there to protect her and try to break up the lynch mob. Besides, she's not alone. Miss Jennifer is with her."

"Jennifer!"

"Yep, she wouldn't have it any other way. There's a lot of spirit in that woman."

"Are they safe? Want me to go back there?"

Billie thought for a minute before shaking his head. "Might could use your help here more. I'd ask Ed to go, but don't have the time." Having reached the Slipper, he climbed the steps to the porch and was immediately confronted by drunken men.

"What do ya say we just take her off your hands, Sheriff?"

"Yeah, what do ya say?" added another man who was holding himself upright by wrapping his arms around a post.

"Not tonight, boys." Billie eased past the men. "Can't have the circuit judge come to town and have nothin' to do."

"It'll save some time."

"Maybe." Billie had reached the door and pulled it open. "But I can't let ya do it." Once inside, he saw Bette Mae and the other girls huddled near the saloon door. One look at them and he knew the situation was bad. He couldn't remember ever seeing Bette Mae scared, but right now, she looked down right petrified. He flashed a brief smile in the women's direction before entering the saloon, where he knew he would have to confront the real troublemakers on this night that he was already wishing he could forget.

"'Bout time you showed up," Conrad Billingsley yelled from his spot against the room's long bar. "We were just going to come get you."

Billie knew that the rancher was drunk. Hell, he knew that everyone in the room was drunk with the exception of himself, Thaddeus, and Sally, tending bar. One glance around the room and he knew he could be in serious trouble. Two sober men standing against a liquor-fortified lynch mob did not bode well for Jesse's chances.

"Here goes," he muttered to Thaddeus as they made their way through the crowd. Reaching the bar, he hopped up onto the well-cared-for surface and looked down at the men in the room. "Bar's closed." Shouting over the protests that followed, he continued, "You've all had more than enough. I'm asking you to go home and sleep it off. We can talk about Jesse when you are sober and thinking right."

"Like hell." The rancher Butler slammed his fist down on the bar at the sheriff's feet. "We'll hang the bitch tonight." Several other men in the room voiced their agreement to the declaration.

The newspaperman appealed to the richest and most respected rancher in the valley. "Billingsley, put an end to this before you all make a serious mistake."

"Why, Thaddeus? She stole the cattle. Let her pay the price."

"Conrad, you know she didn't steal any cattle." The sheriff took up the appeal for reason. "I've heard Jesse's side, and I can assure you that she had nothing to do with this."

The shouts for hanging were getting louder and more adamant. Many of the men who had been outside had now come in to hear what was being said and were adding their voices to the chaos. The sheriff's voice was nearly lost in the increasing noise and he stood on the bar watching any influence he might have had slipping away. Trying one more time to take control, the sheriff shouted, "I'm ordering you all to *go home now!*"

As Billie looked over the crowd to see if any would do as he had ordered, a shot rang out. He was thrown sideways by the force of a bullet ripping through his arm. Unable to protect himself as he fell, he could not avoid cracking his jaw on the edge of the bar. Before his body reached the floor, unconsciousness had claimed him.

A moment of silence filled the room as the men watched the limp body disappear behind the bar. Then a voice shattered the stillness: "Now's our chance, boys. Ain't got to worry 'bout the sheriff tryin' to stop us now." As if all of their bodies were somehow linked together, the throng surged towards the saloon's door. The first man had barely reached the opening when another shot exploded in the room.

The men turned to see Sally standing behind the bar, a shotgun in her hands pointed into the crowd. A deadly silence took over the room as the men hastened to check to see if anyone had been wounded.

Before they could regain their momentum, Sally calmly aimed the shotgun at Conrad Billingsley's chest. "Next man who talks of lynching Miss Jesse, I'll blow *your* head off."

"Come on, boys." The voice in the crowd spoke again. "She won't shoot anyone."

"She might not." Bette Mae now stood in the doorway leading into the kitchen, a shotgun leveled at the throng. "But I sure as hell will."

"Come on. Two women ain't gonna stop us."

"Two women and one man," Thaddeus said from his place behind the bar. After the sheriff had been shot, the newspaperman had ducked behind the bar to check on his condition. Seeing that the bullet had gone clean through his arm,

he took a handkerchief from his jacket pocket and wrapped it
around the wound. Then he pulled a pistol from the unconscious
man's holster and took his place behind the bar. "And it look's
like there's a few more women out there just hoping you'll try to
leave." He nodded to the open door leading into the dining room
where some of the girls had gathered, many holding weapons.

"All right!" Billingsley shouted to the men stirring about
him. "This has gone far enough."

"Like hell it has," the voice called out.

Cutting off further conversation, Billingsley commanded, "I
said *enough*! Everyone sit down. Now."

Slowly, the intoxicated men obeyed. One by one, they sat in
the nearest chair and when all the chairs were taken, they sat on
the floor until no one was left standing except Billingsley, the
newspaperman, and women with their weapons pointed.

"Tha's better." Bette Mae kept post at the kitchen's door.
"How's Billie?"

Sally placed the shotgun on the bar in front of Thaddeus
then knelt down to the sheriff slumped on the floor. "He's
coming around." She stood back up. "Bullet went clean through,
but he's going to have a headache for a few days."

Bette Mae signaled to Ruthie standing behind her. The
woman ducked under Bette Mae's arms and made her way
through the men cramped together in the saloon. She and Sally
helped the sheriff up and half-carried him into the kitchen area
so that they could attend to his injuries.

"Now," Bette Mae addressed the men. "Y'all are goin' ta
stay right here 'til mornin'. Ya won't move, ya won't say
anythin'. I suggest that ya git some sleep 'cause you're goin' ta
wish ya had come sunrise." Hearing more than a few grumbles
from her captive audience, she continued, "My girls and I ain't
goin' nowheres, so don' git any ideas." After a long look at the
men sitting about the room, she added, "Sweetwater's
population of jackasses sure done grown tonight. And ya can put
that in your paper, Thaddeus."

A rippling of laughter was heard from the women.

"I'll make it my headline," Thaddeus agreed as he took a
more comfortable position sitting atop the bar, then exchanged
the pistol for the shotgun and laid it across his legs.

Chapter
Four

IT TOOK A couple of hours, but Billie's vision was finally clear and the ringing in his head was down to a loud roar. His arm was wrapped in a clean bandage and a piece of ice wrapped in a towel was pressed against his jaw. He sat in the kitchen, attended to by one of the women who worked at the Slipper. The sheriff didn't know her name, but knew that she very shy and said very little. She worked in the kitchen and laundry of the Slipper and rarely came into contact with the guests who might comment about the scar on her face. As his mind cleared, the sheriff wondered why he hadn't taken notice of the pretty girl before. Maybe after this mess was over, he would come by the Slipper and see if he could get her attention.

"How's the head?" Bette Mae sat beside the sheriff, effectively bringing his thoughts back to the events at hand.

"Feels like my horse kicked me." He spoke cautiously so as not to jar his injured face too much.

"Probably will for a while." Bette Mae handed him a fresh piece of ice and took the wet towel from him. "What now, Billie?" she asked, her voice heavy with concern.

"You keep them here and I'll go check on Jesse." He nodded a *thank-you* for the ice before pressing it against his jaw. "She probably thinks something happened to me by now."

"Somethin' did happen ta ya." She wrung out the drenched towel before handing it back.

"Yeah." He wrapped the towel around the chunk of ice. "Good thing it happened at the Slipper and you stood up to them." He rose from the chair, swaying a bit as he stood.

"Hang on, Billie." She reached out to place a steadying arm on the sheriff's. "Maybe one of us should walk with ya."

"Nah." He tried to smile but it quickly turned into a grimace when his jaw protested. "I'll be okay once I get going. Besides, I'd rather you stay and help Thaddeus keep an eye on them." He tilted his head in the direction of the saloon.

"Okay. I'll have Ruthie keep an eye on ya from the porch. She can make sure ya make it back ta your office."

"Sounds good." Billie reached for his hat resting on a shelf near the door. Without care, he placed it on his head, mashing his disheveled hair under it. "Thanks again."

"Ya give our love ta Jesse." The older woman squeezed the arm that she still gripped. "And send Miss Jennifer back here so's I can see that she's all right."

"I will."

It was still dark out, and this surprised the sheriff. It felt like the night's events had lasted several days instead of just a few hours. He stepped into the moonlit street and stopped in the middle of it. Careful not to move his jaw any more than necessary, he took several deep breaths. The cold, night air felt good as it filled his lungs, and the lingering dizziness from his fall seemed to dissipate as he continued to draw in the crisp air. After several minutes, he continued his journey, gaining strength as he walked towards his office.

Reaching the jail, he was grateful to find that Jennifer had locked the front door as he had instructed her to do upon his departure just hours earlier. He knocked lightly, sorry to have to wake the women he was sure were asleep inside. As his knocking received no answer, he knocked louder and called to Jennifer. Silence continued to be the only response. Moving to the window beside the door, he peered into his office. He could see nothing; no lamp was lit inside the building. He rapped his knuckles strongly against the windowpane in hopes that the sharper sound would wake the women.

No movement came from inside the dark building. "Strange," he mumbled. He had always heard that Jesse was a light sleeper and would awake at the slightest sound. "Must really have been worn out after tonight's excitement."

He was about to try the other window when something caught his eye. It wasn't much, just the flash of moonlight reflecting off the cell's bars. He stood frozen in place while he tried to reason out why that had caught his attention. It was just the moonlight, and it wasn't unusual on a clear night for the moon to penetrate into his office.

"Damn." He jerked away from the window. The moonlight, that was the answer. There was no way for the moon to reach that part of the jail unless it came through the building's back door. And the only way for it to come through the back door was if the door was open.

He raced down the boardwalk until he reached the end at the opposite side of the general store. Jumping off the boardwalk, he ran to the back of the store and around to the back of the jail, sliding to a stop in front of the wide open door. He entered the building already knowing what he would find. It was empty. The cell that he had left Jesse securely locked in was open and vacant. And his desk was pushed up against the front door to keep out any unwanted visitors.

"Damn. Why, Jesse?" His voice echoed in the empty room. "They'll hang you for sure when they catch you."

"Then you'll have to make sure they don't catch her."

He swung around to see the storekeeper, Ed Granger, standing in the open doorway. "Did you know?" Billie shot the accusing question at the big man.

"No." Ed shook his head. "Didn't think she'd break her way out."

"She didn't. She had help from Miss Jennifer." He pointed at the key ring still hanging from the cell door's lock.

A smile slowly made its way across Ed's face, and his belly laugh filled the air. "Dang, that schoolteacher has sure got some spunk."

"Yeah." Billie pulled his desk away from the front door. "That spunk may get them both killed."

ED ACCOMPANIED THE sheriff back to the Silver Slipper. The short walk was made in silence as both contemplated the opinion the sheriff had voiced in his office. They knew that a posse would have to be formed, and Jesse and Jennifer would be hunted down and brought back to face judgment for the jailbreak. Any hope of the judge letting Jesse off after hearing her testimony regarding the rustled cattle was gone. The sheriff wondered how he could keep control of a posse of men who would now be angry that they had been forced to sit in the Slipper's saloon while Jesse made her escape. Ed wondered if Jesse could keep herself and the schoolteacher safe until they could uncover the truth behind the rustlers and clear both their names.

As the sheriff was about to enter the Slipper to inform the now-sobering men of the jailbreak, Ed stopped him with a large hand on his arm. "Give Jesse the time she needs." There was no need for the storekeeper to explain his request.

"I'll do what I can," Billie agreed, and then entered the saloon.

Ed followed close behind as they stepped over the men on the floor and made their way back to the bar where Thaddeus still sat. A few men were talking quietly, but most were sleeping or just sitting, waiting to see what would happen now that morning had arrived. Dislodging a cowboy, the sheriff pulled a chair behind the bar and stood on it. Still a little unsure on his feet after his injury, he did not want to chance climbing on top of the bar.

Thaddeus slipped off the bar and handed Ed the shotgun. "You'd probably be more comfortable with this than I am."

"Thanks." The large man accepted the gun and stood beside Billie.

Thaddeus took up a position at the end of the bar where he could watch the proceedings and make notes.

Once everyone was situated to his satisfaction, the sheriff picked his pistol up from the bar and rapped it hard on the wood surface.

The men who were already awake had been watching the sheriff's actions, and were ready for the sharp noise of his gun hitting the wooden surface. The sleeping men were not, and woke in various stages of alarm. After a few moments, the sheriff rapped again. "I hope I have everyone's attention now."

"Hey, what's with all the noise?" one man asked. "Thought you wanted us to sleep?"

"Listen to me. Something has happened and I need to form a posse."

This news quickly brought the men back to life, with several of the men shouting questions at the same time.

The sheriff held up his hands to quiet them. "Hold your questions and listen to me. I'll tell you want happened, but first I'm setting some ground rules."

A few grumbles could be heard, but since the men wanted to find out what was going on, most remained silent to encourage the sheriff to continue.

"All right. I'm naming the posse members. The rest of you are to return to your homes and ranches and go back to your own business. If any of you try to interfere with the posse, I'll arrest you. And you can answer to the circuit judge when he gets here."

More grumbles were heard, but were shushed by those around them.

"Billingsley and Butler, name three of your best trackers."

"That's it?"

"No, I'm asking Thaddeus and Ed to join us," the sheriff said. "And *that's* it."

Billie wasn't sure that putting the two ranchers on the posse was the best of ideas, but he knew he would never leave town without Billingsley. And it was better to have Butler, who had a major dislike for Jesse, where he could keep an eye on him. Plus, both men employed the best trackers in the valley. The best, that is, besides Jesse. That little piece of information gave the sheriff some peace of mind, as he knew Jesse probably would not make it easy for the posse to follow her.

The sheriff's decision to add the newspaper editor and the storekeeper to the posse was two-fold; first, it would give him two extra sets of eyes and ears that were not out to harm Jesse and Jennifer. And the two men would provide neutral testimony when the women went on trial. The sheriff knew he had to bring the women back, but he wasn't going to bring them back to hang.

"All right, Billie." Conrad Billingsley rose from the chair he had been occupying. "You've named your posse. Now do you mind telling us what the hell is going on?"

"Jesse broke out of jail last night."

Shouts arose from every man in the room, but the sheriff cut them off by firing his pistol in the air.

"Miss Jesse isn't going to like all those bullet holes in her new ceiling," Ruthie whispered to Bette Mae as they watched the proceedings from the kitchen.

"Hush, child," Bette Mae scolded. "Them's the least of our worries right now."

"All right!" the sheriff tried to out-shout the men. Calls for the sheriff's arrest, and worse, for letting a prisoner escape, started to make their way about the room.

Realizing that he couldn't hold back the men alone, the sheriff turned to the rancher standing on the other side of the bar. "Billingsley, you know this has gone too far. We have to work together or Sweetwater will pay the price for years to come."

Studying the sheriff and listening to the growing anger of the crowd, the rancher gave in for the second time in the last few days. He nodded and walked behind the bar to stand beside the sheriff and storekeeper. "Quiet!" Billingsley's bellow rolled around the room and the men paused. The smart ones saw the intensity in the eyes of the men behind the bar and quieted. The not-so-smart ones and the ones still too intoxicated to notice foolishly continued to protest. "I said, *quiet!*" A second, more forceful bellow rattled the glasses behind the bar and got everyone's attention. "Last night was a mistake." He lowered his voice. "We're ranchers, not a lynch mob. Jesse has been a good friend since she came to Sweetwater."

"Speak for yourself."

"Shut up, Butler." Ed glared at the man. "You don't like Jesse 'cause she's a woman and she runs a ranch. That doesn't mean she should hang for something she didn't do."

"Is that how you treat cattle rustlers in Sweetwater?" a voice shouted from the back of the room.

The sheriff looked in the direction of the voice. "Who said that? Someone has been trying to stir you men up all night. Always pushing you towards a lynching. Look around, who do you see? You see your friends and neighbors. People you have known for several years. Not people who would want to hang a friend."

Billingsley nodded at the truth of the sheriff's words. Someone had been stirring the pot most of the night, but why? Maybe Jesse was innocent.

As the men searched the faces of those standing or sitting near them, no one took notice of the lanky cowboy who sat at a table in the back of the room. To all that looked in his direction, he appeared to be just another of the young cowboys employed by one of the valley's ranches. His outward calmness hid the fact that his heart was in his throat and the hands he concealed under the table were shaking so bad he was afraid they would give him away. The boy concentrated on whether or not he could manage to escape from the room alive. He was in way over his head and he had long ago decided that no amount of money Johnson was going to pay him and his brother would compensate for the fear he was experiencing.

As the men continued to search for the owner of the voice, the sheriff drew their attention back to the front of the room. "Okay, any more questions, or problems, before we break this up?"

Some of the men shook their heads, but most just stood quietly.

"Good. Billingsley, you and Butler pick your men and meet me at the jail in half an hour. Bette Mae, Sally, the Slipper is closed until the posse gets back," the sheriff told the women watching from the kitchen. Without waiting for a response, he continued, "I expect no harm to come to the Slipper or to Jesse's ranch and livestock. There's no real proof she had anything to do with the rustling. But we will bring her back and let the judge decide."

The sheriff bent to step down from the chair, then changed his mind and straightened back up. "Now for the last time, *go home.*"

Half an hour later, a small group of somber men sat on their horses in the street outside of the jailhouse. Sheriff Monroe, with a bandage wrapped around his upper arm and sporting a nasty bruise on his jaw, stood on the boardwalk in front of the building. The newspaperman and storekeeper were astride their own horses standing slightly apart from the ranchers.

With one final look at his posse, the sheriff mounted his horse and turned it in the direction that would take them to Jesse's ranch. "Let's go."

"WHERE ARE WE going?"

After leaving Jesse's ranch, Dusty had maintained a steady pace. They rode east from the ranch and into the thick forest on that side of the valley. Jesse led them deep into the trees before changing directions to travel south in the direction where she had lost the rustlers' tracks the previous day. *Was it really only one day?* So much had happened.

"Jesse." Jennifer twisted in an effort to see Jesse's face. "Are you okay?"

"Yes." Jesse patted the arms wrapped tightly around her waist. "Just thinking." She turned in the saddle to smile back at her passenger and was surprised to again see the genuine concern in Jennifer's eyes. "Guess I got myself in a pretty good mess, huh?"

"We'll get you out of it." She didn't know how and she didn't know why, but somehow she knew it was important to her future, both their futures, to see Jesse cleared of the charges against her.

"Wish I was as sure as you are." Jesse turned back around to guide Dusty around yet another rocky stretch of ground.

"Wouldn't it be faster to ride across here than around it?"

"Yes. But it would also be harder on Dusty. And it would make it rough for Billie to follow our trail."

Jennifer turned to look behind them. All she saw were trees. "I didn't think you wanted them to follow us."

"Not too close. But we don't know what's up ahead. If we run into trouble, might not be a bad thing for Billie to ride in on it too."

"Are they following?"

"Probably." After taking note of the location and length of the sun's shadows, she added, "Should have reached the ranch by this time." She wondered if Billie would be able to stop the ranchers from tearing it apart looking for more evidence that she had stolen their cattle. There wasn't much she could do about it now.

"So where are we going?" Jennifer repeated.

"South, to the spot where I tracked the rustlers yesterday. Hopefully, I can pick up their tracks again."

"Then what?"

"Then I try to find out who they are and why they want me to hang."

Jennifer stiffened. "Don't say that."

"Hey." Jesse gently stroked Jennifer's arm. "I have no intention of being the guest of honor at a necktie party. But you have to admit, someone is trying real hard to make me look guilty."

"I know." Jennifer's voice was soft as she laid her head against Jesse's back.

IT WAS LATE morning when Dusty left the cover of the forest. They quickly made their way across the south end of Jesse's property, Dusty carrying them on a path that would cross the rustlers' trail.

"That's the canyon I found the cattle in yesterday." Jesse pointed.

Jennifer lifted her head. "Shouldn't we check it out?"

"Nah, I doubt they would go back there." Jesse shook her head at her own stupidity. If only she had left the cattle where she had found them and had gone to find Billie. But the animals had been hungry and thirsty, and she knew she had done the right thing for them. Unfortunately, it wasn't the best thing for her.

Though Jesse tried to urge her forward, Dusty insisted on stopping at a small creek their path crossed. Jesse had to admit her horse was right; a break was in order. Unlocking Jennifer's arms from her waist, she swung her leg over the saddle horn and slipped to the ground, then reached up to help Jennifer from Dusty's back. Free of her riders, Dusty dropped her neck to enjoy a drink of cold water.

As soon as her feet touched the ground, Jennifer groaned at her sore and protesting muscles. She arched her back into a stretch. "Goodness, I never knew riding a horse was so hard on one's body."

Jesse laughed as she stretched out her own tired muscles. "Takes some getting used to. I take it you didn't do much riding back home?"

"Only if you count horse-drawn buggies." Jennifer took a few tentative steps, hoping to get the blood flowing again in her legs.

"Here." Jesse offered the canteen. "Drink. Won't be long 'til the sun is really beating down on us."

Jennifer accepted the offer and took a long drink before

handing it back. As Jesse knelt to refill the canteen from the creek, Jennifer joined her. After rolling her sleeves above her elbows, she cupped her hands and filled them with the cool water, splashing some on her arms and face.

Watching, Jesse pulled the bandanna from her neck, soaked it in the creek, and partially wrung it out. "Put this around your neck." She held the still-dripping cloth out. "It will help keep you cool."

Jennifer smiled gratefully as she took the bandanna from Jesse. "What about you?"

"I'm used to the heat," she lied. She knew that in a short time the sun would make their ride miserable, but it was a small sacrifice to give Jennifer some relief from the heat. "Keep that wet," she added. "Let me know if the canteen gets low."

Dusty was ready to continue and Jesse mounted up. She reached down for Jennifer and as soon as the schoolteacher was settled, urged Dusty into a trot.

Jesse soon picked up the rustlers' trail, following it back into the forest where the riders had split up. Guessing that the three riders would eventually rejoin each other, she followed the trail that led to the south. It was a direction that would keep them in the trees and out of the sun. And would make for an easier ride for Dusty and them.

DUSTY CAREFULLY PICKED her way around the scattered stones of a dry creek bed. Jesse and Jennifer were walking alongside to give the tired horse a break. It was hot, but the large ponderosa pines around them served to block the sun's intensity and provided some much-appreciated shade. Jennifer had long ago given up on keeping Jesse's bandanna wet. The afternoon's oven-like conditions dried it almost as fast as she could pour water over it. They had been following the same set of hoof prints for so long that Jennifer was able to pick them out almost as easily as Jesse could.

Jesse needed to break the heavy silence that had grown between them. "So, what brought you to Sweetwater? Other than the schoolteacher position, I mean."

Jennifer was quiet for several moments while she debated how much she wanted to tell her companion. But, considering that she had not hesitated to break Jesse out of jail after knowing her for only a few days, she figured there wasn't much reason to not just tell the truth. "I come from a family where girls are raised to marry, have children, and not question their father's or husband's decisions. I wanted more than that. A friend gave me a newspaper from Denver, I saw the ad for schoolteachers, and I answered it."

"Your father, or...or husband must have had something to say about you leaving." She held her breath, not really sure she wanted to know the answer to her unspoken question.

Jennifer laughed softly. "Oh, I'm not married, not that my father didn't do everything in his power to make sure that I was. I didn't tell anyone I was leaving. Oh, except for Matt," she smiled as she remembered the librarian, "he's the friend. He helped me, bought the train ticket and gave me some money to live on until I received my schoolteacher's pay. He kept my secret even though he works for my father. I knew if my father found out what I was planning, he would have had my brothers watch my every move. To him, I wasn't anything more than the incentive part of a business deal. Just a way to make his shipping business more profitable by marrying me off to the son of one of his associates."

Jesse, saddened by Jennifer's words, wanted nothing more than to pull the schoolteacher to her and hug her tight. Refusing to give into her instincts, she instead asked, "What about your mother? Is that how she felt?"

"Like I said, the women in my family are taught to obey. I don't think I ever heard my mother question my father. Whatever he decided was fine with her. And my brothers will go along with Father as long as he controls the family business. It may have been good enough for Mother, but I was not going to end up like that. So," she shrugged, "here I am."

"I'm glad you're here."

Jennifer smiled back shyly. "Me too. What about you?"

"I'm sure Bette Mae or one of the girls has told you the story. I won the Slipper in a poker game. Not much else to tell."

"Sure there is," Jennifer protested. "I mean, it's not usual for a woman to be riding around the West by herself. What about your family?"

"I was born on my folk's ranch outside of Bozeman. It was just the three of us. My mom had a baby boy a year after me, but he died the same day. She couldn't have any more children after that. I don't think my dad ever forgave her. He'd always wanted a son."

"But he had you."

"Yeah, he worked me liked he would have a son, that's for sure. I worked that ranch since the day I learned to ride, and I was riding before I could walk. Guess I just figured one day the place would be mine. He figured it differently." Jesse's voice betrayed the hurt and bitterness she still felt over events that had happened a couple of years before.

"What happened?"

"Came home one day after riding fence to find them packing up and moving into town. Said he'd sold the ranch and I was on my own."

Jennifer gasped. "He threw you out?"

"Guess you could say that. Seems I had taken too long to find myself a husband and the son that he could finally pass the ranch on to. So he took the money when it was offered."

"What did you do?"

"Got on Dusty and never looked back. Found myself in Denver one night and decided to try my luck in a poker game. You know the rest."

"Some pair we are, huh? Neither of us any good to our families because we wouldn't get married."

"Yeah. Looks like we'll be a pair of old spinsters, puttering around Sweetwater in our old age."

"As long as we do it together, you won't hear me complain," Jennifer said before she could stop herself.

"Me too," Jesse whispered, and this time she didn't hesitate; she wrapped her arms around Jennifer and hugged her tight. It felt so good to hold the schoolteacher, and she was pleased when Jennifer returned her embrace without any indecision. If only she could stay in this moment forever, she would be a very happy woman. No one's touch had ever affected Jesse the way the schoolteacher's did. And Jesse was going to do everything in her power not to lose the feeling.

Jennifer melted into the rancher's arms. She looked into Jesse's eyes and saw the same affection she felt for the rancher reflected back at her. Now she knew why she had turned away every suitor her father had arranged for her. None had looked at her like Jesse was looking at her now; none had made her feel important like Jesse did by just holding her. She had left the place of her birth, traveled halfway across the country, and had finally found her home. Snaking her arms around the rancher, she couldn't think of a better place to spend the rest of her life.

After several moments, Jesse gently broke their embrace. "We need to keep moving."

Jennifer sighed, but knew Jesse was right. "When this is all over, I want to pick up where we left off."

Jesse smiled. "That's a promise."

They resumed their journey, stepping around the larger rocks in the dry creek bed.

"You would think that he would try to hide his tracks." Jennifer referred to the rustler they were following.

"Um." Jesse had had the same thought more than once. It was almost as if the rider wanted to be followed. "Maybe."

"Maybe? It's almost as if he wants us to follow."

"If that's the case, I guess we're obliging him."

"Jesse." Jennifer reached out a hand and gently rested it on Jesse's forearm. "What do you plan to do when we catch up with the rustlers?"

Jesse stopped and looked down at the hand on her arm before raising her eyes to meet Jennifer's. "I plan to find out why they are doing this to me, and then I plan to figure out a way to get them back to Sweetwater and let Billie deal with them."

"But what if—"

Jesse reached up, tenderly placing two fingers on Jennifer's lips to quiet her. Those lips were soft, and Jesse's heart raced as she considered what it would be like to kiss them. She slowly dropped her hand, relishing the tingle that remained on her fingertips. "It'll be okay," Jesse said with a confidence she didn't really feel. "Come on." She pulled herself back into the saddle. "Let's ride."

Jennifer reached up to take Jesse's outstretched hand and soon found herself seated behind Jesse in a position she was quickly becoming accustomed to. She reached up and touched her lips where only moments before Jesse's fingers had rested, smiling at the memory.

THE TRACKS EVENTUALLY left the dry creek bed, leading them along a forest path to a large meadow. As Dusty walked out from the trees into the clearing, she came to an abrupt stop.

"What's wrong?" Jennifer cried out at the sudden lack of motion.

"Shh. Look, but don't make any noise."

Jennifer peeked over Jesse's broad shoulders and saw several dozen large deer-like animals grazing on the meadow's grasses. "What are they?"

"Elk."

"They're beautiful." Jennifer was immediately taken with the magnificent animals. Some stood as tall as Dusty and carried the early growth of antlers on the heads. Their brown coats blended in with the late afternoon shadows, and if it hadn't been for the patch of lighter coloring around their almost non-existent tails, Jennifer would have had trouble picking some of them out in the fading light. A few lifted their heads to look at the intruders, but sensing that they were not in danger, they promptly went back to grazing. Several of the younger animals skirted around to put their mothers between themselves and the women.

"It'll be dark soon." Jesse looked to the western sky. The sun stayed in the sky late this time of year, but when it started to drop, it fell fast, and night was a short time coming. "Guess this is as good a spot as any to set up camp."

"We're going to camp here with them?" Jennifer was a little nervous thinking of trying to sleep with the big animals wandering around.

"No." Jesse nudged Dusty around the elk herd to the edge of a small creek running through the clearing. "They'll be gone by nightfall. They don't stay in one spot for very long."

"Oh." Jennifer continued to watch the elk, impressed at the way they moved with their heads held high. "They're so majestic when they move."

"Yeah." Jesse swung her leg over Dusty's neck and slipped from the saddle. "I could sit and watch them all day."

Jennifer slid down from the saddle and landed next to Jesse. "I can see why." She stretched her back and legs.

Jesse pulled the saddlebags and gear off Dusty and placed it on the ground. Then she pulled the saddle and saddle blanket off. Rummaging around in one of the saddlebags, she found the grooming tools and began to give Dusty a good rubdown. "Been a long day for you, girl. Hasn't it?"

Dusty raised her head in agreement.

"Let me get you cleaned up and then you can run free for the night."

"Aren't you afraid she'll run off?"

"Nah. Raised her from a foal. She and I are good pals, we look out for each other. I'd never leave her, and she'd never leave me. Right, girl?" Jesse patted the mare's neck before removing the bridle.

Dusty whinnied her response, then took off at a run right through the center of the herd, the elk scurrying out of her way.

Both women laughed at the mare's antics.

"Best get camp set up while we still have light."

"What can I do?" Jennifer had never, in her entire life, slept outside. She had no idea how it was done. Where would they sleep? What would they eat?

"You could gather up firewood."

Jennifer wasn't sure where she would find a stack of chopped firewood. She scanned the meadow. "Ah, Jesse?"

"Yes?" Jesse was gathering rocks for a fire ring.

"Where is the firewood?"

Looking up, Jesse was puzzled at Jennifer's question. "Well

you could start with that dead branch you're almost standing on."

Reaching down, Jennifer lifted the branch in her hand. "You mean this?"

"Yes. What did you think I meant by firewood?"

"I guessed you meant like the chopped wood Ed brings to the school house every day."

"Oh." Realization slowly dawned on Jesse. "Sorry, I should have known you probably never did anything like this before." She smiled apologetically.

"I can truthfully say that I've never set up a camp before." Jennifer grinned back.

"Okay. Let's start again. You can go around and pick up all the pieces like that branch you can find. Just stay in the meadow and don't get near the elk."

"Right." Jennifer set off on her task.

After setting up the fire ring and clearing the loose debris around it so that a spark wouldn't set the meadow on fire, Jesse rolled out her bedroll and placed her blanket next to it. "Guess I'll be sleeping on the grass tonight," she muttered as she looked down at her only bedroll.

"Did you say something?" Jennifer returned with an armload of wood. She dropped it next to the fire ring.

"Just thinking I should have picked up another bedroll when we stopped at the ranch." Jesse reached for a few of the smaller branches and placed them inside the ring.

"Oh." Jennifer studied the lone bedroll, pondering its possible advantages.

"We'll need more wood. It'll get cool tonight."

"I bet I know one way to keep warm tonight," Jennifer mumbled as she set off on another foray of firewood-gathering.

"Did you say something?" Jesse took out a match from the small box in the saddlebag.

"No, nothing at all."

When she brought her second armful of branches back to the camp, Jennifer was surprised to see a fire blazing, a small pot of water warming on a rock placed amidst the burning wood, and Jesse gutting two large fish. "Where did those come from?"

"The creek." Jesse gave her a very self-satisfied grin.

Jennifer walked over and looked into the small body of water flowing between the creek's banks; it didn't look deep enough to hold fish the size the rancher was cleaning. "In there?"

"Yep."

"Jesse, there's barely enough water in there for me to get my boots wet."

"Wanna bet?"

Jennifer considered meeting the challenge, then shook her head and walked back to the fire. "They're big. What are they?"

"Trout, rainbows. Ever taste one?"

"Don't think so."

"Then you are in for a treat. Rainbows are the best when they're fresh from the water and cooked over an open fire." Jesse finished cleaning the fish and placed them in a frying pan. Soon the smell of grilling fish filled the air.

"Smells wonderful." Jennifer sat on a short section of log Jesse had found not far from their camp and had rolled close to fire.

Night had fallen by the time the fish were ready to eat.

JENNIFER LAY ON her back on the bedroll, staring up into the night sky. "I have never seen so many stars."

"You don't have stars back home?" Jesse looked up from where she was washing up in the creek.

"Not as many as these." The more Jennifer stared, the more the stars took on shapes and forms. She had once read a book that talked about the stars and she remembered the book had called various groupings constellations. But she had never been able to compare the book's descriptions to the actual stars in the sky because her father had told her it was nonsense for a woman to do such things and had forbade her to stay out at night to try. "This is so different from back home." She sighed.

"How so?" Jesse sat on the log, tossing a few more branches onto the fire.

"I don't know if I can describe it." Jennifer sat up to face Jesse. "I felt so restricted back there. So controlled. But here," she swept her arm around the meadow, "I feel so free. Like I can do anything."

"You can do anything, Jennifer."

She cocked her head and looked at Jesse. "That sounds nice."

"What? That you can do anything?"

"No." Jennifer tucked her head, suddenly embarrassed by her feelings. Raising her eyes to look at Jesse, she softly continued, "The way you say my name. You put so much feeling into it when you say it. No one has ever done that before."

Neither woman knew what to say after that. They sat quietly, each entranced by the way the fire's light reflected off the other's face.

Dusty trotted back to the camp, breaking the spell.

"Tired of irritating the elk?" Jesse asked the mare who had spent much of the evening chasing the large animals around the meadow.

After a long drink in the creek, Dusty walked over and pushed her still-dripping muzzle into Jesse's face and blew out a long breath through her nostrils. She then turned and trotted away from Jesse with a spring to her gait.

Jennifer did everything she could to not laugh.

"Smart ass," Jesse grumbled as she wiped her face dry on her shirtsleeve.

Dusty whinnied her response to the glaring rancher.

Jesse looked over at the schoolteacher struggling to hold in her laughter. "Oh, go ahead and let it out before you bust a gut."

Howls of laughter rang out, scaring away any elk that remained in the meadow. After several minutes of uncontrollable laughter, Jennifer began to hiccup and couldn't stop.

Now it was Jesse's turn to laugh. "Serves you right," she chortled.

Jennifer was unable to respond as every time she opened her mouth to say something, a hiccup escaped. She looked at Jesse helplessly.

Taking pity on the schoolteacher, Jesse handed her the canteen. "Take a large gulp but don't swallow until you feel a hiccup coming. Swallow at the same time."

Jennifer did as she was instructed and the hiccups stopped. Taking a large lungful of air, she handed back the canteen. "Where'd you learned that?" she wheezed out.

"Don't know. Just always worked for me." Jesse walked over to her saddle and picked up the saddle blanket tossed over it. She lay down on the ground next to the log, pulling the blanket over her. "We better get some sleep."

Her breathing back to normal, Jennifer watched Jesse pull the blanket tightly around her body. "What are you doing?"

"Going to sleep. What does it look like?"

"It looks like you plan to sleep wrapped in that smelly blanket."

"I do."

Jennifer paused, then said what she had been thinking all evening. "Jesse, come share the bedroll with me."

Jesse took a deep breath; she wanted so much to do as Jennifer suggested. Her feelings for Jennifer made the idea of sleeping close to her both spine-tingling and terrifying. "I don't know."

"Please." Jennifer opened the bedroll and crawled inside. Then, holding it open, she added, "We'll both be warmer."

Jesse got up and slowly walked around the fire to where Jennifer lay waiting. She settled beside the schoolteacher. Nervously, she lay on her back and waited to see what Jennifer would do. The bedroll wasn't really wide enough for two people, but Jesse wasn't going to move now that she was here.

Jennifer smiled at Jesse before moving to lie on her side next to Jesse. She placed her head on Jesse's shoulder and timidly wrapped an arm around her waist. "Is this okay?"

"Yes," Jesse breathed as she felt the weight of Jennifer's body pressed against her own. "Are you comfortable?"

"Very." Jennifer snuggled closer and was surprised, but very pleased, when she felt Jesse's arms pull her even closer.

"Jennifer." Jesse paused before continuing awkwardly, "What would you think if I said that I was having feelings for you?"

Jennifer's heart leaped into her throat. *Was it possible that Jesse felt the same way about her that she felt for the rancher?* She was afraid to ask but she had to know, "What kind of feelings?"

"The kind of feelings a woman must have for a man when she wants to spend the rest of her life with him." The words tumbled out in one long burst. Not hearing a response from Jennifer, Jesse realized she had made a mistake in putting voice to her feelings. She tried to get up.

Sensing Jesse's panic, Jennifer placed a hand on her chest to stop her and looked deep into her eyes.

"I'm so sorry." Jesse saw tears rolling down Jennifer's cheeks.

"No, Jesse." Jennifer smiled through the tears. "I'm glad you said it because I feel the same way."

"Then why are you crying?" Jesse gently wiped the tears away.

"Because you've just made me very happy." Jennifer captured Jesse's hand in her own and pulled it to her chest as she laid her head back down on Jesse's shoulder. She could hear Jesse's heart racing and knew that her own was beating just as rapidly. "Good night, Jesse."

Jesse wrapped the blankets around their bodies. "Good night, Jennifer."

IT WAS EARLY afternoon and the women had been back on the rustlers' trail since dawn. For the past hour, the trail had led them in a southwesterly direction and was sloping more downhill. Jesse knew that they would soon leave the relative safety of the forest and would be back in the open canyon country at the south end of the valley. She pulled Dusty to a stop. "Listen." She twisted in the saddle so she could see Jennifer. "I don't know what we're going to find when we leave the trees. Maybe it would be best if you stayed here and..."

"No. Leaving me here is not an option. You're right, you don't know what we'll find, but whatever it is, we'll have a better chance if we stay together."

Jesse hesitated. She didn't want to put Jennifer in danger, but it did make better sense to stay together. She looked into Jennifer's eyes and saw the schoolteacher's determination. "Okay, but if we run into trouble, you do as I say. Deal?"

Jennifer nodded. "Deal."

Twisting back around in the saddle, Jesse nudged Dusty forward at a walk. This end of the valley was mostly box canyons and scrub brush ravines. Whoever they had been following could now be waiting in ambush in any number of places. Other than turning around and traveling back through the forest to meet the posse following them, there really wasn't much choice than to ride out and face head-on whatever, and whoever, awaited them. She only hoped that Billie had some good trackers in the posse and that they would catch up with the women soon.

As the forest thinned, she was able to see the open country beyond. The trail led to a small meadow before leaving the forest completely. Dusty walked into the clearing and stopped, nervously pawing the ground. She had already spotted the source of her mare's apprehension. Across the meadow, a camp was set up and a fire was burning. Three horses stood tied to a picket line, but their owners were nowhere in sight. "Damn."

"What?" Jennifer had a death-grip on Jesse's waist.

"Trouble."

"Maybe," Jennifer whispered fearfully as she peeked over Jesse's shoulder, "we should go back."

Jesse continued to search the meadow and surrounding trees for any movement. "Too late for that."

A man stepped out from the trees, his rifle leveled at the women. He waved two younger men out from their hiding places both also armed with rifles.

"Been a long time, bitch."

"Johnson?" Jesse was surprised to recognize the previous owner of the Silver Slipper.

"So you remember me."

Jesse didn't answer, but took the time to study the three men facing them. Johnson's younger companions looked uneasy, almost like they didn't want to be there. Johnson, on the other hand, looked jubilant, like he had fully expected Jesse to ride into his camp. "What do you want, Johnson?"

"The Slipper."

"It's not for sale." She stalled as she tried to devise a plan to get herself and Jennifer safely out of the trap Johnson had sprung.

"Don't plan to pay for what I already own, bitch."

"Game was fair. You lost."

"Come over here. Nice and slow."

"If I refuse?"

"I'll shoot that pretty schoolteacher."

In response to a gentle flip of the reins, Dusty moved forward.

"Hold it!" Johnson shouted. "Throw down any weapons you have on you first. And you get off and walk. Don't want you tryin' anything."

"All right." She slowly swung her leg over the saddle horn and slid easily to the ground. They were a good fifty feet from the men and she knew she had to use the opportunity this presented. Turning to pull her rifle from the saddle's scabbard, she whispered to Jennifer, "Keep looking at Johnson. I need you to listen to me and do as I say." She felt Jennifer's body stiffen, and patted her leg to reassure her. "Please, Jennifer. We don't have time to argue."

"What's taking you so long?"

"Rifle's caught in the scabbard, give me a minute." She turned to face the man. Seeing him stop, she turned back so he couldn't see her face. "I want you to ride Dusty back through the forest and find Billie."

"I can't."

"Yes, you can. I'm going to distract Johnson and his pals, then I'll signal Dusty. Hold on tight to the saddle horn so you won't be thrown off when Dusty starts to run. Find Billie and tell him to bring the posse as fast as he can."

"How will I find him?" Jennifer asked as Jesse pulled the rifle free and tossed it on the ground.

Jesse wrapped the reins loosely around the saddle horn. "Just hang on. Dusty will take you to him." She looked up and smiled confidently. "You can do it." She reached into the saddlebag and pulled her pistols from it, slipping one pistol into the back waistband of her pants while she made a show of tossing the other one down next to her rifle. Then she walked up and patted the mare's neck. "Take care of Jennifer for me, girl."

Jesse stepped away from Dusty and spread her arms wide,

away from her sides. "Get ready," she whispered.

"Wait! Jesse, you can't do this." Jennifer kneed Dusty's sides in an attempt to move her closer to Jesse, but the horse wouldn't budge. "Please, Jesse," she cried out as Jesse moved further away from her.

"Bring her with you," Johnson commanded.

"No!"

Johnson raised his rifle and pointed it at Jennifer.

Jesse pulled the pistol from its hiding spot and dropped to the ground rolling. She fired a couple of shots at Johnson, the bullets digging into the trees behind him. Johnson dove to the ground, and Jesse used this moment to whistle to Dusty.

Jennifer felt Dusty's muscles tense and just had time to grab the saddle horn with all her might before the golden horse sprang into action. In a few strong steps, Dusty had turned and reached full speed as she sped for the safety of the forest. Jennifer tried to rein the horse in, but the racing mare ignored her attempts. She heard more gunshots behind her and a cry of pain that she was sure came from Jesse, but before she could turn around to look, Dusty had entered the forest and the trees blocked her view of the disappearing meadow.

Holding on as tight as she could, Jennifer let Dusty carry her away from Jesse. Tears streamed down her face as she imagined the worst had happened. "Please, let her be all right."

IT SEEMED LIKE an eternity had passed when Dusty broke out of the forest and into the meadow where they had spent the previous night. Jennifer saw the sheriff and posse examining what remained of their campfire. Dusty was already making her way towards the men when Jennifer started shouting. "Sheriff! Sheriff!"

Dusty galloped right up to the posse before skidding to a stop literally at their feet.

"Thank God, we found you," she cried in relief.

"Miss Jennifer? Is that you?" It was hard to tell that the sweaty and dirt-covered rider dressed in denim pants and a flannel shirt was indeed the pretty schoolteacher from Sweetwater.

"Yes, it's me." Jennifer's breath came in ragged gasps as she tried to control her emotions.

"Arrest her, Sheriff." Butler grabbed for Dusty's reins. The horse snorted and reared, pulling the reins from the rancher's hands.

"Stop that!" Jennifer screamed as she almost fell from the

saddle. Dusty settled back on all fours, but shied away from the man still attempting to grab at her.

Ed stepped out of the group of men and eased his way up to the horse. "Take it easy. There now, Dusty. No one is going to hurt you or Jennifer." His gentle voice and smooth movements calmed the mare, and she did not resist when the storekeeper took hold of her reins.

Thaddeus also stepped forward and the two men attempted to help Jennifer off the horse, but she refused to dismount. "You have to save Jesse," the frantic schoolteacher gasped. "Please, we don't have time to wait."

"Hang on there, Jennifer. We can't help if we don't know what the problem is. Now, why don't you get down off that horse and get yourself calmed down enough to tell us what's wrong."

"No! There isn't time."

"Jennifer." Thaddeus looked up into Jennifer's tear-streaked face. "Ed's right. We can't do Jesse any good until you tell us what's going on. Come on and get down." He reached up to help her, but was nudged out of the way by the taller storekeeper. Ed put his large hands around her waist and lifted her out of the saddle.

"Just get her to tell us where Jesse is so we can get this over with and go home." Butler shoved the sheriff toward the woman. "And arrest this one, too."

"Hold on."

"He's right, Billie," Billingsley agreed. "She broke Jesse out of jail. Arrest her."

"Look, she's not going anywhere. Let's hear what she has to say."

"Shut up!" Jennifer screamed at the men standing around her. When Butler started to speak, she looked him straight in the eye. "I said to *shut up!*"

Ed handed her a canteen. She smiled weakly at the big man as she accepted his offering and took a drink. It tasted so good, and as she drank she wondered if Jesse had been given something to drink or if she was even still alive. Tears filled her eyes and she wiped them away with the dirty sleeve of her shirt. "They shot Jesse." Her voice was so full of emotion she could barely get the words out.

"Is she dead?" Butler smirked.

"I don't know." Jennifer felt her heart shatter. She might never again feel Jesse's strong arms gently holding her.

"Why don't you tell us what happened." Ed reached out, covering her shaking hands with his much larger ones and gently squeezed.

"We were following the rustlers' tracks when we came to a meadow. A man named Johnson and two others," Jennifer began.

"Johnson? What the hell does Johnson have to do with anything?"

"He said he wanted the Slipper back."

"Where are they?"

"At the south end of the valley where the forest meets the canyons." She pointed in the direction she had last seen Jesse. "I heard gunshots."

JESSE FELT A searing pain as the bullet ripped through her upper arm. The force twisted her around and out of the way of the other bullets shot at her. As she hit the ground, she looked to see if Jennifer had escaped. Dusty was well on her way to the tree line and in a few more strides would disappear safely into the forest.

She heard Johnson yell at his cohorts to shoot Dusty and stop Jennifer from getting away. She turned back around, firing her remaining bullets at Johnson and the other men. It wasn't much, but it did keep them from injuring her mare or the schoolteacher. When her pistol clicked on an empty chamber, she threw it away in disgust. Seeing that she was too far away to reach her rifle and other pistol, she called out to Johnson and his companions, "Hold your fire."

"Save your bullets, boys. Show yourself." Johnson directed to Jesse.

She sat up, ripped a sleeve off her shirt and wrapped it tightly around her bleeding arm. The wound stung, but she was grateful to see that the bullet had only grazed her. Tending to her wound gave her time to think about her predicament, and it wasn't good. She was just glad that Jennifer had gotten away, and hoped the woman could hang on as Dusty took her for the ride of her life.

"Bring her here."

She watched as the two younger men cautiously approached her.

"Can you stand?" Clinton, the oldest of the pair asked her.

"Yeah." She struggled to her feet.

"Ya got any more guns hidden on ya?" Jimmy, the younger brother, asked from behind the gun shaking in his own hand.

Jesse looked at the trembling boy, and it became obvious why she hadn't been hit by more of the bullets fired at her. "No.

If I did, I would have used them. Why don't you point that somewhere else before it goes off."

Jimmy looked at his quivering hand and dropped his arm. "Not used to pointin' one of these at anyone," he mumbled.

"What's taking you two so long? Bring her here."

"Come on," Clinton growled as he grabbed Jesse's wounded arm.

"Hey." She winced at the jolt of pain that resulted. "If you need to grab something, try the other arm."

"Sorry." Clinton released her arm. "Come on, he ain't gonna wait forever."

The brothers escorted her to an impatiently waiting Johnson. "Well," Johnson gloated. "Looks like the cards are all in my hand now."

"Look, I'm not sure what exactly you want, but you might want to know that there's a posse just a couple of hours behind me."

"They'll be lookin' for a cattle thief, and," Johnson jabbed a finger in her chest, "that would be you." Johnson glared at Jesse, and before she knew what was happening, a huge fist slammed into her face. She dropped to the ground like a stone.

"Why'd ya do that?" Jimmy cried.

"Tie her to that tree." Johnson pointed at the broken trunk of a ponderosa pine near their camp. "Then go find the other one and bring her back."

"What about the posse?"

"What about 'em? They ain't looking for you. Now, git."

The boys dragged the unconscious Jesse against the tree and propped her up before tying her to it. After securing her, they claimed their horses and rode toward the forest. Once they were safely deep enough into the trees to be hidden from the meadow, Clinton pulled his horse to a stop.

Jimmy followed suit, looking at his brother quizzically, "You thinkin' what I'm thinkin'?"

"Yeah." Clinton looked back in the direction of the camp. "Let's get the hell out of Montana while we still have a chance." He kicked his horse into action and led his brother away from Johnson as fast as their horses could run.

IT WAS NEARLY dusk when Jesse started to come to. The throbbing of her arm was nothing compared to the pounding going on in her head. She shook her head trying to clear it, groaning in pain. She could hear laughter, but was unable to focus on its source. Slowly, she lifted her head from where it rested on her chest and tried to focus her blurry eyes. She blinked several times, but her vision still didn't clear. With a grunt, she laid her head back against the rough trunk she was tied to.

Johnson rose from his spot next to the fire. "Bout time you woke up." The rustler glared down at Jesse, but it was lost on the woman who could only see a blur standing over her. "How's the head?" He laughed.

"Fine," she lied; no use in him knowing the truth.

"Right." He laughed again as he returned to the warmth of the fire.

As the vision in her right eye gradually cleared, she discovered that her left one was swollen shut. Squinting to focus the best she could, she saw Johnson huddled next to the fire, his companions nowhere in sight. The sound of movement caught her attention, and she turned her head to see a horse grazing a dozen feet away. "Ugh," she moaned, the movement causing her head to throb even more.

Johnson looked up from the fire. "Thought you was fine," he chuckled. He reached for the coffeepot warming by the fire, refilling his cup.

"Could I have some water?" Her throat was so dry she could barely get the words to come out.

Johnson looked at the woman, considering her request. He didn't want to get too close to the troublesome woman, but he had checked the ropes several times while she was unconscious and was sure she wouldn't be able to get loose. He put down his coffee cup and stood. Walking to his horse, he removed a canteen from his saddle and ambled back over to her. Holding the canteen above her head, he emptied the contents in the general direction of her open mouth.

More water missed than hit the mark, but she was able to capture enough to give her throat some relief. "Thanks," she sneered after swallowing.

"You're welcome." He dropped the empty canteen onto the ground next to her before returning to the fire.

Jesse watched the man as she recalled the day's events. Something he had said earlier continued to run around in her mind. It didn't make sense, unless... "You knew the posse was looking for a rustler. How?"

"Because I set you up." He shrugged.

"Why?"

"The Slipper. By the way, I hear you've turned it into a respectable business," he mocked. "Won't take too much to change it back. I will even give you odds that the whores will be happy to return to their previous duties."

"You're a pig," she spat. Thinking of Johnson regaining ownership of the Slipper and forcing her employees and friends back into their previous livelihoods filled her with rage. After a few moments to calm her rapidly beating heart and throbbing head, she asked, "If you wanted the Slipper back, why not just make me an offer?"

"You think I'm that stupid? I know you'd never sell the Slipper to me. Besides, you cleaned me out that night in Denver."

She considered replying to his question, then thought better of it. As the darkness grew, she wondered about Jennifer. Was she safe? Did she find the posse? Did they believe her story? If they did, where were they? Calculating the time she had been unconscious, she wondered why they hadn't found Johnson's camp yet. They couldn't have been that far behind, not with the trail she had left for Billie to follow. *Until they show up, it's best to keep Johnson talking.*

"So how would setting me up for rustling get you the Slipper back?"

"Easy." He grinned as he described his "perfect" plan. "Once the good folk of Sweetwater discovered you was nothin' but a cattle thief, it would be easy to convince them that you was probably a card cheat, too. I would get the Slipper back because you had cheated me out of it in the first place."

"You don't really think they'd believe that, do you?"

"Why not? Clinton had them ready to hang you the other night. If that damn schoolteacher hadn't butted in, you'd be crow-bait by now."

She shuddered, understanding just how close to the truth Johnson was.

"Yep." He added a few branches to the fire. "Clinton had them going good. Even got a shot off at the sheriff. Only winged him, but it would have been enough to get him out of the way if it hadn't been for Bette Mae. Known I should have killed that bitch years ago, but she kept the other whores in line," Johnson grumbled.

"What did Bette Mae do?"

"Clinton said she and the other girls held the entire group at gun-point until they sobered up. Wouldn't let anyone leave, even made Billingsley stay put. Bet he liked being told what to do by the ol' whore."

"Must you be so crude?" Jesse sighed. She grinned as she imagined Bette Mae standing up to Billingsley and the other ranchers. So that's how she and Jennifer were able to leave town unnoticed. *Gotta remember to thank her if I ever get out of this.* "So now what? Your plan didn't exactly play out the way you were expecting."

"Now what? Now I'll just have to shoot you myself. Then I'll take your carcass back to Sweetwater. I'll tell them I caught you with some stolen cattle, you tried to shoot me, but I got you first."

"If you're just going to shoot me, why haven't you already done so?"

"Waiting for the boys to get back with your schoolteacher."

Jesse's heart clenched. That's where the other two men had gone—to get Jennifer. She fought against the ropes. She had to make sure Jennifer was safe.

"Hey." Johnson looked at the struggling woman. "What got your bloomers twisted all of a sudden?"

"Why can't you leave her out of this? She hasn't done anything to you." Jesse was frantic, but the ropes were too tight and the more she fought them the more her head throbbed. "Just leave her alone," she begged, collapsing back against the tree, her heart racing so fast she felt she might pass out again. She closed her good eye. "I'm sorry, Jennifer," she whispered too quietly for Johnson to hear. "I love you."

THE POSSE WAS surprised when two riders came charging up the path, almost crashing into them. "Hold up, there. I'm Sheriff Monroe from Sweetwater. What are you two running from in such a hurry?"

Pulling their horses to a stop, Clinton and Jimmy instantly threw their hands into the air, figuring taking their chances with the posse were much better odds than Johnson would ever give them.

"We got nothin' to do with murder, Sheriff," Jimmy blurted out. "We helped rustle cattle, but we didn't sign on to kill anyone."

Jennifer went pale at the boy's words, and fresh tears ran down her cheeks. "Is Jesse dead?"

Ed reached over to comfort the woman then barked at the brothers. "Answer her question."

"No!" Clinton shouted as he looked at the angry man. "She was alive when we left, but he plans to kill her. At least, that's what he told us."

"Take their guns," Billie instructed the cowboys circling the brothers. "Tie 'em to their saddle horns and let's get moving."

The posse continued as quickly as possible; still, it was

almost dark when they finally reached the meadow. The men dismounted and left the horses hidden in the forest, so as not to alert Johnson to their presence. The brothers were questioned, and Clinton pointed out where they had left Johnson and Jesse. Billie sent a cowboy ahead to verify they were still in the meadow, who returned after several long, anxious minutes.

"He's there, just where they said he was. Jesse's there, too."

"Is she all right?"

"Can't tell. She's still tied to the stump. Didn't move the whole time I was watching."

"Okay, you stay here with them," Billie told a couple of the cowboys, referring to the brothers. "Miss Jennifer, I want you to stay here, too."

"No." She shook her head violently. "I need to see Jesse."

"He's right." Thaddeus placed a hand on Jennifer's shoulder. "It might be better for you to stay here until we know more."

"No!" She shook off his hand. "I'm coming." She started out of the forest.

Thaddeus put out an arm and stopped her. "If you're going, you'll stay with us." He motioned for Ed to join them. "Jesse won't be too happy if we let anything happen to you."

She started to protest, but the resolve on the faces of the two men made her think better of it. "All right, but let's quit wasting time."

"Okay." The sheriff took charge. "Stay to the trees and get positions as close to the camp as you can. Get to them quickly, but don't alert Johnson. Then wait for my signal. Let's go." Billie led the men into the shadows and they faded into the forest.

Ed and Thaddeus guided Jennifer into a small field of boulders at the edge of the meadow, and they hid behind one of the larger rocks. Their hiding spot provided a good view of the meadow and camp and allowed Jennifer to observe Jesse's still form. In the firelight, she could see the bloody bandage wrapped around Jesse's arm, but was unable to see Jesse's face because her head was hanging down onto her chest.

Somehow, Jennifer knew Jesse was alive, and her body ached to hold the injured woman. "We're here, Jesse. Hang on, we're here," Jennifer whispered.

The sheriff had reached his vantage point, hidden in the trees approximately twenty feet from Johnson who was calmly sitting next to the fire drinking coffee. Jesse was between Johnson and the sheriff, and he briefly contemplated trying to reach her without Johnson noticing. But he rejected that idea when Jesse groaned, drawing Johnson's attention.

Johnson stood up. "'Bout time you woke up. How's the head?"

At Johnson's words, Billie took a closer look at Jesse. Her face was bruised and one eye appeared to be swollen shut. "Damn," he muttered under his breath. Johnson had returned to the fire and Billie was about to signal the posse members into action when Jesse asked for water. Johnson again stood and Billie waited. He didn't want Johnson too close to Jesse when the posse made its move.

Jennifer watched as Johnson carried a canteen to Jesse and poured the water over her head. It took all the strength Ed and Thaddeus possessed to keep the schoolteacher from rushing out from their hiding spot and taking Johnson on single-handed.

Billie also watched as Johnson drenched Jesse with water. "Come on," Billie said to himself. "Go back to your nice fire." Again, Billie was just about ready to signal the posse when Jesse began to speak.

"You knew the posse was looking for a rustler. How?"

Knowing that Butler and some of the others had not believed the brothers' story, Billie decided that it might be a good idea to hear Johnson's answer. Besides, it didn't look like Jesse was in any immediate danger. And Billie could, at any time, signal the posse to move in to stop Johnson from further hurting Jesse.

Billie and the others listened as Johnson bragged of his plot to have Jesse hang as a cattle thief and to retake ownership of the Silver Slipper. Billie felt they had heard more than enough to convince even Butler of Jesse's innocence when Johnson threatened Jennifer. Billie was surprised at Jesse's violent reaction to Johnson's words until he heard her whispered pledge of love for the schoolteacher.

A movement across the small meadow caught Billie's attention. "Damn," he muttered when he recognized Jennifer moving rapidly down from the boulders, Ed and Thaddeus hot on her heels. He saw Johnson pick up Jennifer's movements and reach for his gun.

Billie stepped from his hiding place and leveled his rifle at Johnson. "Don't. It's over, Johnson. Put your hands up." At his words, the rest of the posse members stepped from their hiding places, and Johnson saw that he was surrounded.

Jesse lifted her head when she heard Billie's familiar voice.

Johnson, seeing his plans of revenge collapsing, swung around and aimed at Jesse's head.

For Jesse, time seemed to stand still as she stared into the barrel of Johnson's six-shooter. Somewhere, she heard someone screaming, but her eyes refused to leave the sight of the gun pointing at her. With explosions going off all around her, Jesse could only think of a pretty schoolteacher and what they might have had.

Then everything went black again.

"GIVE HER SOME room before you smother her," Ed was saying.

Jesse felt hands tending to her wounds, including a new one where Johnson's bullet had skimmed along the side of her head. But the only touch she was thinking about were the hands caressing her face. Without opening her eyes, she knew the hands belonged to Jennifer, and she spent several moments enjoying the caress.

"Wake up, sweetheart. Please, wake up," Jennifer cried, mindless of the ranchers and cowboys surrounding her, who were giving each other strange looks over her use of the endearment.

The schoolteacher had sprung from her hiding place and raced across the meadow when she saw Jesse start to fight against the ropes that held her. Her heart had stopped when she saw Johnson point his gun at Jesse's head and she had screamed at him not to shoot. When a burst of gunfire exploded in the meadow, Jennifer had not missed a step in her dash to reach Jesse.

Ed and Thaddeus arrived immediately behind Jennifer and helped lay Jesse on the ground where her wounds could be tended. Fresh blood covered Jesse's face and her head hung down against her chest. Jennifer had tried to untie the ropes but her shaking hands couldn't grab hold of the knots. Billie knelt beside Jennifer, pulling the knife hidden in Jesse's boot and slicing through the ropes freeing the injured woman.

Jennifer sat beside Jesse, trying to pull her bleeding head into her lap.

"Give her some room." Ed gently pulled Jesse from Jennifer's grasp and poured water on a rag before carefully cleaning the cut left by the bullet. Jennifer leaned over Jesse, begging her to wake up.

"Ugh." Jesse opened her good eye. She looked up into the bluest eyes she had ever seen or ever wanted to see.

"You're awake. Thank God, you're awake." Tears streamed from Jennifer's eyes.

"Hi." Jesse tried to smile, but it quickly turned into a grimace of pain.

Jennifer winced, seeing the agony on Jesse's face. "Don't

move, sweetheart. You're hurt."

"Kinda figured that one out myself."

"That's the best I can do until we get you back to Sweetwater." Ed finished bandaging Jesse's head. "You're gonna feel this for a good while."

"Thanks, I think."

"Ain't nothin'." Ed patted her shoulder, then stood and motioned the men away to give the two women some privacy.

"How are you?" Jesse wanted to reach up and pull Jennifer into her arms. But even blinking hurt, so she decided it probably wouldn't be a good idea.

"I'm fine." Jennifer gently stroked Jesse's bandaged head. "This must really hurt."

"I won't say it doesn't, but," Jesse reached up and took Jennifer's hand into her own, "seeing you makes the pain go away."

"Then I'll just have to stay right by you at all times."

"I think I'd like that." It hurt, but, damn it, she couldn't stop herself. Looking at Jennifer just made her want to smile.

Ed returned with the sheriff and some blankets. "Here. It'll get cold tonight."

Thaddeus walked up, carrying an armful of gathered branches and twigs to feed the fire next to Jesse. The existing fire was too far away to provide the women much warmth and no one wanted Jesse moved before morning. "This should help, too. How you feeling?"

"Just fine." She looked into Jennifer's eyes. "I'm feeling just fine."

The man laughed as he and Ed walked back to the other fire. The sheriff stayed behind.

"You look like you've had a couple of rough days," Jesse said to her bandaged friend.

Nodding, Billie replied, "'Bout the same as you. What happened to your eye?"

"Johnson's fist."

"Didn't think Johnson had that in him."

"You trying to make me feel good by saying it was a lucky punch?"

"Is it working?"

"No." Jesse winced. "Hurts like a son of a..."

Jennifer placed her fingers over Jesse's mouth. "Sweetheart, is that any way to talk in front of a respectable woman?"

"Sorry." Jesse looked chastised. "Guess I just don't think about you in that way."

Billie laughed as Jennifer slugged Jesse in her good arm.

"Hey, I'm wounded here."

"You're lucky I didn't hit the other arm. Now behave yourself."

"I see that you're in good hands, Jesse." Billie laughed at the pouting woman. "We'll be heading for Sweetwater at first light, so get some sleep."

Jennifer picked up the extra blankets, arranging them on the ground so that she could lie close to Jesse but not with her. Not that she didn't want to do just that, but she wasn't sure how the rancher would feel about it.

"Hey," Jesse interrupted her actions.

"What?"

"Put those blankets over here." Jesse patted the ground.

Jennifer looked questioningly at her.

"I'd like to hold you."

Jennifer nodded happily. When the blankets were re-arranged to Jesse's satisfaction, Jennifer lay down beside her. She carefully placed her head on Jesse's shoulder and wrapped an arm around her waist. "How's this?"

"Wonderful," Jesse sighed.

Moments later, both women were fast asleep.

Chapter
Five

THE TRIP BACK to Sweetwater was pure agony for Jesse, even with Jennifer riding behind her helping to hold her in the saddle. Every step Dusty took caused jolts of pain to explode in her head. Only Jennifer's non-stop encouragement and support kept her from screaming out her distress. The group stopped regularly to afford Jesse breaks from the constant pounding. This was both a blessing and a curse. The breaks allowed Jesse much needed rest, but they also extended the length of the trip. She was sure that she would be unable to take any more just as Sweetwater finally came into the riders' view. Her salvation had been having Jennifer's arms wrapped tightly around her and the constant whispering of endearments in her ear.

Ruthie was keeping watch on the porch of the Silver Slipper, so she saw the posse appear over a rise some distance from town. She ran to the building's main door shouting, "They're back!"

Bette Mae came rushing out of the kitchen, followed closely by the other girls. "Where?" Bette Mae hurried out onto the porch.

Just about that time, a couple of the riders broke from the group. As they neared the edge of town, Bette Mae recognized them as the storekeeper and the newspaper editor. The two men rode directly for the Slipper.

"Is Jesse...?"

"She's hurt but alive," Ed answered before Bette Mae could finish her question. "She'll need some looking after."

"Ruthie," Bette Mae called, "go in and fix up the room first off the stairs."

"No." Thaddeus smirked. "Best you fix up Jennifer's room for Jesse."

A grin broke across Bette Mae's face. "Well, I'll be. Go on, girl," Bette Mae said to Ruthie, who was standing with a look of puzzlement on her face. "Ya heard him. Fix up Miss Jennifer's room. Go on, git."

Ruthie scurried into the building.

"How is Miss Jennifer?" Bette Mae asked.

"She's fine. Just worried about Jesse. Won't leave her side, not for a minute," Ed climbed down from his horse. "Damn, I'm too old to spend that much time in the saddle." He rubbed his sore backside, stretching out his legs.

"Me too," Thaddeus agreed as he joined Ed on solid ground. "It'll be good to get back into my desk chair."

The rest of the posse rode up with the sheriff leading the way. Ed and Thaddeus moved immediately to Dusty's side and gently eased Jesse out of the saddle. Instantly, Jennifer was on the ground holding the injured rancher around the waist.

"Come on," Jennifer whispered. "We'll get you into a nice, soft bed and you can rest."

Unable to speak because of the pain, Jesse barely managed a nod as she allowed Jennifer to lead her to the stairs going up to the Slipper's porch. It was clear to everyone that Jesse would never be able to climb the few steps on her wobbly legs.

Without asking, Ed lifted Jesse into his powerful arms and carried her up the steps. Jennifer shadowed the big man all the way into the building and up the stairs to her room where Ruthie stood with the door open. As soon as Ed placed Jesse on the bed, Jennifer took back Jesse's hand.

Bette Mae shooed everyone but Jennifer out of the room. "Let's see what we got here." She unwrapped Jesse's bandages.

"She needs a doctor." Jennifer watched anxiously.

"Bette Mae's the best doctor this town has got," Jesse assured the worried schoolteacher. "Aren't you?"

"Can't argue with that. Got any other wounds I need ta know 'bout?" The older woman carefully washed the blood and dirt from Jesse's face after filling a bowl from the room's water pitcher.

"No."

"How 'bout you?"

"No, I'm okay." Jennifer sat on the edge of the bed. "Is she going to be all right?"

"She'll be fine. Lucky she got hit in the head. It's her hardest part," Bette Mae chuckled.

"When I'm feeling better, I'll make you pay for that." Jesse tried to swat at her friend. Realizing too late that she was using her injured arm, she hissed at the pain.

"Lay still." Bette Mae grabbed her arm and gently laid it back on the bed. She wrapped a fresh bandage around Jesse's head and then started on her arm. "Damn, you are one lucky woman, Jesse. Two bullets and both only grazed ya."

"They hurt like they more than just grazed me."

"I bet they do. Few days rest will fix 'em right up. The blow ta your head and that eye is wha's goin' ta cause ya the most bother. What'd ya get hit with?"

"Johnson's fist."

"Johnson? What does that bastard have ta do with all this?"

Jennifer supplied the answer. "He set Jesse up for the cattle rustling. Thought if she hanged, he'd get the Slipper back."

"Always figured he was a card or two short of a full deck." Bette Mae finished with Jesse's wounds. She took the dirty bowl of water and tossed it out the window.

"Might be someone standing under there," Jesse remarked.

"Hope it's Butler," Jennifer muttered, and was surprised to hear Bette Mae snicker at her comment.

"Yep, she's a feisty one." Bette Mae winked at Jesse as she started to remove her boots. "Ya best git some sleep and give your body time ta heal. I'll have a bath prepared for ya, Miss Jennifer. Your bath, Jesse, will have ta wait another day."

Jesse made no argument.

"I can wait, too. I don't want to leave Jesse."

"Go on. You'll feel better. Besides I'm not goin' anywhere."

"You sure?" Jennifer thought that a hot bath did sound pretty good.

"I'm sure. Just," Jesse whispered, "hurry back."

Jennifer bent down and softly kissed Jesse's cheek. "I won't be but a minute."

The pain in Jesse's head disappeared when she felt the warmth from Jennifer's lips. Her eye closed as she savored the touch. "I'll be waiting."

When Jennifer pulled her head back, Jesse was already asleep.

RUTHIE CAME OUT of the kitchen carrying a tray with three plates heaped with food. She placed the dishes in front of Billie, Ed, and Thaddeus. Bette Mae had offered hot meals to all the posse members, but the ranchers had declined stating that they wanted to return to their ranches. Bette Mae believed their decision to leave immediately was based more on their embarrassment at accusing Jesse of rustling than any desire to get right home.

The sheriff, storekeeper, and newspaper editor accepted the offer and were enthusiastically digging into their meals after eating trail food for the past several days.

"How's Jesse and Miss Jennifer?" the sheriff asked between bites.

"Sound asleep." Bette Mae took a long drink from her glass of lemonade. She had helped the schoolteacher with her bath, then had to practically carry the young woman back upstairs to her room when exhaustion overcame her. She tucked Jennifer under the blankets and smiled as the two sleeping women snuggled close to each other.

"Seems like the two of them got to be real good friends out on the trail." Billie shoved a forkful of ham into his mouth.

"I do believe you are right." Thaddeus chuckled.

"Now, ya stop that," Bette Mae playfully scolded the men. "It was only a matter of time 'fore they figured out they had a likin' for each other. Being out there jus' gave 'em the little push they needed."

"They do make a cute couple, if I say so myself." Ed smiled. "Any chance of getting more of this ham, Bette Mae?" He held up an empty plate.

"After bringin' my girls home, ya can have the whole damn pig," Bette Mae announced, rising from the table to disappear into the kitchen. Reappearing a few moments later with a large platter of ham and potatoes, she rejoined the men. "I take it that's Johnson in the blanket?"

"Yep." the sheriff stabbed a large potato off the platter. "Tried to shoot Jesse after we caught up to him."

"Tried?" she snorted. "Seems he managed ta put two holes in her."

"Yeah, well, he was aimin' between her eyes on the last one." Billie cut the potato into chewable pieces. "Didn't give us much choice but to shoot him first."

"Jus' as well."

"What's next, Billie? Will Jesse have to stand trial?"

"Nope," the sheriff answered around a mouthful of potato. "Johnson confessed, everyone heard him. Hell, even Butler couldn't argue it. When the circuit judge gets here, I'll tell him what happened and Jesse will be in the clear. Miss Jennifer, too."

"Why? What did Miss Jennifer do?" Bette Mae asked.

"She broke Jesse out of jail. If Jesse had been guilty, she would have had some big trouble over it."

"But Jesse wasn't guilty."

"Yep. So Miss Jennifer won't get more than a talkin' to by the judge."

"What do you bet it's the judge that will be getting the talking to?" Thaddeus laughed and the others joined in, remembering how, on the ride back to town, the schoolteacher had not shied away from telling the posse members what she thought of the accusations against Jesse.

THE FOLLOWING MORNING, Jesse was still asleep when Jennifer quietly dressed to reluctantly return to her teaching duties. Being so new to the position, she was afraid the parents of her students would not be happy to have school postponed any longer. Before she left the room, she sat on the edge of the bed and studied the rancher. Gently, she stroked Jesse's cheek, smiling when the sleeping woman nuzzled against her hand. She leaned over and placed a kiss on Jesse's forehead. "Sleep well, love."

Moments later, she pulled the room's door shut and went downstairs for breakfast.

THE MID-MORNING SUN was beating through the room's windows when Bette Mae entered to check on her friend. She was surprised to see Jesse awake and standing by the window that faced town.

"Mornin'. Didn' think ya'd be up."

Jesse took a deep breath and let it out slowly. She had been watching the schoolhouse, hoping for a glimpse of Jennifer. When she had awakened a short time before, the first thing she noticed was how empty the room seemed. She missed the young woman who had come to mean so much to her the last few days.

"How 'bout a nice, hot bath to wash all that dirt off?" Bette Mae walked across the room to stand beside the rancher.

"Hmm." Jesse's eyes never left the schoolhouse.

Bette Mae peered out the window, smiling because she knew what was holding Jesse's attention. "Come on." The older woman gently steered Jesse to the door. "A good scrub, a change of clothes, a hot meal, and ya might jus' be presentable by the time Miss Jennifer is done teachin' for the day."

Jesse allowed herself to be led from the room and helped downstairs without complaint. The bath did feel wonderful, and it was indeed good to get the dirt and grime scrubbed off her skin and out of her hair. When she returned to the room freshly bandaged, she found that the bed linens had been changed and a tray of hot food had been set out on the desk. She didn't have much of an appetite, but she did her best to eat.

"Now, ya git some rest." Bette Mae cleaned up the dirty dishes. "It'll be a while 'fore Miss Jennifer gets back and your head can use it."

Jesse snuggled between the clean sheets; the quilt had been removed, as the day's heat was already too much to need its extra warmth. She looked up at the woman who had become her first friend after arriving in Sweetwater. There was much she didn't know about Bette Mae, but the one thing she did know was that she trusted the older woman's advice.

Jesse was confused. She had feelings for Jennifer that she had never had for anyone else. And she knew Jennifer felt the same. But was it right? Could they? No, should they respect those feelings? She needed to ask.

"Bette Mae," she nervously called out before the other woman could leave the room. "Bette Mae, what would you do?"

Knowing what Jesse was asking, Bette Mae recalled a moment many years before when she had asked herself that very same question. A faraway look crossed her face as she remembered her own choice. Smiling sadly at Jesse, Bette Mae quietly answered, "Follow your heart, Jesse. Follow your heart."

As the door closed behind the departing woman, Jesse rolled her head to gaze out the room's window. She couldn't see the schoolhouse from where she lay, but she could visualize it out on the small knoll. And she knew that at this very moment that schoolhouse held her heart.

Smiling, Jesse let the sleep she had been fighting reclaim her.

JENNIFER RUSHED FROM the schoolhouse as soon as the day's lessons were over. She missed Jesse terribly and she couldn't wait to see her. Bette Mae was clearing a table in the dining room when she burst through the Slipper's door.

"Afternoon, Miss Jennifer." Bette Mae brushed the crumbs off the table. "How was school today?"

Although she wanted to run up the stairs to her room, Jennifer paused long enough to answer the woman. "Just fine. How's Jesse?" Jennifer saw the grim expression on Bette Mae's face.

Bette Mae straightened from her task. "Well, now, let's see. She's had a bath, put on clean bedclothes, ate some breakfast, took a nap, jus' had lunch. And..."

Jennifer's heart clenched. "Is something wrong?"

"Yep." Bette Mae was having trouble maintaining a straight face. "She's been missin' ya, somethin' awful."

"She has?"

"Yep." Bette Mae laughed, unable to hold back any longer. "Suggest ya don' spend too much time down here talkin' ta this old woman when ya can be up there with her." Jennifer was halfway up the stairs before Bette Mae finished.

Jesse was again standing by the window, where she had watched Jennifer leave the schoolhouse and hurry toward the

Slipper. She couldn't wait for Jennifer to walk into the room, but she was unsure what to do when that happened. Hearing Jennifer's footsteps moving rapidly down the hallway, she turned to face the door. Without hesitation, she threw open her arms as soon as Jennifer appeared in the doorway.

Jennifer ran into the welcoming embrace.

"I've missed you." Jesse held the schoolteacher tight.

"So I've heard."

After several long minutes the women separated just enough for the schoolteacher to examine the rancher's wounds. Jennifer's fingers lightly traced over Jesse's bandages. "How do you feel?"

"Head's still a little on the dizzy side. But overall, I feel pretty good. Considering..."

"Considering that in the last few days, you've been accused of cattle rustling, punched in the face, shot twice, tied to a tree stump, and bounced senseless on the back of a horse. I certainly hope that doesn't describe a normal week for you."

"Nope." Jesse shook her head, then instantly wished she hadn't. "I can honestly say that nothing even close to that has ever happened to me before you showed up." Jesse paused for a moment before adding, "Say, you don't think..."

Jennifer scowled.

Jesse looked at the schoolteacher and Bette Mae's words came back to her. *Follow your heart.*

Jennifer held her breath as Jesse reached out, cupping her hands around Jennifer's face and pulling her close until their faces were almost touching. Looking into the schoolteacher's eyes, Jesse whispered, "I love you."

Jennifer leaned forward to close the gap, timidly placing her lips against Jesse's. At the touch, a tingling spread throughout her body, causing her to press harder.

Jesse happily returned the kiss.

It was a new experience for both women and they tentatively explored each other's soft lips and warm mouth until a need for air caused them to part.

Jesse released a long breath. "Wow."

"Yeah, wow," Jennifer sighed before recapturing Jesse's lips.

"SEE THAT LINE of three stars?" Jesse was sitting on the wide plank that topped the cross rails on the Slipper's porch. She and Jennifer had come out on the porch after finishing their supper to enjoy the cooler evening air. When the sun dropped from the sky, the women had moved to the porch balustrade to observe the stars twinkling in the crystal clear night sky.

"You mean those three?" Jennifer, sitting beside the rancher, pointed into the night sky.

"Yep. See how that one is a little out o' step with the others?"

"Yes."

"That's me. I've always been a little out o' step with other folks."

Jennifer gazed at the stars. "I'm glad you are."

"You are?"

"Yes." Jennifer leaned against the rancher. "It's what makes you so special."

"Special, huh?"

"Very special." She slipped her arm around Jesse's.

"I think you're pretty special, too." Jesse reached up, gently placing her hand against the schoolteacher's face. She leaned close until their lips were almost touching. "I love you."

Jennifer closed the gap, pressing her lips against the rancher's.

After several long moments, they broke apart.

"Whoa," Jesse sighed. "Your kisses leave me light-headed."

"Sure that isn't because of this?" Jennifer ran her fingers along the bandage still wrapped around Jesse's head.

"Nope." Jesse pulled Jennifer close. "It's definitely because of you."

"I love you, Jesse." The schoolteacher laid her head on the rancher's shoulder and gazed back up into the sky. "I like your star, too."

"You do?"

"Yes. Whenever I look up at night, I'm going to look for it and it'll always remind me of how much I love you."

Jesse tilted her head to look up. "I like that."

AFTER A COUPLE of days of doing little else than napping during the mornings and spending the afternoons talking with Jennifer, Jesse was feeling restless. Her eye had finally re-opened enough that she could see out of it, and she decided to walk to the schoolhouse and meet Jennifer at the end of her school day.

Jesse took her time to walk from the Slipper to the top of the knoll; she could tell by the absence of any children outside that class was still in session. Just as she reached the school yard, the building's door burst open and the children ran out.

One boy, the second oldest son of the town's mayor, ran up

to Jesse. "Did you really get shot in the head?" He stared up at Jesse's bandaged head.

"Yep." The rancher was a little unsure what to tell the boy of her experience.

"Boy, my pop was right," the boy said in awe.

"How's that?"

"He said you had the hardest head in the valley."

Jesse could hear someone chuckling nearby and looked up to see Jennifer standing on the schoolhouse porch.

"Go on home, Tyler," the schoolteacher instructed the young boy. "Miss Jesse shouldn't be standing out in the hot sun. Come on inside," she told the scowling rancher.

"Think that's funny, do ya?" Jesse muttered as she entered the schoolhouse.

"Sit down." Jennifer pulled out the chair behind her desk, it being the only chair in the room to occupy, as the students sat on long benches for their lessons. "Seems you have a reputation for hard-headedness."

"Is that a word?"

"Doubt it." Jennifer bent over to examine the rancher's eye. "Can you see okay?"

"Okay enough to do this." She reached out, pulling the schoolteacher into her lap. "And this." She slipped a hand behind Jennifer's neck and brought their lips together.

The sound of giggling forced the women to end the kiss they were enjoying.

Jesse glanced over Jennifer's shoulder to see young Tyler and a few of the other children standing in the doorway. "Ya kids best be gettin' on home or I'll really show ya how hard my head is," Jesse growled.

"Jesse, you scared them," Jennifer laughed when the children ran away.

"Good," the rancher smirked. "Now, where were we?" She pulled Jennifer back to her and resumed their kiss.

Jennifer wondered if she should go check on the children, but once Jesse's lips pressed against her own, she could think of nothing else.

A FEW DAYS later Jennifer returned to the Slipper at the end of the school day to find Jesse placing her saddlebags on Dusty's back. "Jesse?" she approached the rancher apprehensively.

Jesse finished securing the bags to her saddle before she tried to answer. She walked to where Jennifer waited, then stood shuffling nervously from one foot to the other. Johnson was dead, the brothers he had talked into helping in his plot were behind bars, the stolen cattle had been returned to their rightful owners, and she had been cleared of all charges. So why was she so fearful? "I kinda figure it's time for me to get back to the ranch," she mumbled, staring down at her dirty boots. She wanted to ask Jennifer to join her, but didn't know if it was too soon. After all, their growing relationship was only days old.

It was obvious that the women were in love, but neither of them had been confident enough to take their relationship to the next level.

Standing at the bottom step, Jennifer quietly watched Jesse. She smiled when the rancher quit studying her boots and looked up to face her. She had hoped Jesse would ask her to accompany her to the ranch, but had been too afraid to make the first move. Now, seeing her own feelings reflected back at her, her fears melted.

She stepped forward to meet the nervous rancher, wrapping her arms around Jesse and pressing their lips together in a tender kiss.

Surprised but very pleased, Jesse slipped her arms around Jennifer and pulled her close. The kiss deepened as the women spent the next several moments enjoying the intimate touch of the other.

After much too short a time, Jennifer pulled away and laid her head on Jesse's shoulder. "Let's go home, love."

A smile spread across Jesse's face. Taking Jennifer's hand, Jesse led her to a patiently waiting Dusty. She helped Jennifer up into the saddle, then swung up behind her, wrapping an arm around her waist. With her free hand, she took the reins from around the saddle horn.

"I love you," Jesse whispered into Jennifer's ear.

Jennifer leaned back into her warm body and entwined her hand with Jesse's. "I love you, too."

Dusty raised her head and whinnied before moving off at a walk. She would carry her two mistresses home and neither one would ever remember the trip.

DUSTY WALKED UP to the porch of the ranch and stopped. Only after the mare snorted several minutes later did one of her riders notice that they were no longer moving. Jennifer, leaning back into the warm cocoon Jesse had created for her, opened one eye and looked at their surroundings. "Um, Jesse," she tenderly rubbed the arms wrapped around her. "I think Dusty is trying to tell us that we're home."

"Too soon," Jesse murmured in her ear. "Haven't been riding that long." She had spent the entire ride from Sweetwater with her head nestled next to Jennifer's. Her eyes were open, but all she saw was the woman sitting in the saddle in front of her.

"Sweetheart." Jennifer reached up and took a gentle hold of Jesse's chin, turning her head to the cabin. "What would you call that?"

Jesse was forced to break her gaze away from the woman in her arms. "Um, sure looks like the ranch." She squeezed Jennifer tight before releasing her and swinging down from the saddle.

Jennifer giggled as she swung her leg over the saddle horn and waited for the rancher to help her to the ground. After pulling the saddlebags free, Jesse led her to the door of the cabin.

"Welcome home." Jesse pulled open the cabin's door, then stood aside to allow Jennifer to enter first. "It's not much, still needs some work. But it's ours."

A lump formed in Jennifer's throat when she heard Jesse describe the cabin as "ours." She stepped in front of Jesse, capturing her lips in a tender kiss. "Do you know how much I love you?" She looked into Jesse's soft brown eyes.

Jesse grinned. "Got a pretty good notion."

"Good," Jennifer smiled back and entered the house.

Jesse followed, placing the saddlebags on a small table in the room. "I've got to see to Dusty. Make yourself comfortable. I won't be long."

"Can I do anything to help?"

"Nah." She stopped when her stomach rumbled. She smirked at Jennifer, who had heard the noise. "Unless you can cook."

"I think I can manage something edible." Jennifer realized the rancher didn't know she was a good cook since she had always taken her meals in the dining room of the Silver Slipper.

Jesse was interrupted by the sound of Dusty's impatient whinnying. Frowning, she shrugged at Jennifer before walking back outside.

Jennifer stood by the door and took in the place she could now call home. The few minutes they had spent at the ranch after she'd broken Jesse out of jail hadn't given her much time to really appreciate the ranch house.

She found herself standing in a large open room that made up the inside of a structure built of entire logs laid atop one another. The log cabin was rectangular in shape with a fireplace at each end. The door they had used to enter the cabin was in the middle of the west wall and she saw a matching door on the opposing wall. Windows had been cut into the logs between the doors and end walls, allowing plenty of light into what otherwise would have been a rather dark interior.

Under the window to her left, a small, crudely made table held Jesse's saddlebags. Two rickety chairs were tucked under it. A larger, sturdier table was pushed under the window on the back wall, canisters and boxes of foodstuffs crammed underneath. Shelves had been nailed to the log wall on either side of the table and held some plates, cups, and a few cooking utensils. The fireplace at that end of the cabin obviously served as the cook stove and heated water for the tub sitting in the corner between the fireplace and the small table.

On her right was the sitting/sleeping area. A bed, piled with blankets, was positioned lengthwise under the window on the east wall. She was pleased to see that the bed was bigger than the one in her room at the Slipper on which, when sharing with Jesse, she had been afraid to move lest one of them be pushed off the mattress and onto the floor. The trunk of clothes left by the building's previous owner still rested at the foot of the bed. A small dresser stood against the wall next to the fireplace, a broken corner propped up by a piece of wood. Along the front wall, between the window and door, a neatly constructed bookcase provided space for several books. She grinned, knowing that it had to be Jesse's handiwork.

The fireplace at that end was smaller than the other, but plenty large enough to warm the sleeping area. A chair, badly in need of having its stuffing replaced, sat facing the fireplace, a well-used quilt hanging over its back. The only other piece of furniture in the room was the tall cabinet near the back door that Jesse kept her guns and ammunition in.

Jennifer let out a long sigh. "Jesse's right, it's not much. But," a smile slowly spread across her face, "it's home."

JESSE WAS GREETED by the smell of frying bacon when she entered the cabin after rubbing Dusty down and checking on the other horse in her barn. Jennifer was stirring a pot hanging on the cooking hook and the rancher quickly crossed the room to wrap her arms around the schoolteacher.

"Something smells awfully good in here." She peered over Jennifer's shoulder.

"Glad you think so." Jennifer leaned back into Jesse's embrace. "Go on, get washed up." She pointed to a bowl of warm water she had filled moments before. "This is just about ready."

Jesse reluctantly relinquished her hold on Jennifer. "You find everything you needed?" She rolled her sleeves up to wash her hands and face.

"No." Jennifer filled two plates with bacon, beans, and gravy-covered biscuits. "Sweetheart, you really need more than flour and beans if you expect me to cook for you."

"Sorry." Jesse shrugged apologetically as she pulled one of the boxes out from under the kitchen table and sat down. "Meant to get supplies at Ed's last week. You best start a list." Jennifer placed the plates on the table where Jesse sat and looked around for a chair, but saw only the ones at the small table under the window. And they definitely didn't look safe to use. "Jesse?"

"Hey, this is really good," Jesse said around a mouthful of biscuit and gravy.

"I'm glad you like it," Jennifer beamed, then returned to her quest. "Jesse, don't you have any *good* chairs?"

"Damn." Jesse sprang from her box. "I've been meaning to make me a couple. Just haven't found the time yet. Here you go." She pulled a second box out from under the table and gestured for Jennifer to sit.

"Guess we should add chairs to the shopping list," Jennifer chuckled.

"Yep." Jesse took another spoonful of gravy-covered biscuit. "We can take the wagon into town tomorrow. You make out your list and I'll have Ed fill it while you're at school. Don't know if he'll have any chairs, though. Probably can take a couple from the Slipper."

"Okay." Jennifer took a bite and was surprised at how good the food tasted considering what she'd had to work with.

"This is really good," Jesse repeated as she finished off her biscuits. "I didn't know you could cook."

"One of the few things my father allowed was proper for a girl to learn."

Jesse heard the sadness in Jennifer's voice. "I'm sorry, Jennifer."

Jennifer turned and saw the hurt in Jesse's eyes. "It's okay." She laid her head on Jesse's shoulder. "I'm here and that's all that matters now."

Jesse leaned close and softly kissed the top of Jennifer's head. "I'm glad you're here."

After several long moments, Jennifer sat back up and returned to her meal. "If I need to make a list of supplies, you're going to have to tell me what you like to eat."

"That's easy." Jesse tore a biscuit in half and used it to clean the remaining gravy off her plate. "You cook it and I'll eat it."

"We'll see," Jennifer smirked.

Jesse looked at the schoolteacher suspiciously. "Something you're not telling me?"

"Not really." Jennifer popped the last piece of bacon from her plate into her mouth. "I just like to experiment."

"Uh, oh."

JENNIFER FINISHED HER bath and stepped from the tub drying herself with the tattered towel Jesse had provided. After cleaning up the supper dishes, Jesse had filled the tub and offered Jennifer first use of the hot water.

The rancher was sitting in the chair near the bed waiting her turn at a bath and trying desperately not to turn around and look at what she knew would be Jennifer's naked body. She wanted to look. She *really* wanted to look. But she thought it best to give Jennifer some privacy. Even though they had shared a room at the Slipper, the bathing room was downstairs and they had taken their baths privately before coming to bed already dressed in their nightshirts. As she sat, she remembered a moment a few days earlier when she had caught a glimpse of the schoolteacher's body.

"Jesse," Jennifer broke into her musing, "I, ah. I just remembered that all my clothes are at the Slipper. Do you have an extra nightshirt?"

Jesse rose from the chair, being careful to keep her back to Jennifer. "I'm pretty sure I have one in here." She pulled open a drawer in the dresser and began rooting around until she found the requested item.

Moving with her back still to Jennifer, she made her way across the room and handed the garment to the schoolteacher.

"Thanks." Jennifer took the nightshirt. She was disappointed when Jesse immediately retreated to the far end of the cabin without showing any interest in taking advantage of her current undressed condition. She pulled the nightshirt over her head, wondering if Jesse would ever look at her again the way she had only days earlier in this very room. Jesse had said she was beautiful. *Had she already changed her mind?* Tears sprang to her eyes as she considered that possibility.

Sensing Jennifer's distress, Jesse twisted in the chair. She immediately rushed to her side when she saw the tears. "Hey," Jesse reached for the schoolteacher, "why are you crying?"

Jennifer let Jesse pull her into a warm hug. Jesse may not want her, but she craved Jesse. "When you didn't want to look at me..." she blushed, but seeing only concern in Jesse's eyes, she continued, "I thought maybe you had changed your mind about me."

"Never," Jesse assured the trembling woman in her arms. "I was..." It was now Jesse's turn to blush. "I wanted to look, but I was afraid it would bother you."

"Oh." Jennifer rested her head against Jesse's. "It wouldn't bother me." She sighed.

For several minutes, the women stood in the embrace, soaking up the other's affection. It was a feeling both women found themselves to be enjoying more each time they did it.

"Jesse." Jennifer patted Jesse's side.

"Um."

"You better get your bath before the water is too cold."

"Yeah." Jesse continued to hold Jennifer until she was gently pushed away.

"Go."

Jesse made quick work of her bath because the water was, indeed, cold, but more so because Jennifer was in bed waiting for her. She climbed from the tub, quickly drying off before pulling on her own nightshirt. When her head popped through the shirt's opening, she saw that Jennifer was observing her. She felt a blush start in her toes and rise all the way to her face as she followed Jennifer's eyes taking a long, lazy tour of her body.

"Ready for bed, sweetheart." Jennifer held open the blankets that covered her.

"No fair," Jesse groused, climbing under the blankets to join Jennifer. "You peeked."

"Guess you'll just have to wait until my next bath." Jennifer snuggled next to the pouting woman.

"I could start heating the water now." Jesse threw back the blankets.

"Uh-uh." Jennifer pulled her back into bed, recovering their bodies. "You lost your chance for tonight, honey."

"Spoilsport."

Settling back on the bed, Jesse turned onto her side, arm bent at the elbow and her head propped up on her hand. "You are so beautiful," she murmured, her eyes gazing at the woman lying beside her. Her free hand lifted, but before she touched Jennifer, she pulled it back. "I'm sorry," she whispered as she ducked her head so Jennifer couldn't see the blush coloring her face.

Jennifer remained silent for several heartbeats. A part of her had hoped the rancher would be experienced in the ways of making love, but it was clear the embarrassed woman beside her was as nervous as she was and a larger part of her was truly glad of that. As she lay listening to Jesse's ragged breathing, she was sure of three things. One, she loved Jesse more than she could say. Two, she planned to spend the rest of her life with the shy rancher. And three, knowing the first two, there was no reason to force events this night and ruin what she was sure would be a most pleasurable experience. No, they had the time to take things slow and to express their love when they were both ready.

At Jennifer's silence, Jesse cautiously raised her head, sure that her inability to go further had upset the woman she loved.

Jennifer looked at the rancher, her eyes expressing all the love, hope, and dreams she held in her heart. "Hold me." She smiled, snuggling closer to Jesse.

Misty-eyed, Jesse rolled onto her back, pulling Jennifer tight against her in a silent, and relieved, gesture of gratitude for understanding. "With pleasure," she sighed, kissing the top of Jennifer's head.

THE NEXT MORNING, Jesse was backing the draft horse into the buckboard's harness. Except for pulling the wagon when she brought supplies from town, she didn't have much need for the large workhorse that had come with the ranch. But she liked the gentle giant and it provided a companion for Dusty. Dusty, however, had a different opinion on the subject and complained loudly whenever Jesse left her at the ranch in favor of the draft horse.

"Stop it," Jesse grumbled at a snorting Dusty. "You know you don't like pulling this wagon, so stop whining."

Dusty snorted again, shook her head several times and stomped her front hoofs.

Jesse finished attaching all the buckles of the harness and turned to face her normal ride. "You want me to tie you to the back of the wagon and you can eat dust all the way to town?" She glared at the annoyed horse.

Dusty whinnied, snorted, and stomped, then took one last look at Jesse before running to the far corner of the corral, turning her rump to her mistress.

"Just once I'd like to take the buckboard to town without you throwing a fit," she mumbled as she led the big horse to the cabin porch.

Jennifer came out of the cabin just as Jesse pulled the horse to a stop. She was wearing a spare pair of Jesse's denim pants and one of the rancher's flannel shirts, her dress tucked under her arm. "I'm going to change when we get to town. I can't teach school dressed like this." Although she would really like to.

Jennifer had surprisingly discovered she enjoyed wearing the denim pants; they seemed to give her a sense of freedom that being bundled in a dress did not. She had already decided that she would wear the more comfortable pants whenever she could. After all, Jesse wore pants all the time and no one seemed to mind.

"Okay." Jesse helped Jennifer up into the buckboard before climbing up herself. "'Course, now if I were one of your students, I wouldn't mind what you wore to class, just as long as I could look at you all day."

"Oh, really." Jennifer blushed and nudged Jesse in the arm.

"Yep."

"What's his name?"

"Who?"

"The big, bad, horse that has Dusty so upset."

"You noticed," Jesse grumbled.

"Hard to miss the commotion she was making."

"She hates being left behind."

"I'd never know," Jennifer laughed. "So what's his name?"

"Boy."

"Boy?"

"Yep, he's my big Boy."

"You'd think with all the books you read you could have come up with something more..." Jennifer's arms flailed wildly. "Oh, I don't know. Something more original." She shook in head in amazement at the rancher.

"I like 'Boy.' So does he. Don't ya, Boy?" The rancher gently slapped of the reins on the horse's broad back.

Boy, hearing his name, raised his head and whinnied while the women laughed.

JESSE PULLED THE buckboard to a stop in front of the Slipper. She jumped down from the wagon seat, then helped Jennifer down. As they entered the Slipper, Bette Mae was coming out of the kitchen with a fresh pot of coffee.

"Oh," Jennifer moaned. "I've love a cup of that."

Bette Mae smiled at the couple. "Sit yourself down and I'll pour ya one. Didn' have any at the ranch this mornin'?"

"No." Jennifer settled into a chair at the nearest table. "Jesse was out of coffee beans and just about everything else."

Bette Mae filled a cup with the hot liquid and placed it in front of the schoolteacher, then poured one for Jesse, seeing the sheepish look on Jesse's face. "Now, don' ya be tellin' me ya took this little lady home without any food in the place." She put her free hand on her ample hip and glared at Jesse.

"Hey, I was going to get supplies last week, but something," Jesse smirked at Jennifer, "or should I say someone, came up."

"Don't worry, Bette Mae. She'll be spending time with Ed today," Jennifer assured the older woman.

Jesse patted the pocket of her shirt. "Yep, got me a nice, long list of *e-ssentials* to buy."

Bette Mae winked at Jennifer as she continued to tease Jesse. "Good thing you picked a smart one. Now what about breakfast?"

"Oh, yeah," Jennifer groaned. "We are definitely having that."

Bette Mae chuckled on her way back into the kitchen.

AFTER BREAKFAST, JENNIFER went up to her old room and changed into her one and only dress. She carefully folded the pants and shirt and left them on the dresser. Grabbing her bag of lessons and notes, she headed back downstairs.

Not seeing Jesse in the dining room, she knocked lightly on the door to Jesse's office.

"Come on in, darlin'," Jesse called. She knew it was either Jennifer or Bette Mae, and the older woman would have just entered after knocking.

Jennifer paused. Jesse had never used that particular endearment before and Jennifer found that she rather liked it.

When no one entered, Jesse rose from her desk. Pulling open the door, she was surprised to see Jennifer standing in front of her. "Didn't you hear me?"

Jennifer looked at Jesse with a big smile. "Oh, I heard you all right."

"Then why didn't you come in?"

Jennifer leaned in and kissed Jesse. "You've never called me that before. And I was just standing here considering how much I liked it."

"Oh." Jesse pulled Jennifer to her and returned the kiss. "Then, *darlin'*, I'll just have to remember that." She took the bag. "Walk you to school?"

"I'd love that."

AFTER BIDDING JENNIFER goodbye at the schoolhouse, Jesse walked to the general store. Entering the building, she saw Sweetwater's sheriff and her friend, Billie Monroe, grabbing a handful of crackers from a wooden barrel.

"You paying for those, Sheriff? Or confiscating them as evidence?"

"Dammit, Jesse." The startled sheriff dropped the top of the barrel down on his hand. "You could stop a man's heart doing that." He smiled at his friend while he rubbed his hand.

Jesse noticed that he still maintained a firm grip on the crackers he had taken.

"Morning, Jesse." Ed Granger, the storekeeper, stood in his usual place behind the store's scarred wooden counter. "Don't worry about Billie. Anything he doesn't pay for, I just add to Mayor Perkins' bill."

Jesse joined in the amusement at the expense of Sweetwater's pompous mayor. "Knowing the way he and his kids eat, I doubt if he'd ever notice."

"They surely do keep the freight wagons busy." Ed laughed.

"How's the head, Billie?" She asked when the laughter died down.

"Hardly bothers me any more. How's yours?" Billie pointed at the very noticeable scar tracing the bullet's path along the side of Jesse's head. An unnecessary reminder of just how close she had come to being killed.

"Twitch, now and again, but not enough to bother me. Headache was the worst part."

"Yep." Billie nodded. "I didn't think my head would ever stop ringing."

"Guess we both came away lucky." She patted her friend on the shoulder. "Just let's not do it again."

"Right with ya on that," Billie agreed heartily. Johnson's plot against Jesse was the worst criminal act the sheriff had yet to deal with since being appointed to the position. And he was more than happy to go back to dealing with the occasional drunk or card cheat. "I best be gettin' back to the office." Billie tossed a couple of coins on the counter to pay for his crackers.

"Thanks, Billie." The storekeeper gathered up the coins before turning his attention to the rancher. "Something I can do for you today, Jesse?"

"Yep, need some supplies for the ranch." She pulled the paper from her pocket and handed it to the storekeeper.

Ed read through the items. "Gosh, Jesse, I didn't know you could cook." He was surprised to read many of the spices and other ingredients listed.

"I can't." She grinned. "Jennifer made it out. I don't know what half that stuff is."

"That explains it." He finished reading the list before looking up at the rancher. "Not sure I have all of this, Jesse. If I don't, I can always order it from Bozeman."

"Nah." She flinched at hearing the name of the town. It had been years since her parents had sold the family ranch and moved into Bozeman, leaving her to fend for herself. Yet the hurt was still heavy in her heart. "Just give us what you've got. For the rest, Jennifer can decide if she wants it bad enough to special order."

"Okay." Ed nodded. "You in a hurry for it?"

"Nope. Jennifer won't be done at school until after noon. Send word to the Slipper when you've got it ready."

"Sounds good." He was already pulling items off the shelves when she exited the store.

Jesse stood on the boardwalk for several minutes. Was it really such a short time since she had stood in this very spot and watched the town's new schoolteacher step down from the stage? She smiled as she remembered seeing Jennifer for the first time and how unsettled she had been over her reaction to the newcomer. Now she realized she had fallen in love with Jennifer at that very moment.

"Yep. She hooked me on the first look." Whistling happily, she started back to the Slipper.

IT WAS AFTER noon when Bette Mae knocked on the office door before carrying a tray into Jesse's office. Jesse had spent the morning working on the Slipper's ledgers. Bette Mae was responsible for the day to day running of the boarding house and saloon, but Jesse did the books and paid the bills. It wasn't that Bette Mae was incapable of doing everything; Jesse just didn't feel right asking the older woman to carry the entire burden. So even though she would much rather spend all her time at the ranch, Jesse came into town several times a week to take care of the Slipper's business.

Bette Mae placed the contents of the tray on the desk in front of Jesse before settling onto the couch Jesse used for sleeping if she had to work late at the Slipper. "Guess we won' be seeing the boss workin' late anymore," Bette Mae chuckled to herself.

Jesse took a bite of the ham sandwich set before her. "Care to let me know what you find so humorous?"

"Nope." Bette Mae smiled, then changed the subject. "Didn' think I'd see the two of ya in town this morning."

"Why not?" Jesse washed down the bite of sandwich with a swallow of cold milk. "You know Jennifer had to teach today."

"Jus' figured ya'd have other things ta keep ya busy." Bette Mae raised an eyebrow at the rancher.

Jesse put down the glass, gazing at the older woman. "I love her so much, Bette Mae. But..." She stopped, too embarrassed to tell her that she hadn't been brave enough to try to make love with Jennifer.

"Wanna talk 'bout it?" Bette Mae saw the distress in Jesse's face.

"I," Jesse started. "I wanted to, you know."

Bette Mae nodded.

"But, I... I don't know what to do."

Bette Mae looked across the room and instead of the confident business owner and rancher she knew, she saw a frightened young woman who was experiencing love for the first time. She smiled compassionately at Jesse. "Come over here, child." She patted the cushion next to her.

Jesse rose from the desk and, on shaky legs, crossed to sit next to the woman she hoped could help her. She had once before. When she had been unsure of how to act on her feelings for Jennifer, Bette Mae had told her to *Follow your heart*. It was the best advice she had ever received. She hoped Bette Mae was up for a repeat performance.

Bette Mae took Jesse's hands into her own. "What do ya want ta do?"

Reassured by her friend's caring tone, Jesse began, "I want to hold her so tight I'm afraid I'll squeeze the breath right out of her. I want to touch her, to feel every inch of her soft skin. I want to kiss her, not just her lips but her neck, her shoulders. I just... I just want so much to show her how I feel."

"Then tha's what ya should do," Bette Mae encouraged her.

"But..."

"But what?"

"What do I do?" Her voice trembled. She had never even kissed anyone before Jennifer. Boys had never held any attraction for her. She hadn't really avoided them, but the idea of doing anything on the romantic side had simply never occurred to her. She was completely unprepared for affairs of the heart.

The question was asked in a voice so pitiful that Bette Mae had a hard time keeping a straight face. "Believe me, once ya git started, ya won' have any trouble figurin' out what ta do next."

"I won't?"

Bette Mae lifted Jesse's head, looking into her doubting eyes. "No, ya mos' certainly won't."

Outside, the school bell rang, sounding the end of the school day.

"Now, ya go wash your face 'fore your sweetie gits here. Then ya take her home and show her jus' how much ya love her."

Wiping the tears from her eyes, Jesse couldn't help but feel encouraged by Bette Mae's words.

JESSE MET JENNIFER on the porch of the Slipper, planting a passionate kiss on her lips.

"What did I do to deserve that?" Jennifer was gasping for air but it was well worth the effort.

"I've missed you, darlin'."

"I'll have to make it a point to go away more often." Jennifer laid her head against Jesse's, foreheads touching. "I've missed you, too."

"Come on." Jesse took Jennifer's hand and started off the porch. "Ed's got the supplies ready."

"Wait." Jennifer tugged her to a stop. "I want to change first. And get my things."

"Already thought of that." Jesse pointed to the buckboard.

Jennifer saw her small canvas bag resting under the seat.

"Thought you might like to have them at the ranch."

"Thank you, Jesse." Jennifer kissed the rancher on the cheek. "That was very sweet of you."

Jesse looked down at her boots, hoping Jennifer didn't notice the blush coloring her face. Darn, the schoolteacher could sure turn her to mush.

Pretending not to notice Jesse's embarrassment, Jennifer told her, "You stay right here. It won't take me but a minute to change clothes." She disappeared inside the Slipper, thinking how cute Jesse was when she blushed.

True to her word, moments later Jennifer bounced back out onto the Slipper's porch wearing the more comfortable denim pants and flannel shirt. "Let's go."

Jesse helped Jennifer into the buckboard and then climbed up into the seat beside her. She flicked the reins and Boy started down the street.

"Say, Jesse." Jennifer watched as a cloud of dust rose from Boy's hoofs. "Does it ever rain here?"

"Yep." Jesse took off her Stetson and waved it around in an effort to clear the cloud. "But when it does the dust turns to muck. I prefer the dust."

Jennifer snatched the hat and placed it on her own head. "Then you better get another one of these from Ed."

Jesse looked at her hat now resting on Jennifer's head. She liked the way it looked. "I think I can do that."

Boy stopped in front of the general store's boardwalk stacked high with boxes and sacks of supplies.

"Wow." Jennifer's eyes fell on the huge pile. "Are all of those ours?"

"Let's hope not." Jesse jumped from the wagon. "We'll have to make two trips to get all of that home."

Jennifer climbed down from the wagon without Jesse's help. She immediately regretted her actions when she saw the disappointment in Jesse's eyes. It was at that moment she understood Jesse didn't assist her in getting down from the wagon or off Dusty's back because she didn't think Jennifer could manage it on her own but because she genuinely enjoyed doing it. And the schoolteacher made a silent vow to stay put in the future so that Jesse could have her pleasure. She reached out and grabbed Jesse's hand, giving it a loving squeeze as an apology, and Jesse accepted it for what it was.

"I was beginning to wonder if you forgot me." Ed stepped out of the store onto the boardwalk.

"Sorry, Ed." Jesse turned to the big man. "I hope Jennifer's list didn't include all of this." She indicated the pile of goods next to the man.

"Nope. Freight wagon dropped a delivery this morning. Just haven't got it all put away yet. Yours is that stack there. The rest is inside."

"Freight wagon!" Jennifer was excited to hear the storekeeper had received a delivery. Maybe it included the dress material they had ordered.

"Sorry, Jennifer." He shook his head. "Wagon was sent out before they got your order. Should be on the next one, though."

"Oh." Jennifer couldn't hide her disappointment. "Say, Ed. You have any pants in your store?"

Both Jesse and Ed looked at her, perplexed.

"Well," she informed them as she crossed the boardwalk to enter the store, "I need to get me some britches that fit. And a hat." She flipped Jesse's Stetson back to her.

"You heard the lady." Jesse grinned at the storekeeper. "Best you get in there and see to her needs while I load the wagon."

An hour later, Jesse had the wagon loaded and Jennifer had found not one but two pairs of pants that fit her. She had also added a couple of new shirts each for herself and Jesse. And a new Stetson hat sat smartly atop her head.

Ed tallied up the damage for the women and pushed the ledger across the counter for Jesse to see. "Here you go."

Jesse whistled as she counted out enough money to cover the tab. "Darn it, woman. That's more than I pay for supplies at the Slipper."

"The Slipper doesn't have bare cupboards in its kitchen,"

Jennifer retorted.

"This better last you awhile." Jesse winked at Ed. "If not, I'll have to raise the prices in the dining room."

"That might not be a bad idea." Ed patted his ever-growing paunch. It was well known about Sweetwater that Ed loved Bette Mae's cooking and ate at the Slipper almost every meal. "Just might encourage me to eat at home more often."

"Oh, don't say that," Jesse laughed. "You're my best customer."

"It was just a thought," he assured her. "A bad thought, but just a thought." Ed's jovial laugh rumbled through the store and the women couldn't help but add theirs.

"Ready, darlin'?" Jesse turned to the woman standing beside her.

"Yes, sweetheart."

They blushed simultaneously at their use of the endearments in front of the burly storekeeper.

"Ah," Ed smirked at the matching red faces, "now ain't that just the cutest thing."

"Come on." Jesse grabbed Jennifer's hand, pulling her from the store. The women started to giggle as soon as Boy pulled the buckboard away from the boardwalk to pass in front of the jail and newspaper office.

"Stop!" Jennifer cried out, pulling on Jesse's arm.

"What's wrong?" Jesse looked around to find the cause of Jennifer's alarm.

"I completely forgot about Thaddeus."

"What about Thaddeus?" Jesse still didn't understand Jennifer's distress.

"I promised to work afternoons for the Gazette."

"I thought I heard voices out here." The door to the newspaper office opened and the man being discussed stepped out onto the boardwalk.

"I'm sorry, Thaddeus. I completely forgot about my commitment to you."

"What commitment?" Thaddeus began, then caught himself and smiled. "Jennifer, I don't expect to hold you to that. Fact is, I kinda figured you'd have other things to keep your afternoons busy now."

"No, Thaddeus. I agreed to work afternoons for you, and if my father taught me anything, it was to live up to my responsibilities. Jesse, I'll meet you at the Slipper when I'm done here."

"Hold on, there." He held up both hands and waved them at the determined woman climbing down from the buckboard.

"You just go on with Jesse. I'll get along just fine without you."

Jennifer stood in the dusty street, looking at the newspaper editor. "But you said you needed help with the paper."

Thaddeus chortled. "To be honest, Jennifer, when I heard you discussing your problem with Bette Mae that day, you seemed so desperate that I made up needing an assistant. You go on and don't worry 'bout me. Not enough news in this town to need two people to write it. Unless Jesse goes and gets herself into trouble again."

"Are you sure, Thaddeus?" She was relieved but, if he wanted, she would fulfill her end of their agreement.

"Yes, I'm sure. Go on now."

Jennifer started to climb back into the wagon and wordlessly accepted Jesse's outstretched hand. Once she was resettled next to Jesse, she turned to the newspaper editor. "Thank you, Thaddeus. You keep whatever wages I have coming. I don't really feel like I earned them."

"Doesn't seem fair, but if it will make you feel better."

"It will."

"All right. Good to see you, Jesse," he nodded to the woman silently listening to the exchange.

"You too, Thaddeus." Jesse watched as the newspaperman went back into his office. She sat quietly, thinking about what she had just heard. "Jennifer," she twisted on the bench seat to face the schoolteacher. "Why were you desperate to find another job? Isn't your teaching salary enough?"

Jennifer hesitated. So much had changed since the day she had arrived in Sweetwater. She had barely known who Jesse was when the Slipper's owner arranged for her to have new dresses and paid for them. But now Jesse was no longer a mysterious benefactor. She was the woman who held Jennifer's heart and though she still fully intended to pay Jesse back, she didn't know how Jesse would react to hearing her reason for accepting Thaddeus' offer.

Jesse waited patiently for Jennifer to answer.

Figuring that the truth was the best course, Jennifer told Jesse, "I wanted to make enough money to pay you back for the dresses. And my salary, when I receive it at the end of the school year, is just enough to pay Matt back."

"Matt?"

"He's the friend I told you about. He paid for my ticket to Denver and I promised to pay him back as soon as I could. So I had to find another way to pay you back."

Jesse smiled at the anxious face watching her. "Well, darlin'," Jesse drawled out slowly, "I would say that you definitely found a way to pay me back. In fact," she flicked the reins to restart Boy, "I'd say that you have more than paid that debt in full."

Jennifer scooted close to Jesse and snaked her arm around the rancher's. "Have I told you how much I love you?"

"Can't say I recall hearing it recently," Jesse teased.

"I love you."

"I love you, too, darlin'."

"Chairs." Jennifer slapped Jesse's arm. "We forgot chairs." She was not going back to the ranch without something decent to sit on.

Jesse pulled the wagon to a stop in front of the Slipper. "Be right back." She hopped from the wagon, ran up the steps to the porch and quickly disappeared inside. Moments later, she reappeared with two chairs taken from the dining room. She stood on the porch and held them up for Jennifer's inspection. At Jennifer's nod, the chairs were added to the back of the wagon.

Jesse was climbing back up into the buckboard when Bette Mae came out on the porch.

"Hi, Bette Mae," Jennifer cheerfully greeted the older woman.

"Ya headed home?"

"Yep," Jesse nodded. She smiled when she felt Jennifer rest a warm hand on her thigh.

"Good. Don' 'spect to see ya back around here 'fore Monday, ya hear?"

"Yep." Jesse smirked. "I'll do my best to make sure that doesn't happen."

"Best make sure ya do."

Jesse slapped the reins on Boy's back. "Come on, Boy. Let's get home. Dusty's probably chewed through the new corral fence by now."

"Jus' remember wha' I told ya," Bette Mae called after them.

"What does she mean by that?"

"I'll tell you later."

THAT NIGHT, WHEN Jennifer stepped from the tub Jesse was waiting with a brand new towel bought that day in the general store. Rubbing gently, she dried the wetness from the schoolteacher's skin.

Jennifer's body was on fire by the time Jesse finished rubbing her dry.

"There." Jesse wrapped the slightly damp cloth around Jennifer. "Now go get in bed before you get chilled."

Jennifer didn't think that was likely. Not with the inferno raging inside her from Jesse's touch. She reached for the nightshirt she had placed near the tub before her bath, but Jesse stopped her.

Pulling Jennifer's hand to her mouth, she tenderly kissed it. "You won't be needing that tonight," she boldly, but nervously, informed her soon-to-be lover.

"Oh." Jennifer shyly retrieved her hand before leaving Jesse to her bath.

The bed sheets felt cool on her heated skin and Jennifer snuggled comfortably between them. As she watched the rancher bathe, she worried about making love with Jesse. Beyond kissing, she really had no clue what two people did to make love except for the whispered comments she had sometimes heard exchanged between the women in her mother's quilting circle. And most of them had not put a very positive spin on the experience.

Jennifer's body came alive with never-before-experienced feelings as she watched Jesse rise from the tub, water cascading down her long frame. She put aside her concerns and hoped that Jesse had some idea as to what to do, because she definitely wanted a more intimate relationship with the woman walking toward her.

Oh yeah, a much more intimate relationship.

"Hi, beautiful." Jesse slipped between the sheets and pulled her close. With a confidence she really didn't possess, she put Bette Mae's words, *Show her how much you love her,* into action.

Jesse leaned down, tenderly pressing her lips against Jennifer's. She loved how soft the schoolteacher's lips were and allowed herself the pleasure of exploring every bit of them. She soon wanted more, her tongue seeking to taste the luscious lips and, when it was offered, slipping inside a warm, wet mouth. She pressed against the tongue waiting within and teased it into her own mouth, smiling when she was rewarded with a deep moan.

Separating just enough to draw needed breath into her lungs, Jesse placed one more loving kiss on Jennifer's lips before shifting to place a trail of gentle kisses around the schoolteacher's face and down her neck.

"Oh, my," Jennifer moaned when Jesse's lips reached the base of her neck. Unthinking, she tossed her head to the side permitting the rancher all the room she needed to continue torturing the sensitive spot.

As Jesse's lips and tongue gave Jennifer's body special attention, the schoolteacher's legs wrapped around hers and warm hands begin to explore her back. A fire burned in her belly and spread throughout her body, the heat settling at the apex of her legs. The new and unexpected sensation spurred Jesse on and she threw off the coverings so she could gaze at the body writhing beneath her. "I want to see you," Jesse whispered when Jennifer shyly tried to pull the blankets back over their nakedness. Reaching a long arm down, Jesse slowly caressed her way up Jennifer's leg, past the knee to the curve of a hip and over a silky smooth stomach, her light touch raising goose bumps as they passed. "So soft," she sighed. Hesitating for only a moment, Jesse's hand moved upward, cupping a supple breast.

Jennifer moaned in pleasure, her back arching into the touch, forcing her aroused nipple into Jesse's callused hand.

After that, Jesse had to agree with Bette Mae, she did indeed have no trouble figuring out what to do next.

Chapter
Six

THE MOON'S SOFT light shone through the window and fell on two entwined bodies. Jennifer lay on her back, absentmindedly weaving her fingers through the auburn hair spread across her chest. Jesse's head rested between her breasts, the rancher's arms wrapped around her waist.

Jennifer marveled at the memory of what had recently occurred between them. Their lovemaking had started out tenderly, but soon became fervent. At one point she had been sure she would pass out from the intensity of the reactions Jesse was causing within her. For two people new to the experience, she believed they had done quite well for themselves. Smiling to herself, she wondered how long it was proper to wait until they could repeat their actions.

Jennifer felt more than heard a quiet sob escape from her new lover.

"Jesse." She timidly reached out to stroke Jesse's face, suddenly frightened that though she had found their lovemaking more than satisfying it had somehow displeased her lover. Receiving no response, she tried again, her voice shaking with fear. "Jesse, please tell me what's wrong."

A deeply inhaled breath followed by more sobs was her only answer.

Close to panicking, she cupped Jesse's face, turning it towards her. "Please, sweetheart. If I disappointed you, I'm sorry. It was my first time, I'll do better..."

Realizing that Jennifer had misinterpreted her emotions, Jesse sat up. Leaning against the headboard, she pulled her concerned lover into her arms. "Shh," she stilled Jennifer's words. "I wasn't disappointed, darlin'. That was the most beautiful..." Her words caught in her throat. "It was just..." She choked up again, unable to continue.

Jennifer scooted around so that she could hold Jesse. Soothingly, she rocked the sobbing woman giving her the time to regain her composure. When the sobs eased, Jennifer whispered, "Tell me what's wrong, sweetheart."

Slowly, and between the occasional sob, Jesse explained. "I never thought I would ever have this in my life. I grew up so lonely. Never had many friends even when I started school, I was too isolated out on the ranch. As I got older, I wasn't the kind of girl the boys wanted to ask to a social. Once or twice, my pop took me so I could find a beau, but the boys would never ask me to dance. Guess I just came to believe that love wasn't meant for me. I thought I'd learn to accept it," she wiped at her tears. "Then I met you." A deep sob stopped Jesse's words. When she spoke once more, her voice was so full of emotion that she could barely get the words out. "You...you changed so much. I don't know what I ever did to deserve this, but tonight, tonight, you made me feel more loved than I've ever felt in my life." Lifting her head from Jennifer's shoulder, Jesse looked into the sapphire eyes of the woman who meant so much to her. "I love you so much, Jennifer Kensington."

Tears streaming down from her own eyes, Jennifer choked out, "I love you too, Jesse..." She paused, her nose scrunching up as she searched her memory for something she was sure she must know. "Um, Jesse." Yet she couldn't recall ever being told this one bit of information, this one very important bit of information. "Jesse, just what is your last name anyway?"

"Uh?" Jesse was caught off-guard by the question.

"Don't *uh* me," Jennifer scowled. "I just realized that I've broken you out of jail, helped you track down rustlers, hung on for dear life like a maniac on the back of a racing horse to get you help, watched you get shot, *and* fallen in love with you." Jennifer paused to inhale a deep breath of much-needed oxygen after her tirade. "And I don't even know your full name."

Jesse's mood lightened at Jennifer's outburst and she grinned. "Sure you do. I'm sure I told you."

The irritated schoolteacher poked a finger into the rancher's chest, right above one very lovely, very bare, breast. "You never, ever said your full name. Now give."

Laughing, Jesse gave. "Jesse Marie Branson," she proudly confessed.

Jennifer contemplated this new information. She nodded once, then again. "Jesse Marie Branson. I like it."

"Me too." Jesse snuggled back down on the bed, pulling Jennifer with her. "And now Jesse Marie Branson would like to show Jennifer." She paused. "Any middle name?"

"Stancey."

Jesse wrinkled her nose.

"Don't blame me, it's a family thing."

"Okay. Jesse Marie Branson would like to show Jennifer Stancey Kensington just how much she loves her."

Jennifer stretched her body out atop Jesse's and leaned down until she was nose to nose with her lover. "Jennifer Stancey Kensington can think of nothing better than to have Jesse Marie Branson do just that," she purred as their lips met.

The moon was on its way out of the sky by the time their declarations of love finally ceased.

JESSE SAT ON the cabin's porch, her back resting against the logs that made up the cabin's front wall. Jennifer sat between her legs wrapped in her arms. In the cool morning air, steam rose from two cups of freshly made coffee placed within easy reach on the porch's surface. Songs of morning birds fractured the stillness as the sun peeked over the mountains to the east.

"We need more chairs." Jennifer squirmed, lifting a cup to her lips. The hard, uneven and splintered porch wasn't very comfortable to sit on.

Jesse watched a squirrel race across the yard and scamper up a pine tree. "I was thinking that a swing might be nice."

Jennifer tilted back her head, scrutinizing the porch roof above them. "You sure that can hold a swing?" She pointed to the roof in question.

Jesse bent her head back and took a long look at the overhang. She smirked at the numerous places where she could see the lightening sky above. "Seems you're gettin' smarter about things." Looking back down at the woman in her arms, she said, "Chairs are good. I'll pick up a couple more from the Slipper next time we take the wagon to town."

"Until then," Jennifer snuggled back against her, "this is pretty nice."

"Yep, it sure is." She took a swallow of coffee. "So, darlin'." She was becoming quite fond of the endearment. Especially since she knew Jennifer was extremely fond of it. "What would you like to do today?"

"Um." Jennifer took another sip from her cup. "How about you show me the ranch?"

"Really?" Jesse smiled. She loved the ranch but had doubted the schoolteacher would share her enthusiasm.

"Yes, I would really like to see what you have here, Jesse. I'd like to feel a part of it."

"You are a part of it, darlin'. A very big part of it." Jesse tightened her hold on the schoolteacher.

Jennifer's heart almost burst at her words. How could she love this woman any more? She pushed herself up from the porch's rough planks. "What say, you go do your chores while I make breakfast. Afterward you can give me the grand tour."

Allowing Jennifer to pull her to her feet, Jesse smiled. "Okay." She drank the last of her coffee before placing the empty cup in Jennifer's outstretched hand. "I'll let Dusty know we'll be taking our lady out for a ride later."

Jennifer shook her head at her lover. "Go on, you nut. I'll have breakfast ready when you're done."

As Jesse walked to the barn, Jennifer thought how nice it would be to eat on the small table under the window and look out across their yard at the neighboring forest and distant mountains. Then, remembering the condition of that particular piece of furniture, she called out, "A table, Jesse. We need a table."

"Add it to the list," Jesse called back. With the speed Jennifer was coming up with things the cabin needed, she knew it wouldn't be long before she would be hitching Boy to the buckboard for another trip to town.

AFTER BREAKFAST, JESSE helped Jennifer wash the dishes before she led the schoolteacher outside. She took Jennifer into each of the buildings scattered about the yard, explaining their purpose and use. She demonstrated every tool and piece of equipment and even let her try her hand at some. She showed Jennifer the barn, corrals, tack room, chicken-less chicken coop — add chickens to the list — and told her of her plans for the ranch's future.

Having grown up in a more civilized environment, everything was new to Jennifer and she pestered Jesse with enthusiastic questions, then listened intently while her lover patiently provided the answers.

Early afternoon found the women standing, hand in hand, at the rear of the cabin inspecting a long neglected garden.

"It needs some work but we could grow our own vegetables. Be real nice to have some flowers too."

"We had a small garden back home—" Jennifer stopped herself. What was she saying, she was home. "Back east," she revised. She didn't want Jesse to think she considered the ranch less than what she had left behind.

"It's okay, darlin'." Jesse squeezed her hand. "I sometimes think that about my folks' ranch."

"It's so hard to know what to call...back east." Jennifer sat on the edge of the cabin's wrap-a-round porch. "In only a few days," she swept her arms out encompassing their surroundings, "this has become more of a home to me than back there ever was. But still, it was my home. Before."

Jesse joined her. "I know. It's really okay if you say it." After a few heartbeats, "Do you miss them?"

She knew whom Jesse meant. "It's funny, but since I arrived in Sweetwater, I really haven't given them much thought. I guess I just wasn't that much a part of the family. My brothers were older and they spent their days, for as long as I can remember, with Father at the business. Mother..." Jennifer saddened as she remembered the woman who had, at one time, meant so much to her. "When I was young, Mother used to spend all day with me. She'd tell me stories and teach me how to do things. We'd take long walks to the parks around town. But as I got older and started to question some of Father's rules we seemed to grow apart."

Jesse wrapped an arm around her waist and the schoolteacher leaned into her.

"It was almost like she didn't know what to do with a daughter who asked 'why' so often. She never questioned Father and couldn't understand when I insisted on doing so."

"Did you ever ask her?"

"Several times, but she would only smile and tell me that some day I would have a husband of my own and would understand. Eventually, I just stopped asking."

Jesse softened her voice, knowing there must be a lot of hurt in her past, but sure that the woman beside her still had feelings for her family. "Do you think they miss you?"

"My brothers, no. I was just a nuisance to them. Father, I doubt if he would miss *me*, but I'm sure he misses the opportunity I represented to him." Her voice dropped and Jesse had to strain to hear her next words. "Mother, maybe," she sighed.

"Do you want to send word to them?"

"No." Jennifer's response was quick and sharp. "They have their life, now I have mine. And I have no intention of letting them try to ruin it."

"But don't you think they'd want to know you were all right?" Jesse was more than a little concerned with her lover's adamant response. "They are your family."

Jennifer took Jesse's hand into her own. "You're my family now, Jesse." She tenderly kissed each finger on the hand she held. "I don't want them to know where I am. Please, Jesse."

"Okay." Jesse nodded. "Guess you know what's best."

"I do." Jennifer held Jesse's hand against her heart, entwining their fingers. "What about you? Do you ever miss your folks?"

"Yeah," Jesse sighed. "But I think I loved them a lot more than they ever loved me. I was a disappointment from the moment I was born. They'd always wanted a son, Pop especially. Even had the name picked out."

"Not..." Jennifer gasped.

"Yep." Jesse nodded. "Never even decided on a girl's name, they were so sure I'd be a boy. Guess it's lucky for me they had decided not to use my pop's name, Stanley." She chuckled but she really didn't find much humor in the thought. "Anyway, once they figured out they got a girl on their first try they spent the next year trying again. My brother only lived one day, but my folks grieved for the last nineteen years. The older Pop got, the more he seemed to hold it against me. I wrote them once I got settled in Sweetwater, hoped they might want to come visit. Never got an answer, though." Her shoulders slumped. "Figured that kind of said it all."

"I'm so sorry, sweetheart." Jennifer wiped her wet cheeks with the back of her hand.

"Thanks." Jesse tightened her hold on the woman she loved and placed a kiss on her forehead. "But I've got you now and that's all I need."

The women sat in silence as they considered the life fate had dealt them.

"How about some lunch?" Jesse quickly tired of the dark mood hanging over the pair and tried to lighten it. "And then we can take Dusty out and introduce you to the girls."

"The girls?"

"Yep." Smiling broadly, she playfully bumped shoulders with the schoolteacher. "Fifteen of the sweetest heifers you'll ever meet."

Jennifer playfully swatted Jesse.

DUSTY STOOD QUIETLY on a small rise in a sea of gently rolling hills less than a mile from the ranch house. Sitting atop the golden mare, Jesse and Jennifer surveyed the small herd in the field before them, the young cows munching happily on the thick grass.

"Soon as we get a breeding bull, we'll be able to start a real herd."

"How soon?"

"Hopefully, by the end of the year."

Jennifer turned her head and studied the land around them. "How much do you own?"

"Just under a hundred acres. McPherson's been talking about selling, now that his sons took off for the gold fields. He'll let me know if he decides. His land would double what we have."

She used we *again.* Jennifer smiled.

"See that stand of trees over yonder?" Jesse was pointing to the west. "There's a small creek running behind them. That marks the west boundary. The badlands mark the south and the east boundary is about a mile into the pine forest. And the gate marks the north."

Jennifer knew she was referring to the archway they passed under every day as they traveled the road to and from town. Jesse had carved *J's Dream* into the archway, the name bestowed on the ranch after she'd purchased it and the inspiration for her brand. Looking at the cows in Jesse's herd, Jennifer could make out the connected JD, the top of the J curving out and down to reconnect near the bottom of the J to form the D.

Jesse twisted in the saddle. "So what do you think, darlin'? Is it big enough for the two of us?"

"Oh, I think we'll manage." Jennifer laughed as Jesse turned Dusty back to the ranch buildings.

"I reckon we will." Jesse chuckled before calling out a warning. "Hold on!"

Before Jennifer could question why, Jesse released Dusty from her lazy trot and the mare took off for home at a breakneck gallop. "Not again," she moaned, grabbing onto the saddle horn and thankful for the strong arms wrapped around her.

"WHAT DO YOU think?" Jennifer leaned against the hoe she had been using most of the afternoon. After their ride to see the cattle, she and Jesse had tackled the job of getting the garden into planting condition. It was still early summer and they wanted to try to get a few late-season vegetables and flowers planted.

"I didn't think this many weeds could grow in such a small space." Jesse pulled yet another fistful of the unwanted plants from the ground.

"If the flowers grow as well as the weeds, we should have quite the garden." She lifted her Stetson and wiped her brow before attacking another overgrown row.

Jesse rose from where she had been kneeling, stretching her long legs. "Didn't know gardening was this much work," she muttered, walking to a bucket placed in the shade of the porch and pulling a full dipper of water from it. Carefully, so as not to spill the precious contents, she carried the dipper to the schoolteacher. "Here, darlin'."

"Thank you." Jennifer accepted the dipper, tilting it up to allow the cool water to slide down her parched throat. When she finished, she handed it back to the rancher. "I'm not sure I'll ever get used to this heat."

Jesse walked back to the porch to refill the dipper so she could enjoy a drink. "Sure you will." She removed the bandanna from her neck and drenched it with water. Tying it back around her neck, she commented, "Come winter, you'll be wishing to have some of it back."

Jennifer had returned to her hoeing. "How cold does it get here, Jesse?"

"Cold enough. And if the wind is blowing, it'll freeze your words before you can get them out." Jesse returned to the task of pulling weeds from the dry earth. "But it's not as bad here as it gets on the eastern side of the mountains. Wind blows over there all the time and the snow can build into drifts higher than my head." More weeds were thrown from the garden. "We had a pretty mild winter in the valley last year. Not too much snow and I hardly ever had to wear my heavy coat. Which reminds me, you'll be needing some winter clothes."

"Oh." Jennifer was hesitant, embarrassed to have to again tell Jesse of her poor financial condition. "Um, Jesse," she nervously chewed on her lower lip before continuing. "I, ah, I don't think I'll be able to afford any new clothes this year."

Jesse looked up at the schoolteacher, puzzled. "What do you mean, can't afford any?"

Jennifer studied the ground at her feet for a few moments before the words starting rushing out. "You know I don't get my salary until the end of the school term. And most of that I have to use to pay Matt back. That's why I took the job at the Gazette. I hoped it would pay me enough to pay you both back."

"Whoa." Jesse threw aside the weeds she had just yanked from the ground. Brushing her hands free of the dirt clinging to them, she stood and walked to Jennifer's side. Cupping a finger under her chin, Jesse gently lifted it up until she could look into Jennifer's eyes. "Don't you know that I'll buy you anything you need?"

"I can't let you do that."

"You're not letting me, darlin'. I want to." Leaning forward, she placed a kiss on the distressed woman's cheek. "Besides," she smiled at the woman she loved and would gladly spend

every dime she had to make happy, "the Slipper makes enough
for both of us."

"But, Jesse—"

"Nope." Jesse gently placed two fingers on Jennifer's lips,
stifling her objection. "No buts. Whatever I have, is ours," the
rancher stated before resuming her weed pulling chores. "Now,"
she grabbed another handful of unwanted vegetation, "just how
much money do you owe this Matt fellow?"

Jennifer stood in a daze. She couldn't believe what Jesse had
just said; the rancher was willing to share all she had with her.
Jennifer's heart melted all over again.

"Darlin'?"

"Ow." Jennifer was brought out of her cloud by a dirt clod
striking her arm.

"Asked you how much you owed your friend."

"You didn't have to throw that at me," Jennifer whined as
she rubbed her arm.

"Did, too." Jesse snickered at the frown on her face. "So how
much?"

"Jesse, I'll pay him back as soon as I receive my salary."

Figuring that she wasn't going to get an answer out of the
stubborn woman glaring at her, Jesse tried a new approach. "You
know," she pulled out another clump of weeds, "seems to me
that Mayor Perkins can let loose of that money before the school
year is over."

"But that was the agreement. Room and board would be
provided and I wouldn't be paid until I finished the year."

"That's my point. Sweetwater is no longer having to pay for
your room and board." She smirked at the blushing
schoolteacher. "So there ought to be enough funds for you to get
paid now."

"I don't know, Jesse. That's not what I agreed to."

"I'll have a talk with the mayor. I think he'll be more than
happy to pay your salary early. Then you can pay your friend.
And as for your clothes, you don't need to fret none about that. I
can't have my sweetie walking around without decent clothes,
now can I? Nope." she shook her head, "Bette Mae would tan my
hide if I didn't take proper care of you."

Jennifer laughed, picturing the rancher spread across the
older woman's knees. "I just bet she would do it, too."

"Oh, she most definitely would." Jesse rose, pushing her
long frame up once again from the ground. "That's enough
weed-pulling for today. What say we call it a day? I'll check on
Dusty and Boy while you fix dinner. Then we can have an early
bath," she suggested to her lover.

"Oh." Jennifer dropped the hoe. "What say we skip dinner and go straight to the bath?"

"I'd say you were a *baaaad* woman." Jesse grabbed her around the waist, swinging her around in a circle. "But you're my bad woman." She pressed their lips together.

THE LONG, HOT days of summer were rapidly passing and the women had fallen into a comfortable routine. During the week, Dusty would carry the rancher and schoolteacher to the Silver Slipper. They would share breakfast with Bette Mae; that way they could spend a few more minutes in bed cuddled together. After breakfast, Jesse would walk Jennifer to the schoolhouse, leaving her with a kiss. Jesse would spend the rest of the morning taking care of the Slipper's business matters or talking with her friends around town. Afternoons were spent at the ranch, the schoolteacher working alongside the rancher to make their home more livable. The dress material finally arrived from Bozeman and Ruthie, utilizing her natural talent for sewing, made Jennifer some new dresses. She had done a wonderful job with the material the general store had received even though, regrettably, it was not the most flattering, and Jesse wished she could have provided better for her love. However, Jennifer refused to complain and wore the dresses proudly.

The school year would soon be over and the women were looking forward to spending more time together at the ranch.

"MORNING, ED," JESSE sang out as she entered the general store.

"Morning, Jesse." Ed pulled a large jar of buttons from a shelf. "Be with you in a minute."

She leaned against the counter and waited for the big man to finish with his other customer. "Morning, Mrs. Perkins."

"Morning, Jesse. I'll take those, Ed." The woman pointed to several buttons now spread out on the counter. "I do declare, the way Miles, Jr. is growing, I'll never keep him in clothes."

"He does seem to be part bean spout." Ed laughed as he placed the buttons in a small bag. "I'll put these on your bill."

"Thank you, Ed." Mrs. Perkins, unlike her husband, was always cordial to others. "Jesse, I do want you to tell Jennifer how happy I am with her teaching. My boys actually like going to school. And Miles Jr. is reading more every day."

"I've seen him in the Slipper a time or two." Jesse's

collection of books was available to any who asked. "I'll be sure
and pass on what you said."

"You make sure you do." Mrs. Perkins smiled at the rancher
and gently patted her arm. "You do make such a nice couple."
She walked out, leaving the rancher blushing.

After a few moments, Jesse felt the blush finally receding
from her cheeks and turned to the storekeeper. "Damn, I wish
people would quit telling us that," she muttered. But she had to
admit, the comment made her proud.

Ed was reading a letter and didn't seem to hear her; a scowl
had replaced his normal smile.

"Problem, Ed?"

"No." He crumbled the paper into a ball, tossing it into a
basket of trash under the counter. He thought for a moment
before bending down and retrieving the paper. "My no-good
brother-in-law got himself in some trouble in Bannack. Wants me
to come help him out."

"You going?"

"Gosh, Jesse. You know I can't leave the store for that long.
It's what? Four, maybe five, days' ride to Bannack. For all I care,
he can rot in jail. But I do care about my sister. And the bastard
didn't put one word about her in this." He shook the letter at
her. "Not one word."

Jesse considered Ed's dilemma for a minute, and a smile
slowly crossed her face. "What say I take a ride to Bannack for
you?"

"Ah, that's mighty nice of you to offer. But I can't ask you to
do that. You've got the ranch to look after, and I doubt Miss
Jennifer would want to see you gone for that long."

"Actually, I was thinking of taking her with me. And Billie
can keep an eye on the ranch."

"No, I can't ask." Ed shook his head.

"Hear me out, Ed. One of Jennifer's reasons for wanting to
come west was she had heard how beautiful the country is. This
would give me the chance to show her some of it. Besides," she
grinned, "I hear there's a dress shop in Bannack."

"What about her teaching?"

"School term ends this week."

"Are you sure?" He was worried about his sister, but
frowned when he thought of what else could be waiting in
Bannack. "I mean, who knows what my brother-in-law has
gotten himself into this time. I don't expect you to get in the
middle of whatever it is."

"We won't," Jesse assured her friend. "We'll see to your
sister and make sure she's okay. Whatever trouble it is, we'll just

find out and let you know when we get back. That way, you can decide if you want to help him or not."

"Sounds fair." The storekeeper really didn't want to travel all the way to Bannack just to find out his sister's husband had again been caught cheating at cards or trying to jump some miner's claim. How the man had lived this long without being shot was a mystery. "All I really want to know is if my sister is okay. So if you're sure," he held out his hand, "I'll thank you for your offer. That is, if Miss Jennifer has no objection."

Jesse took the large hand and gave it a firm shake. "Don't worry, I'll talk to her soon as she's done teaching today." After the storekeeper released her hand, she added, "Now, Jennifer's made out another list." She pulled a paper from her shirt pocket and handed it to the storekeeper.

"Way she keeps making out lists I should just move my store next to your ranch." Ed chuckled. It was a rare week that Jesse didn't come in at least once with a list of items Jennifer discovered lacking at the ranch.

"Actually, I think she's planning on having the freight wagon stop there before coming into Sweetwater. That way, she gets first pick and it saves us having to bring the buckboard to town."

"BANNACK." BETTE MAE had settled on the couch in Jesse's office. "Lordy, tha's a long ride jus' ta show your sweetie some pretty country."

"Maybe so." Jesse sat behind her desk. "But it's got what Sweetwater doesn't: a dress shop."

"Ah. So tha's wha's got ya so excited."

Jesse ignored the woman's smirk. "Besides, I told Ed we'd check in on his sister."

"Wha's she got ta do with this?" Bette Mae's mood instantly shifted from playful to troubled at the mention of the storekeeper's sister.

"He got a letter saying his brother-in-law was in trouble in Bannack, didn't make any mention of his sister. He didn't want to leave the store for two weeks, so I said we'd go."

"Wha' kind a trouble?"

"Don't know. Letter didn't say."

"You're not tellin' me that you're takin' Jennifer all the way ta Bannack ta git into the middle of some trouble ya don' even know what it is?"

Jesse wondered how Bette Mae managed to get all that into one sentence. Shaking her head in disbelief, she answered the perturbed woman. "No. I'm taking Jennifer to Bannack so she can see the country between here and there. Check on Ed's sister and ask what trouble her husband has managed to get himself into. Spend a little time at the dressmaker's. Show my girl the town. Maybe take her to eat at one of the fancy restaurants I hear Bannack has." Jesse grinned at the best cook in the territory. "Then we'll come home after enjoying a few trouble free days."

Bette Mae glared at the rancher. "That all?"

"That's all." She pulled a ledger from her desk drawer and opened it.

"Fancy restaurants, my foot," Bette Mae grumbled. As she watched Jesse making notations in the large book, Bette Mae settled back on the couch.

"You know," Jesse didn't look up as she continued her work, "I don't think I've ever heard Ed call his sister by name. Her husband, either. Usually just says 'my no good brother-in-law' or 'that bastard.' Sometimes wonder if they even have names." Jesse wasn't really expecting an answer and, therefore, wasn't surprised when she received none.

Bette Mae sat silently, lost in memories of a time long ago.

She had been about the same age as Jesse was now and living in Fort Benton working the gambling halls for the money that could be made seeing to the needs of the gold seekers, gamblers, adventurers, soldiers, and other travelers the steamboats brought to town.

It was a typical night in the saloon. The noisy, smoke-filled room was full of men fresh off the boats and looking for a little action before they left on the morning stage or as part of one of the freight-wagon trains heading to Bozeman, Virginia City and other points west.

She glanced toward the front door when she heard boisterous whistles and catcalls coming from that side of the saloon. A girl stood just inside the doorway, looking terrified of her surroundings but determined to accomplish whatever mission had brought her into the establishment. As Bette Mae watched, the terrified girl scanned the men in the saloon, her eyes resting on a face for an instant before she rejected it and looked to the next. The drunken men were becoming more vocal, and she moved to intercept the girl before anything worse than rude remarks could darken her path.

"Come with me." She grabbed the girl's arm, pulling her back outside through the saloon's swinging doors.

"Let go of me!" The girl tried to yank her arm free but found it caught in a surprisingly strong grasp.

"*Saloon ain't no place fer a lady ta be.*" She continued to pull the girl away from the brightly lit building.

The banks of the Missouri River weren't too far from the saloon and she angled for them. That time of night the river was usually deserted, any men about would be in the saloons and gambling halls.

"*Stop it,*" the girl cried, "*you're hurting me.*"

She immediately released the girl, yanking back her hand as if it had been burned. "*Damn, I'm sorry. Never meant ta cause ya no harm. Jus' wanted ta git ya out a that place 'fore them men decided ya was there fer their pleasurin' and tried ta take ya upstairs.*"

"*I was looking for my husband,*" the girl declared, offended at the implication.

"*You're married?*"

"*Yes,*" the girl answered indignantly.

"*Who's ya husband?*" Bette Mae sat on a crate that had tumbled off the edge of one of the steamboat docks and lay upside down on the sandy shore.

"*Mr. Stuart Cassidy.*"

She felt a knot twist around her guts. The girl's husband was well known in the saloons and gambling halls of Fort Benton. He had been coming into her place of business the past couple of nights, throwing money around like it grew on trees. What he didn't lose at the poker tables, he spent on the women that plied their trade in the upstairs rooms. Which is where he was at the current moment.

"*Do you know him?*"

Bette Mae didn't answer. She couldn't. How could she tell the girl that her husband was in the arms of another woman? A woman who expected to be paid for sharing her bed with complete strangers.

"*You don't have to protect me.*" The girl's soft voice was almost lost in the rhythmical lapping of the river against the shore. "*I know he's in there. And I know he's with one of them.*"

"*I'm sorry.*" She couldn't think of anything else to say to the distraught girl. At least, not anything that would remove the look of hurt on the girl's face.

"*I can smell them on his clothes when he finally comes back to our hotel room. He thinks the cigar smoke and smell of whiskey hides it, but I can smell them.*"

"*Why do ya stay?*" She scooted over to make room for the girl to share the crate.

"*I have no place else to go.*" The girl sighed as she sat down.

"*Can't ya go back ta your family?*"

"They don't want me back." Tears filled the girl's eyes. "Momma thinks the world of him. She'd never believe it if I told her he turned out to be no good."

"Then go some place else." She wasn't sure why she cared what the girl did. But something deep inside was telling her the girl needed her, and she didn't know how to ignore it.

"He's spent most of our money. Even started to sell some of the supplies back to the merchants."

"Supplies?"

"We're going to the gold camps where he's going to open a store. 'Make his fortune', that's what he kept telling Momma. Made it sound so good he even got my brother to join him as a partner; he's going to meet up with us after he finishes the planting back home. Anyway, everything seemed to be all right until we got here. That's when we found out the wagon train we were supposed to travel with had left a day before we arrived."

"What happened?"

"Our steamboat was slowed down by a wreck a few days out of St. Louis. The captain kept promising to make up the time but he never did. By the time we landed here, the wagons were gone and we were told we had to wait for the next wagon train. It doesn't leave for another few days. My husband had made arrangements for the supplies for our store to be here when we arrived. Last couple of days, he's been selling them back to the merchants to get money for gambling and..."

"Tha's not right," Bette Mae spat, wanting to go back inside and tell Mr. Stuart Cassidy exactly what she thought of him and the way he was treating this beautiful young woman.

"He's my husband. He has a right to do as he sees fit."

"Horse pucky," Bette Mae grunted. "Man ain't got no right ta treat his wife like that jus' 'cause he's a horse's ass."

The girl snickered. "I've never heard a woman talk like you." She smiled shyly, the moonlight reflecting in her eyes.

"Guess it jus' comes naturally. Grown up 'round saloons all my life. My momma pleasured the men and I never known who my daddy was. Had me lots of aunts that helped raise me. Must o' picked up some of their sayin's along the way. Name's Bette Mae." She grinned, holding out her hand.

"Elizabeth," the girl grasped the proffered hand. "My friends call me Lizzie. I'm glad to meet you."

"Pleasure is all mine." Bette Mae felt a tingling moving up her arm from their clasped hands. It was a sensation that was new to her, but one she was most undeniably enjoying. "Mos' definitely, the pleasure is all mine."

The women saw a lot of each other during the following days.

Every afternoon when her husband would leave their room for the gambling halls and saloons, Lizzie would hurry down to the river where Bette Mae would be waiting. They would spend the next several hours talking about nothing in particular, then she would escort Lizzie back to her hotel room to await her husband's reappearance.

She wasn't sure exactly when it happened, but some time during one of the evenings they spent together she realized she had fallen in love with the girl. She found herself waiting anxiously for the sun to set and she would hurry to the river to wait breathlessly for Lizzie to appear. Casual touches set her skin afire and she yearned for the courage to kiss the sweet lips that spoke so sweetly to her.

Much too quickly, their time together came to an end.

Bette Mae's heart would forever feel the pain of the day Lizzie had come to her with the news of her departure from Fort Benton. "So soon?" Tears flooded her eyes and she couldn't stop them from falling. Thankfully, the dark night kept them from being seen by her companion.

"Yes. The wagons are packed and we will leave at dawn." Lizzie could not contain her excitement, unaware of the misery her words were causing.

"Where will ya go?"

"Bozeman to start. If there are already too many stores there, Stuart says we will go to the other side of the mountains. He says that there are a lot of new mining camps sprouting up around the Sweetwater Valley and the miners will be wanting someplace close to get their supplies."

"I'll miss ya," she whispered as her heart shattered into pieces never to be mended.

"I'll miss you, too, Bette Mae. I have never known anyone that I could talk to so freely. I feel as if I've known you forever and I'm so glad that I met you. I just don't know how else I would have made it through these last few days."

The tears flowing down her cheeks and the lump in her throat made it almost impossible to speak. "Goodbye." She turned to walk away from the young woman who had come to mean so much to her.

"Wait," Lizzie called after her friend. "Bette Mae, where are you going? We still have several hours before I have to be back at the hotel."

"I have ta git back ta work." She kept walking, refusing to look back.

On shaky legs, Bette Mae staggered away from the woman she loved and into the night, stopping only when she reached a small abandoned shack at the edge of town. Not caring about the squalid conditions of the forsaken building, she pushed her way inside through a door barely hanging on rusty hinges attached to what was left of the wood frame. Blinded by tears, she stumbled in the dark until her progress was halted by bumping into the back wall of the shack. No longer able to hold back the sobs, she slumped to the filthy floor to cry until sleep finally claimed her long past dawn.

Weeks later, unable to get the woman out of her thoughts, Bette Mae left Fort Benton to try to find Lizzie and a way to proclaim her love. She arrived in Bozeman only to learn that Stuart Cassidy and his wife had continued on to Sweetwater. Disappointed by the setback, she felt her heart soar when she rode the stage into Sweetwater and saw the sign proclaiming "Cassidy's Mercantile" on a building across from the stage station. But her hopes were soon crushed when she questioned the boy operating the store. He informed her that Cassidy had left him in charge until his brother-in-law arrived to take over. Cassidy had gone to the gold fields to seek his fortune, and Lizzie had obediently accompanied her husband.

"Elizabeth," the older woman quietly murmured.

"What was that?" Jesse looked up.

"Elizabeth. Tha's her name." Bette Mae's voice was soft as she reminisced on a summer many years ago.

"Whose name?"

"Ed's sister."

Jesse put her pencil down. "Didn't know you and she were acquainted."

"It was a long time ago."

Jesse studied her friend, who had never looked sadder. "You were friends?"

"S'pose ya could say that." Bette Mae squirmed uncomfortably on the couch but continued. "We met in Fort Benton. I was working in one of the saloons on the river and they'd just arrived on one of them steamboats. She was just a spit of a girl back then. I wasn't much older but I'd been around some. She was fresh out of her mama's house and been drug west by that worthless excuse of a man wit' nothin' but gold in his eyes."

Jesse remained silent when Bette Mae paused to gather her thoughts. Bette Mae had never spoken about her life prior to coming to Sweetwater, and, not wishing to invade her privacy, the rancher had never asked any questions. It was obviously a painful memory, and Jesse allowed the older woman all the time she needed to continue.

"Anyways, over the next several days we spent many a hour jus' talkin'. Seemed ta have a natural feeling 'bout us bein' together. I found that I liked her. Liked her a lot." Bette Mae smiled sadly, looking up at Jesse. "Kinda like you and Jennifer."

Jesse remembered the discussion she'd had with Bette Mae concerning her feelings for Jennifer and how Bette Mae had seemed to understand. "Did you follow your heart?"

A deep sigh preceded the answer. "I didn' think it would be proper. Considerin' she was married and all."

"You never told her?"

Tears tracked down the older woman's cheeks as she slowly shook her head.

Jesse left her desk chair and crossed to the couch. She sat, wrapping her long arms around the sobbing woman. "What about when you met up again here in Sweetwater?"

"It was too late." She sniffled. "By the time I got here, she'd been drug off ta another gold camp. Only found out by accident that Ed was her kin." Pulling a hankie from her sleeve, she blew her nose. "Always wanted ta ask 'bout her well-bein' but could never build up the nerve."

"Maybe it's not too late." Jesse needed to offer some hope even if the chance was slim. "Maybe she'll come back to Sweetwater."

"Sun's done set on that day, Jesse." Fresh tears flooded from the older woman's eyes as Jesse held her.

WHEN JENNIFER RETURNED to the Slipper after the school day ended, Jesse repeated her conversation with Ed. She barely had the words out before Jennifer agreed.

"Really?" Jennifer was literally jumping up and down in front of Jesse's desk. "Oh, Jesse, I'd love to go." The stage that carried her from Denver to Sweetwater had stopped for one night in Bannack. But it had arrived after dark and had left just before dawn the next day. Unable to explore the bustling mining camp, Jennifer had promised herself that if she ever had the chance, she would return to Bannack. Much sooner than she would have ever anticipated, it looked like she was getting that chance.

"Ed says he'll agree to us going, but only if you're okay with it." Jesse smiled at her happy lover.

"Oh, sweetheart," Jennifer flung herself into Jesse's lap, "I'm very much okay with it. When can we leave?"

"School finishes this week, right?"

"Yes." Jennifer was planting sweet kisses all over her face.

"Then I'd say first of next week."

"How will we get there? Will we go by stage?"

"No." Jesse hugged her close, burying her face in the schoolteacher's hair and breathing deeply.

The stage would get them to Bannack faster, but Jesse wanted to be able to take their time. What she had in mind was to ride over the mountains using little known and less-traveled trails, exposing Jennifer to parts of the territory that were virtually untouched by settlement. There would be little in the way of civilization on their route except a few isolated mining camps, and those she would guide them clear of because a traveler never knew what trouble they were likely to run into in the camps, especially women travelers. She wanted this trip to be fun for Jennifer.

Yep, this trip would have no unnecessary adventures. Just the two of them and the beautiful Montana country that Jennifer wanted to see.

"We'll ride Dusty. Go south out of the valley and pick up an Indian trail that will take us over the pass into the Big Hole."

"Big Hole?"

"That's what the fur trappers called the valley on the other side of the pass. It's big, a lot bigger than our valley. It'll be a little longer ride but we won't be eating dust the whole way like we would if we took the wagon road. Besides, the scenery is much prettier."

"Great." Jennifer leapt up and pulled Jesse from her chair. "Let's go tell Ed we're going."

Chuckling, Jesse allowed the schoolteacher to tug her away from her desk and out of the office.

JESSE'S BREATH CAME in ragged gasps. It wouldn't take much more for Jennifer to bring her to climax and her lover didn't keep her waiting. Jesse's body stiffened as the explosion built and with a cry of her lover's name, she released, her back arching off the mattress. After reaching her pinnacle she dropped back to the bed's surface, spent but very satisfied.

Jennifer crawled up to lie beside Jesse, kissing her satiated lover. "You sure we aren't hurting something by doing it so often?" She traced lazy patterns around Jesse's sweat-covered breasts and down to her still-fluttering stomach. "I mean, we can't go blind or anything, can we?"

"Nah." Jesse twitched as Jennifer's tracings crossed a particularly ticklish spot. "I asked Bette Mae. She said that was an old wives' tale."

"Good, 'cause I'm not sure I could stop even if it was true." Jennifer laid her head on Jesse's shoulder, draping a leg over her body. "It sure is a lot more fun than what I expected after listening to some of my mother's friends discussing it."

Jesse caressed the leg placed so conveniently within her reach. "Bette Mae says that how much you enjoy it depends a lot on the person you're doing it with." She stopped Jennifer's busy hand and brought it to her mouth to suck on the fingers.

"Hmm." Jennifer pushed up onto an elbow to look at her lover. "If that's the case, I must be doing it with the right person, because I'm *really* enjoying it."

"Oh, are you?"

"Oh, yes, very much so." She repositioned herself atop Jesse, resting her chin between Jesse's breasts and wrapping her arms around her lover's warm body.

"Well, darlin'," Jesse drawled, stroking her hands up and down Jennifer's back, "want to do it some more?"

"I thought you'd never ask."

Jennifer giggled as she was flipped over and a new exploration of her body began.

Chapter
Seven

"OKAY, YOU READY?"

On the morning they were to leave for Bannack, Jesse stood in front of the ranch house waiting for Jennifer as she considered mounting the caramel-colored mare that Jesse had surprised her with a few days earlier.

Jennifer had dismissed the students for the last day of the school year and walked back to the Slipper where she knew she would find Jesse. As she neared the large two-story building, she spotted the rancher sitting in the shade on the porch steps, holding the reins of a strange horse.

"What's this?" she asked as she neared the grinning woman.

"Thought you might want to learn to ride on our trip to Bannack." As Jesse spoke the words, she felt disappointment, knowing if Jennifer agreed she wouldn't be able to wrap her arms around her lover as they rode. However, she knew Dusty would tire easily if she had to carry both women and their supplies on the long ride. *In either case*, she reminded herself, *we'll still be able to snuggle at night.*

"She's beautiful," Jennifer commented, reaching up to rub the horse's soft muzzle. "Where did you get her?"

"Butler."

"Butler?" Jennifer bristled. She had a mammoth dislike for the man who had almost cost Jesse her life. He had been more than willing to accept the flimsy evidence that she had stolen cattle, allowing his aversion of women ranchers to cloud his judgment as he encouraged the lynch mob. "I'm surprised you'd buy a horse from him, of all the ranchers in the valley," she huffed.

"He might not have much good to say about me, but he is the best horse breeder in the territory. Besides, he gave me a real good deal." Jesse stood. "Threw the saddle and tack in for no charge. Seems he's been feeling right shameful over accusing me of rustlin'."

"I should think so." Jennifer ducked under the horse's neck to wrap her arms around Jesse's waist and receive the kiss Jesse offered her.

"What's her name?"

"Hasn't got one. Thought you might want to christen her. After all, you don't seem to care much for my taste in names."

Jennifer chuckled at their draft horse named Boy. "Good idea, sweetheart." She stepped back to give the horse a good looking over.

The mare stood as tall as Dusty but not as broad across the back, and except for one patch of white, she was a solid, light-brown color. On her nose, a mark in the shape of a thunderbolt stood out against her cinnamon coat.

She studied the unusual marking before declaring, "Blaze. I'm going to call you Blaze," she told the horse now nuzzling her head.

"I'm ready, I think." Jennifer wavered. "Jesse, are you sure this is a good idea? I mean, I haven't had that much practice."

"You'll do just fine, darlin'," Jesse assured her. "We'll take it nice and slow until you get more comfortable. Besides, you've had no trouble the last couple of days."

Jesse had given Jennifer a lesson each afternoon after they returned to the ranch. The schoolteacher showed a natural talent that would take over once her nervousness faded.

"Okay." Jennifer positioned a booted foot in the stirrup and pulled herself into the saddle. She watched as Jesse mounted Dusty. "I'm ready when you are, partner."

"Well, then," Jesse nudged Dusty forward, knowing Blaze would follow, "let's go."

The women left the ranch buildings behind as they rode toward the southern end of the Sweetwater Valley.

As the day stretched toward late afternoon, Jennifer did, indeed, become more comfortable on Blaze. The mare was a good match for the schoolteacher and provided her an easy ride. By riding both horses, they could take fewer breaks and they made good time, already skirting around the edge of the badlands and the site of Jesse's almost murder. The rancher led them in a wide berth around the meadow, not wanting Jennifer to begin their trip reliving the events that had taken place mere weeks earlier.

"How you doing?" The trail grade was becoming steeper. The valley was now behind them as they followed an Indian trail that would eventually take them over the crest of the Rockies.

"All right."

Jennifer missed having Jesse's arms wrapped around her, but she enjoyed the freedom of her own horse. Never, not even when she would sit for hours and contemplate what life might be like in the West, had she dreamed she would one day be astride a horse, riding in the wilds of the Montana territory, free to do as she pleased. Or that such a beautiful woman would be both her companion and the love of her life. As she rode, she hoped that this was not just a dream from which she would wake in the morning to find herself back in her father's house. She was saddened at the idea of not having Jesse in her life, the thought causing her such sorrow that her heart nearly stopped beating.

"Darlin'." Jesse saw the dark cloud cross her features. "Is something wrong?"

"No." Jennifer shook her head to rid it of the unimaginable vision. She gazed at Jesse. "It's just sometimes I can't believe how lucky I was to end up in Sweetwater. I mean, of all the towns the company in Denver could have sent me to, they sent me to you. Sometimes it just seems so fantastic. Almost like it's unreal."

"Nah, darlin'." Jesse nudged Dusty alongside Blaze, leaning over to kiss Jennifer. "It's very real."

"So it is." Jennifer returned the kiss.

Dusty, not liking being that close to Blaze, stepped away, inconveniently breaking apart the lovers.

"Dusty, be sociable," Jesse chastised, but Dusty refused to close the distance between herself and the other horse. She shrugged at Jennifer. "Guess we'll just have to do our kissing on the ground."

Jennifer giggled at the palomino's actions. "Speaking of the ground..." She had begun to notice some unusual pain and soreness in her back and thighs. "How much longer are we riding today?"

Jesse looked at the position of the sun in the sky and noted it was still a couple of hours before dusk. "I'd like to get a few more miles up the trail. The last stretch before the pass gets pretty rough. Rather not have the girls have to do too much before we reach that section tomorrow."

"Oh." Jennifer had been hoping they would be stopping sooner.

Seeing the look of disappointment cross Jennifer's face, Jesse rushed to continue, "But we could stop now if you want. We'll just take it easy in the morning and give 'em a breather when we reach the bad stuff."

Jennifer considered Jesse's offer and decided it really wouldn't be fair to make the horses work harder than necessary just because she was tired. After all, she had the easy task of being the rider while Blaze and Dusty had the harder task of actually having to climb the rocky trail. "No, that's okay. Let's keep going. Although, you may have to give me a rubdown when you're done giving the girls theirs tonight."

"Ooh." Jesse dropped her voice down to a seductive purr. "I'll look forward to doin' just that, darlin'."

JUST BEFORE DUSK, Jesse called a halt to the day's travels. They set up camp in a small clearing beside the trail. A creek gurgled nearby and Jesse picketed Blaze next to it. Dusty was set free, but did not go far due to the unfamiliar forest surrounding them.

Jennifer was gathering firewood, her chore made easier by the many fallen branches close to the campsite. Dropping her armful of wood, she returned to gather more. She had quickly learned how the temperature dropped in the mountains and wanted to have an ample supply for the night. She dropped her second armful and looked around for Jesse. She found the rancher squatting beside the creek cleaning two freshly caught rainbow trout. "Don't you dare tell me you found those in that little, bitty creek," she confronted the rancher.

"Okay, I won't," Jesse snickered, standing with their meal. "You want to cook them now or after your rubdown?"

"Now. I'm not sure I'll be awake later."

"Ah, darlin'," Jesse sighed, her smirk turning into a frown. "You just ruined my plans for the evening."

Shaking her head at Jesse's antics, she laughed as she poked through the packs looking for their frying pan.

JESSE SAT WITH her back against a tall pine tree close to the fire. Jennifer was nestled between her legs, her back resting on Jesse's chest and her arms lying atop the ones wrapped around her.

Their campsite allowed them a panoramic view of the forest-covered mountain ridges that stretched for miles. An endless sea of deep green spread out before them, broken only by the occasional bare rocky slope or wildflower-carpeted meadow. Above them in the darkening sky, a bald eagle circled, scanning the ground for a late meal, while off in the distance calls of coyotes echoed. Occasionally they heard the howl of a wolf or hoot of an owl over the crackling of their fire and the rustling of the grazing horses.

"It's so beautiful." Jennifer watched as the disappearing sun painted the sky in a rainbow of brilliant colors. "So peaceful."

She jerked upright seconds later when deep grunting shattered
the serenity of the evening. Alarmed, she scanned the forest for
the source of the sounds of something large moving rapidly
through the trees not too far from their camp. "What's that?" she
cried, fully expecting a vicious animal to come bursting out from
the trees at them.

"Bull elk." Jesse reached out, placing a comforting hand on
the schoolteacher's shoulder. "He's probably just letting the
other bulls know he's in the area."

Relieved, Jennifer settled back against Jesse.

The rancher sighed deeply and tightened her hold on
Jennifer. "This is nice," she murmured in Jennifer's ear.

As the last of the sun's colored beams disappeared from the
sky, Jennifer purred, "I know something that would be nicer."
She turned her head to kiss Jesse. After several moments,
Jennifer broke the kiss and pushed herself up from the ground
before turning to offer her hand to the rancher, pulling her up
beside her.

Taking a few moments to check on the horses, Jesse wasted
no time in removing her clothes to snuggle under their blankets
where Jennifer lay waiting.

"You're chilled." Jennifer shivered when the rancher's
cooled skin rubbed against her.

"Bet you know how to fix that." Jesse lay on her back,
invitingly.

"Hmm." Jennifer shifted, stretching her body on top of the
rancher's and loving the feel of their breasts pressed together. "I
have one or two ideas that might work." She leaned down,
pressing her lips to Jesse's.

"Way you're goin', darlin'," Jesse panted when Jennifer
began a trail of kisses down her neck, "I'll be needin' a dip in
that creek 'fore too long."

"Shut up," Jennifer murmured as she reclaimed the
rancher's lips.

AFTER WALKING THE horses up the last mile of the trail to
the summit of the mountain pass, the women had stopped to
rest. Expecting to be looking down the opposite side of a
mountain, Jennifer was astonished to see more mountain ridges
extending before them.

"Thanks." The schoolteacher tilted her head back, taking a
welcomed drink from the canteen Jesse had passed to her. "Jesse,
how wide are these mountains?" She passed the canteen back.

"We'll be out of them by nightfall, but you won't hardly

know we're traveling downhill from here. It'll seem that we're riding along the top and then all of a sudden we'll be out of the mountains and in the Big Hole. It sits higher than the Sweetwater Valley, so the drop isn't as much."

"I've never seen mountains that go on like this. The ones back east don't come close to comparing to these."

"What about on your trip, darlin'?" Jesse secured the canteen to her saddle before remounting Dusty. "You traveled through these mountains on your trip from Denver."

Jennifer squirmed on Blaze's saddle; her legs were sore and it took some doing to find a comfortable spot. "Guess I wasn't really paying much attention. I was too excited just to be making the trip. Besides, the dust those stagecoaches throw up can block out the sun at noon."

"Yep, that's for sure. I've found there's only two ways of traveling by stage, dusty or muddy. Best to avoid either one, if you ask me. Horseback may be a little rough on your behind, but it's the best way to go."

The trail down from the pass proved to be an easy ride, just as Jesse had predicted. Jennifer looked in wonderment at the scenery and wildlife they encountered. The path they followed kept them mostly within the confines of a thick forest of pine trees towering high above them, their trunks reaching straight up for the deep blue sky above. Wherever the trees parted, she could glimpse the snow-covered peaks of the mountain range they were crossing, and they rode through a beautiful mountain meadow alive with activity. Colorful birds flew in and out of the trees and squirrels and chipmunks scurried about, chattering their unhappiness at being disturbed. Beaver and muskrat busily worked building homes in the creeks and streams, and moose foraged on tasty water plants while giving the women little more than a casual glance as they rode by. The teacher was even startled to see a young black bear tumble out of a tangle of berry bushes before rambling back into the forest.

She could not get enough of the wide-open sky and the beautiful land they were riding through. They were two days out of Sweetwater and had not seen a single cabin or even another traveler. For the young schoolteacher, this vast uninhabited land was a bit overwhelming, and she couldn't imagine making such a trip alone. She was very glad that Jesse was riding beside her. For many reasons.

"Jesse, what's that?" She pointed to the side of an escarpment several hundred feet away. The boulder-strewn slope was covered with loose rock and an animal was carefully picking its way across the slippery precipice, a smaller version of itself struggling to keep up.

Jesse turned to look. "Bighorn sheep, and she's got a lamb with her."

"Bighorn sheep," Jennifer idly repeated, watching the animals' progress.

"Yep. The rams have horns that wrap around in a circle. When they fight over the ewes, you can hear the clash of their horns for miles." Catching the movement of a third animal hiding among the boulders, Jesse reached back, pulling her rifle from the saddle scabbard.

"What's wrong?" Jennifer grew alarmed, seeing the weapon in Jesse's hands.

"Hold tight to your reins," Jesse warned, leveling the rifle at the third animal, then gently pulling against the weapon's trigger.

The loud crack of the shot startled both Jennifer and Blaze.

Had Jesse not warned her, the horse's sudden rearing would, most probably, have unseated Jennifer. Quickly regaining control of her mare, she turned to look where Jesse had fired. The ewe and her lamb were running straight up the rocky slope, seemingly unaffected by the loose surface. Jesse fired a second shot and Jennifer saw rock explode less than ten feet from where she had first spied the ewe. After Jesse fired a third shot, Jennifer saw a large cat-like animal emerge from of its hiding place and run down the rocky ledge away from the ewe and lamb.

Jesse lowered her rifle, but kept close watch on the retreating animals.

"That's the biggest cat I've ever seen," Jennifer exclaimed. From head to tail, the cat had to be longer than Jesse was tall.

"Mountain lion." Jesse kept her eyes on the cat.

Jennifer had heard of the big cats, but had not imagined them to be so large. "Shouldn't we be getting away from here?"

"Nah, it's climbed up a tree. It'll wait a while, then go after the lamb again." Jesse replaced the rifle into its scabbard.

"It's too bad you missed it."

"Wasn't aiming to kill it."

"Why not?" Jennifer asked, perplexed that the rancher would allow the large predator to live.

"Darlin'." Jesse turned to the schoolteacher. "We can't go about killing everything we fear or don't like. It serves a purpose. Without the mountain lions, the sheep and other wild animals would become overpopulated. That would weaken the herds and, eventually, you'd have fewer and smaller animals."

"But if that's the case, why did you chase it away?" Jennifer was now puzzled — if Jesse felt as she did, why take any action at all?

Jesse gazed at her as she considered her question. If she'd been riding alone, she would have let nature take its course. So why did she prevent it this time? She was looking at her answer. She hadn't wanted Jennifer to witness the death of the small lamb. She shrugged, not willing to tell Jennifer the truth. "Don't rightly know. Come on, let's get going." She nudged Dusty and the mare moved away, Blaze following.

Jennifer smiled at Jesse's back. She had seen the look in Jesse's eyes as the rancher mulled over her question. It was the same look Jesse had when she'd tried to protect Jennifer from Johnson, the crazed ex-owner of the Slipper. *She was protecting me. That is so sweet.* As Blaze pulled alongside of Dusty, Jennifer reached over and took her lover's hand in her own.

Knowing she had been figured out, Jesse smiled sheepishly at Jennifer.

Later that afternoon, with the high summer sun beginning to drop, Jesse suggested making camp in a small meadow. As Jennifer gathered firewood, Jesse performed her magic and caught a pair of trout in the meadow's creek. After dinner, Jennifer received another rubdown before the women crawled into their blankets and snuggled together. Then Jennifer spent the better part of the night showing Jesse just how much she loved her.

JENNIFER WAS SORRY to see the forest fade behind them. Without the cover of the trees, the sun's rays beat down on the riders and horses, and Jesse called a halt at every creek they crossed to allow time to rest. Before them lay the biggest valley the schoolteacher had ever seen. It was ringed by mountain ranges, and she traced their peaks for as far as she could see. Within the ring, gently rolling mounds of grassland flowed unbroken except for the sporadic stands of willows and cottonwoods along meandering creeks. In the huge expanse of open land, she could see absolutely no sign of human occupation.

"Doesn't anyone live in this valley?"

"Wasn't anyone the last time I came this way." Jesse led Dusty down the side of a hillock. "Trappers come through every so often to trap the beaver. And the Indians come to hunt the antelope and elk."

"Antelope?" Jennifer had never heard the name before.

"Yeah, kinda like a small deer but lighter in color. And," she chuckled, remembering her many failed attempts to shoot one, "faster than any animal you've seen. I swear they can outrun a bullet. Just as well, since they're not too good for eatin'."

"Think we'll see any?" The schoolteacher scanned the horizon for any evidence of the fast-moving creatures.

"Probably." Jesse turned Dusty in a more southerly direction. "There's a lot of 'em in this valley."

"Jesse, is that smoke?" Jennifer rode Blaze up the slope of the next hillock. Far in the distance, a column of gray-black smoke rose from behind a small ridge.

"Seems so." Jesse pulled Dusty to a stop and searched for signs of any activity. "Strange, I don't recall a cabin being around there."

"Maybe it's just someone's campfire." Jennifer had also stopped Blaze, who was standing patiently alongside Dusty.

"That's a lot of smoke for a campfire."

Dusty raised her head, sniffing the air. The golden mare sidestepped uneasily. Blaze picked up on this and twitched nervously.

Jennifer patted the mare's neck. "Whoa, girl. What's got into you?"

Jesse patted Dusty's neck to calm the agitated animal. "Settle down, Dusty. You're upsetting Blaze."

A loud whinny and vigorous shake of the head were Dusty's answers, but she calmed. Blaze seemed to understand the reason for Dusty's agitation and also raised her head to sniff the air.

"What's wrong?"

"Don't know." Jesse reached for her rifle as she nudged Dusty forward. "Could be trouble." Jesse spotted some buzzards circling high above the smoke.

Nearing the source of the smoke, the horses became more skittish and balked at moving in the direction they were being urged to go. Taking on their mounts' moods, the women were not anticipating a welcome sight, but nothing could have prepared them for the shock of what awaited them.

A Conestoga wagon lay partially on its side, its contents scattered about on the ground. Both wagon and contents had been set on fire. The body of a man was lying face down next to the wagon, his body covering a woman's. As they rode closer, the women could see that both had been shot in the head.

Jennifer gasped, burying her face in her hands to block out the horrific sight. Jesse was on the ground instantly, gently pulling her from her saddle and wrapping her in protective arms.

"Don't look." Jesse felt her own cheeks wet with tears.

"Please, darlin'. Don't look."

"Why?" Jennifer moaned into Jesse's shoulder. "Why would someone do this?"

Jesse looked at the burning wagon and wondered that herself.

It took several minutes for the women to compose themselves enough to deal with the tragedy before them.

"Sit here." Jesse lowered Jennifer onto a convenient rock. "Let me get them buried."

"I'll help." The schoolteacher tried to stand even as Jesse gently pushed her back down.

"No, darlin'," Jesse whispered. "I don't want you to see..."

Jennifer reached up and cupped Jesse's tear-streaked face in her hands. "Jesse, I want to help. Please, sweetheart. I need to help them."

Understanding, Jesse nodded.

JESSE CAREFULLY ROLLED the lifeless body of the man off the woman's remains.

"He must have been trying to protect her," Jennifer commented as she helped carry the body to where she and Jesse had dug side-by-side graves. After laying the man out in one of the graves, they returned for the woman.

"Why don't you see if you can find anything with their names or their next of kin," Jesse suggested as she filled in the graves. A search of the victim's clothing had turned up nothing to identify them.

Jennifer nodded before returning to search the items scattered about the smoldering wagon. It was obvious that whoever was responsible for the couple's death had ransacked the wagon and contents before setting them on fire. There wasn't much left worth trying to save. She flipped upright a small travel trunk and found it to be empty. Tossing it aside, she froze, thinking she had heard a faint noise coming from under the wagon. Cocking her head to listen, she heard the noise again. She was astonished to realize that it sounded like a child's whimper. "Jesse," she called, cautiously stepping closer to the wagon. "Jesse, come here. There's someone under the wagon."

Dropping the shovel, Jesse rushed to her side. "Watch out!" She grabbed Jennifer's arm, stopping her from crawling under the still-smoldering wagon box.

"Jesse, I heard a child," Jennifer cried out, struggling to pull loose of Jesse's hold.

"Hold on." Jesse pulled Jennifer back. "It's not safe." She

whistled for Dusty. "Let's get it back upright." Taking a rope out of her saddlebag, Jesse slipped it around one of the wagon bed's ribs and gave it a strong tug to make sure it would hold. She then swung herself up on Dusty, looping the other end of the rope around her saddle horn as she backed the horse away from the wagon until the rope was stretched taut. "Okay, girl," she patted Dusty's neck, "let's get her back on her wheels."

Dusty started backing again, and slowly the wagon eased upright, teetering for an instant before the airborne wheels dropped heavily down onto the ground.

The women held their breath, waiting to see if the damaged wheels would support the wagon's weight.

When she was satisfied the wood was sound, Jesse said, "All right, let's see what's under it." Before she could dismount, Jennifer was crawling under the wagon.

Jennifer could no longer hear the sound that had caught her attention and she worried that moving the wagon could have injured a child if one were underneath it. At first, her search through the jumble of clothing and household objects revealed nothing. Then she heard the tiny whimper again. Pushing aside a pile of clothing, her hand hit something solid. She quickly cleared the rest of the pile to reveal a small wooden crate lying upside down. Lifting it carefully, Jennifer was shocked to see a small baby staring back at her.

Carefully cradling the infant, she scooted out from under the wagon. "It's a baby." She held her arms out for Jesse to see.

Amazed and bewildered, Jesse tilted her head to one side staring at the small bundle.

Dusty took one look at the little person, shook her head and sneezed.

The noise startled the baby and an earsplitting wail erupted from the tiny body.

"HUSH, LITTLE ONE," Jennifer cooed, rocking the crying infant. "You're okay."

Jesse carefully poured water from a canteen, drenching a clean cloth she'd removed from their packs. She handed the dripping material to Jennifer. "It's not milk, but it will have to do for now." She watched as Jennifer placed the wet cloth in the infant's mouth.

The baby sucked on the cloth for a few moments before spitting it out, crying again. The women looked helplessly at each other.

"Here," Jesse sat next to Jennifer, "let me try something."

Wrapping an arm around Jennifer, she bent down close to the upset baby and began to sing an old lullaby, repeating words she remembered her own mother singing to her as a child.

Jennifer smiled as the baby quieted. She leaned into Jesse, soothed herself by the rancher's soft, melodic voice. "That's beautiful," she whispered. "I didn't know you could sing."

"Don't do it much," Jesse shyly replied. "Let's see if she'll stay quiet until I can finish burying her folks."

Jesse left Jennifer to look after the baby as she returned to the task of filling in the graves. When she had finished, she carried the shovel back to where Jennifer sat with the now-sleeping child. "Did you find anything saying who they were?" She spoke softly, so as not to wake the baby.

Jennifer shook her head.

"I'm going to take a look around. Tracks show they had a cow tied to the wagon. I doubt whoever did this would have had much use for it; they probably just cut it loose. It shouldn't be too far. If you have any trouble, use this." She placed a revolver on the rock next to Jennifer. "I'll come back."

"Jesse." Jennifer looked up at the rancher, concern clearly written on her face.

"I won't be long, darlin'." Jesse bent to place a tender kiss on her forehead. "I promise."

Unable to do anything but watch Jesse ride away, Jennifer nervously hummed to the sleeping baby. She was greatly relieved when Jesse returned less than an hour later with a milk cow trailing behind Dusty at the end of a long rope.

Jennifer walked up to Jesse as she dropped from the saddle. "Thank goodness you found that. This little one is starting to fuss again."

"Found this, too." Jesse held up a wallet. "Money, if they had any, is gone. But it says their names were Kenneth and Catherine Williams. No name for the baby, though." Jesse tucked the wallet into her saddlebag, then pulled a small pot from one of their packs. "Let's see what we can get."

Jesse knelt beside the cow and massaged its teats, coaxing out the warm milk. It didn't take long for the pot to be filled. "Now how do we get this into that little thing?" she pointed at the baby's small mouth. She was surprised when the baby wrapped its tiny hand around her finger and held tight.

"Since she's already got a hold of you," Jennifer laughed, "you hold her while I see if I can find something to use to feed her." She traded the baby for the pot of milk.

"How do you know it's a her?"

"She needed her diaper changed while you were gone. I

checked her over, didn't find any injuries. The box she was in must have protected her." She again searched through the wagon's contents, looking for something they could use to feed the baby.

"So how old do you think she is?" Jesse gently ran a finger down the baby's soft downy cheek taking a good look at the infant. She was small, barely stretching the length of the rancher's arm from elbow to hand. Soft feathery hair almost the same ginger color as Jennifer's covered her small head. Bright, curious blue eyes looked up at Jesse.

"Can't be very old. I'm guessing eight, maybe nine months."

"Damn, that's young."

Not finding any unbroken bottles for feeding the baby, Jennifer decided to improvise and emptied one of their canteens. "Give me your knife." She held out her hand.

Jesse obeyed, pulling the knife from her boot. "What are you planning to do?" She was careful to keep the sharp blade away from the baby playing with her fingers.

"I'm planning to put a small hole in the cap so we can pour small amounts of milk into her mouth. It's not the best way to feed a baby, but it'll have to do until we get to Bannack." Jennifer finished with the knife and handed it back to Jesse. Then she poured the milk into the canteen and tightened the cap down. "Shall we give it a try?"

Jesse sat on the ground, providing a nest for Jennifer to sit in while she carefully fed the infant the milk. Both women sat mesmerized by the tiny person in their arms.

Jennifer turned to look into Jesse's eyes. "What are we going to do with her?"

"Take her into Bannack. That's probably where her folks were coming from. We'll see if anyone there knows who they were. The sheriff might be able to help. Need to report the bandits to him anyway."

"Think he'll find them?"

"Hard to tell."

"Jesse, are we in danger?" Jennifer was scared. She had heard of bandits attacking travelers, but had never imagined the consequences could be so terrible.

"It'll be okay, darlin'," Jesse assured the schoolteacher.

"Promise?" Jennifer rested her head against Jesse's shoulder as she continued to pour tiny swallows of milk into the baby's mouth.

"Promise." Jesse hoped she could fulfill the promise to her lover. "Country is pretty open between here and Bannack. We'll keep a sharp eye out."

After the baby fell asleep, Jesse patted Jennifer's leg. "Come on, let's get out of here. It'll be safer."

Jennifer looked down at the baby sleeping peacefully in her arms. Feeling a tiny tug on her heart, she readily agreed.

JENNIFER TUCKED WHAT clothes for the baby they could salvage from the burned wagon into her one of their packs. She had also found some cloth that could serve as diapers until they reached Bannack.

"Here, put this over your head." Jesse stepped next to Jennifer. She had torn a dress into strips to made a makeshift sling that she placed over Jennifer's head. Next, the baby was placed into the pocket of the sling. "It'll make carrying her easier. We can take turns."

Jennifer adjusted the baby in the sling, pleased to see the infant didn't seem to mind what appeared to be a somewhat awkward position.

Before mounting their horses, Jesse and Jennifer stood at the foot of the newly dug graves paying their respects to the couple they had known only in death. The mounds of earth had been carefully covered with rocks to keep animals from digging up the bodies. Two crosses made from pieces of wood pulled from the wagon's side were placed at the head of the graves. Using a piece of charred wood, Jesse had scratched the couple's names onto the crosses.

"We'll take care of your baby," Jennifer vowed to the graves' occupants. "I promise."

"Let's go." Jesse helped her onto Blaze before handing up the baby. Once Jennifer was settled with the infant, she pulled herself up onto Dusty and checked the cow's lead rope wrapped around the saddle horn. "Ready?"

Jennifer, who was making sure the infant was comfortable, nodded, and the women rode away, glad to be leaving the scene of the grisly attack behind them, but sure that the memories of what they had found this day would never leave them.

JESSE AND JENNIFER rode until dark, stopping only to rest the horses or feed and change the baby. They had kept a lookout for any other riders, but had seen none as they rode. With the sun dropping out of the sky, they set up camp alongside a small creek. Jesse tended the horses and cow while Jennifer took care of the baby and set out their bedroll and blankets.

"Best we do without a fire tonight." Jesse joined Jennifer, a fresh pot of milk in hand.

"Won't it be cold?" Jennifer had laid the baby on their blankets where she was happily playing with her toes.

"Yes, but an open fire can be seen for miles at night. I think we better do without." Jesse sat beside the blanket, tickling the child's tummy.

The baby smiled at the rancher, happily kicking her feet.

"She likes you." Jennifer poured the milk into the canteen used for feeding the baby.

"Nah." Jesse lifted the infant to place her on a gently bouncing leg. "She just likes the fact I bring the milk. Don't ya?" she teased the giggling baby.

"Come on, little one." Jennifer took the baby to feed her.

"You know, we should come up with something to call her besides 'baby' and 'little one'." Jesse twisted around, rummaging through their packs looking for the jerky and hard biscuits they had brought with them.

"Hmm." Jennifer was trying not to put too much milk in the baby's mouth, but it was difficult in the growing darkness. "Any suggestions?"

"Nope." Jesse found the food and placed it near the blankets. "She done eating? We better get under cover before we start to get cold." Jesse crawled into the blankets, holding them open for Jennifer, whose arms were full of tired baby.

"I think she was too worn out to eat much. She'll probably wake up during the night to finish."

Rolling onto her back, Jesse took the baby and placed her on her chest, thinking it would be warmer for the infant than laying her on the ground. She gently rubbed the tiny back as the baby sleepily played with the buttons on her shirt. With her other hand, she reached for the jerky and biscuits. "Here, this will have to do for dinner."

"Thanks," Jennifer turned onto her side, snuggling up to Jesse. "What about KC?"

"Uh?" Jesse mumbled, chewing on a piece of jerky.

"For the baby? KC after her parents, Kenneth and Catherine."

"Oh." Jesse wrapped an arm around Jennifer, pulling her close. "That's a good idea, she'll always have a reason to remember her folks."

"Jesse, what's going to happen to her?" Jennifer tucked the blankets securely around their bodies.

"Don't know. If she has relatives, she'll probably go to them. If not, there's probably an orphans' home in Bannack. Or maybe a church that will take her in."

"Oh." Jennifer placed a hand on top of Jesse's. For several long moments, she watched as the tiny child slowly fell asleep. "Jesse, did you ever think about having children?"

Jesse was surprised to admit that she never had. "No, can't say I ever gave it much thought." She wove her fingers into her lover's. "What about you?"

"I always hoped I would have a big family with lots of children. But I guess that isn't going to happen now."

Jesse heard the sadness in Jennifer's voice. She knew her lover loved children, and it wasn't unexpected that she would have wanted to have her own. But Jennifer was right, there wasn't much chance of her having children with another woman. "Guess that's one thing I can't give you, darlin'." Jesse sadly turned her head to face Jennifer.

Seeing the anguish in her lover's eyes, Jennifer reached up to gently caress Jesse's face. "I love you, Jesse. And I wouldn't trade a day with you for all the children in the West." She laid her head back on Jesse's shoulder. Carefully, so as not to wake the baby, she draped an arm and leg across Jesse and settled into her favorite sleeping position.

Jesse kissed the top of her head.

In the distance the moon was rising over the mountain peaks, its pale glow not enough to brighten the dark night. Jesse felt Jennifer's body relax as sleep claimed her. It wasn't long before the only sounds in their camp were the peaceful breathing noises of her lover at her side and the baby on her chest. Jesse smiled. She felt content. It was a good feeling. "I love you, too, darlin'," she whispered.

JESSE WOKE JUST after dawn with Jennifer snoring softly in her ear. She took a few moments to enjoy the pleasure she always felt when waking up with her lover in her arms. For some reason, this morning seemed even more of a treat and the rancher wondered if the tiny baby sleeping on her chest had anything to do with that.

She scanned the horizon, seeing nothing to cause concern. Knowing the mares would have alerted them to any danger, she was additionally comforted that Dusty and Blaze were calmly grazing not too far from where the women lay.

Carefully slipping out from under Jennifer, Jesse placed the baby in the warm blankets she had just vacated. In her sleep, Jennifer reached out a protective arm and covered the child.

It didn't take long for Jesse to get a fire going and to put a pot of coffee in the flames to heat. She milked the cow so the baby would have warm milk for breakfast and then went to the nearby creek to look for fish. Pickings were slim but she managed to catch a couple of trout for their morning meal. She had just placed the fish in the frying pan when Jennifer woke.

"Morning." Jennifer stretched under the blanket. "And good morning to you, KC." She felt the baby grab onto her shirt. "Uh, oh. Someone needs some dry britches." She made a face as she picked up the baby.

"Not me." Jesse knelt beside the fire, patting her backside. "My britches are nice and dry. But I do thank you for the offer."

"Funny." Jennifer pushed the blanket out of the way. "Sweetheart, can you get me a diaper?"

"Right there." Jesse pointed to a cloth resting on top of the baby's canteen. A rag sat in a bowl of water beside it. "Figured she'd be needing a change when she woke up."

Jennifer removed the soiled diaper and grabbed the wet cloth. "Hey, this is warm water," she noted, picking up the bowl.

"Yep. Pretty sure she wouldn't want us to use water straight from that creek. It's a mite on the chilly side."

"You're pretty smart for an old rancher," Jennifer teased, washing the baby before putting on the fresh diaper.

"Who you callin' old?" Jesse scowled, handing her a clean baby gown. "Here you go. And there's warm milk in the canteen."

"You've been busy." Jennifer finished dressing KC, then settled the baby in her arms for feeding. The baby swallowed the milk as quickly as Jennifer could pour the liquid into her mouth. "Looks like she's hungry this morning."

"Don't doubt that." Jesse returned to cooking the fish.

Jennifer looked at the fire quizzically. "You said it was safer not to have a fire?"

"Last night it was." Jesse turned the fish in the frying pan. "But whoever it was is long gone by now." She sincerely hoped her words were true, since she'd decided not to have Jennifer and the baby brave the crisp morning without a fire to warm them.

KC finally drank her fill and pushed the canteen away.

Jennifer wiped the baby's face clean, then joined Jesse by the fire. "Oh, that feels good." Jennifer could feel the fire's warmth against her chilled skin.

Jesse handed her a plate of fried fish, then poured a cup full of coffee and set it on the ground at Jennifer's side. "Here, let me hold her while you eat." She lifted the baby from Jennifer. KC smiled and wrapped her fingers around Jesse's much larger ones. "She's sure got a good grip for such a tiny thing." She played with the child, making faces and funny sounds to entertain KC.

As Jennifer watched the pair, she considered what it would be like to raise KC as their own. She sighed dejectedly, knowing that in another day they would have to give the baby up.

"What's wrong, darlin'?" Jesse looked up to see the sad look on Jennifer's face.

"I was just thinking."

"Must not have been anything good, by your expression." She lifted the baby's gown and tickled KC's belly, eliciting a small baby laugh.

"Don't know that I would say it was bad. I was just thinking about having to leave her in Bannack." Jennifer finished her fish and picked up the cup of coffee, sipping the hot drink.

"Yeah," Jesse sat KC in her lap, "guess we shouldn't get too attached to her." But as she spoke the words, both women knew that they already were.

"Yeah. You better eat before it gets cold, sweetheart. You want me to hold her?"

"Nah." Jesse picked up her plate, trying to juggle it and the baby. "She can help me eat this fish."

"Jesse, she's too young to eat fish," Jennifer laughed.

"Maybe." Jesse smirked as a tiny hand plopped down squarely in the middle of her plate. "But she ain't too young to play with 'em."

Jennifer left Jesse to her game of grabbing pieces of fish away from KC's busy hands. By the time she had rolled up their bedrolls and tied them in place on their saddles, both rancher and baby were in need of a good scrubbing. Jennifer warmed water to wash KC, but Jesse was sent to clean up in the frosty water of the creek. It was mid-morning before the rancher quit grumbling about life's injustices.

JESSE CALLED A halt to the day's travels earlier than she had the previous day. They hadn't seen any sign of the bandits all day and she felt there was no need to ride until dark. KC had been placed on her back in the middle of a blanket so the women could set up camp.

"Jesse, look!" Jennifer called excitedly to the rancher.

"What?" Jesse was rubbing down the horses after the day's ride.

"KC. She just rolled over." Jennifer was focused on the blanket. KC was now lying on her stomach trying to push up on her tiny arms.

"I'll be." Jesse walked over to the blanket, lying flat on the ground so she would be nose to nose with the baby. "Showing off, are ya?"

The baby answered by trying to reach out and grab Jesse's nose. Unfortunately, the movement left her with only one hand on the ground and her tiny body couldn't balance. She fell to the side and the motion rolled her back over to the position she had originally started in. Surprised by all the unexpected action, KC whimpered.

"Hey, there." Jesse stretched her head over the blanket so she could look down at the baby. "Nothing to be upset over. You're just learning somethin' new."

Looking up into the smiling upside-down face above her, KC's whimper changed into a giggle.

Jesse laughed with the girl. "That's better."

Jennifer sat on the blanket, tickling the baby. "Won't be long and you'll be crawling. Bet you'll be a handful then."

"Heck, darlin'," Jesse winked, spreading her fingers to denote the baby's small size, "she ain't much more than a handful now."

Jennifer reached out and grabbed Jesse's hand, pulling her onto the blanket. She quickly covered her lover's body with her own, planting kisses all over her face.

Jesse's hands found their way to Jennifer's back, working her shirt loose of her pants.

Jennifer felt Jesse's warm hands on her bare skin and her body instantly reacted. She pressed her lips against her lover's.

Suddenly, feeling like they were being watched, Jesse broke the kiss and looked at the baby lying beside them. KC was happily carrying on a gibberish conversation with herself, but turned to look at Jesse at the exact same moment.

"Should we be doing this with her right there?"

Jennifer straddled Jesse's hips, unbuttoning her shirt. "I don't think she minds."

"Maybe not, but it feels kinda strange." Jesse stopped Jennifer's hands. "I mean, shouldn't we wait until she's asleep, at least?"

"Jesse, she's just a baby. She doesn't' know what we're doing."

"Maybe." Jesse rolled her eyes towards the baby, only to see KC looking straight back at her. "Still, it seems strange having her watch."

Jennifer collapsed down onto Jesse. "What are you saying, sweetheart?"

"I think I want to wait until she's," Jesse shrugged,

sheepishly, "asleep."

"Tonight?" Jennifer groaned in disappointment.

"I promise." Relieved, Jesse kissed the top of Jennifer's head before rolling the schoolteacher off her. She stood and walked back to the horses, buttoning up her shirt on her way.

Frustrated with her unexpectedly shy lover, Jennifer remained on the blanket, thinking of the promise she would definitely hold Jesse to later that day. Her thoughts were interrupted by a small arm smacking her side as KC again experimented with her newly discovered skill. "You, little one." She rolled onto her side to watch the baby. "You had better learn to look the other way when I want to make love with that gorgeous woman."

KC giggled.

Later that evening, with KC soundly asleep, Jesse made good on her promise.

DUSTY AND BLAZE carried their riders down a small hill, then climbed up the backside of another. At the crest, a road could be seen less than a mile in the distance. A wagon rumbled along it, a cloud of dust billowing behind. The few riders sharing the road pulled to the side and let the wagon pass.

"That's the road into Bannack," Jesse answered Jennifer's unasked question. "We should be in town by noon."

Jennifer adjusted KC, who had fallen asleep. She looked at Jesse, both women feeling a deep sadness that they would soon need to part with the infant.

"She'll be okay, won't she, Jesse?"

Jesse could hear the distress in the schoolteacher's voice. "Yes, darlin'. We'll make sure of it."

"All right." Jennifer urged Blaze forward. "Let's not prolong this."

"Whoa, hold up there," Jesse called.

"What?" Jennifer pulled Blaze to a stop.

Jesse nudged Dusty alongside Blaze. "People in Bannack might not be as accepting of us as our friends in Sweetwater. Might be best if we tell folks we're sisters."

At first, Jennifer wondered what Jesse was talking about. After reflecting on the rancher's comments, she had to agree that she was regrettably right. She turned to Jesse, smiling. "Hmmm, Jennifer Branson. Kinda has a nice ring to it, don't you think?" She rode on, leaving an open-mouthed Jesse staring after her.

Jesse sighed. "Ya know, it does sound right pretty."

Dusty trotted ahead to catch up with Blaze.

Chapter
Eight

BILLIE MONROE ENTERED the Silver Slipper's dining room, taking his usual place at the table that afforded him the best view of the kitchen. Maybe today was the day he would finally find the nerve to speak with Ruthie. Though he often thought of the pretty young girl who had seen to his injuries the night he protected Jesse from the lynch mob, he had yet to actually do more than nod a quick greeting to the shy young woman.

"Plannin' on havin' your usual, Sheriff?" Bette Mae filled a cup with hot coffee.

"What?" His attention on the activity in the kitchen, Billie was startled by the sudden appearance of the older woman. "Ah, yeah," he quickly gathered his wits. "Yes, Bette Mae, breakfast, please."

Bending down to place the cup on the table, Bette Mae whispered, "Why don' ya jus' ask her ta have breakfast with ya? She hasn't had any yet."

"Uh." Billie looked bewildered, embarrassed that Bette Mae had seemingly read his thoughts. "Oh, I'm sure she's busy with her chores," he mumbled.

"She's got stuff ta do," Bette Mae grinned at the man's discomfort, "but she's got ta eat, too."

"I doubt she'd want to join me," Billie said, partly disappointed and partly hopeful.

"Well, now." She glanced into the kitchen where Ruthie was busily peeling potatoes. She chuckled, noticing the young woman had pulled the heavy bucket of tubers into a position where she could unobtrusively keep an eye on the sheriff. "Seems right interestin' ta me that every mornin' she finds herself a task that keeps her right in your line a sight. But," she shrugged casually, "suit yourself."

Billie scratched his chin as Bette Mae's words repeated in his head. *Could she really be as interested in me as I am with her?* he wondered. Deciding that there would be no better time than the present to find out, he gathered his courage and stood. Hesitantly, he entered the kitchen, walking to where Ruthie sat working. "Miss Ruth," his nervousness showed in his voice and sweating hands. "I was wondering if you would like to join me for breakfast."

Ruthie started to look up at the sheriff before timidly ducking her head back down so he couldn't see the smile on her face.

"I'm sorry," he whispered when he received no response. "I didn't..."

"I'd like that."

"Excuse me?"

She raised her head so he could see her face. "I'd like to join you."

"You would?"

"Yes."

Billie held out his hand.

"Let me get cleaned up first." Ruthie wiped her hands on the towel draped over her shoulder.

"All right." He could tell the young woman wanted a few moments to prepare herself. And to be honest he was happy to have the time himself. His heart was beating so fast he wasn't sure it wouldn't burst right out of his chest. "I'll be waiting at the table," he smiled at Ruthie. "Take all the time you need. Bette Mae," he called out as he turned to leave the kitchen, "make that two for breakfast this morning."

"'Bout time," Bette Mae muttered to herself, placing two plates with eggs, bacon, potatoes and toast onto a serving tray. "Wha' is it with the young folks in this town? It's easier pullin' teeth than ta git them ta see how much they cares 'bout one 'nother."

AFTER BREAKFAST, RUTHIE accompanied Billie out onto the porch of the Silver Slipper. "Thank you for breakfast."

"You're very welcome." Billie strode over to a pair of chairs; stretching out a hand, he silently asked the young woman if she'd like to sit.

Ruthie, glad that the sheriff wasn't in a hurry to leave, settled in one of the chairs. The pair sat without speaking for several minutes.

"I, um." He cleared his throat, breaking the silence. "I've been wanting to ask you if you'd agree to me courting you."

She blushed, a pinkish glow coloring her fair skin as she

ducked her head demurely. "I'm sure there's prettier girls in town you could ask," she said, even though she knew there weren't many single women in Sweetwater, and most of them worked at the Slipper.

"Why, Miss Ruth." He gazed adoringly at the shy woman. "I do believe you are the prettiest girl in the valley, and I'd be right proud if you'd accept my offer."

Self-consciously, Ruthie reached up to cover the scar that marked her cheek.

Billie gently pulled her hand away. "I mean what I say. Will you allow me to call on you?"

With tear-filled eyes, Ruthie whispered, "Yes."

JESSE AND JENNIFER rode slowly toward Bannack. As the road curved to parallel Grasshopper Creek, they rode past miners working along the gravel creek bed. Jesse explained the different methods the miners engaged to coax the gold from the gravel as Jennifer took note of the dirty, backbreaking labor. She questioned why men who would not accept a regular job would work so hard for the chance of finding a nugget or two of the shiny metal.

The women rode across the creek and through the small community of Yankee Flats. The small town consisted of several roughly thrown together shacks and lean-tos where Union sympathizers separated themselves from the more southern-leaning population of Bannack.

Several more sturdily constructed houses announced their arrival in Bannack. The residences at this end of the main street soon gave way to buildings housing businesses of every description. Stores selling a variety of goods were intermingled with saloons, laundries, doctors' offices, hotels, fraternity lodges, boarding houses, mining offices, and much more. At the far end of the road, Jesse recognized the unique rooftops of churches. In the surrounding hills, Jesse and Jennifer could see activity at several mines dug into the slopes.

Dusty and Blaze walked down the center of the main street, which was bordered on either side by a wide boardwalk running along the front of the buildings. As they walked, the structures became closer together until they reached the center of town, where space was in such demand that the walls of adjoining buildings literally touched. Both street and boardwalk were bustling with activity as men, women, and children hurried about their business.

Most of the buildings were made from rough-hewn logs or

wood planks, attesting to the town's young age. A few businesses were still housed in canvas tents, the owners having arrived recently and having not yet earned enough money to replace them with more permanent structures. Freight and ore wagons juggled for room on the street and both horses and people scurried to avoid being run over by the large vehicles.

Bannack was a hive of activity, and the women were quickly overwhelmed by it all. Jesse pulled Dusty to a stop in front of a two-story, wooden structure. Joining her, Jennifer looked the building over. It had a plain front with four pillars supporting a second-floor balcony and the building's over-hanging roof. A wood sign nailed into the side of the building and jutting out over the boardwalk and street proclaimed it to be the Goodrich Hotel.

"Let's get a room and find out where we can find the sheriff." Jesse slipped down from Dusty's saddle. then reached up to take the baby from Jennifer so the schoolteacher could dismount.

"Sounds good," Jennifer agreed, stepping up onto the boardwalk with Jesse.

As soon as they opened the door to the Goodrich Hotel, they were greeted by a man standing behind a counter on the far side of the hotel's small lobby. A good foot shorter than the women and well on his way to losing what was left of his hair, he wore a black vest over a smartly pressed white shirt. "Good afternoon, ladies," the man merrily greeted them. "How can I be of service to you this fine day?"

"Afternoon." Jesse nodded at the overly cheerful clerk. "My sister and I need a room for a few nights."

The man opened the hotel register, handing Jesse a pen as he continued, "Good thing you came in when you did. I have only one room available and the stage is due in an hour. It only has the one bed, though," he apologized.

"That's okay." Jesse signed the register. "My sister and I are used to sleeping together."

Jennifer hid her smile behind a hand, coughing in a fruitless attempt to cover the chuckle that had burst forth.

Jesse glared at her lover and raised an eyebrow, warning her to behave.

Jennifer shrugged.

"Good, good." The man turned the register back around, reading what Jesse had just written. "Sweetwater, huh? What brings you to Bannack? Business or meeting up with your husbands?" It wasn't uncommon for women to travel alone, but it happened seldom enough that it was always noticed.

"Business," Jesse answered, leaving out the fact that they had no husbands.

The clerk watched as the baby in Jesse's arms began to fidget. He noticed the remarkable resemblance the baby showed to the woman's sister and smiled at Jennifer. "Beautiful baby, ma'am. You and your husband must be very happy."

Jennifer smiled at the man. "Yes, she is beautiful, but, regrettably, she's not mine. We found her parents on the trail, murdered."

"Bandits." The clerk sadly shook his head. "So they've struck again."

Both women were shocked that he showed no surprise at the news.

"You don't seem too surprised." Jesse settled the fussing baby on her shoulder, soothingly rubbing her back. KC snuggled against the rancher and calmed.

"I wish it wasn't so." The clerk reached for a key from the rows of hooks hanging on the wall behind him. "But bandits have been attacking travelers on the roads between here and Virginia City for the last few months. Somehow they always seem to know who's carrying gold dust or other valuables."

"Hasn't the sheriff been able to do anything?"

"He goes out looking, but always comes back empty-handed." The man made a notation next to Jesse's name. "The room is six bits a night. Bath is two bits extra. Supper is served between six and nine in the dining room in the back and breakfast from five to nine in the morning. Meals are extra."

"We'll need a cradle for the baby." Jesse handed him a bill. *Bannack is going to cost some.* At the Slipper, meals and bath came with the room; she considered changing her prices when they returned to Sweetwater.

"Sorry." The man took the money and made another notation next to Jesse's name. "Don't have any. Never have much call for them and the owner doesn't see any reason to keep any on hand."

"That's okay. We'll make do," Jennifer said.

"Need a place to board our horses," Jesse added.

"Livery is on the north road, you can board them there. Tell Jasper you're a guest of the Goodrich. He'll take care of you. Your room is at the top of the stairs, front of the building. Let me know when you want your bath." The clerk handed Jesse the room key.

Jesse took it, but wasn't through with the man. "You happen to remember a Conestoga wagon coming through town few days back?"

"That what you found?"

"Yes."

"Let me think. Conestoga. Hmm, don't see many of those in these parts. Most stay further south on the Oregon Trail, country around here is too rough for 'em."

"Did you see one?" Jesse asked impatiently. She wasn't looking for a lesson in transportation.

"Seems I do recall one coming through. Didn't stay long. Was parked across the street for a spell in front of Carpenter's Mercantile. Sheriff might know more."

"Where can we find the jailhouse?"

"Across the street in the alley behind the store. But you won't find the sheriff there. He keeps an office in the back of the mercantile."

"Thanks." Jesse started to re-cross the lobby, but thought better of it when she felt a growing wetness on her arm, beneath the baby. She grinned at Jennifer. "I think someone needs fresh britches."

Jennifer took the baby and key from Jesse. "You get the saddle bags. I'll take KC up to the room. She's probably hungry too."

AS JENNIFER FINISHED cleaning up KC, Jesse looked out the room's window.

"Jennifer, I don't want you wandering around Bannack alone," the rancher grimly said, watching the activity on the street below.

Jennifer lifted KC into her arms, carrying her over to the window. "Jesse, you don't have to watch over me every minute of the day. I can take care of myself, you know."

Jesse draped her arm around the schoolteacher, pulling her close. "It's not you I'm worried about, darlin'. It's them." She nodded down at the street.

Jennifer looked where Jesse had indicated, seeing numerous cowboys, miners and other men hustling along the boardwalks and spilling out into the street. It was early afternoon and many of them were already showing signs of having had too much to drink. There were a few women moving about, but all were accompanied by at least one male companion. She saw the wisdom of Jesse's concern. "All right, sweetheart."

"Thank you." Jesse leaned down and captured Jennifer's lips. "Now let's go get Dusty and Blaze boarded, and the cow. Then we'll go find the sheriff."

AFTER TAKING THE horses and cow to the livery and arranging for their feed and care over the next few days, the women strolled the length of the main street and started back toward Carpenter's Mercantile. Jesse didn't seem to be in much of a hurry to find the sheriff, and Jennifer wasn't about to question her reasons.

They discovered that the eastern end of the street mirrored the western, being populated mostly with private residences. Thankfully, this area was relatively free of drunken cowboys and men looking for trouble, the majority of that activity taking place in the center of town where the businesses and saloons were located.

Crossing the street to walk back on the opposite side, Jennifer stopped in front of a lot where a log cabin sat back several feet from the boardwalk. Occupying the ground between the street and cabin were a swing, teeter-totter, and other toys. This was obviously the town's school.

Jennifer left Jesse standing on the boardwalk while she investigated the building. "It's empty," she said when she rejoined Jesse. Excited at finding the schoolhouse, she was greatly disappointed to discover it vacant.

"School must be out for the year, just like in Sweetwater," Jesse guessed. Knowing Jennifer was anxious to have the opportunity to talk to another schoolteacher, she offered, "Why don't we ask the hotel clerk if he knows where the teacher lives? I'm sure she must have a place close to town."

"I'd like that." Jennifer smiled adoringly at the rancher.

The women continued their stroll along the boardwalk and eventually found themselves in front of Carpenter's Mercantile. Jesse held the door to the store open for Jennifer to enter; she wasn't too surprised that the interior of the store wasn't much different from the general store in Sweetwater. They walked up to the counter where the storekeeper stood warily watching them.

"Afternoon, ladies." The man's greeting was guarded. He stood of medium height and was so skinny his apron strings were wrapped twice around his body before being tied in a crooked bow.

"Afternoon." Jesse nodded at the man. "We're looking for the sheriff. We were told he has an office here."

"You ladies got trouble?"

"You might say that," Jesse said impatiently. "Rather discuss it with the sheriff, if you don't mind." She wondered why it was that nothing seemed to be simple in Bannack. Even worse, she was getting a real uneasy feeling about the town.

"Office is around back." The man jerked a thumb towards the back of the building. "You'll have to enter from the alley. He ain't got a door into the store."

While Jesse was talking to the storekeeper, Jennifer had searched the shelves for the supplies they needed for KC. She smiled at Jennifer as she placed two baby bottles and some cloth she could cut up for diapers on the counter. "How much for these?"

"Four bits." He reached under the counter and produced a bag to put the items in. Taking the money from Jesse, he handed her the bag in return.

"Thank you." Jesse carefully passed KC to Jennifer.

Jesse led Jennifer outside. Standing on the boardwalk, she looked for the easiest way to access the alley in back of the row of commercial buildings. She noticed a gap between the mercantile and the next building. "Come on." She led Jennifer into the narrow, dark passageway.

The women soon stepped back into daylight when they reached the alley at the back of the building. Looking around, they saw a short pair of uneven steps leading to an unmarked door at the back of the mercantile. Jesse placed a booted foot on the top step and pulled the door open, cautiously looking inside.

A large man with a handlebar mustache sat behind a small table. He eyed Jesse and then Jennifer as they opened the door into his small office. Standing slowly when they entered, he asked, "Something I can do for you ladies?" He looked both women over carefully before his eyes came to rest on Jennifer.

"You can if you're the sheriff." Jesse stood slightly in front of Jennifer, in an obvious protective stance.

"Sheriff Logan," the lawman informed them. "What's your business?"

Jesse pulled a chair from the front of the table and offered it to Jennifer. "We just rode in from Sweetwater. Had some trouble on the trail."

"What kind of trouble?" The sheriff slumped back into his chair, leaving Jesse standing.

"Found a wagon overturned. Man and woman it belonged to had been shot."

"They dead?" the sheriff asked tensely.

"Yes." Jesse watched the sheriff closely, the knot in her stomach tightening. The lawman's reaction to her story didn't seem right. He seemed to relax after being told the couple hadn't survived. "Found this not too far from the wagon." Jesse tossed Kenneth Williams' wallet at the seemingly uninterested lawman.

The sheriff opened the billfold and pulled out a piece of

paper. "Hmm, Williams. Seem to remember a couple by that name came through here a few days back. They were driving an old Conestoga they'd bought south somewhere. Trailing a cow, if I remember."

"That would be them. Wagon was burned. Bandits took the horses, but the cow is over at the livery."

"Never could figure out why they were dragging around that old milk cow." The sheriff put the paper back into the wallet.

"For her." Jesse motioned to KC sitting happily in Jennifer's arms. "Found her under the wagon."

"I'll be damned. Didn't know they had a young 'un with 'em." The sheriff pushed back his hat and scratched his head, to all appearances confused to be confronted with the baby.

"We were hoping you could tell us if the Williams's had any family in the area."

"Don't know much about 'em. Like I say, they came through here like a lot of folks do. Most only stopping long enough to buy supplies and check on which roads are safest to travel. Don't usually say much about where they're going or where they've been."

"Did the Williams?"

"Did they what?" the sheriff looked suspiciously at the tall woman glaring at him.

"Did they check on how safe the roads were?"

"Yep, he came in and we talked. I told them bandits were in the area. They always are around mining camps, but most of their thieving has taken place between here and Virginia City. Asked if they were carrying anything of value. They denied it. Guess they figured if they kept it a secret, they'd be all right. Guess they was wrong."

"Looks that way." The knot in Jesse's stomach grew.

"I'll ride out tomorrow and take a look. Where exactly did you find the wagon?"

"'Bout a day and half ride into the Big Hole, northwest of the cutoff."

The sheriff shrugged. "I should be able to find it. Though, ain't much I can do this long after it happened. Bandits have probably split up by now."

"You will try?" Jennifer didn't care for the sheriff's obvious lack of enthusiasm.

"Like I said, I'll ride out there tomorrow." The sheriff sat up in his chair, visibly anxious for the women to leave. "Anything else I can help you with?"

"Yes. Stuart Cassidy. Got word he was in your jail."

"That's right. You related to him?"

"No." Jesse shook her head. "We're checking for a friend. Mind telling us what he's done?"

"Shot his wife."

Jennifer gasped at the sheriff's words, and Jesse rested a comforting hand on her shoulder. "What happened?"

"Cassidy had a problem with gambling. Problem was, he couldn't win no matter how much he played." The sheriff laughed at his own joke. "And he played a lot. Wife came in to town one night looking for him. He was losing and drunk, as usual. Didn't take too kindly to her ordering him home. Pulled his revolver and shot her. She died two days later. Trial starts next week if you're interested."

"We're not."

"What will happen to him?" Jennifer's eyes were brimming with unshed tears. She had never realized the West could be so brutal for women. First the women working at the Slipper and the way had been forced to earn a living before Jesse took over, then Mrs. Williams being killed when her baby was only months old, and now Ed's sister. She couldn't understand how such a beautiful country could hold such hardship for the people who made it their home.

"Not much doubt as to him being guilty. Once the judge arrives, he'll hang."

KC, sensing Jennifer's sudden sadness, whimpered. Jesse bent down and lifted KC from Jennifer's trembling arms.

"What do you plan to do with the young 'un?"

"If we can't locate any kin, I guess we'll see if one of the churches will take her in." Jesse helped Jennifer stand.

"Shouldn't be a problem. Folks are always looking for extra hands to help with chores. 'Course most folks prefer boys than girls. They can do more work."

Jennifer looked at the man as if he had just sprouted a second head. Was he really saying that orphaned children were treated like nothing more than extra plow horses? Why, it was no different then the way her own father had treated her. Then and there, she determined that she would never allow KC to face such a future. *Never.*

As the women turned to leave his office, Sheriff Logan asked, "You want to see the prisoner?"

"No." There was nothing they had to say to the man.

"Say, you never told me your names." The sheriff pushed back his chair and stood.

"Jesse Branson," Jesse turned back to the sheriff. "And this is my sister, Jennifer."

"Going to be in town long?"

"Couple of days. We're staying at the Goodrich Hotel. Appreciate it if you'd let us know if you find out anything on the bandits."

"All right. See me 'fore you leave town. Especially if you'll be carrying anything of value."

Jesse looked at the man, puzzled. *Why would he need to know that?* "Thanks for the information, Sheriff. By the way, where is Mrs. Cassidy buried?"

"Up on the hill. Cassidy didn't have enough for a tombstone. Gravedigger can point out her grave, if you have a mind to ask."

Jesse could feel her anger rising. The sheriff spoke as if he was talking about the morning's weather instead of someone's loved one. How could he be so indifferent to what was happening around him? Before she could grab the man around the neck and throttle some compassion into him, Jennifer placed a warm hand on her back.

"Let's go back to the hotel, Jesse. The baby's tired."

Without saying a word, Jesse followed Jennifer outside.

Sheriff Logan waited until the women disappeared around the corner of the building before he left his office to cross the alley to the jail buildings. He had two jails at his disposal; one was used for men needing a place to sleep off a drunk, while the other held the more dangerous prisoners. Sheriff Logan unlocked the door to the second.

The jail was built with coarsely squared logs and separated into three parts. Half of the building consisted of a room where a guard sat to keep watch on the prisoners. It could also be used to hold prisoners if the cells were occupied. The other half of the building consisted of two jail cells approximately six feet square. These cells had thick log walls and were entered through a small opening that forced even a normal-sized man to bend down to avoid cracking his head. A heavy ring was anchored into the logs that made up the building's floor and prisoners were chained to the ring, thus preventing escape attempts through the building's sod roof. The cells had no windows, and when the door was closed, a prisoner sat shackled in total darkness.

Sheriff Logan nodded at his deputy before opening the small shutter used to pass a prisoner's meals through on the only occupied cell. After looking inside, the sheriff unlocked the door. In the cell sat his prisoner, Stuart Cassidy. The man looked dazed and slowly raised his head when he heard the door pulled open.

"Any word from Sweetwater?"

Leaning against the doorframe, Sheriff Logan pondered how much he should tell the prisoner about his recent visitors. "You know a Jesse and Jennifer Branson?"

"No."

"Too bad." The sheriff stepped back and started to close the cell door.

"Are you sure my letter was sent?" The prisoner was desperate.

"Yep, it got sent. Maybe they just don't give a damn." The sheriff slammed the heavy door shut and locked it. "Probably just as well."

"SWEETHEART, WE'RE GOING to need more milk before morning." Jennifer poured the last of the milk from the canteen into one of the bottles they'd purchased at the store.

"Okay, I'll take a walk to the livery. Want to check on Dusty and Blaze anyway."

Jesse sat on the hotel room's bed, her long legs spread wide. KC lay between her legs, playing with a piece of cloth that would soon serve as her diaper. The baby's giggles helped lighten the moods of the women.

Jennifer sat beside Jesse and leaned against her. "Are we going to the grave today?"

"Nah." Jesse draped her arm across Jennifer's shoulders, kissing her brow. "I think I've had enough for one day. What about you?"

"Yeah, more than enough."

Outside, the sun was beginning its long drop from the sky as the women weighed all the things they'd heard since arriving in town, KC's happy playing noises the only sound in the quiet room.

"Jesse." Jennifer entwined her hand with her lover's.

"Hmm?" Jesse looked down, studying the joined hands. It never failed to amaze her how Jennifer's touch made her tingle all over. It was a nice feeling and she smiled.

"I don't think I like that sheriff."

"My stomach's been in a knot ever since we talked to the clerk downstairs. Knot got bigger when we talked to Logan. I think it's best we stay to ourselves the rest of our time here." Jesse looked into Jennifer's eyes. "I'm sorry, darlin'."

"For what?"

"This isn't exactly the trip to Bannack I was hoping for. I wanted you to have a good time."

"Ah, Jesse." Tears came to Jennifer's eyes. "Sweetheart, you couldn't have known we'd find the Williams. Besides I wouldn't say it's all been bad." She smiled down at KC, who had managed to roll herself over and was pushing up on her tiny arms, looking at the two women sharing her bed. "We found her."

"That we did." Jesse lifted the baby up, planting a kiss on KC's soft cheek before passing her to Jennifer. "I'll go to the livery and get her some fresh milk. Then, what say I take my girls to supper in the dining room?"

"KC and I would love to." Jennifer accepted the offer and squirming baby.

"Good." Jesse climbed off the bed. "I won't be long. Lock the door and don't open it for anyone except me. There's a pistol in the saddlebag."

"Be careful." Jennifer followed Jesse to the door.

"I will."

"ANY NEWS FROM Bannack?"

"Wasn't expecting to hear from them." Ed carried a flour barrel to the back of his store. "What can I do for you, Billie?" he asked, steadying the barrel next to an identical one.

"Need me a courtin' shirt and pair of pants."

"Courtin'?" Ed peered at the nervous lawman. "Do I have to ask who the lucky young lady is?" he teased, already knowing the answer. He and Jennifer had spent one entire afternoon recently discussing how long it would take the shy sheriff to ask the even more reticent Ruthie for a date.

"Miss Ruth has agreed that I can come calling." Billie scowled at the chuckling man. "And I plan to dress appropriately when I do."

"I certainly hope so," Ed laughed. "Otherwise Bette Mae will chase you out of the Slipper before you have a chance to do much courting."

"Ah, Ed." Billie slumped against the counter. "This is hard enough for me without you reminding me about Bette Mae watching over us like a bear sow ready to take a bite out of my britches."

Ed took pity on the sheriff. "Come on, Billie." He slapped the young man on the shoulder. "Let's get you fixed up with some duds that even Bette Mae can't find fault with. But speaking of bears, you know she thinks of all those girls as her cubs. So you better only have good intentions when it comes to Ruthie, or she'll do more than bite your arse."

"Believe me, Ed," the sheriff smiled, "I only have the very best of intentions when it comes to Miss Ruth."

"Good lad," Ed declared as he led Billie to the corner of the store where he kept his limited supply of clothing.

JESSE CARRIED KC as she and Jennifer entered the hotel's dining room. An isolated table was pushed against the back wall, and the women headed for it and the privacy it offered. Immediately after they were seated, they were greeted by a friendly girl who filled their coffee cups while regaling them with the different attributes of each meal on the restaurant's menu. Both women ordered steak with all the fixin's and apple pie. Assuring them it would not take long for their meals to be prepared, the girl rushed off to the kitchen to place their order.

Jesse and Jennifer talked quietly as they waited for their steaks to arrive. KC, held in the crook of Jesse's arm, was curiously looking around the room. Quickly becoming bored with the lack of activity, the baby yawned and promptly fell asleep.

Their meals arrived and the women attacked the food after they realized it had been some time since they had last eaten. Jesse was finishing the last bite of her apple pie when a distinguished-looking man wearing a brilliant white shirt, black string tie, and long black coat walked into the dining room. He scanned the diners before making a beeline to their table.

"Excuse me," the man addressed the women as he approached them. "Are you the young women from Sweetwater with the baby?" Spotting KC asleep in Jesse's lap, he continued, "Ah, I see that you are. I am Reverend Tobias. I must say that we don't normally get children this young, but let me assure you that we do find them all nice, decent homes. Why, just last week, we sent a young boy to a family near Dillon where he'll have a fine home."

Jennifer looked at Jesse, panic written all over her face.

"Whoa there, Reverend. I think you've got the cart before the horse." Jesse held a hand up, stopping the man as he leaned down to take KC from her.

"But, I thought..." the man looked quizzically from one woman to the other.

"You thought wrong. We're looking for her kin."

"I'm sorry to say, Miss," he hesitated a moment. "Branson, isn't it?" When Jesse nodded, he continued, "Yes, Miss Branson. I'm sorry to say that you won't be finding any of her kin. I, myself, talked to the Williams when they passed through. They had no kin, and that's why they were traveling west. Indians attacked their settlement in Wyoming and kilt most everyone.

They lost their entire families, poor things. And so young they were. Why, not much older than yourselves."

Having to know the answer, Jennifer asked, "The boy you sent to Dillon. What does the family do?"

"Why, they have a farm just outside of town. Nice family; they've taken in two other boys, so the young lad will have brothers to grow up with. Why do you ask?"

"Just wondering." Jennifer smiled sadly at the reverend but her heart was breaking as she imagined the life ahead for the boys.

"Now, about this child." He returned his attention to KC.

"Thank you for your offer, Reverend." Jesse lifted KC from her lap and placed the sleeping infant against her shoulder. "But I think we'd still like to try to find any family. If we can't..." She paused, looking at Jennifer to see the fear in her pale eyes. She was as attached to the small baby as she knew Jennifer was, but could they take on the responsibility of raising the tiny girl as their own? They were so young themselves, and just starting their own lives. "If we can't find any kin, we'll let you know." She stood. "If you'll excuse us, it's been a long day, and KC isn't the only one needing sleep."

"Of course." The reverend backed away as Jennifer rose and joined Jesse. "My church is just down the street. You can come by anytime. The doors are always open."

"Thank you, Reverend."

Jennifer followed Jesse from the room. She said nothing. She couldn't. The thought of leaving KC in Bannack cut her heart in half, and she knew if she tried to speak, she would not be able to control the emotions flowing through her.

That night the two women clung to each other as the object of their distress slept beside them.

THE NEXT MORNING, after finishing a quiet breakfast, Jesse and Jennifer made the steep climb up to the cemetery. The hotel clerk had told them the gravedigger lived at the foot of the trail and they stopped at his small cabin. Finding no one home, they decided to chance that he would be at the cemetery performing his duties.

The graveyard occupied the top of a knoll just behind the north side of town. The trail leading up to it was steep and rocky, and Jesse took care not to lose her footing while carrying KC. The path led to a gate in a sturdy wooden fence surrounding the obviously well cared for plot of land. Passing through the opening, the women could see a man working at the far end of the graveyard. Jesse and Jennifer walked to where the man was struggling to dig a fresh grave in the hard, rocky ground.

The man stopped his work to look at his visitors. "Morning." He leaned on his shovel, pulling a bandanna from his pant's pocket to wipe his brow. "Don't recall seeing you before. Visiting kin?" He regarded the numerous graves around them.

"Friend," Jesse replied. "Elizabeth Cassidy."

The man shoved the dirty bandanna back into his pocket. "Cassidy? Ain't that the missus got herself shot?"

"Yes." Jennifer nodded. "We were hoping you could point out her resting place."

"Sure, be glad to show you." The man dropped his shovel into the hole he had begun and walked to the western side of the graveyard. "She'd be right here." He stood beside a recently covered grave. "I thought she'd like a nice view of town and the hills."

"It's a lovely view. I'm sure she appreciates it."

From the site of the grave, the women had a panoramic view of the hills surrounding Bannack and Yankee Flats. And they had an excellent view of the streets of Bannack and the buildings lining them.

"Least I could do. Not many folks showed up for her burying. Don't know why not. She was a pleasant sort, always having a kind word. Not at all like her husband. I'm surprised someone hadn't plugged him 'fore now. Guess the hangman will take care of him, from what I hear."

"Can we arrange for a headstone?" Jesse ignored the comment, not wanting to voice her opinion of Stuart Cassidy.

"Stonemason's shop is behind the livery. Take a couple of weeks. You gonna be in town for long?"

"Another day or two."

"You go ahead and tell him what you want and I'll make sure it gets placed right. Nice lady like her deserves a stone."

"Thank you." Jesse pulled a bill from her pocket and handed it to the man. "We'd appreciate it if you'd keep care of her grave. It would mean a lot to a friend of ours."

The man took the offering, his eyes widening as he saw more money than he made in a month of digging graves. "I'd be might' proud to look after her. Yes, ma'am, might' proud." The man tucked the bill into his pocket. "I best be gettin' back to my digging. Like to get it done 'fore the sun gets too high. 'Spose you'd like to be spending some time alone with her."

"Thank you." Jennifer watched the man walk away.

Jesse reached out and placed her arm around Jennifer's waist. She didn't care what the gravedigger thought, she needed the closeness of her lover. And she knew Jennifer felt the same when the schoolteacher leaned against her.

"Poor woman," Jennifer sighed softly. "What are we going to tell Ed?"

"I'm more concerned in breaking the news to Bette Mae."

Tears filled Jennifer's eyes, overflowing down her cheeks.

As they paid their respects, Jesse noticed three men come out of Finney's saloon and mount horses tied to the hitching rail in front of the building. The men rode down the main street to the intersection with the north road, where they turned, their horses charging at full gallop up the grade past the livery and around the sweeping turn, circling the far end of the cemetery. They quickly disappeared over the hill behind the graveyard.

"Wonder where they're going in such a hurry." Jennifer placed her Stetson over KC's face to protect her from the dust cloud the horses kicked up.

"I wonder." Jesse absently watched another figure come out of the saloon and walk across the main street to disappear down the passage alongside Carpenter's store.

"Isn't that the sheriff?" Jennifer caught a glimpse of the man.

"Yep."

"Do you think he had anything to do with those riders?"

"Maybe."

"Jesse, what have we gotten into?"

"Not sure, darlin'." Jesse shifted the restless baby in her arms. "But let's try to stay as far away from it as we can."

"How are we going to do that?"

"By going down to that dress shop and buying you some pretty dresses." Jesse smiled at her lover. "Then we'll go see if we can find the schoolteacher and you two can talk the rest of the afternoon."

"Like you'd sit still for that." Jennifer laughed as they made their way amongst the graves and back to the gate.

"Yep, I surely will, darlin'. Me and KC here will sit nice and quiet." Jesse tickled the baby and received a baby chuckle in response. "'Course, we'll be sound asleep. But we'll be nice and quiet."

"Brat." Jennifer swatted Jesse.

As the women carefully picked their way back down the stony path, they observed the sheriff walking from his office to the livery. After a few minutes, he casually rode out of town towards Yankee Flats.

"Think he's going out to look for the Williams?" Jennifer asked as they reached the bottom of the path.

"Nope."

Surprised, Jennifer turned to Jesse. "Why not?"

"No saddle bags. Go out there and back is a three day ride. Isn't going to do that without taking some supplies. Probably just making a show of going. Then he'll come back and tell us the trail was too cold."

"What are we going to do?"

"Believe what he says."

"Jesse, are you sure about this?"

Jesse stopped and looked around to see if anyone was paying them any attention. But it was early morning; the streets were almost empty, as the miners and cowboys had other places to be. And the few people on the boardwalks were hurrying about their business, paying them no mind. "Darlin', we are in a town we don't know. We don't know the good folks from the bad. Let's just do what we came to do and get back to Sweetwater. We can tell Billie about the bandits and the sheriff and let him decide what to do. I don't want you or KC to get hurt because I guessed wrong. All right?"

Jennifer looked into her eyes and was shocked to see the fear in them. She couldn't conceive of Jesse being afraid of anything or anyone.

But she was afraid. She was afraid for her lover and she was afraid for the baby.

"I love you." Jennifer smiled, wordlessly agreeing to the rancher's plan.

"Love you too, darlin'." Jesse smiled back. "Now let's go buy you some pretty duds."

Jesse and Jennifer decided to visit the stonemason before going to the dressmaker, and walked past the livery to a small shack behind. Stones of various shapes and sizes littered the ground in front of the shack, many with engravings already started in their hard surfaces.

"Mornin'." A boy appearing to be no older than some of Jennifer's students came out of the shack.

"Good morning," Jennifer greeted him. "We're looking for the stonemason."

"That would be my pa. But he ain't here right now."

"When's the best time to talk to him? We want to arrange for a stone."

"I can do it. What kinda stone you lookin' for?"

Jesse started to say they'd wait until they could talk to the boy's father, then decided it probably wouldn't make much difference. "A headstone for a friend."

"Okay." The boy scrounged around for a paper and pencil.

"Write down the name you want on it," he instructed.

Jennifer took the items from the boy. "Elizabeth..."

"Granger," Jesse supplied.

Without comment, Jennifer wrote the name on the paper, then added "beloved sister and friend." Holding the paper up for Jesse to read, she smiled when Jesse nodded her agreement. She handed the paper back to the boy.

"And an angel. Put a nice angel above her name."

The boy read the paper. "Don't recall any Granger being buried lately. Don't know if'n I can locate a grave."

"She was buried last week. Name of Cassidy."

The boy looked at Jesse. "You ain't puttin' her man's name on the stone?"

"No." She shook her head. "No need for her to carry it where she's going."

"All right. Guess it don't much matter."

"How much?"

"Let's see." The boy counted out the letters on the paper. "Two bits a letter and with the angel will cost ya... Ten dollars, total."

Jesse handed the boy the money. "Let the gravedigger know when it's ready. He'll take care of it."

"All right." The boy stuck the money into his pocket. "Thanks." He grinned at the departing women.

JENNIFER STOPPED IN front of the dress shop, gazing pensively at the dress displayed in the glass window, a simple but beautiful wedding gown.

Jesse opened the shop's door and paused when Jennifer didn't follow. She looked to see what was holding the schoolteacher's attention. The look on her lover's face almost broke her heart. She thought for a minute, an idea beginning to take shape, and a smile flickered across her face as she made up her mind. "Jennifer? Coming?"

"Yes." Jennifer pulled her eyes away from the dress and joined Jesse.

Entering the shop, the women were addressed by a petite woman sewing precise stitches into a child's dress.

"Good morning, ladies. What can I do for you?"

"My sister needs some dresses. She's a schoolteacher and needs something fit to wear," Jesse proudly told the woman as Jennifer looked around at the dresses and other garments in the shop.

The dressmaker smiled and put down her work. "You look

familiar. Have we met before?"

"No, I don't believe we have," Jennifer replied. "I've only been in Bannack once before and that was only overnight for the stage."

"Oh." the woman brought a tape measure to where Jennifer stood. "Perhaps back east? My husband and I left there a short time ago."

"I'm sorry." Jennifer spoke calmly, but inside she was tied in knots. *What if this woman knew her father?* She frantically searched her memory for any hint that she had met the woman before. She could come up with nothing.

"Jennifer." Jesse picked up on her lover's distress. "Is something wrong?"

Turning to see the worry on the rancher's face, Jennifer hurried to assure her. "No, I'm fine." She smiled but her eyes reflected the uneasiness she was experiencing.

"Do you want to go back to the hotel?"

Not wanting to draw any more attention to herself by running out of the shop, Jennifer shook her head. "No, I'm fine. Really." She turned her attention back to the dressmaker. "Why don't you show me what you have?"

After measuring Jennifer and showing her several different designs and bolts of material, the dressmaker helped the schoolteacher settle on six dresses, each a different color and style. She would have happily settled for half as many, but Jesse insisted she have *a dress for every day of the week.*

Jesse sat with KC, offering her opinion when asked. The baby had intently watched Jennifer comparing bolts of cloth and dress patterns before tiring and falling asleep in the rancher's arms.

"If there is nothing else you'll be needing?" The dressmaker finished making notes on Jennifer's selections and looked up at the women now standing next to her desk.

"No," Jennifer began.

"Yes," Jesse said. "We'll take the dress in the window."

Jennifer looked confused. "But, Jesse, that's a wedding dress."

"I know." Jesse smiled at the schoolteacher.

"But—" Jennifer stopped. Could Jesse be saying... "Are you sure?"

"Very sure. That is," Jesse hesitated, worried Jennifer might not feel as she did. "I mean, if it's all right with you," she shyly said.

"Nothing would make me happier." Jennifer reached out, lovingly caressing Jesse's cheek.

"Um, excuse me." The dressmaker was uncomfortable. For

sisters, the women showed an unnatural closeness. "I would have to lengthen that dress for you."

Reminded of their present surroundings, Jennifer stepped away from the rancher as Jesse answered the dressmaker, "That's all right."

"It'll cost more." The dressmaker retrieved the dress from the window, a sharp edge in her tone.

Jesse picked up on the woman's mood change. "If you would rather we take our business somewhere else..." She left the rest of the comment hanging.

"No," the woman quickly assured the now-angry rancher. "Let me recheck your *sister's* measurements. It won't take much to let out the hem. She's a bit taller than most." The woman scrambled to regain her customers' good will.

"How long before the dresses are ready?"

"Three weeks. Maybe more."

"Make it two." Jesse didn't want Jennifer to have to wait any longer for the much-needed dresses. "We'll be in town another day and will take the wedding dress with us. You'll have to ship the rest to Sweetwater. If you need anything, we're staying at the Goodrich." She carefully passed the sleeping baby to Jennifer and pulled her wallet out. "How much do we owe you?" After paying for the dresses and the cost of having them shipped to Sweetwater, she led Jennifer from the shop.

As she pulled the door shut after bidding the women goodbye, the dressmaker's husband entered the shop from their living quarters in the back half of the building. He studied the two women walking past the shop's large front windows, his attention more on Jennifer.

"Isn't that Martin Kensington's daughter?"

"I knew she looked familiar. Called herself Branson and said they were sisters. But they were awfully close for sisters."

"What do you mean?" The man continued to watch from the window.

"Oh, it's nothing." The dressmaker decided it was really no concern of hers. After all, they had paid up-front for the dresses, unlike most of her customers, so who was she to question their relationship?

"Where'd they say they were from?"

"Sweetwater. Why?"

"Think I'll send Kensington a telegram."

"WHERE DID THE hotel clerk say the schoolteacher lived?" Jesse asked as they walked along the boardwalk.

"East end of town in a small cabin. But he said we might find her at the school."

Jesse walked beside Jennifer, who was carrying KC. The baby was snuggled into Jennifer's shoulder, her tiny eyes tracking the passing sights.

"I'll sure be glad to get back to Sweetwater." Jesse approached the old cabin that served as the school.

"Why's that?"

"Well for one thing, Sweetwater ain't so big. We could have walked the length of town, and back, half a dozen times by now. For another, Bannack is just too noisy." She had to raise her voice to be heard over the racket of a passing ore wagon. An unceasing parade of the noisy wagons clamored through town day and night. Jesse, Jennifer, and KC had all had trouble sleeping the night before.

"There's one more reason I'll be glad to get home," Jennifer added.

"What?"

Leaning close so only Jesse could hear, Jennifer whispered, "Because we can't touch one another. And I need your touch, sweetheart," she purred.

Jesse grinned at the smirking schoolteacher. "Darlin'," she purred right back, "your touch isn't all that I'm needing."

Jennifer blushed a deep shade of red.

The women had refrained from any physical activity to keep their true relationship hidden while in Bannack — and because of the thin walls between the hotel's rooms.

Jesse waited at the walk leading to the school building as Jennifer composed herself. When her lover brushed by, Jesse heard her growl, "I'll get you for that."

"Ah," she chuckled, "I'm definitely counting on it."

Pulling the door open, Jennifer entered the log building. From outside it had looked large, but she discovered the inside was smaller than her own schoolhouse. Jennifer surmised that the size of the logs used to build the cabin was the reason for the deception. Three rows of benches stretched the length of the building. A blackboard was nailed to the logs at the front of the room. On the back wall, a heat stove occupied one corner and in the other, a small desk sat. But the room was currently unoccupied.

"Guess we try to find her cabin." Jesse followed Jennifer out of the schoolhouse.

Continuing their walk on the boardwalk, the women passed a small restaurant. As they walked by the clean windows, a pretty Chinese woman working inside the building smiled at them.

"Jesse." Jennifer smiled back at the woman. "Have you ever eaten Chinese food?"

"Once or twice," the rancher replied. It was common for western towns to have a significant population of Chinese. Especially the mining and railroad camps.

"Did you like it?"

"Yep, it's pretty good."

The smells coming from inside the restaurant intrigued Jennifer as she walked beside Jesse, wanting desperately to hold her lover's hand but refraining from doing so. "Can we try it tonight?"

"Sure."

After reaching the last of the commercial buildings, they walked on to the private residences. A small log cabin sat back off the boardwalk, a dirt path leading to a covered porch. Sitting on the porch was a young woman, appearing to be not much older than the lovers themselves.

"Good morning," the woman stood. "Is there something I can help you with?"

Taking a chance that this was the woman they sought, Jennifer said, "I'm the schoolteacher in Sweetwater and I was hoping to talk with you.   That is, if you're not busy," she hastened to add.

"Another teacher. That's wonderful. Oh, what a beautiful baby."

"Thank you." Jennifer smiled at KC. "Her parents were killed by bandits. We're hoping to find someone who might know if she has any other family."

"Terrible." The woman shook her head. "It's a shame that Sheriff Logan can't find those men."

"We heard there's been several attacks," Jesse said.

"Yes. It's amazing, but the bandits always seem to know who is carrying valuables and who isn't. Travelers with nothing to steal are left alone. But have a gold nugget in your pocket when you leave Bannack or Virginia City, and, most likely, you won't get far."

Jennifer looked at Jesse; she could tell by the look on her lover's face that she was not happy with what they had just heard.

"My, look at my manners," the young woman chastised herself. "I haven't even asked your names. I'm Leevie Temple, and you are?"

"Jennifer Branson. And this is my sister, Jesse."

"Please to meet you both," the schoolteacher acknowledged Jesse. "I was just about to enjoy some cold lemonade. Would you join me?"

"Yes, we'd like that."

The woman reached up to tickle the baby, but KC buried her head against Jennifer's shoulder, refusing to look at the stranger.

"My, she seems to have taken a liking to you, hasn't she? Who did you say her parents were?"

"Kenneth and Catherine Williams. Came through Bannack three or four days ago."

"Driving a Conestoga and trailing a milk cow," Jesse added.

"Oh, yes. I remember them. Don't see too many of those this far off the Oregon Trail. Young couple from Wyoming, I believe."

"Did you talk with them?" Jennifer was ashamed that she was secretly hoping the local teacher would not have any knowledge about KC's family.

"Spoke with her a little when I saw the wagon in front of Carpenter's Mercantile one morning. She was sitting in it and I said 'good morning'. He must have been inside the store, never did see him. But I do know that Reverend Tobias spoke with them. Have you talked to him?"

"Yes," Jennifer sighed. "Unfortunately, he did not have good news." She referred to more than just the lack of information regarding KC's origins.

KC started to fuss and whimper. She was hungry.

"I'm sorry." Jennifer pulled a bottle of milk from the small bag Jesse was carrying.

"Don't you be apologizing. Just go ahead and feed her." Miss Temple offered the women chairs in the shade of the front porch. Jesse settled with KC and fed the baby while Jennifer engaged the woman in conversation.

As the schoolteacher talked, both Jesse and Jennifer were surprised to learn that, although she wasn't much older than Jesse, she had been teaching for almost five years. Jennifer was thrilled to be able to ask all the questions she had been storing up since taking on the teaching duties in Sweetwater. And Jesse smiled as her lover gleaned all the information she could from the more experienced teacher. It was late afternoon by the time both women had exhausted their subject and sat back in their chairs.

"I guess I can tell which of you is the talker," Miss Temple teased Jesse, who had barely said more then ten words all afternoon.

Jesse smiled and shrugged.

"Yes, but my *sister*," Jennifer emphasized the word, "has other talents that make up for it."

Jesse choked on the sip of lemonade she had just taken from her glass. KC looked up at the gagging woman, puzzled as to why her afternoon playmate was suddenly jerking about and turning red. Once Jesse regained her breath, she rose from the chair, anxious to leave before Jennifer could say any more.

Miss Temple ignored the rancher's extreme reaction to what should have been an innocent comment. "I can't tell you how much I've enjoyed this. It isn't often I get to talk with someone who understands the difficulty of teaching so many different levels of students at the same time."

"I'm happy to say my students in Sweetwater don't seem to cause me quite the challenges yours do. And they should cause me even less with the ideas you've given me. If you ever get to Sweetwater, you must come visit my school."

"I'd love the opportunity but I don't see me doing any traveling for a while. At least, not until the bandits are dealt with. And speaking of that, you be careful on your ride back."

"We will," Jennifer assured her.

"What will you do with KC?"

"We'll..." Jennifer stopped. "If we can't find any family, Reverend Tobias has offered to find her a home."

Jesse heard the heartbreak in Jennifer's words and knew exactly how she felt. She guided Jennifer away from the cabin.

"Seems to me that baby has already found a home," the woman murmured, watching the little family walk away.

JESSE AND JENNIFER returned to their hotel room. KC was tired, wet, and hungry, and the women saw to her needs.

"There you go, KC." Jennifer laid her in Jesse's arms. "You've got nice dry britches and a full belly. And I bet Jesse will sing you a lullaby if you promise to go to sleep."

Jesse smiled at KC as the baby snuggled against her chest. She started to sing in low, soothing tones and it wasn't long before KC was asleep. She placed the baby in the middle of the bed, carefully tucking a blanket around the small body.

"She should be out for a while." Jesse joined Jennifer standing by the room's window. Wrapping her arms around her lover, she nuzzled Jennifer's hair. "What's going on in this pretty head?"

"What makes you think anything is going on?" Jennifer leaned back into Jesse's embrace.

"You always get real quiet when you're bothered by something." Jesse tightened her hold. "Want to talk about it?"

Jennifer remained quiet, just enjoying the feel of Jesse

pressed against her. She could feel her body tingling wherever it touched Jesse's, and she wanted nothing more than to take the rancher to the bed and show her how much she loved her. "I'm not sure going into that dress shop was such a good idea."

"Why?"

The schoolteacher turned in her lover's arms so she could face the rancher. "I can't stop feeling something bad will come of it."

"Maybe you just remind her of someone," Jesse offered, remembering how upset Jennifer had become when the dressmaker mentioned the possibility that they had previously met.

"No, she definitely had seen or met me before. I just know it." Jennifer leaned against the rancher. "I just wish I could remember."

"I'm sure it's nothing." Jesse tightened her arms around the schoolteacher. "She'll forget about you as soon as she's done with your dresses."

"Jesse, about the wedding dress." Jennifer tilted her head up, looking into her lover's eyes.

"What about it?" Jesse tensed. Had Jennifer changed her mind? Was she upset over the crude proposal in the dress shop? "I know it wasn't too romantic the way I sort of sprung it on you. But I love you so much, darlin'. And I would be honored if you would like to, you know. I mean, that is, if you feel the same." The words tumbled out of Jesse.

Jennifer replied, "I love you too. It's just..." she hesitated. "I know things are different out here in the West, but will a church really marry us?"

Jesse looked into the blue eyes she adored. "Don't rightly know about that. But then Sweetwater doesn't have any churches. Mayor Perkins presides over marriages and funerals. So we just have to ask him to marry us. That is, if you want to," she added nervously.

Jennifer smiled at the woman she desperately loved. "Sweetheart, I would be very proud to be your wife."

Jesse dipped her head to place a tender kiss on Jennifer's lips.

When their lips parted, Jennifer asked, "But how do you know Mayor Perkins will do it?"

"Oh, he'll do it, all right. Mrs. Perkins will make sure of that."

Jennifer looked puzzled.

"She thinks we make a nice couple," Jesse explained.

"How do you know that?"

"She told me one day in Ed's store. And besides, Bette Mae will tan his hide good if he refuses."

Jennifer laughed. "All right, sweetheart. Then I think when we get back to Sweetwater we should announce that we're getting... How do you say it out West? Getting hitched."

Jesse pulled Jennifer tight, reclaiming the sweet lips of her soon-to-be wife.

JESSE CARRIED KC as she and Jennifer walked to the Chinese restaurant where the schoolteacher wanted to dine, Jennifer staying close to Jesse's side. It was early evening and the boardwalk was becoming crowded with miners and cowboys in town to sample the entertainment in the numerous gambling establishments and saloons. Luckily, the section of street where the restaurant was located was far enough away from the rougher area of town that the women didn't have much trouble with the growing throng of men.

The restaurant was located on the ground floor of a two-story wood plank building, a sign painted on the front of the building advertised rooms for rent on the top floor. As soon as Jesse pulled open the restaurant's door, the pretty woman they had seen earlier in the day welcomed them. She motioned the women inside. "Come in, please."

Jesse and Jennifer were led to a table near the front window and a hot pot of tea was quickly placed on the table with two small cups for drinking. Having sampled Chinese cooking before, Jesse ordered for both women and they were left alone to enjoy the tea.

KC tried to reach for Jesse's cup but her hand was gently captured in a much larger one.

"Uh-uh," Jesse cautioned the baby. "That's too hot for you. What say you play with this instead?" She pulled a small toy horse from her shirt pocket and handed it to the baby.

KC took hold of the toy, studying it before lifting it to her mouth to chew on it.

"Where'd you get that?" Jennifer motioned to the toy.

"When I went to check on Dusty and Blaze this afternoon, saw it in the window of the candy store. Figured she might like something to play with besides her toes." Jesse watched as the baby waved the slobber-covered horse around.

"Seems she likes it." Jennifer smiled.

Their meals were brought to them and Jesse grinned as the schoolteacher entertained her with much ooh-ing and ah-ing over the exotic food.

When her plate was empty, Jennifer pushed it away. "That was delicious," she told the woman who came to clear their table.

"I pleased you like," the woman said in broken English. "You like more?"

"Oh, no thank you." Jennifer shook her head. "I couldn't eat another bite. But I would like more tea."

The woman nodded and left to refill the empty pot. Coming quickly back, she refilled Jennifer's cup before placing the pot on the table. The woman glanced around the small dining room, and seemed relieved. Jennifer looked around as well, and realized that all the diners were Chinese except Jesse and herself. Was that what the waitress had noticed?

The woman whispered, "You be very careful. Sheriff is very bad."

Jennifer looked at Jesse and saw that she had also heard the woman's words. "Why do you say that?"

"He sends bandits to hurt people. You not trust."

Everything was starting to make sense. Why the sheriff had not been surprised when told of the bandits' activities. Why he was so interested in any valuables that travelers might be carrying. Why he had come out of Finney's saloon right after the men who had left town so quickly.

"If you know this, why doesn't the town do something about him?"

"They don't want to believe. Many die. Baby's parents died. They talked to sheriff before leave town and now they dead. If you trust sheriff, you die."

A man standing in the doorway of the kitchen called to the woman, speaking in a language Jesse and Jennifer couldn't understand. The woman nodded rapidly at the man before turning back to the women. "I glad you enjoy. Four bits, please."

Jesse handed the woman the money. "Thank you."

Before the woman returned to the kitchen, she again whispered, "Be careful. No trust sheriff."

Jesse and Jennifer made their way back to the hotel. Neither spoke. Both women wanted nothing more than to leave Bannack behind them. Far behind them.

Entering the Goodrich Hotel's lobby, they were immediately greeted by the friendly desk clerk. "Evening, ladies. Sheriff Logan was in earlier looking for you."

Jennifer instinctively reached out and grabbed Jesse's hand.

Jesse gently squeezed it while she asked the clerk. "Did he say what he wanted?"

"No. Word is there was another attack today."

"Where?"

"North road. Wagon coming from Virginia City. Some say it was carrying the payroll for one of the mines."

"Thanks." Jesse led Jennifer upstairs.

Once the room's door was securely closed behind them, Jennifer turned to face her lover. "Jesse, let's go home. There's really no reason for us to say here any longer. Who knows what that sheriff wants with us. Let's just go home."

Jesse placed the baby on the bed so she could hug and reassure her upset lover. "We'll go home, darlin'. But tomorrow, we have to finish our business here. We'll go the next day, I promise. I'm sure Logan wants nothin' more than to tell us he tried but couldn't find anything. Even though he probably just went for a ride and came back."

Jennifer leaned into Jesse's embrace. "All right. One more day."

Jesse glanced at the saddlebags that had been neatly tucked in the corner of the room. To a casual observer, they appeared to be untouched, but she knew better. She wondered what the sheriff had thought when he discovered no valuables in the bags. She had been carrying their money and, except for her weapons, the bags contained only spare clothes and items for the care of KC. "Tell you what, tomorrow we'll ask around town to see if anyone else might have talked to the Williams and learn what we can. We'll stop by the dress shop and get your wedding dress. Then we'll go to bed early so we can leave at daybreak. How's that sound?"

"Sounds good." Jennifer didn't sound convinced. "Jesse, what if we don't find out any more about KC's family? We're not going to leave her with the Reverend, are we?"

"Darlin'," Jesse sighed, "I don't want to any more than you do. But can we take care of a baby? I mean, we're barely old enough to have one of our own. And we've got the Slipper to run and the ranch. And you've got your teaching. I don't think it would be very good for her, do you?"

"She'd be loved, Jesse. Isn't that all that's important?" Jennifer cried, tears streaming down her face. "Please, Jesse. My heart would break if we left her behind."

Jesse felt the same. The tiny baby had taken a firm hold on Jesse's heart and she could no more bear the thought of leaving her than Jennifer could. A baby. A little girl. *Their* little girl. She would finally have her family. *Well it really isn't that bad of an idea, is it?* "All right, darlin'." Jesse hugged Jennifer tight. "We'll keep her. Doesn't seem likely she's got any other kin." As she spoke the words, a huge weight lifted from her heart.

Jennifer sobbed in Jesse's arms. "Thank you."

Later that night, the women lay in bed with KC sleeping on Jesse's chest.

"If we're not going to leave her here, do we have to stay another day? I'd really like to get home, Jesse."

"Fair enough," Jesse agreed; she was also ready to get back to their home. "We'll leave right after we pick up your dress."

"Jesse," the schoolteacher snuggled close to the rancher, "I love you."

"I love you too, darlin'. And I love you, KC," Jesse spoke the words that both women had been carefully avoiding the past few days.

"I love you, KC," Jennifer happily repeated.

Chapter
Nine

JESSE AND JENNIFER woke early and, while KC continued to sleep, quietly prepared to leave Bannack. Saddlebags were packed neatly with their belongings, and Jennifer hummed softly as she carefully folded the infant's clothing. She hadn't expected to be taking the items with them and now that they had decided to keep KC, she bubbled with delight. Even Jesse seemed to move about the room with a lighter step.

"What's the plan, sweetheart?" Jennifer removed her nightshirt and tucked it into the saddlebag.

Jesse stopped in the process of pulling on her boots to observe her disrobed lover and soon-to-be wife. *Oh, will I be happy to put Bannack behind us.* She felt her body respond to Jennifer's nakedness. She said nothing, satisfied to simply watch Jennifer dress.

"Sweetheart?" Jennifer turned when she received no response. "Is something wrong?"

"Nope, darlin'. I was just enjoying the view."

Jennifer smiled. She loved it when Jesse looked at her in that way, for she knew the rancher wanted her in the same way she wanted the rancher. *Oh, will I be ever so glad to get out of Bannack.*

"Figured we might as well eat here," Jesse said once Jennifer's body was covered. "Then we'll go get Dusty and Blaze, and KC's cow. We'll find the Reverend and let him know we're keeping KC with us in case any of her kin show up. Then we just need to pick up your dress on the way out of town."

"What about the sheriff?" Jennifer asked, remembering the sheriff had come looking for them the previous evening.

"What about him?" Jesse finished with her boots and stood from the room's only chair so that Jennifer could use it. "If he wants to talk to us, he can come and find us. Otherwise, we leave town without talking to him. He's not going to tell us anything we want to hear anyway."

"Okay." Jennifer picked up her boots and carried them to

the chair. "Why do you think the town doesn't do something about him?"

"Don't know, darlin'." Jesse tied the flaps on the saddlebags, making sure they were secure. "Maybe they don't think they can. Or maybe they just haven't got a gutful of him yet."

"Think they ever will?" Jennifer tugged her pant legs over the top of her boots.

"Eventually." Jesse placed the saddlebags by the bed. She looked around the room to make sure they weren't forgetting anything.

"Sad to think how many more people will fall victim to the sheriff before they do." Jennifer walked to where Jesse stood, wrapping her arms around her.

Jesse twisted in her arms to be able to return the hug.

As the women stood content in each other's embrace, KC stirred. The women watched as the tiny child that was now so much a part of their lives opened her eyes, looking around until she spotted them. As soon as KC's eyes settled on the women, a smile spread across the baby's face and little arms reached out.

"Morning, sunshine," Jesse greeted the baby. "Let me guess, you need dry britches and you're hungry."

Jennifer laughed as she sat on the bed, tickling the baby's tummy. KC rolled over onto her stomach and pushed herself up on her hands and knees. She rocked for a few moments in the position before falling face first back to the bed.

"I think you need a little more practice on that." Jennifer rolled the annoyed baby over and kissed her tenderly on the forehead. "Let's get you changed and cleaned up. I'm starving."

"After all you ate last night?" Jesse filled the water bowl from the pot she had been warming on the room's stove. She soaked a cloth in the warm water.

"Yep." Jennifer removed the soiled diaper from the baby and accepted the damp cloth from Jesse. The naked baby shivered in the morning coolness. Jennifer quickly washed KC and dressed her in clean clothes.

Jesse sat on the bed next to her with a bottle of milk. "Here you go sunshine." She offered the bottle to the baby as Jennifer placed KC in her arms. It didn't take long for KC to start sucking down the bottle's contents.

"Looks like we've got another milk drinker in the family," Jennifer chuckled, knowing that Jesse's favorite beverage was a cold glass of milk.

"Family, huh." Jesse pondered the concept as she watched the baby drink.

Jennifer wrapped an arm around Jesse. "Family," she repeated.

Jesse turned to look at her fiancée. "Kinda has a nice ring to it, doesn't it?"

Jennifer smiled. "It sure does." She leaned her head against Jesse's and they watched the baby watching them.

BREAKFAST WAS A quiet affair as Jesse and Jennifer ate quickly, both wanting to leave Bannack as soon as possible. KC seemed to sense their mood and calmly sat propped in Jesse's lap happily playing with her toy horse.

"Ready?"

"You bet." Finishing the last of her coffee, Jennifer pushed away from the table and stood. "I want to check her britches before we go."

"All right. Why don't you do that and I'll settle up with the clerk, then meet you up in the room." Jesse followed Jennifer from the hotel's dining room.

"Okay."

Jennifer carried KC upstairs to their room. She inserted the key into the door, swinging it open so she could carry the baby inside and placed her on the bed.

KC looked around for her tall playmate, frowning when she couldn't locate her. She started to whimper and reach out for the missing woman.

"It's all right, sweetie." Jennifer tickled the unhappy baby. "Your mommy is downstairs." She paused hearing her description of Jesse. It was true, wasn't it? They were going to be KC's mothers. The enormity hit Jennifer and she dropped on the bed like a ton of bricks were on her shoulders.

A baby. *Their* baby. Were they really ready for that responsibility? "Momma." She took a deep breath and blew it out slowly. Then she took another. "Momma." Jennifer smiled as she repeated the word. It sounded good.

KC looked up at the woman and reached for her. When Jennifer picked her up, the baby wrapped her arms around Jennifer's neck, holding tight.

"Think I'll make you a good momma?"

"I think you'll make a wonderful mother." Jesse stood in the doorway. She walked over and sat next to Jennifer. "Everything all right?"

"Everything is fine. It just dawned on me, the responsibility we're taking on with KC." Jennifer rubbed light circles around the baby's back as KC snuggled into her touch. "Guess you could say we were having our first mother-daughter conversation."

Jesse draped an arm over Jennifer's shoulders. "You know, it's not too late..."

"No." Jennifer shook her head, stopping Jesse from finishing her thought. "I want to keep her, sweetheart. It's just I never really appreciated what that meant until now. Guess it was when I said 'momma' that it really hit me. She's going to count on us to be her mommas. That's a lot to take on."

"Darlin'." Jesse took Jennifer's hand into her own. "I don't want you to do this unless you really want to."

Jennifer turned to look into Jesse's eyes; she saw concern and more. Much more. Love. She saw the depth of Jesse's love for her and she knew that Jesse could see her love reflected back.

"Sweetheart," Jennifer smiled at her lover, "let's take our daughter home."

Jesse nodded. "I'd like that." She glanced over her shoulder, making sure the room's door was shut before claiming Jennifer's lips in a tender kiss.

IT DIDN'T TAKE long for the women to retrieve Dusty and Blaze from the livery. With the milk cow trailing behind they rode to Reverend Tobias' church.

The reverend was opening the large wooden doors to the building as the women rode up. "Ah, good morning, ladies," the reverend greeted them. "Looks like you're leaving town." He walked down the building's steps to stand on the boardwalk. "Guess that means you'll be leaving the child with me. I talked to a nice couple just yesterday that are looking for a daughter."

"Sorry, Reverend," Jesse cut the man off. "We've decided to keep KC with us. If any of her family makes inquiries, you can have them contact us in Sweetwater."

"Miss Branson," the reverend sputtered. "You can't expect to arrive back in Sweetwater with a child you know nothing about and expect your sister's intended to provide for it." Word had obviously spread about the women's purchase of a wedding dress. "A child needs to be raised in a decent home with both a loving mother and *father*."

"Don't worry, Reverend." Jennifer readjusted the restless baby in her arms. "KC will be raised with all the love she'll need. As for a loving father, mine didn't hold much in that."

"We thank you for your concern, Reverend, but KC is going home with us. Come on, Jennifer." Jesse turned Dusty back to the street.

"I must protest," the reverend called after them.

Jennifer sadly shook her head at the angry man. "You can protest all you want. But KC is not going to grow up in a home where she is no better thought of than the family mule." With that, she turned Blaze to follow Dusty, leaving a still-sputtering reverend on the boardwalk.

The women had not ridden fifty feet when they heard someone calling to them. Looking to the opposite side of the street, they spied Leevie Temple standing on the small porch of her cabin. As the women rode over, she walked to meet them.

"You're leaving?"

"Yes."

"From the look of the reverend over there, I'd say you decided to keep KC with you."

"If you hear from any of her kin, please let them know where we are."

"I'll do that, but I doubt if we will. There are too many children without any family in the mining camps for anyone to take notice of one more. It's a real shame, but what can you do?" The schoolteacher had seen her share of orphans and abandoned children to know that most were never sought even if they did have family living. "Besides, I'd say that KC is one lucky little girl to grow up with two loving mothers." The schoolteacher winked at the women. "You take care of each other. You have something special, don't lose it."

Jennifer was speechless. Could this woman know their true relationship?

Jesse reached down and offered her hand to the schoolteacher, who instantly took it. "Thank you. I promise, I'll take care of them both." As she sat back up in the saddle, she added, "You come visit us in Sweetwater anytime you like. We'd be glad to have you."

"I'll keep that in mind. Be careful, those bandits are still out there." The schoolteacher waved as Jesse nudged Dusty down the street, Blaze following.

"We will. Goodbye." Jennifer waved back. "Thank you."

Blaze walked up alongside Dusty.

"Jesse, do you think she knows about us?"

"Seems so."

"How?"

"Don't know. Maybe she sensed it."

"You think maybe she's like us?"

"Could be." Jesse smiled at her lover. "We can't be the only ones."

"No, I guess we can't," Jennifer smirked. "At least I hope not. Think how much the others are missing."

Jesse playfully shook her head at her lover.

The laughing women stopped in front of the dress shop.

"Stay here. I won't be long." Jesse swung down from the saddle.

When she entered the shop, Jesse was surprised to see a man standing inside the shop staring intently at Jennifer outside. His interest in her lover made Jesse more than a little apprehensive.

"Good morning." The dressmaker reached for a neatly tied package on a shelf. "I have your sister's dress right here. I must say that she'll make a beautiful bride. Who's the lucky man?"

Jesse turned to the woman and took the package, but refused to answer the question. "You'll send the rest as agreed?"

"Oh, yes. Two weeks, as you requested."

Jesse turned to leave. The man watching Jennifer had moved to the back of the shop; he no longer was paying any attention to Jennifer and Jesse tried to shrug off her uneasy feeling as she left the shop.

Once Jesse was outside, the man returned to stand by the window and watched as she placed the package into one of the saddlebags. "That's definitely Kensington's daughter."

"What do you think he'll do when he receives your telegram?"

"Who knows? Probably come out here and drag her home." He turned away from the window as the women rode off.

The dressmaker's eyes followed the women as they rode away. "I think he'll have a fight on his hands if he tries."

"From her 'sister'?"

"No. From her."

"What makes you say that?"

"She's got something worth fighting for," the woman informed her husband, who looked at her, puzzled, before wandering to the back of the shop.

Outside on the street, Dusty and Blaze were walking past Carpenter's Mercantile. Sheriff Logan stepped off the boardwalk and into the street. He reached out for Dusty's reins but the mare snorted and pulled her head away.

"Something we can do for you, Sheriff?" Jesse settled Dusty down.

"Leaving town?" Giving up on grabbing the uncooperative horse's reins, the sheriff leaned against the horse hitch in front of the store.

"Looks that way." She pushed her Stetson back on her head.

"I was looking for you last night. Did Jackson tell you?"

"Yes, he told us."

"Aren't you interested in why?"

"Not particularly. But I have the feeling you're going to insist on telling us." She leaned nonchalantly back in her saddle. Not trusting the sheriff, she casually dropped a hand until it was within easy reach of her rifle.

Logan laughed, but there was no humor in it. "You interested in what I found yesterday?"

"Do tell."

He looked hard at Jesse before answering. "Ain't no point in telling if you're not interested." He decided to try a different tack with the women. "Asked you to stop by before you left town."

"Had no reason to, we're not carrying anything of value unless you count my sister's wedding dress."

The sheriff looked at Jennifer who was sitting quietly, allowing Jesse to do the talking for the pair.

"Word is, you've been spending pretty freely since you hit town. You sure you aren't taking any back with you?"

"No secrets in your town, are there, sheriff?" Jesse asked, not expecting an answer. "If you know we've been spending freely, as you put it, then you know we're tapped out. That's why we're going home."

"Takin' the young 'un with you, I see. Reverend Tobias okay with that?"

Jesse smiled at the man, but her eyes held no amusement as they bored into the sheriff. She was tired of this conversation, tired of this man. "Wasn't up to the Reverend. Now if you've finished with your questions, we'd like to get moving."

"Best you keep a sharp lookout, the bandits may still be in the Big Hole," the sheriff warned, his voice edged with more menace than necessary.

"Maybe you'd do better out looking for them than bothering two women and a baby." Jesse flicked Dusty's reins. The big mare snorted before moving away from the sheriff.

"Don't say I didn't warn you," he called after the women as they moved off.

"Don't worry, Sheriff, we'll be looking out for you," Jesse muttered in a voice too low for the sheriff to hear. She nudged Dusty into a trot, and Blaze immediately matched her pace. Even the horses seemed to feel that they couldn't be out of Bannack soon enough.

The women didn't notice the three pairs of eyes following their progress from within Finney's saloon. After they had passed from sight, Logan walked across the street and entered the saloon.

"We going after them?"

"Yes. Give 'em a couple hours lead." Logan threw a coin on the bar's surface and received a glass of whiskey in return.

"What are they carrying?"

"Nothing."

"Nothing? Then why bother?"

"I don't trust 'em. If they go back and say something to the sheriff in Sweetwater, we might as well pack up and move on. You know there's already talk in Virginia City of vigilantes forming a posse to put an end to the road bandits."

"So what do you want us to do?"

"Kill 'em. And make sure you get the brat this time. I don't want it showing up again and people askin' questions." He slammed his empty glass on the table and stormed out of the saloon.

"I don't know, boys. Killin' babies ain't what I signed on for."

"If you can't stomach this, I can take care of that right now." One of the men pulled a pistol from his holster and placed it on the table, its barrel pointing at the reluctant man.

"Didn't say I won't do it. Just said I didn't like it."

"You can stay here if'n you ain't willing to hold up your end. We'll tell Logan you chickened out."

"Hell, he'd shoot me 'fore I could leave town."

"Your choice. Make it."

"Shit. I'll go get the horses."

DUSTY AND BLAZE trotted comfortably as Jesse and Jennifer rode in silence, the baby asleep in the sling resting on Jennifer's shoulders. Jesse turned the horses northwest into the Big Hole valley and away from the mining camps; they would ride a more direct route back to the mountain pass and cut a full day's ride off their return journey. The sooner they were back in Sweetwater, the happier the women would be.

Around mid-day, KC woke, hungry and out of sorts due to being confined in the sling. Jennifer tried to calm the unhappy baby, but she would have none of it.

"I think we need to stop."

"All right, let's head for those trees. It'll be cooler there." Jesse turned Dusty toward a small stand of cottonwoods not too far off their route.

Jennifer turned Blaze to follow.

The horses had covered half the distance to the trees when a shot shattered the stillness. Jesse turned just in time to see Jennifer knocked from her saddle; she hit the ground hard and lay still.

"No!" Jesse screamed. Pulling her rifle from the scabbard, she turned to fire in the direction the shot had come from. As soon as her last bullet was fired, she hit the ground running. She covered the short distance to Jennifer's prone body, diving to the ground next to it.

Jennifer was lying on her back, the baby still tucked securely in the sling. As soon as KC saw Jesse, she let out a wail.

"It's okay, sunshine. It's okay," she whispered, trying to calm the baby and hoping that her words were true. Jesse tried to find Jennifer's injury, but with the struggling baby, it was impossible. Having no other option, she gently pulled the baby free. "Please, KC, I need you to be quiet," she begged the crying child.

Panicked by the fall and Jesse's obvious concern, the baby continued to wail. Holding the child in one arm, Jesse examined Jennifer with her other hand. She was relieved to find no bullet wounds. "It's okay," Jesse told herself as well as the baby. "She just had the breath knocked out of her when she hit the ground."

Knowing her lover was not seriously injured, Jesse's concern switched back to whoever had fired the shot. She laid the crying baby next to Jennifer. "You stay right here and keep an eye on your momma." She placed a kiss on the baby's forehead. "I'm going to take care of whoever is shooting at us."

By chance, Jennifer had fallen into a small depression. It wasn't much, but it did provide some protection from the gunmen's bullets. Jesse carefully crawled to the side of the hollow and raised her head just enough to peer over the top of its shallow side. Dusty and Blaze stood between her and the cluster of trees the shot had come out of.

Being careful to keep the horses between her and the unseen gunmen, Jesse quickly pulled the saddlebags with her extra ammunition from Dusty, dropping them into the depression. "Go on, find somewhere safe, but don't go too far."

Dusty raised her head and whinnied before taking off at a gallop, Blaze on her heels. The milk cow, still tied to Dusty's saddle horn, struggled to keep up with the racing horses.

As soon as Dusty took off, Jesse leaped back into the protection of the small depression.

HIDDEN IN THE stand of cottonwoods, the three bandits waited. They had kept to the backside of hills as they followed the women, and ridden in gulches and ravines to keep themselves out of sight. The men had managed to get in front of the women and made their way to a small stand of cottonwoods next to a small creek. They waited in the shade of the large trees, watching as the women turned their horses toward the cottonwoods.

"They're headed straight this way."

"Good. Let them get good and close, then shoot. Make your shots count, remember what Logan said. He wants them dead. *All* of them."

"I ain't shootin' no kid." An outlaw muttered to himself, moving slightly away from the other two.

As the women neared the stand of trees, the first gunman got antsy and fired. His shot went wide, but one of the horses reared, throwing its rider to the ground. The other rider pulled a rifle and fired several shots at the trees, forcing the men to seek cover behind the thick trunks.

"You fool. Now they know we're here."

"So what? What can a couple of women and a kid do to us?" the man who had fired shouted back.

"I guess we're about to find out."

"Look! One of them is standing behind the horses." The gunman took aim at the closest horse. But before he could fire, the rifle was knocked from his hands.

"Don't shoot the animals. If they ain't got nothin' on 'em, we can at least sell the horses and make some money out of this."

As the gunman bent to pick up his rifle, the horses took off at a gallop. He straightened and watched the horses disappeared over a rise. "How you gonna sell them now?" He glared at the other man, disgusted.

The third gunman fired at the woman, but it was too late as she had already dived back to safety.

JESSE HIT THE ground and rolled. A bullet screamed overhead, burying itself in the dirt about five feet beyond the depression. Her roll came to a stop next to Jennifer and KC.

Scared by all the events happening around her and by the lack of response from the woman she lay beside, KC was crying loudly. Careful to keep her head below the level of the depression's sides, Jesse placed a loving hand on the baby's tear-soaked face. "It's okay, sunshine. It's okay."

With her other hand, Jesse pulled the saddlebags close. She untied the flap of one and reached in for the box of rifle cartridges it carried. Pulling the box out, she quickly reloaded her rifle.

"Ugh," Jennifer groaned as she regained consciousness.

Jesse turned to the sound. "Jennifer," her voice was thick with concern. "Darlin', can you hear me?"

"Yeah." A shaky reply. "What happened?"

"You got thrown off Blaze and landed hard. Knocked the breath out of you." Jesse filled her shirt pockets with the rest of the bullets.

Hearing the baby's wails, Jennifer immediately became concerned. "KC?"

"She's fine, just scared."

Jennifer started to sit up.

"Whoa." Jesse gently held her down. "Keep down."

Jennifer looked around and saw that they were in the bottom of a shallow hollow. She rolled onto her side to pull the wailing baby into her protective arms.

"Try to get her to quiet down." Jesse crawled to the depression's edge.

Jennifer spoke soothingly to the baby and rocked her as best she could in the prone position she was forced to remain in. "What's going on, Jesse?"

"We were ambushed. They're hiding in that stand of trees we were heading for." Jesse carefully lifted her head only high enough out to steady her rifle on the depression's rim and take aim on the trees.

"Logan's men?"

"Probably." Jesse could see movement in the trees, but couldn't get a clear shot at any of the gunmen. She waited patiently.

"If they're in those trees, why didn't they wait until we rode closer?"

"Don't know. But I'm sure glad they didn't."

KC had stopped crying and was clinging to Jennifer. "It's okay, sweetie, Mommy will take care of us." Jennifer gently rubbed the infant's back.

Jesse heard the words and her heart swelled. Jennifer's faith in her under the circumstances was all it took to fill her eyes with tears. It made her realize how much Jennifer, and now KC, meant to her. She knew that with Jennifer's trust spurring her on, she'd find a way to get her family home safely. She blinked the tears away; now was not the time, the safety of her family required clear vision.

As her eyes dried, Jesse saw a man step out from behind a tree. She took aim and squeezed the trigger.

THE BANDITS HAD been watching the ground where the women were holed up. After several minutes with no movement, one gunman decided to get a closer look. He started to inch his way from behind the cottonwood tree where he had been hiding.

"Stay where you are," another of the gunmen commanded.

"Why? They're obviously hurt or dead, or they'd be doing something. Listen. The kid quit crying."

The first gunman stepped clear of the protective tree. Before he could take another step, a shot rang out. He stood a moment longer before slowly collapsing backwards, coming to rest on his back. Blood oozed out of a hole in his forehead.

"Damn. Logan didn't say they could shoot like that."

"Logan didn't say a lot of things."

The bandits began firing at the women's hiding spot.

AFTER SEEING THE man fall, Jesse ducked back down and covered Jennifer and KC with her body. Seconds later, the ground around the depression came alive with bullets striking the earth. When the firing stopped, Jesse rolled off and crawled back to where she could watch the trees shielding the bandits.

KC started to whimper again, her arms and legs flaying and kicking. Jennifer tightened her hold on the frightened child. She reached into one of the saddlebags and pulled out a bottle they had filled before leaving Bannack. Fortunately, the bottle had not broken when Jesse dropped the bags into the depression. Rolling on her side, so the baby could lay flat beside her, she offered the bottle to KC, who accepted it and sucked hungrily.

"That's my girl." Jennifer smiled down at the baby before turning her attention to the rancher. "Jesse, how many are there?"

Jesse eyes constantly scanned the trees for movement. "One less than there was before."

"You mean one left?" Jennifer hated not being able to see what was happening.

"Not quite. How's KC?"

"Scared. But she took a bottle, so that's a good sign." Jennifer gently stroked the baby's cheek as she drank.

"How about you?"

"I'm scared, too."

"Yeah, guess that makes three of us." Jesse wiped her sweating hands on her shirt. "Don't worry, darlin', we'll get out of this."

"Jesse, is there anything I can do? Just lying here is starting to drive me crazy."

"You are doing something. You're taking care of our daughter." Jesse took a moment to smile at her lover.

Jennifer smiled back.

"WHAT DO WE do now?" One of the two remaining gunmen looked over at his companion.

"We wait them out. Come dark, we'll move in closer and take care of them."

Not happy with the answer but not having any real choice, the other gunman looked around for a more comfortable place to wait. He was about to move to a small stump near the creek when the other man stepped away from his hiding spot to claim the stump. Just as the man reached the broken tree, a shot took his leg out from under him. Before he hit the ground, a second shot slammed into his shoulder, the bullet exploding out his back.

Frozen in place, the third bandit watched as the gunman fell.

"Shit," was all the wounded man could manage.

JESSE SAW THE MAN step from his hiding place and move deeper into the shadows of the trees. Probably thinking he was out of her range, he didn't count on the determination of a woman protecting her family. She took careful aim and squeezed off two shots, one right after the other. She watched the man fall and was satisfied with her aim when the man did not get back up.

Jennifer jumped at the sound of the rifle blasts. "Jesse?"

"It's okay. Now they're two short." She reached into her pocket, removing bullets to reload the rifle.

"Did you kill him?" Jennifer wasn't sure how she felt about that possibility.

"Sure hope so." Jesse resumed her vigil.

The sound of horses running reached her ears before Jesse saw the solitary rider leaving the stand of trees. He rode away from the women at full gallop with two riderless horses chasing behind. Jesse watched until the man disappeared from sight.

"Stay here. The pistols are in the saddlebags. Get them out and use them if you have to."

Jennifer reached out and grabbed Jesse's boot before she could leave the depression. "Jesse, where are you going?" The fear in Jennifer's voice stopped the rancher.

"I think they've gone. I'm going to check it out."

"Jesse, please don't go." Tears filled Jennifer's eyes and flowed down her cheeks.

Jesse reached down and took Jennifer's hand in her own. "I have to."

"Come back to me." Jennifer refused to release her lover's hand.

"I promise." Jesse smiled at the schoolteacher. "I love you too much to leave you now." With that, she disappeared from the depression.

Jennifer clutched the baby to her. "Your mommy better come back." She pulled a pistol from the saddlebag. "Because if she doesn't, I don't think I can go on without her." Her throat was so choked with emotion that Jennifer barely managed to force the words out. Slowly she edged her way to the rim of the depression so that she could keep an eye on Jesse.

THE DYING BANDIT groaned. He had fallen with half his frame in the creek and the cold water was quickly freezing his already numb body. The bullets had done major damage to his leg and shoulder and the water flowed red with his blood.

The other bandit stood rooted in place, watching his comrade's life slowly ebbing away. He could only think of how much he did not want to suffer the same fate. Ignoring the fallen man's calls for assistance, he cautiously eased his way to where their horses were tied.

"You can't leave me," the injured man begged, watching the other bandit mount his horse.

"Like you said at Finney's, it's my choice," the man grabbed the reins of the horses, "and I'm making it."

Spurring his horse, the bandit left the protection of the trees and rode as fast as he could away from the women and the comrade cursing his name. He would not return to Bannack to face the sheriff, but would ride to the mining camps in the mountains to the northeast where he could sell the horses. They should get him enough money to get out of the territory. He figured his days in Montana were numbered; he just didn't know how true that was.

"Come back here, you bastard," the gunman called weakly. Loss of blood and the cold water were draining his strength. He tried to pull himself out of the water, but the pain in his shoulder prevented him from moving. As he struggled, he became aware of someone standing near him. Turning his head, he saw a woman cradling a rifle in her arms. "Help me."

"Why should I? Seems you got what was coming to you." Jesse's voice was hard and her expression held no sympathy for the man who had attempted to kill her and her family.

Assuring herself that there were no other gunmen hiding in the trees, Jesse turned to go back to where Jennifer and KC waited.

"You can't leave me." The man's voice was so weak it could

barely be heard.

Jesse turned back to the man. "Seems your friends left you. So why shouldn't I?"

"Please. At least finish it," the bandit begged.

Jesse studied the man for a moment before responding. "You're already finished." She turned away and walked back to her family.

"Damn you, Logan," the man swore with his last breath.

Before she left the shadows of the trees, the bandit was dead.

"ARE THEY GONE?" Jennifer asked as soon as Jesse returned to the depression.

"Yes." Jesse wasn't about to tell the schoolteacher of the two bodies left in the trees. "You okay?" She opened her arms to the woman she loved.

Jennifer rushed into the embrace and the women held on to each other.

When KC started to whimper, Jesse bent down and lifted the baby into her arms. KC's arms encircled Jesse's neck while Jennifer's encircled her waist.

After several minutes, Jesse hooked a finger under Jennifer's chin and lifted her face. She leaned forward and kissed her. Jennifer returned the kiss and the women reassured each other of their love.

"Let's go home," Jesse whispered when their lips broke apart. She whistled for Dusty and Blaze. Moments later, the mares trotted up with the milk cow. She placed the saddlebags back onto the horses while Jennifer prepared the baby for travel.

When Jennifer went to mount Blaze, she found her saddle full of Jesse's saddlebags and their packs. She looked quizzically at the rancher.

"Maybe you'd like to ride with me for a while." Jesse gently lifted the baby from Jennifer's arms.

Smiling, Jennifer pulled herself up onto Dusty and took the baby back when Jesse held her up.

Jesse swung up in the saddle. Holding the reins in one hand, she wrapped her other arm around Jennifer and KC.

Jennifer leaned back against Jesse's chest.

Without any encouragement from Jesse, Dusty started to carry her family home.

SHERIFF LOGAN STOOD next to the bar in Finney's saloon.

"They're not coming back." The bartender used a dirty rag to wipe the bar's surface. "I told you killin' women and children would be trouble."

"Shut up." The sheriff slammed a fist down on the bar. "Give me some whiskey."

Finney poured a glass and set it on the bar before the sheriff, placing the opened bottle next to it.

Emptying the glass in one gulp, Logan snatched up the bottle and refilled it. He looked to the saloon's door when the sound of boots striking the boardwalk outside could be heard. Logan grunted as several cowboys walked past the saloon, none stopping to enter. Turning back to the bar, he retrieved his glass and downed the whiskey.

"Where ya goin'?" Finney asked as the sheriff walked to the door.

"Think I'll go out and have a look around."

"Hell, it's dark outside. You ain't gonna see nothin'."

Logan turned to glare at Finney. "You got a better idea?"

Figuring he'd pushed the sheriff as far as he could without getting shot, Finney shrugged. "Nope."

AFTER WANDERING AIMLESSLY in the darkness, Logan welcomed the morning sun's rays. He scanned the valley for any sign of his missing men. Circling buzzards alerting him to their location.

As Logan approached the stand of cottonwoods, he could see a body crumbled next to one of the big trees. He pulled his horse to a stop next the corpse, looking down at it. "Damn fool," Logan spat at the carcass, "to let a woman shoot ya."

Looking around, he spotted a second body stretched across the creek and spurred his horse forward.

"Damn." He shook his head. "Thought you was better than that."

Expecting to find a third body, Logan searched the area. He discovered the tracks of three horses leading away from the trees. Sitting on his horse, his eyes followed the tracks until they could no longer be seen.

"Ran out on me, did ya?" Logan muttered at the missing bandit. "You better hope we don't cross paths again." He turned his horse back toward Bannack.

Chapter
Ten

JESSE WAS CARRYING KC when Dusty and Blaze walked into the shade of the Slipper. Bette Mae was sitting on one of the porch's rockers and stood to greet the women.

"Lordy be." Bette Mae smiled broadly at the return of her friends. "Looky what the cat done drug in."

Jennifer slid from Blaze's saddle and reached up to take the baby from Jesse.

"My goodness." Bette Mae was surprised to see the tiny child emerge from the sling around Jesse's shoulders. "What in the world is *that?*"

"*That,*" Jesse dropped to the ground, "is a baby."

"Lordy," Bette Mae chuckled. "Didn' know ya could buy those in Bannack."

The women mounted the stairs to the porch.

"You can't." Jesse hugged her friend. "It's a long story and we'll tell you all about it just as soon as we talk to Billie."

"Ya might as well come inside, then. He's in there courtin' Ruthie." Bette Mae looked at the child clinging to Jennifer; since the ambush, KC had refused to be out of her mothers' arms.

"Told you so," Jennifer whispered to Jesse as they followed Bette Mae inside. She had told Jesse weeks before that Sweetwater's sheriff looked to be sweet on the shy girl who worked at the Slipper.

"Think you're so smart, don't ya?" Jesse stuck her tongue out at the schoolteacher.

"Yep." Jennifer wrapped her free arm around Jesse's waist. "I found you, didn't I?"

"BOY." BILLIE MONROE, Sweetwater's sheriff, whistled, leaning back in his chair. "Sounds like you had yourselves quite the adventure."

Jesse and Jennifer had spent the past two hours relating the events of their trip to the sheriff and Bette Mae. They left out the news about the storekeeper's sister and brother-in-law, preferring to unveil that information to Ed and Bette Mae in private. Neither was looking forward to the task.

"Guess you could put it that way." Jesse played with the baby in her lap. "Billie, can you do anything about Logan?"

"Yeah, I'll send word to Virginia City. Seems I heard something about citizens there forming a vigilante group to track down the outlaws. Haven't been too successful so far. Problem is, Logan is sheriff of both towns, but this might just be the information they're needing."

"How can a lawman do that?" Jennifer asked.

"Oh, hell," Billie started, then stopped when he saw the look on Jesse's face. "Sorry, Jennifer. Half the lawmen in the West have spent time on the other side of the badge, some even spending time in prison. If what I've heard about Logan is true, he got himself run out of the California gold camps for being on the wrong side of the law."

"Hard ta git men ta wear the badge," Bette Mae added. "Most that do, don' live too long."

"Ain't that the truth," Billie added with a grin. He had no complaints being sheriff in a small town like Sweetwater. At least his life expectancy was longer than most lawmen.

"So." Bette Mae looked at Jesse. "Ya plannin' on raisin' the little one yourselves, eh?"

"Yes." Jesse tickled KC and was rewarded with a hearty baby laugh.

"We couldn't leave her in Bannack. Who knows what kind of life she would have been forced into." Jennifer pulled KC into her own lap before continuing. "At least this way she'll be raised with love."

Billie pushed his chair away from the table. "If I get this all written down quick, I can get it out on the afternoon stage."

"There is one more thing," Jennifer said shyly. She looked at Jesse, who nodded her approval. Smiling broadly, Jennifer announced, "Jesse asked me to marry her."

"Lordy be," Bette Mae exclaimed. "A weddin'. I don't think we've ever had one in Sweetwater."

"That's wonderful news." Billie slapped Jesse on the back. "But Bette Mae has a point. Most folks go to Bozeman with there being no church here. You planning on that?"

"No." Jesse shook her head; she definitely wasn't going to the town where her parents lived to marry her love. "We were hoping that Mayor Perkins would do the honors."

"Don' ya worry 'bout the mayor. I'll have a little talk with his missus." Bette Mae patted Jennifer's hand. "Now we got some plannin' ta do. You'll be needin' a dress..."

Jesse chuckled. "Already taken care of. Bought her the prettiest wedding dress in Bannack."

"I'll leave you ladies to your planning." The sheriff stood.

"One more thing, Billie." Jesse stopped the man from leaving. "I was hopin' that you'd agree to be my best man."

Billie puffed out his chest at the unexpected request. "I'd be right honored to, Jesse. Right honored."

"Thanks," Jesse smiled.

Billie nodded and left.

"Okay." Bette Mae took possession of the women's attention. "Jus' when do ya plan ta hold this here weddin'?"

"Oh." Jennifer was testing KC's britches and wasn't surprised to find them wet. "I guess we haven't given that much thought." Turning to Jesse, "Sweetheart, KC needs changing."

Standing to retrieve a fresh diaper from the saddlebags outside on the horses, Jesse answered Bette Mae's question, "Just as soon as possible."

"I'm thinkin' it'll take 'bout two weeks ta git everythin' ready and ta notify folks in the valley. How's that sound?"

"It sounds just fine," Jennifer said, more to a squirming KC than to Bette Mae.

Jesse came back in with the diaper and offered to take care of the baby, but Jennifer shook her head and carried the baby into Jesse's office.

"Gettin' hitched, huh?" Bette Mae smiled at the rancher. "I'm mighty proud of you." The woman tried to fight the tears welling in her eyes.

Jesse didn't know what to say. It was the first time she had heard those words. For years, she had hoped to hear them from her parents, but had eventually given up. Now, to hear them from someone who had become more to her than just a friend meant so much to the rancher. She struggled to get words out of her choked throat. "I was kinda hopin' that you'd stand up for me at the wedding, bein's that I don't have any kin to do it. I mean, you're the closest I've got to a mom and all. It would mean a great deal to me, if..." Jesse knew she was babbling but she couldn't get the words to come out right.

Letting the tears fall, Bette Mae stood and wrapped Jesse in her arms. "I can't think of anythin' that would make me happier."

Jennifer came out of Jesse's office to see her lover encircled in Bette Mae's arms. Both women were crying, but it was obvious to the schoolteacher that something good had just happened. She stood quietly and allowed the women their moment.

JESSE, CARRYING KC, and Jennifer slowly walked toward the general store. They had just left the Silver Slipper, after breaking the news about Elizabeth Cassidy to Bette Mae. Their friend had sat emotionless on the couch in Jesse's office as she listened of the death of her long-lost love. It was only after the women left Bette Mae alone to deal with her grief that they heard the mournful cries coming from the room. It had been heart-wrenching, and they weren't looking forward to going through it again with the dead woman's brother.

"Boy, I'll be glad to get this over with." Jennifer sighed, the devastated look on Bette Mae's face haunting her.

"Yeah." Jesse reached down and took Jennifer's hand. "Let's hope he takes the news better than Bette Mae. I'm not sure I can handle any more."

Jennifer leaned against Jesse's shoulder as they walked. "It must be so painful to hear such terrible news. I really feel for Bette Mae."

"Me too," Jesse whispered as they neared the store.

Ed was just walking outside when the women climbed up onto the boardwalk in front of the general store. The storekeeper smiled. "Just who do we have here?" He grinned at the women as he studied KC.

"This is KC, our daughter," Jennifer said proudly.

"Daughter?" Ed looked puzzled. "Just what kind of stores do they have in Bannack?"

Jesse laughed. "Not those kind. Let's go inside and we'll tell you all about it."

"DAMN." ED SLUMPED down on the stool behind the counter. "I knew he was a no-good excuse for a husband but I never figured him for doin' somethin' like that."

Jesse and Jennifer told the storekeeper about the events of their trip, finishing with the news of his sister's death.

"I'm so sorry, Ed." Jennifer hugged the man who had become a second father to her. In fact, the gentle man had become the father she had always dreamed of. "She has a beautiful spot. You can see for miles. It really is lovely."

"And you gave her a stone?"

"Yes. A real nice one. I think she'd like it."

"I'll pay you back, Jesse."

"No." Jesse reached out and gave the man's arm a gentle squeeze. "It was the least we could do."

"But it weren't your responsibility."

"We were glad we could do it for her."

"All right, then I'll thank you." He nodded. "You said the trial should be this week. Think they'll hang the bastard?"

"From what Logan said, seems likely. If you want to go and check on things, we'll keep an eye on the store," Jesse offered.

"No point to it." Ed pulled a kerchief from his pocket, wiping at his tearful eyes. "She's at peace now. I'm happy with that. Law can deal with him."

"Offer's open." Jesse wrapped her arm around Jennifer's shoulder. "Now we've got some good news for you."

"Well I'm ready to hear some of that." Ed perked up at the opportunity to chase away the mood that had settled in the store. He would grieve for his sister in private, but now was time to get on with life.

"Jesse and I are getting married," Jennifer blurted out. Jesse's proposal made her so happy she wanted everyone to know.

"I'll be." Ed looked from one woman to the other. "That is good news. Goin' to Bozeman?"

"Nope, going to do it right here in Sweetwater. Bette Mae is making all the plans. She'll probably be coming in here with a list a mile long," Jesse grumbled good-naturedly and received a playful slap on the arm from her fiancée.

"I'll make sure she gets everything she needs." The storekeeper laughed. "I think your credit is good."

"Thanks." Jesse reached out and took the man's hand. "We need to be getting back to the ranch. I'm real sorry about your sister, Ed."

Jennifer timidly looked up at the large man. "Ed, I was wondering if you'd like to give me away?"

"Why Miss Jennifer," Ed was startled at the request, "ain't that somethin' your own papa should do?"

"Even if my father knew about our wedding, he wouldn't come. Besides, you're more a father to me than he ever was. But if you don't want to—"

"I'd be proud to," Ed cut her off.

Beaming, Jennifer hugged the big man. "Thank you. And considering that, don't you think it's time you dropped the 'Miss' and just called me Jennifer?"

Smiling down at the schoolteacher, Ed chuckled. "All right, *Jennifer*. Now get and take that baby home. You all look exhausted."

Ed shooed the women out of the store and watched them as they returned to the Slipper. As he returned to his duties inside the store, he smiled to himself. "A weddin' in Sweetwater. I'll be."

And, Playing the Role of Herself

by K. E. Lane

Actress Caidance Harris is living her dreams after landing a leading role among the star-studded, veteran cast of *9th Precinct*, a hot new police drama shot on location in glitzy LA. Her sometimes-costar Robyn Ward is magnetic, glamorous, and devastatingly beautiful, the quintessential A-List celebrity on the fast-track to super-stardom. When the two meet on the set of *9th Precinct*, Caid is instantly infatuated but settles for friendship, positive that Robyn is both unavailable and uninterested. Soon Caid sees that all is not as it appears, but can she take a chance and risk her heart when the outcome is so uncertain?

The leading ladies and supporting cast of this debut novel by newcomer K. E. Lane will charm you, entertain you, and leave you with a smile on your face, eager for Ms. Lane's next offering.

Coming February 2007

Butch Girls Can Fix Anything

by Paula Offutt

Kelly Walker can fix anything—except herself. Grace Owens seeks a stable community of friends for herself and her daughter. Lucy Owens wants help with her fourth-grade math. As their stories unfold in the fictional town of High Pond, NC, each must deal with her own version of trust, risks, and what makes someone strong.

Coming February 2007

OTHER YELLOW ROSE TITLES

You may also enjoy:

Learning to Trust

by J. Y. Morgan

Jace, the director of a college Achievement Center, has a new graduate assistant, Taryn Murphy. Both women cannot avoid spending time with each other, as they are part of an extended family. Both have their secrets and reasons not to trust, but when they find themselves opening up to each other, they realize their problems are very similar. Can a friendship develop between them or will their pasts haunt them forever.

ISBN 978-1-932300-59-8

Tropical Storm

by Melissa Good

From best-selling author Melissa Good comes a tale of heartache, longing, family strife, lust for love, and redemption. *Tropical Storm* took the lesbian reading world by storm when it was first written...now read this exciting revised "author's cut" edition.

Dar Roberts, corporate raider for a multi-national tech company, is cold, practical, and merciless. She does her job with razor-sharp accuracy. Friends are a luxury she cannot allow herself, and love is something she knows she'll never attain.

Kerry Stuart left Michigan for Florida in an attempt to get away from her domineering politician father and the constraints of the overly conservative life her family forced upon her. After college she worked her way into supervision at a small tech company, only to have it taken over by Dar Roberts' organization. Her association with Dar begins in disbelief, hatred and disappointment, but when Dar unexpectedly hires Kerry as her work assistant, the dynamics of their relationship change. Over time, a bond begins to form.

But can Dar overcome years of habit and conditioning to open herself up to the uncertainty of love? And, will Kerry escape from teh clutches of her powerful father in order to live a better life?

ISBN 978-1-932300-60-4

OTHER YELLOW ROSE PUBLICATIONS

Georgia Beers	Thy Neighbor's Wife	1-932300-15-5
Carrie Brennan	Curve	1-932300-41-4
Carrie Carr	Destiny's Bridge	1-932300-11-2
Carrie Carr	Faith's Crossing	1-932300-12-0
Carrie Carr	Hope's Path	1-932300-40-6
Carrie Carr	Love's Journey	1-930928-67-X
Carrie Carr	Strength of the Heart	1-930928-75-0
Carrie Carr	Something to Be Thankful For	1-932300-04-X
Carrie Carr	Diving Into the Turn	978-1-932300-54-3
Linda Crist	Galveston 1900: Swept Away	1-932300-44-9
Linda Crist	The Bluest Eyes in Texas	978-1-932300-48-2
Jennifer Fulton	Passion Bay	1-932300-25-2
Jennifer Fulton	Saving Grace	1-932300-26-0
Jennifer Fulton	The Sacred Shore	1-932300-35-X
Jennifer Fulton	A Guarded Heart	1-932300-37-6
Jennifer Fulton	Dark Dreamer	1-932300-46-5
Anna Furtado	The Heart's Desire	1-932300-32-5
Gabrielle Goldsby	The Caretaker's Daughter	1-932300-18-X
Melissa Good	Eye of the Storm	1-932300-13-9
Melissa Good	Thicker Than Water	1-932300-24-4
Melissa Good	Terrors of the High Seas	1-932300-45-7
Melissa Good	Tropical Storm	978-1-932300-60-4
Maya Indigal	Until Soon	1-932300-31-7
Lori L. Lake	Different Dress	1-932300-08-2
Lori L. Lake	Ricochet In Time	1-932300-17-1
J. Y Morgan	Learning To Trust	978-1-932300-59-8
A. K. Naten	Turning Tides	978-1-932300-47-5
Meghan O'Brien	Infinite Loop	1-932300-42-2
Sharon Smith	Into The Dark	1-932300-38-4
Surtees and Dunne	True Colours	978-1-932300-52-9
Surtees and Dunne	Many Roads to Travel	978-1-932300-55-0
Cate Swannell	Heart's Passage	1-932300-09-0
Cate Swannell	No Ocean Deep	1-932300-36-8
L. A. Tucker	The Light Fantastic	1-932300-14-7

About the Author:

Born and raised in Southern California, Mickey Minner has lived in New Mexico, Washington State and, for the past fifteen years, western Montana. Since childhood, she has enjoyed a love of the old west and of writing. She loves living in the Rocky Mountains and enjoys hiking, exploring historical sites and taking long scenic drives. As well as writing fiction, Mickey is a photographer of the disappearing remnants of frontier Montana.

VISIT US ONLINE AT

www.regalcrest.biz

At the Regal Crest Website You'll Find

- The latest news about forthcoming titles and new releases

- Our complete backlist of romance, mystery, thriller and adventure titles

- Information about your favorite authors

- Current bestsellers

Regal Crest titles are available from all progressive booksellers and online at StarCrossed Productions, (www.scp-inc.biz), or at www.amazon.com, www.bamm.com, www.barnesandnoble.com, and many others.

Printed in the United States
64221LVS00006B/106-120

9 781932 300635